HALF-PINT HEX

BOOK ONE OF AURA HEALERS HALL

THOMAS K. CARPENTER

Half-Pint Hex

Book One of Aura Healers Hall

Hardback Version

by Thomas K. Carpenter

Published by Black Moon Books

Cover design by
G&S Cover Designs

Opening Chapter Image by Grand Failure
Chapter Heading by Bourbon-88

Discover other titles by this author on:
www.thomaskcarpenter.com

ISBN-13: 978-1-958498-23-1

The Hundred Halls Universe

Season One

THE HUNDRED HALLS
Trials of Magic
Web of Lies
Alchemy of Souls
Gathering of Shadows
City of Sorcery

THE RELUCTANT ASSASSIN
The Reluctant Assassin
The Sorcerous Spy
The Veiled Diplomat
Agent Unraveled
The Webs That Bind

GAMEMAKERS ONLINE
The Warped Forest
Gladiators of Warsong
Citadel of Broken Dreams
Enter the Daemonpits
Plane of Twilight

ANIMALIANS HALL
Wild Magic
Bane of the Hunter
Mark of the Phoenix
Arcane Mutations
Untamed Destiny

STONE SINGERS HALL
Song of Siren and Blood
House of Snake and Tome
Storm of Dragon and Stone
Sonata of Shadow and Thorn
Well of Demon and Bone

THE ORDER OF MERLIN
The Order of Merlin
Infernal Alliances
Tower of Horn and Blood

The Hundred Halls Universe

Season Two

THE CRYSTAL HALLS
Shadows in Amber
The Emerald Eclipse
The Sapphire Strategem
Chains of Obsidian
The Bloodstone Rebellion

AURA HEALERS HALL
Half-Pint Hex
Full Moon Demon
Blood Witch Curse
Twilight Horn
The Deathless King

Other Works

ALEXANDRIAN SAGA
Fires of Alexandria
Heirs of Alexandria
Legacy of Alexandria
Warmachines of Alexandria
Empire of Alexandria
Voyage of Alexandria
Goddess of Alexandria

KINGMAKERS SAGA
The Stone Tree
The Crystal Bard
The Ghost Tower
The Champion's Prophecy
The Shadow Labyrinth
The Autumn Empire

OTHER SERIES
The Dashkova Memoirs
Gamers
Mirror Shards

HALF-PINT HEX

Arcanium loves books
Coterie adores power
Assassins will kill you
Stone Singers has a stone flower

Animalians is a zoo
Alchemists, you'll devour
Tinkers loves gadgets
Protectors makes you cower

Aura Healers wants to fix you
Blue Flame has a tower
Dramatics loves the spectacle
Oculus has grown sour

One Hundred Halls
Each with their own magic
The Patrons protect
Because faez madness is tragic

In the city of sorcery
Invictus is the Head
His students are many
But the foolish end up dead

- A Children's Rhyme

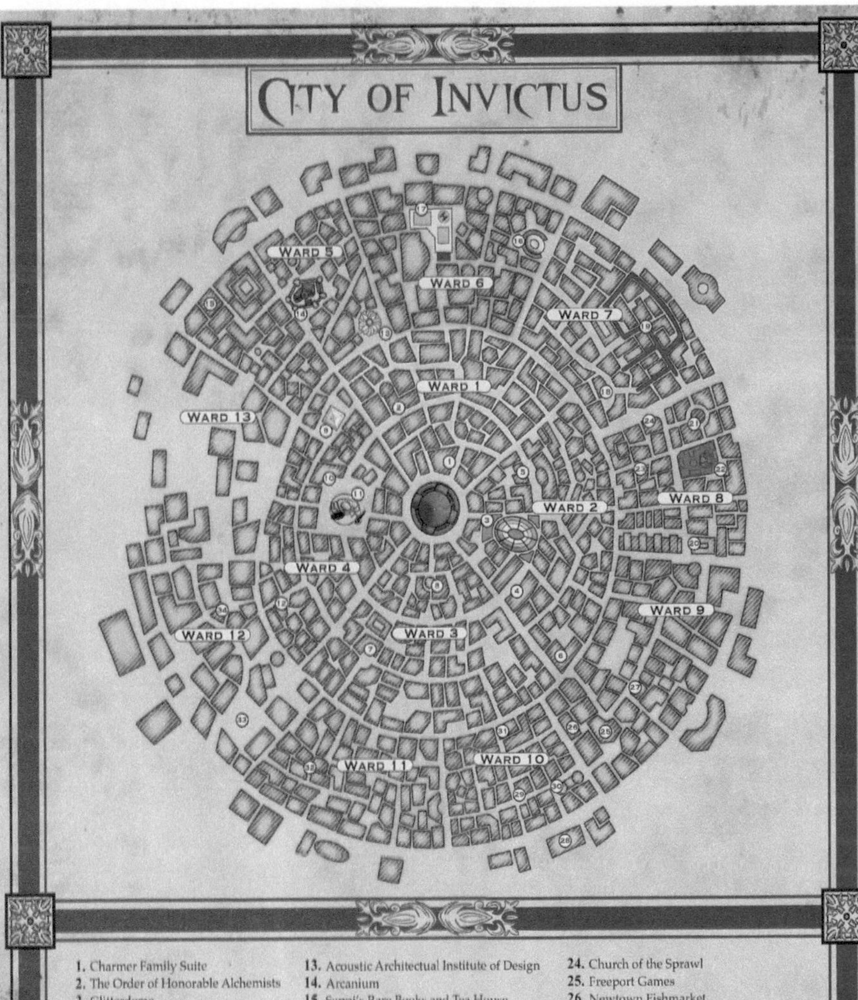

1. Charmer Family Suite
2. The Order of Honorable Alchemists
3. Glitterdome
4. Ashnod's Theater
5. Mystic Chord
6. Herald of the Halls
7. Left Tower Books
8. Protectors
9. Coterie of Mages
10. City Library
11. Statue of Invictus
12. Amber & Smoke
13. Acoustic Architectual Institute of Design
14. Arcanium
15. Seppi's Rare Books and Tea House
16. Museum of Magical Artifacts
17. The Holistic Institute
18. Glass Cabaret
19. The Canal District
20. Oestomancium
21. Animalians
22. Invictus Menagerie and Cryptozoo
23. Goblin's Romp
24. Church of the Sprawl
25. Freeport Games
26. Newtown Fishmarket
27. Uncle Larice's Bodega
28. Royal Society of Illustrius Artificers
29. Wizard's Wax Museum
30. Metallium Nocturn
31. Howling Madwoman's Fortunes and Spells
32. Enoichian District
33. Oba's Autumnal Garden
34. Gamemakers Hall

ONE

A line of vehicles sped past the Utica Magical Juvenile Penitentiary. Remi counted them as they turned the corner. Two hundred and fifty-four cars had passed her since she'd been released. Three and a half hours of waiting for her parents.

She picked up a rock and threw it at the last one, narrowly missing its bright red brake lights. She would have hexed its back tires to go flat, but she had a searing headache from the faez dampeners she'd had to wear for the year she'd been inside.

The gears on the chain-link gate startled Remi to turn around and watch a forest green minivan slip out from the interior of the penitentiary, tires slowly crunching across the gravel. After parking, a woman with curly brown hair wearing a simple A-line dress with a purse hanging on her shoulder climbed out. Her eyes always had dark circles and crease lines at the corners despite the smile on her lips. The rough terrain made her stumble, but she managed to reach Remi without falling.

"I thought you were going to see me for a last session before you left," said Sophia, her face wracked with concern as she glanced down the road at a car speeding past the entrance.

Remi didn't know how Sophia did it, caring for other people all the time. It had to be exhausting to be a therapist.

"I had to get out. Being in solitary for the last week was a shit show," Remi said, staring at her gnawed fingernails and the white lines where the cuts on her knuckles had healed. The blank walls and lack of human contact had left her feeling like an animal in a cage.

Sophia clutched a card between her hands. "I'm sorry, Remi. I should have done a better job of arguing with the warden. Solitary is cruel and should only be used in the most dire situations. You were only protecting your friends. Speaking of. They wanted to hold a party for you." The older woman sighed as she handed over the card. "Happy birthday."

Remi shoved the card in her back pocket. "Thanks? Damn. It's my birthday?"

She should have known what day it was, because she'd been released having reached the ripe old age of eighteen, but her mind was still in a fog from solitary. Or she'd purposely suppressed that knowledge, which if true, brought a new set of concerns.

Sophia inhaled sharply as she frowned at the empty gravel parking lot. "Do you need a ride? Or want me to call you a taxi?"

"No. I'm sure my parents will be here soon. They knew when I was getting out. I'm sure they're caught in traffic or something," said Remi, scraping her foot along the gravel.

Sophia took a step forward. "Remi..."

"They're coming, I swear."

"When was the last time you talked to them?"

Remi ran her hand through her short black hair. "Wasn't long ago. A few weeks?"

The rounding of Sophia's eyes brought heat to Remi's chest. She hated pity.

"I checked your phone records. It was in May."

"May? Damn, three months. Time kinda passes weird in there."

"That's not the first time I've heard that. The magic dampeners don't help either."

Mention of those cursed bracelets brought a surge of tension in her temples, but Remi resisted the urge to massage them in front of Sophia, otherwise she'd get even more clingy and demand to take her to where she wanted to go.

The last thing she needed was for her parents to see her riding in a minivan of all vehicles.

"Remi. I think you have to accept that they might not be coming. Based on everything you've told me, it might be for the best. You're in here because they put you into a terrible situation."

Remi regretted telling her therapist the details of the last job, but after months of sitting in her office, she'd let her guard down. She wouldn't do that again.

"Juvic's better than real jail, and I got my record wiped clean," said Remi with a shrug.

"That's a shit deal, I don't care what your parents said. They shouldn't have used you like that."

"The world is full of users. Better the ones you know."

Sophia checked the watch on her wrist. "I have to go. My daughter needs to be picked up at piano practice."

"Arabesque, right?"

"Yeah," said Sophia, her face brightening. "Recital is next week. Thank you for remembering."

"Hard not to when that's all you talk about," said Remi with her mouth cocked to the side.

Sophia chuckled softly. "I'm going to miss you, Remi. I know this wasn't how you wanted your last year to unfold, but I hope it's been a good experience for you. Given you some time to decide what you want to do with your life." She glanced down the road at an approaching car. "I truly hope you can find a better path."

A better path. It wasn't hard to read between the lines.

Sophia never said it directly, but she'd been hinting about getting away from her parents for months. Another reason Remi regretted letting her guard down with the therapist. The only good thing about those hours in her office was the bowl of hard candy and that the entire conversation was confidential.

"Thanks, Miss Brown," said Remi, holding out her hand.

The therapist smiled wistfully and accepted the handshake. "Are you sure you don't want me to call you a taxi?"

"I'm sure. They'll be here."

Sophia released their hands. "Good luck and happy birthday. I'm rooting for you."

The therapist headed back towards her minivan, but stopped halfway. She held up her wrist and shook it lightly, showing off the watch.

"What gives? I bought this crappy watch expecting you to steal it. You never left my office without draining the candy bowl despite my best efforts to watch you."

A laugh slipped out unexpectantly. Remi held out her other hand, revealing a wad of bills.

"I was wondering why you kept checking back to it. All you did was provide the distraction that I needed to slip my hand into your purse." Remi handed over the money. "Never trust anybody."

Sophia waved off the bills. "Keep 'em. Call it my price of education. And someday, Remi, you're going to have to learn to trust somebody. The world isn't as bad as you think it is."

Remi almost didn't want to take the money, but it was hard to turn down, even if she was sure Sophia had planned the watch bit as a way to give her cash. She waved as her former therapist left the parking lot, her tires slipping as she pulled onto the asphalt road.

She pulled out the card from her friends and stared at the outside. The pencil drawing of the three of them was nearly perfect, even down to the pain reflected in her eyes. She opened the card, then quickly closed it before tearing it up and throwing it into the grass. The last thing she needed was to be seen bawling on the side of the road.

Two more hours of waiting left Remi with the certainty that her parents weren't coming. Maybe they were in the middle of a job, or lying low and couldn't come get her. It was more than possible. When her mom had gotten out of prison in Cleveland, they hadn't been able to pick her up because they were hiding out in a shuttered McDonalds from the local crime boss.

Remi approached the road and stuck out her thumb. To her surprise, it didn't take long for someone to slow down, which made her instantly suspicious until the window rolled down, revealing three older women with gray hair.

"Need a ride, young lady? We're headed into town."

Remi climbed into the backseat and for the next twenty minutes did her best to deflect all questions about why she was in Utica.

They let her out near the park as shadows lengthened. In the middle of the green expanse, a massive oak tree dominated the area. Remi approached the wide roots, checking that no one was near, before reaching into the wide knothole that led deeper into the internal cavity.

"If anything tries to bite me, I'm going to burn this fucking tree down," she said with her arm in the hole up to her shoulder.

A moment of panic set in when she couldn't find the package, but after climbing onto the roots to get more reach, she found it'd slipped lower during the year that it'd remained in the oak tree.

The brick of bills was thinner than she remembered. She opened up part of the package to make sure they hadn't been damaged and to retrieve the pendant which was worth more than the money to Remi. She rubbed her thumb over the raised circular pattern before slipping the chain around her neck and tucking the oblong pendant beneath her shirt.

Using the money Sophia gave her, she bought a burner phone and dialed her parents' place from memory. A rough, pack-a-day voice answered, "Yo?"

"Are the Wildes around?"

"The who?"

"The Wildes," repeated Remi. "Greta and Archer."

"Never heard of 'em. You must have the wrong number."

A click left her staring at the phone. She called again in case she'd misdialed, but when the same voice came on, she quickly hung up.

Remi found a café and ordered a greasy cheeseburger and fries with a massive chocolate milk shake while she considered her options. If her parents weren't at the old place, then she had no idea where they might be. They'd burned multiple hideouts in the months leading up to her getting arrested, but they'd hoped it would be the last job and after that, they'd be set up for life. Every petty thief's dream.

Remi finished with the burger and quietly sang "Happy Birthday," eating the cherry at the bottom of the glass as her cake.

After paying the bill, Remi spotted a bus station across the street. A chart of destinations provided a wealth of ideas. While she didn't know where her parents were, she had other connections, some she'd acquired during her year in juvie. She could find work in Tampa or Chicago, maybe even Memphis if that girl had been honest about her past. But all those places would be one step away from getting thrown back in jail, and this time, it'd be the big house, with real inmates and guards, and fewer idealistic therapists.

It wasn't that she didn't want to pull a job, but every one was another chance to get caught. The only way to win was to hit it big and never cross that line again.

She'd always wanted to visit Paris and eat croissants in the cafés. Maybe even find out what all the fuss was about when it came to museums and art. It was better than the shitholes she'd been living in.

But a life like that required money.

She could get to Paris with the stash she had in her pocket, but she'd quickly run out and be back on the streets. What she needed was that one last job. The one that made everything right. Remi pulled out the pendant, rubbed the oblong metal, and dreamed of flaky, buttery breads.

The only way she was going to hit the big time was pull that last job, and the only way she was going to do that was if she had more than her lame list of tricks up her sleeve. What she needed was real magic, not the side street hexes and sketchy elixirs she knew how to mix.

Remi approached the bus counter.

"One ticket."

"Where would you like to go, young lady?"

Remi checked over her shoulder one last time, hoping to see her parents striding across the street towards the bus station, but when no one appeared she turned back.

"The city of sorcery."

TWO

Damon shut the minivan door with the duffle bag on his shoulder and stepped to the sidewalk as cars sped past the busy street. He craned his neck at the towering building at the center of the city. The Spire was the largest skyscraper in the world by a considerable margin, which wasn't surprising, given that it was in Invictus—the city of sorcery.

"Are you really sure about this?" asked his mother as she came around the vehicle, wetness in her darting eyes. "There are so many people here. Shouldn't we take you closer to the gondola station? I'm afraid you'll get attacked and lose your temper."

"Mom," he said, collecting her in his arms. She barely came up to his armpit. He kissed her on the top of the head. "I'll be fine. I wanted to walk a bit and stretch my legs after the long drive, and the second ward is near here. I was hoping to get a view of the illusionary shows."

She let out a quivering sigh. "I don't know why you want to do this.

So many kids die at the Hundred Halls every year. Not to mention the Event."

She lowered her voice.

"They say there are leftover creatures from when it happened."

"I'm sure there are," said Damon, giving her a reassuring grin.

"Son."

His father stood behind him. Stocky and built like an ironworker despite the lifetime behind a desk, hair sprouting from his ears and other unfortunate locations. He held a large manila envelope in his hands.

"You only get one shot at this. I can't get a third mortgage on the house."

Damon offered a conciliatory grimace. "I won't let you down."

His father glanced sideways at the bum wandering down the sidewalk that everyone was avoiding. He was mumbling and moving his fingers with surprising alacrity while sparks leapt from the tips. The smell of unspent faez—the raw stuff of magic—was a sharpness in the air, making Damon's nose itch.

"It'll be fine, Dad. We have bums in Kansas City too."

"Not like these," said his father. "You know you could study pre-med at UMKC. It's a good program."

"I don't want to be *just* a doctor. There's only so much science can accomplish on its own." He checked his watch. "I should go. The trials start this afternoon. I don't want to cut it too close."

"You don't have to feel guilty anymore. You made things right," said his father. "More than right."

"But I want to make sure it never happens again. Or if it does, I can fix it," said Damon.

"We'll miss you, and don't forget to be proud of who you are, despite what other people think. I'm proud of you, Damon."

His father handed over the manila envelope.

"Don't lose this. It has your letters of recommendation, school history, everything..."

"Don't worry. I worked hard to earn all that. No way I'm going to lose it now," he said, taking the thick envelope and tucking it under his arm.

Damon put his arm around his father's shoulders, squeezing him to his side as he kissed his forehead. "I'll miss you too. Tell the girls I love them and that I expect to be kept up on their lacrosse season."

His father sighed heavily as he shook his head. "It's going to be a long year. Those two don't know how to take it easy."

Damon chuckled, thinking about his sisters. They were the terrors of the league, racking up more penalties and goals than any other player. He was going to miss watching them play. His parents climbed into the minivan and pulled into traffic, waving and telling him they'd miss him, much to the amusement of the people on the sidewalk.

When the vehicle was gone, he was left with a strange sense of relief. He still had to pass the trials of magic to get into the Hundred Halls, but the journey to reach this point had been long and arduous.

It was the same way he felt about test days. The hard work was over. Now he just had to perform.

Hefting the duffle bag on his shoulder, Damon strode down the sidewalk. He was taller than most others, which gave him a good view considering the place was packed. Between the incoming potential students and the tourists visiting the city before the start of the school year, he had to dodge around people every other step.

"Excuse me. Sorry."

He apologized for the first hundred meters until he realized it was unnecessary. No one else had said a word, and many people gave him strange looks.

"Get your wards! Demon wards! Spectral wards! Wards for The King of Vines! Wards to keep the Veil at bay! Protect yourself from the things that go bump in the night! Wards for cheap!"

Damon grinned at the trinket vendor. Like most big cities, there were a few in Kansas City, but the streets of Invictus were packed with people hawking sketchy magical wares. He passed countless shops dedicated to magic: elixirs, trinkets, spell tomes, personal charms, and so on. He wished they'd arrived earlier so he could peruse them, but traffic near the city had been brutal.

A flash of light had him craning his neck at the glass gondola floating overhead, soaring towards the Spire on invisible wires. The interior was packed with people. He couldn't see them due to the reflections on the glass, but he assumed they'd be around his age. As soon as he reached the station, he'd get to ride in one himself, heading to the Spire, where the trials of magic would occur. The anticipation brought a face-splitting grin.

The station was in the third ward, right on the edge of the second. As he turned the corner, he spotted an enormous illusionary dragon flying over the Glitterdome, breathing shadowy mist across the flags. The stadium had been rebuilt after the Event, bigger and better, with arcane installations that made concerts into mind melting happenings. Damon planned on catching a show once he was settled at his Hall of choice.

The line at the gondola station was long, but he had plenty of time to reach the Spire and enter his name for the trials. Damon hugged the folder to his chest. While the letters of recommendation wouldn't help him get into the Hundred Halls, they would help with the selection committee. He'd been volunteering at KC General, learning the ins and outs of the hospital in preparation for getting into the Holistic Institute, which was commonly called Aura Healers.

Damon listened to the chatter around him. The other potential students were a mix of nervous and excited, much like him.

The line went down the sidewalk and into the parking lot. A delivery truck turned around near them, forcing the line to readjust. People were bumping into him, but he held his ground since he was bigger and taller than nearly everyone else.

A new gondola had arrived, and the hectic line was reorienting towards the entrance.

Ahead of him, a girl with short dark hair pushed through the chaos towards the open gondola. No one else but him seemed to notice that she was skipping ahead, and he didn't remember seeing her until the delivery truck had showed up.

Her lack of respect for everyone else waiting annoyed him. It wasn't until he checked the time that he realized his manila envelope was missing. It wasn't on the ground, or anywhere else nearby.

He quickly reviewed the last minute of his memories, sensing someone had bumped into him aggressively. The girl with the short dark hair.

"Hey! You've got my stuff!"

The others in line looked around, confused, but she kept barging forward towards the open doors. If she got in, he was screwed. He needed those documents to ensure he would get into Aura Healers. It was the only reason he'd come to the Hundred Halls.

"Hey! You!"

Damon surged forward, dodging around the others in line. "Excuse me. Sorry."

The girl had been able to make it to the gondola due to her small stature, but he was six foot four and two hundred and twenty pounds. There was no hiding his forward movement.

"She's got my stuff! Please stop her!"

She slipped into the gondola, which was packed full, but he was still twenty feet away. The attendant hit the button and the doors began to close. Damon knocked a girl with rainbow hair, who was holding a small cage close to her chest, onto the sidewalk. He hesitated, wanting to help her back up, but the doors were closing. Damon threw himself forward, launching his duffle bag through the gap while holding onto the straps. He hoped they would open automatically, but then the glass gondola shifted away from the platform, sliding upward at a severe angle.

Damon had a split second to make his decision. Let go or get dragged over the edge.

Everything he'd spent the last four years working towards was in that envelope. He held onto the straps as the gondola lifted upward, dragging him off the platform as the crowd erupted in cries of alarm.

Hanging from a pair of straps wasn't how he wanted to enjoy the experience of the glass gondola ride. Within seconds, the car was a hundred feet in the air, then two hundred, rising as it soared towards the Spire.

He looked up to see the people in the car holding onto his duffle bag. The muffled yells as they tried to get the attendant to stop were lost to him amid the whistling winds. Cars became toys beneath him on the streets as he dangled by the straps. He knew he couldn't hold on forever, so he pulled himself up and shoved his arms through the holes, taking the weight off his shoulders and praying his parents hadn't stayed around to watch him get into the gondola. They were hearty folk, but seeing him dangling from the bottom would give them twin heart attacks.

"I'm gonna kill that girl."

The thought sent a surge of adrenaline through his body. He felt urges building inside, a maelstrom of anger, threatening to trigger a change.

"Not now, not now, not now."

Damon concentrated on his breathing. Inhale for an eight count, then exhale for the same.

Repeat. Repeat. Repeat.

Until the violence receded from his mind.

He opened his eyes in time to see the landing platform approaching. The only problem was he was lower than the concrete pad and would get slammed into the side if he held on. Damon checked below where a road circled around a drainage pond. The drop would be thirty feet to hard asphalt. Maybe if he swung up at the last second he could make it onto the platform and not get cut in half.

As he prepared himself for the final approach, slipping his arms out of the straps and holding on like a gymnast on the rings, he glanced up to see the girl with black hair styled in a messy mullet standing at the door. He didn't see the envelope until it had pushed through the gap. The open end spilled documents into the air. His acrobatic preparation evaporated as he saw his life's work drifting towards the retention pond.

Damon released himself from the straps.

The fall was brief and the impact rattled his bones, straight up through his heels and hips. He tried to gracefully roll forward, but hit his shoulder hard and lay dazed on the concrete as papers floated around him. He staggered to his hands and knees, checking over the edge to see most of the contents of the envelope in the drainage pond.

Damon was about to launch himself into the water to retrieve the papers when he saw the sign: Danger! Stay Out! Grindylows!

Pale, greenish webbed hands snatched the documents from the surface, dragging them into the depths. The surface boiled momentarily and then returned to its eerie calmness. Even if he could retrieve them, the information would be ruined.

"Hey! Are you okay?"

Damon looked up to see the attendant peering over the edge. Too stunned to speak, Damon gave him a thumbs-up, but really he wanted to curl into a ball and forget the day had ever happened.

"There's a ladder on the side if you need to get up here," said the attendant.

Damon nodded as he returned to his feet in a daze. He collected the remaining documents, finding a fraction of what he'd assembled. The only bright spot was the cashiers check for entry to the trials was in his wallet. He collected what he could, folding them in half, and climbed to the platform, where the girl was nowhere to be found.

His pocket buzzed and for a moment he didn't know what was happening until he found a message on his phone from his parents.

[Good luck today!]

Damon didn't have the heart to respond, so he trudged inside, following the line of people heading into the Spire.

For the next hour, he waited in line and signed documents that absolved the Hundred Halls for any injuries, up to and including death, that might occur during the trials. Towards the end, an older woman asked if he had any documents to submit to the selection committee. He handed over the remnants and tried to explain what happened, but she told him that what he had wasn't admissible unless it was complete. Damon dumped what was left in the trash and continued to the last station.

An impressive tome with a feather quill sat on a wooden table.

"Sign your name and list the Halls you're willing to join should you pass the trials," said a woman with a streak of gray in her brown hair.

His hand hovered over the paper.

Most of the students ahead of him listed five or ten Halls, or just wrote "All" next to their name. He'd intended to only put Aura Healers, confident that his preparation would carry him over the line, but without those documents, he felt untethered.

Damon closed his eyes for a second before leaning over and scribbling briefly into the tome. When he was finished, he checked his work.

Damon Arthur Wolfhard

Aura Healers.

He went into the trials.

THREE

The welcome hall was large enough to hold several thousand people. Bigger than the gym in the high school Remi briefly attended a few years ago when she'd been mad at her parents and decided to give a normie life a try. The experiment lasted two months before she realized it was pointless. She knew she was smart, but she'd missed years of schooling, which made it impossible to catch up, and even if she had, she had no interest in the lives they intended to lead after school.

Enormous blank tapestries hung on the outer walls. Remi examined them from the bottom, spotting the runes along the edges that would be used for projecting information. In the rest of the country, magic was usually unobtrusive, constructed in a way that made it look like pure science, but the city of Invictus had been overflowing with it. At first her nose had itched with the excess faez in the air, but she was already getting used to it.

The other potential students appeared frightened by the prospect of the trials. She saw nervous bouncing knees as they sat on the edge of the circular platform in the center, and biting fingernails as they clustered in groups for support.

As if that would help them pass.

For once, Remi didn't feel outclassed by her contemporaries. In high school, she'd felt like an idiot because she didn't understand even the basic unspoken rules, let alone the material presented in the books.

But this.

Even though she had little formal magical training, years of working the system for advantage had left her feeling confident she could manage her way through anything.

Remi was halfway around when she spotted the tall, handsome guy entering the auditorium. She ducked lower and hid behind a knot of people as he craned his neck, probably looking for her.

She regretted the impulse to snatch his documents. It was instinct, drilled by years of hunger when the only way they were going to eat that night was to pilfer a wallet from some rando on the street. She would have never taken it had she known it was full of unimportant documents.

Given his size, he looked like the type that had starred in football at his high school. Even his name, Damon Wolfhard, sounded like a popular kid's name, but the information had portrayed him as a super-volunteer, working at every hospital, clinic, and halfway house in his hometown.

What a waste of talent. She never understood why those born with advantages didn't bother to use them. Hopefully, she only had to avoid him for a few days until the trials were over and then she'd never see him again.

"Have you been practicing?"

She didn't realize the person was talking to her until he repeated his question. Remi turned around to find a pimple-faced guy wearing a red sport coat over a Hundred Halls T-shirt.

"Practicing?" she asked, while checking over her shoulder to make sure Damon hadn't spotted her.

Pimple Face waggled his fingers. "You know, magic, five elements, whatever. Without faez, of course. Don't want to, you know..."

He made wild eyes and stuck out his tongue at a weird angle.

"Die?"

"No," he said, recoiling. "Go mad. Using magic unprotected, like getting an STD without wrapping your rascal, going into battle without a shield, slapping cheeks in the raw. There's a whole rash of it in the city lately. Some think it's because of the Event, but I was reading on the internet..."

Remi blanked her mind and nodded as he went on to explaining his theories about faez madness and the current state of Invictus crime. She wasn't really listening, but hadn't wanted to walk away and get spotted by Damon, who was slowly circulating through the crowd.

"Hey...?"

"Yeah?" he asked. "Oh, right, Bobby."

"Bobby, yeah. Could you do me a *super* special favor? There's a guy here I used to date in high school. He's extra creepy and I don't want him to know I'm here. Would you strike up a conversation and distract him so he doesn't notice me? I would be hella appreciative."

Bobby's expression brightened as he tugged on his jacket as if he were James Bond readying to take down a cat-stroking villain.

"I would be honored."

Once she explained what Damon looked like, Bobby headed straight at him. As soon as her jacketed distraction reached Damon, he was stopped in his tracks, forced to listen to a never-ending soliloquy about theories of crime and faez madness. Remi smirked at the idea Damon was too polite to just tell Bobby to sod off. The straightjacket of society held him fast.

The need to avoid Damon didn't last long, as the striking of a staff on hard wood brought everyone's attention to the center platform.

The woman on the stage elicited gasps from the audience. Remi glanced around, trying to understand the reason for the excitement. The woman had short dark hair that was spiked artfully, and she wore patterned silk robes with runes glowing faintly along the hems. Her skin had the smoothness of youth, but her eyes expressed the exhaustion of experience. She was vaguely familiar, but Remi couldn't figure why.

"Good afternoon. I am Head Patron Pythia Silverthorne. Our intended guide couldn't make it today, so you'll have to suffer through my tortured explanation."

Remi recalled that she'd seen the Head Patron on the internet, but hadn't realized she was so young. Or looked young. Remi wasn't sure, but it was a reminder that magic offered the promise of rewards far beyond normal life, making it well worth the risks.

"Eleven years ago, I stood where you stand, heart full of anticipation and fear, hoping I had what it took to make it into the Halls. I won't lie to you. The trials are dangerous. Deadly, even. Potential students die every year, which seems cruel and capricious—that means fickle, for you C students."

She chuckled to herself as if it were a private joke.

"But there's a reason. Should you pass the trials and survive your five years at the Hundred Halls, the dangers will only increase. Being a mage isn't for the faint of heart, so we keep the trials dangerous to dissuade those that would only succumb later on when their powers were greater and the dangers more acute.

"The trials ahead will test not the height of your magical ability, but the quality of your cunning and the strength of your resolve. Every year we create new games to test our students, not that it would matter if we didn't because you'll be enchanted to keep what happens today a secret."

Remi didn't think that was true, because there were always ways to discover a secret. The richer students probably had information about past trials at the very least.

"There will be three trials," continued Head Patron Pythia. "One per day. The first will test your creativity with magic. The second day will pit you against a current student with a partner, while the third day will be a group test. Score high enough above the cutoff line and you will be invited to join the Hundred Halls, assuming what you wrote in the Tome of Record matches what the selection committee decides."

The Head Patron clasped her hands in front as she slowly rotated until she faced the front doors.

"If the trials are not for you, at any time outside of the trials, you may put your hands on the runed doors and repeat, 'I am defeated,' three times."

She paused, checking to make sure no one was moving towards the doors.

"Mark my words, there will be some of you who will leave after the first trial. But since you've stayed, for now, I will offer you my protection so you can freely use magic without injuring yourselves.

"Open your minds to your magic, close your eyes if it helps, and let it collect into your fist. Then raise your hand and keep it there. When you feel the tingling in your arm, suck the faez back into your mind, completing the connection. It'll feel uncomfortable, like your brain wants to sneeze. Once finished, you can lower your hand. If I have to repeat the connection, you will lose points."

Hundreds of fists thrust into the air. After a moment, Remi joined them. She kept her eyes open, pulling the faez from her mind, which felt both cool and warm as it slipped from the base of her skull. When Head Patron Pythia faced her, she felt a tingle surge down her arm and into her chest. Remi sucked the magic back into her mind, and when it hit the base of her skull, she felt like she'd stepped outside of herself and the world was distant with a pulsing noise in her ears. A spike of pleasure followed when she let her arm down. She checked around her to see the other students had the same slack-jawed elation.

A few potential students botched their connection, which required a second more private ceremony near the platform. Remi was annoyed that they'd been given a second chance. They should have done it right the first time.

"Make sure you report to the red door on the opposite side of the auditorium when your name flashes on the tapestries," said Head Patron Pythia. "And good luck. You're gonna need it."

The anticipation silenced the crowd as the Head Patron walked through a hidden door. Everyone craned their head towards the tapestries. Everyone but Remi, who was watching to make sure Damon hadn't spotted her in the aftermath. She was looking across the auditorium when she heard someone nearby mumble, "What kind of name is Remington Wilde?"

Startled by the implications, she glanced up to see her name listed in the first twenty students to enter the trials.

"Oh, shit."

The nervousness she'd kept at bay came back like a tidal wave, filling her with sudden dread.

FOUR

A girl around her age with pink hair and sleeve tattoos that wriggled as if they were alive stood in the room beyond the red door. She wore a cutoff T-shirt and a golden bracelet with intricate runic designs on her left wrist. Remi had seen the same bracelet on a few other members of the staff.

"Remington Wilde?"

"Just Remi. How did you know?"

The girl pointed to the pin on her chest. "We use those for tracking and scoring."

"Oh. What would happen if I switched with someone else?" asked Remi.

The girl shifted her mouth to the side. "I wouldn't recommend it."

"What's next?"

The attendant pointed to a small round table. Three items sat in a triangle.

"Before you is a proving ground with many dangers. You must reach the other side to pass the first trial. Speed counts towards your score, but not making it to the end will guarantee your exit. You can use each item once and only once. The wand will put up a force shield for thirty seconds, the scroll is a spell that will give you slick shoes to glide across surfaces, and the elixir can give you fire breath. You will be judged not only by the speed of your passage but the methods of your success." She pulled out a round disc. "I'm going to have to scan you for magics. Nothing but what we give you can go in."

The girl stopped with the disc over Remi's heart and held out her hand.

"Sorry."

"This pendant is important to me."

The girl screwed up her mouth. "I can't let you go in with it. Don't worry. It goes in a private lockbox until you get out."

With a heavy sigh, Remi removed the pendant from around her neck and handed it over. For the amount of trouble she'd gone through to acquire it, including a year in juvie, she hated giving it up, even temporarily. The girl finished the scan.

"You're all set."

An archway swirling with mist lay on the opposite side. After collecting her items, Remi approached the girl with pink hair and offered her hand.

"Thanks for the information. Can I use magic as well?"

The girl accepted the handshake hesitantly. "Of course. Anything you do inside will count towards your score."

"Great, well, I hope to see you on the other side," said Remi, pulling away and slipping through the archway.

The sudden dislocation left her dizzy. Remi went through and fell to her knees at the top of a hill. It was the first time she'd traveled by portal and it was as unpleasant as she'd heard.

The sky had a slightly pinkish cast. In the near distance she saw a building with a faint crimson glow indicating where she needed to go. The entire set up was a neat trick. She didn't know where she was at, but it felt real.

Remi took stock of her materials, including the bracelet she'd lifted from the girl. Rather than slip it on, she stuck it in her back pocket. Then she memorized the spell and kept the other two items at the ready.

As she jogged down the grassy hillside, keeping her head on a swivel for danger, she considered using the spell to make her shoes slick so she could descend rapidly, but decided it was better to keep it for obstacles rather than outright speed.

The bottom of the hill was a sharp cliff heading into a canyon, which made her glad she hadn't tried to slide down, as she would have gone right over the edge to her death.

"They're not messing around."

There was no obvious way to cross the gap, which was over a hundred feet wide. She checked to her left to see what looked like points of darkness hanging between the two sides of the canyon. To her right was a flat bridge that would help her cross. She imagined there would be obstacles at each location, but the bridge would be more straightforward. That was her hope.

As she cut across the grass she began to see the problem. A group of short creatures with deep ochre skin and flayed noses held long knives in their taloned hands. They wore grubby clothes that matched their greasy black hair.

Remi knew exactly what they were.

Redcaps.

When she was a kid, she'd been enamored by the Fae. Their realm was a wild place of occult danger and hedonism. The oddities and strange rules had intrigued her because it felt like a more fun version of the real world, which had similarly obtuse laws that she'd never been able to understand.

But reading about redcaps in a book and having to bypass a group of them were two different things. Remi crept to a spot about two hundred feet above the bridge. The redcaps were busy with each other, so they didn't notice her creeping across the hillside. They looked like bored henchmen who'd been left to guard something valuable but had never been told how important it was.

At first glance, the fire breath seemed like the best way to get past the redcaps, but it was a one-time use, which would leave her vulnerable to their counterattacks. Remi had never been much of a fighter, so she didn't entertain that option for long. The slick shoes seemed equally useless as the redcaps could cut her into ribbons as she slid past, but it gave her an idea on how to use her final item.

Remi climbed up the slope until she had a good runway leading to the bridge. The wand was made of a flexible material. They were rarely used in the real world as wood wasn't a great matrix to hold enchantments, but the history of magic made them appealing to non-mages.

"I hope this works, or it's gonna be a really short ride."

With the wand extended forward, she muttered the command word. The thin rod kicked back slightly as a disc of shimmering force appeared three feet beyond the tip. The magical shield was a rounded disc with an eight-foot diameter. Despite the thirty-second-countdown timer in her head, she needed to make sure that it was going to work like she expected. Holding the wand like a gear shifter, Remi pointed it downward until the force shield flattened the grass.

"Let's hope this isn't a short ride," she said as she pushed off and leapt into the cup, letting her momentum carry her forward.

The force disc quickly picked up speed, accelerating down the slope and making her realize the flaw in her plan. She had no way to control the disc and had to hope nothing deflected her off the bridge.

The redcaps alerted to her approach, chattering in a sharp language as they held out their knives in anticipation. She flew down the hill, bouncing at the small imperfections, which threatened to tip her over precariously.

She hit the smooth concrete bridge like a skipping stone bouncing across a calm pond. The redcaps recognized the danger too late, and the front of the force disc smashed into their legs, sending them scattering like bowling pins. Two of them were knocked off the bridge, their screams quickly swallowed by the depths.

Remi feared she would follow them over as impacting the redcaps had changed her trajectory. As she flew towards the edge, which only had a short brick wall, she knew she had to do something or follow the redcaps over.

Remi threw herself out of the disc, letting her makeshift vehicle soar over the edge and out of sight, while she tumbled across the concrete, rolling to a stop.

Afraid that the redcaps would be upon her, she popped to her feet, then stumbled from the dizziness, finding that all but one of the redcaps had been thrown over or incapacitated by the impact. The final creature ambled forward with its blade held high, mumbling in its sharp tongue.

Rolling out of the disc had slammed her knee hard. She wasn't sure she could run, so she faced the redcap and began to mumble nonsense while making random arcane gestures. As the volume of her voice rose, the crimson eyes of the redcap grew larger until she reached a crescendo and the creature squeaked with fright and scurried back to his fallen friends.

With a heavy sigh, Remi limped off the bridge, content that she'd made it past the first obstacle. Her knee loosened up after a few minutes as she crossed a wide field on the way to the building.

Remi stopped outside the opening, peering into the darkness for danger. She wasn't skilled at the five elements, but after three tries managed to send a force bolt through the doorway in case something was lurking on the other side.

Once inside, she crept down an angled hallway that eventually opened up into a much longer space than the building suggested was possible, which meant she'd likely been diverted underground. The room ahead didn't have a flat floor. Instead, it was shaped in a V with a narrow plank headed straight down the middle.

Remi stepped onto the plank, which was sturdier than the thinness of the material suggested. She strode forward, checking for danger.

About two hundred feet across she spotted large bulbous shapes with long spindly legs crawling around the bottom of the V.

Spiders.

Big ones.

She could see the hair on their backs, which gave her the creeps more than the long fangs. There were three of them. Each big as a Great Dane. A few strands of webbing intersected the triangular space, but it was mostly clear. They were hunters rather than web builders.

Remi knew far too much about spiders from living in a run-down house in Kentucky for a few months when they were hiding from a gang they'd double-crossed. The house was infested with brown recluse, which made going to sleep each night a nervous affair.

Once again, she considered the flame breath as a way to get past the obstacle, but there were three of them and she doubted she could hit all of them at once. If she were a better mage, she could defend herself with the five elements, but she didn't want to rely on a barely used skill.

The slick shoes were a consideration again, but after nearly flying off the bridge, she knew it was the wrong choice. There was no way she'd be able to stay on the narrow plank to slip past the spiders.

"Think, Remi. Think."

The best solutions weren't the obvious ones. Her parents never broke into a house like common thieves. The best way to relieve people of their belongings was to get them to invite you in and hand over their precious valuables for reasons that they thought were sound. As a bonus, most people were so embarrassed about being hoodwinked they never went to the police.

Her favorite con was when they set up a security firm in a small Texas town, then flooded the internet with news about burglars and thieves, which invited numerous requests for safes, security boxes, and guards. The only reason the con didn't set them up for longer was the local prosecutor figured out their game before they could escape with all the money.

The lesson remained.

A frontal assault would only end up in failure—a very permanent one. Remi examined the bottom of her shoes and then the spiders. The flame spell didn't have a wide range, but the slick spell did. After practicing the spell without faez until she was certain she could cast it first try, she approached the spiders, taking two steps forward and then pausing in case they surged towards her to attack.

When the spiders were in the spell's range, Remi began the gestures and arcane phrases that would bring the effect into being. In addition to the physical components, she had to rotate a shape in her mind while making it expand.

Halfway through the spell, the giant spiders decided to investigate and came skittering forward along the angled walls. Remi did her best to ignore their advance and focus on completing the spell. The tapping of their approaching feet brought anxious fear. They were much faster than expected, closing the distance within seconds.

The largest spider leapt onto the narrow plank and raced towards her.

Remi rushed through the final components, yelling out the trigger words when the effect was ready.

"Slippery slide!"

A wave of energy spread out from her hands, impacting the spiders and passing through them.

The effect was immediate.

One moment they were bounding forward confidently. The next, their legs were scrambling to find purchase as the ends had been turned as slick as a puck on ice.

The spider on the plank came rushing towards her, spinning on its smooth belly. Remi leapt off at the last second before it impacted her. She hit the angled wall and slid towards the bottom, getting caught halfway down on a sticky cross thread of webbing.

Remi grabbed the thread with her right hand, but immediately realized it was a mistake when her palm stuck. She checked over her shoulder to see the spiders had slid a few dozen feet away, but their momentum was coming to a stop and they were already rotating towards her.

"Not good, Remi. Not good."

The five elements only required one hand, but she had only ever practiced with her right. She had no way to burn away the webbing, and the spiders would return far too soon for her liking. She checked back to see the first one had changed direction with the other two right behind

Remi decided to give the five elements spell for flame a try. The finger movements were sluggish and incorrect. Three unsuccessful attempts gave her a headache.

Remi reached for the vial so she could breathe fire when the lead spider suddenly surged forward faster than expected as the one behind had run into it, transferring its momentum.

With only one hand, she tried to open the vial, but fumbled with the stopper right as the big spider slammed into her, snapping the webbing and knocking the vial out of her hand, which spilled the potion.

The empty glass bounced down the incline and landed at the bottom of the V-shaped room. Remi's momentum sent her sliding down to the bottom.

As she checked back to the spiders, she saw them regaining their footing, as the sliding spell was wearing off. They no longer looked like they were wearing roller skates.

FIVE

The spider looked as big as a horse from her back as she lay in the V at the bottom of the room. It made an awful clacking sound with its mandibles like the victory cry of a Viking raider before he sunk an axe into his foe.

Remi didn't know how she was going to get away.

For the first time, she truly understood the warning the Head Patron had given in the auditorium about the time she spotted the wand near her foot. Remi grabbed it and tried to activate it again, but nothing came out. She tossed it at the spider, which was ambling forward.

The liquid from the vial had run down the slope and collected at the bottom. Remi threw herself forward, chest slamming into the hard surface, then stuck her face into the crack and slurped like she was trying to suck a pool ball through a garden hose. She barely ingested a quarter of the liquid before the giant spider was upon her. Remi rolled on her side and exhaled a lame bubble of flame that barely washed over the many eyes of the spider.

It must have been enough.

The spider recoiled, skittering backwards and screeching in an inhuman voice that grated on Remi's ears.

She stumbled to her feet and fled the opposite way, bouncing from one side to the other to keep from falling over. The spiders chased her, their eight legs more adept at the unusual angles. They were gaining fast, clacking their mandibles in anticipation of her sweet flesh.

The lead spider was only a few feet behind her when it stopped suddenly. She ran a dozen feet more before turning around. The critters had halted at an invisible line. They held up their forelegs and quivered their mandibles before returning the opposite way.

Remi slumped to one knee, putting her face in her hands. Never in all the times she'd been in danger on a job had her life been so close to ending. It took her a moment to collect herself before she was able to continue. The dangers of the trial seemed overblown before she'd entered, but now she understood why some competitors tapped out rather than continue.

The strangely shaped room ended a dozen feet later. She hopped down into a normal hallway that split not long after. A brief foray each direction suggested that she was heading into a maze. Having used up all three of her items, she wondered how much of a chance she had to make it through the next obstacles.

Remi pulled out the bracelet from her back pocket. She'd stolen it on a whim, muscle memory from years of sidewalk pilfers.

"Let's see what this does."

Remi slipped it on, expecting an anticlimactic silence to follow, but when the clasp connected on her wrist she heard a click from somewhere nearby. She headed down the left passage to find the outline of a hidden door. Pushing on the surface revealed a secondary hallway with markers on the wall denoting direction and obstacles within the maze. Further in, she heard the low rumble of a creature stalking through the labyrinth.

"Not this time."

The hidden passage eventually led to a door with a portal outline painted at the center. She stepped into a cavern with an archway waiting. Remi unhooked the bracelet and shoved it into her back pocket before stepping through the portal.

A triumphant gong signaled the end when she stepped through. The rush of adrenaline faded, leaving her with quivering limbs. Concerned that the missing bracelet could be traced to her, Remi tossed it away, letting it slide into the corner before heading out of the exit room, finding herself in a secondary space where others that had completed the first trial were waiting.

Duplicate tapestries hung on these walls, though much smaller in size. Remi had stepped out the same time as another competitor. They both craned their necks at the tapestries as their names popped onto the ledger. The guy next to her pumped his fist when a number in the thousands appeared next to his name, while hers remained empty for a long time. Twice, she thought she saw digits start to appear, but then they faded quickly. Remi feared that stealing the bracelet had been discovered, but then after a long wait, a number appeared. It wasn't as big as the guy who'd come out at the same time, but it was midway through the people that had survived the first trial.

With her heartbeat slowing, Remi noticed that at least half of the potential students that had entered the first trial were listed as DNF. Did Not Finish. The reality of the challenge had been made abundantly clear.

Now she just had to survive two more trials.

SIX

On the morning of the second day, Damon surveyed the room. Half the competitors had been eliminated, or had left after the first trial. He'd managed to score near the top, which made him feel good about his preparation. The only part that had been tricky had been figuring out how to cast the divination spell to make it through the maze without having the reagents he needed, but years of working in hospitals mixing elixirs had given him excellent knowledge about materials that could make workable substitutes. He'd survived his first day with only using the force shield, which he'd wedged in a hallway to block the minotaur from reaching him while he sauntered to the exit.

Damon assumed the girl who had stolen his documents had gotten knocked out. He'd checked the entire dormitory after the first trial and never saw a familiar face. He kept an eye out, but assumed he wouldn't have to worry about her anymore. Fitting that a girl who wasn't above stealing from her fellow competitors wouldn't be able to make it through the first trial.

"Nice score," said Bobby, coming up from behind.

"How's the arm?" he replied, matching a fist bump.

Bobby rotated his shoulder. "Sore, but that's understandable. Looked like a balloon after that spider bit me. Worst pain I've ever experienced. Feel lucky to have made it through the first day, but now I have to keep my score up, or I won't make it past the cutoff."

"It only gets harder from what I hear," said Damon.

"What Hall did you put down?" asked Bobby.

"Aura Healers."

"Just Aura Healers?"

Damon grimaced. "It's the only Hall for me. What about you?"

"Cybermagics, Mathmagics, and Dramatics. After that, I just put all. I'd be happy to be in any Hall, really. As they say, I'm just happy to be nominated."

Damon didn't understand his last comment, but Head Patron Pythia had entered the room and ascended the platform to thunderous applause. He still couldn't believe someone so young had taken over for Invictus, the previous Head Patron, but given her role in the Event, it also wasn't surprising.

"In our complex world," began Pythia, grinning, "it's not enough to have a high Merlin score, or have memorized every spell known to man and mage. Surviving, or thriving, takes a team. Whether you're facing down an infernal manticore, or leading your corporation in this challenging business environment. Our founder, Invictus, created the Hundred Halls because there are one hundred ways to solve a problem, and some problems need the talents of more than one hall.

"In this next challenge you will be paired with another initiate. You and your partner will battle a third-year Hall member in a head-to-head match. You'll each receive items that mimic the skills you will learn in the Hall you placed at the top of your list. The object of the match is to reach the exit before your opponent disables you. You will not only be judged on the way you use your chosen magics, but more importantly, the quality of your teamwork.

"You will find your partner by your pin. Great friendships and even marriages, like my parents, who were both members of the Halls, began because of these pairings. Once I give the signal, a beam of light extending from the pin will point to your partner."

Head Patron Pythia raised her staff, and hundreds of light beams crisscrossed the auditorium. Damon looked down to find his had only gone a short distance.

"Hey! We're partners," said Bobby, relieved. "Lucky me. I was afraid I'd get matched with someone terrible."

Damon put his hand on Bobby's shoulder. "I promise you I'll get us through the second trial."

They didn't have to wait long. Shortly after, their pins flashed red, signaling it was time. When they reached the ready room, there was a potion and a metallic cube on the table. The first item was tagged with Aura Healers, while the second was Dramatics.

"Oh, I know this," said Bobby, picking up the ornate cube. "It's an illusion generator. This is way cool. The tag might say Dramatics, but there's some Cybermagics in this too. You can create realistic illusions with it."

"Mine is a standard enhancer. Strength, speed, that sort of thing," said Damon, tucking the vial in his pocket. "Come on, let's see what's in store."

Beyond the red door no portal was required to reach the competition area. They stepped onto a platform overlooking a large room. From the ceiling hung hundreds of vines that looked capable of holding a person's weight, spaced wide enough to require moderate swinging. The floor, which was thirty feet below their location, was covered in spikes and other obstacles.

A sign near the edge read: Once you step over the edge, the timer starts and your opponent will be free to move as well.

On the opposite side, standing on a similar platform, was a girl in yoga tights with her blonde hair in a businesslike ponytail. She gave them a friendly wave, so Damon responded with the gesture.

"Think she'll take it easy on us?"

"Doubt it." He peered over the edge without going over and triggering the timer. "Looks like we have one of two ways to get past this challenge. Try to evade her on the floor, or try our hand at being king of the jungle."

"We could split up," said Bobby with a sigh. "That way we ensure one of us makes it over."

"No way. I said we're both getting through this trial." Damon pulled the vial out of his pocket and handed it over. "Our best bet is to stay high. This should help you with the physicality."

Bobby frowned at the offer. "What? What about you? Don't you need this?"

"You need it more than I do," said Damon, smirking. "Trust me."

"Yeah, I get it, you look like you work out, but there's no way you're swinging across the entire course without magic. Have something up your sleeve?"

"Something like that." He patted Bobby on the shoulder. "Trust me. The key will be working together to keep her from knocking us off and preventing us from making it to the other side."

Bobby took the vial, staring at his cube. "Potions always taste terrible." He threw back the contents, grimacing, then tucked the cube in his front pocket. He belched and clapped his hands together. "I hope I don't get impaled, but whatever, let's do this."

Damon peered across the competition area, sensing a pattern in the way the vines and obstacles on the floor were placed.

"It looks like the spikes and other stuff on the ground are only in the places between the vines. As long as we stay to the obvious routes, we shouldn't be at risk of getting injured if we fall."

Bobby saluted him. "Whatever you say, boss."

"On three. Stay together," said Damon, approaching the edge. When his toes stuck over the red band, the timer beeped and started counting up. He reached out and grabbed the nearest vine, swinging outward to grab the next with ease. He waited for Bobby, who approached it tentatively. It took him two swings to make it to the next one.

"You got this," said Damon, moving to the next vine. The climbing wall at the gym was a favorite activity. While Bobby worked to catch up, Damon checked ahead to see their opponent headed their way with the skill of a chimpanzee. The blonde girl was fit and had a determined expression. He wondered what Hall she was from. Probably one of the physical ones like Assassins or Protectors.

Bobby's physical inexperience slowed their crossing, but Damon stayed with him. He'd meant it when he'd said he would help him make it across.

The blonde girl moved confidently in their direction. Damon saw she was aiming for Bobby, who was the weaker link of their team.

"Keep going, I'll distract her."

Despite the elixir, Bobby looked drained by the effort staying aloft with only his arms. Damon swung forward on an intercept pattern, catching a furrowed forehead from the blonde girl, who seemed surprised by his direct route. When they neared, she shifted to the left to avoid him, which required him to circle around due to his momentum. He bypassed the closer vines, taking long swings to catch up. The blonde girl spun around suddenly, kicking out with her heel, catching him in the gut.

The impact knocked him loose, but he managed to grab the vine before plummeting to the floor. The pain brought his inner spirits to the surface as his muscles surged with adrenaline and his fingernails grew into sharp claws.

"Not now," he growled.

The blonde girl was closing on Bobby, who looked like a deer about to be creamed by a semi as he tried to swing away. Damon skipped the safer vines, launching himself through the air to catch up, but he feared he'd be too late.

He made two long leaps, soaring through the air on a route the designers probably hadn't intended. He was one vine behind as the girl leapt onto Bobby's back, grabbing him around the shoulders and ripping his hands free.

"Gotcha."

The two started to slide down the vine.

Damon kicked his feet out, sending them like a missile at the girl's back. He hit her squarely, sending them tumbling through the air.

The next moments happened in slow motion.

Damon managed to grab the vine they'd just been knocked from, but he was forced to watch Bobby and the girl fly towards a bed of spikes. She slammed against the side of an obstacle, bouncing off the side and rolling onto her back.

Bobby was not so lucky.

He was in front, so he'd been knocked further. He flew over the tip of the spike, the sharp edge slicing him from his shoulder down to the middle of his left thigh.

Time froze in Damon's mind. The injury would be fatal unless he could fix it right away.

He slid down the vine and ran over to Bobby, who was bleeding profusely in spurts. The tip had nicked the femoral artery and blood pooled rapidly. Damon put his hands on the wound and shouted to no one in particular.

"Help! Stop the game! We need a medic!"

He only heard her approach by the rapid patter of her feet. She hit him from behind, sending him tumbling over Bobby. The rage that he'd been holding back was unleashed, like a dam breaking after the floodwaters had built up.

Damon rolled back onto his feet, and when the girl tried to tackle him, he raked her across the chest with his claws, tearing flesh. The first hit brought bloodlust, and he kept his arms windmilling—clothes and flesh tearing. The girl collapsed, covered in her own blood, as Damon stood over her with a hand raised to finish her.

The realization of what he'd done fell over him like a shroud. The rage turned to emptiness. He stood between two people covered in blood. It wasn't the first time, and he feared it wouldn't be the last.

SEVEN

Blood bubbled from Bobby's thigh. The girl was moaning from his right. Damon couldn't believe that no one had stopped the competition, that no medics were rushing towards them, spells at the ready.

What kind of university would let two people die?

Then his role in their injuries hit him like a meteor. If he hadn't attacked their opponent, kicking her from the vine, Bobby wouldn't have hit the spikes. And she wouldn't be bleeding from many wounds if he hadn't let his rage consume him.

"I won't let you die, Bobby."

He scooped up his partner, throwing him on his shoulder, and after a moment's hesitation, grabbed the girl too. She wasn't as bad as Bobby, but he couldn't be sure.

Damon ran through the obstacles, leaping over small gaps and jumping up ramps carrying their weight. Every bounce and impact splattered more blood across his chest from Bobby's wounds.

After bursting through the exit to a shocked attendant, he shouted, "Medic! Help!" The guy looked stunned by the amount of blood and the two people hanging on his shoulders, so Damon ran up to him.

"Where's the medic area?"

Around that time, a team of medical professionals came rushing in with bags and stretchers. Weight was taken from his shoulders. The two unconscious competitors were laid on the stretchers, and spells were cast on their wounds to stop the bleeding. They had to repeat them for Bobby. Damon had been an observer in the ER countless times, the patients having even worse injuries, but it was the first time he was the cause. He couldn't feel his face as they were carried out of the exit room.

Looking down, he noticed his claws were sticking out, bits of flesh and clothing caught on the tips. The attendant was staring at him in horror. When he approached, the guy stepped back.

"What's her name?"

The attendant's face twisted into a grimace as if he hadn't heard him. "What?"

"The girl. The blonde girl. The one I… the one that was hurt."

"Sara Holmes. Protectors Hall." He checked down the hallway where she'd been taken. "I'm sure she'll be okay. We have the best healers on staff for the trials."

It wasn't Sara he was worried about, but Damon couldn't admit that out loud.

"Are you alright?" asked the attendant.

Damon put his hand over his mouth before he realized the guy was staring at his wrecked clothing.

"I'm fine. I don't think any of the blood is mine."

An attractive woman with lustrous dark skin, her hair pulled back into a tight braid, appeared from the hallway. She wore a healer's white coat and bore the mien of responsibility.

"Damon Wolfhard?"

He swallowed. "Yeah."

She studied him from afar. It was a look he hated, the sizing up of threat and potential for violence. Everything he'd worked to control had come tumbling down, exposing him for a fraud.

"Do you have any immediate life-threatening injuries?"

"I don't think so. I mean, no. I'm fine. None of this blood is mine. I think."

"Come with me. We'll check you out, make sure you're not just in shock. Can you walk?"

He caught up to her, relieved she didn't flinch away when he approached. In fact, as he neared he realized that it wasn't fear in her expression, but cold calculation. Pure analysis. Clearly this wasn't her first time in this kind of situation.

"I'm Dr. Janelle Morrison."

"Nice to meet..."

He let the words trail off, feeling stupid for even muttering them under the circumstances. The doctor led him to the medical area. Cloth screens blocked dozens of the beds. The number of injuries surprised him, even as he knew it shouldn't have. Damon spotted the trail of blood that led through the room.

"They stabilized him as best as they could, but he needs real medical attention, so they took him by portal to Golden Willow Hospital."

"Isn't portal travel with a wound like that dangerous?"

Her forehead furrowed. "How would you know that? But yes, it is. The risk of regular transport was too high."

"I volunteer at my local hospital. I want to be an Aura Healer."

The reaction wasn't what he expected. Normally people either thanked him for choosing that path or commiserated about the amount of study required.

"I see." She studied him. "I'm going to need you to take off your shirt. Actually, strip down to your underwear, or if you prefer I can grab a fresh pair you can change into. I'm not sure there's a place on you not covered in blood."

Damon knew from experience the hospital supplied undergarments were scratchy. He stripped down to his underwear, not sure what to do with his hands. It was one thing to work in a hospital, but it was entirely different to be a patient.

"Merlin's tits, you're covered."

He looked like a horror movie slasher, which only brought more heat to his face. Dr. Janelle handed him a cannister of medical wipes. While he washed himself off, she asked him questions about his health. When he got to his fingernails, which were halfway between his normal ones and the claws, her lips squeezed flat.

"Therianthrope?"

Damon nodded, keeping his chin tucked in.

"There's nothing to be ashamed of. Therianthropes are more common in Invictus. One of my good friends is a therianthrope."

The last part made him lift his head. Of course, they'd be more accommodating in the city of sorcery. His high school had wanted him kicked out when they discovered the truth, but laws protecting the supernatural had kept them from sending him away.

"What kind?"

"Wolf."

"Clan?"

"Clanless. My parents were a part of the Zev Clan before..."

Dr. Janelle's face smoothed with sympathy. "I'm sorry."

"I'm surprised you know about that," said Damon.

"Like I said, I have a good friend who is a therianthrope. Not a wolf, but after I learned about it, I wanted him to know I supported him, so I read everything I could about therianthropy." She glanced down to his naked chest. "You look like you're healthy physically. Do you need someone to talk to about what happened?"

"Could you find out how the girl is doing? Sara. Sara Holmes. I'm afraid I hurt her pretty bad."

Dr. Janelle disappeared for a few minutes before returning. The flat look was not comforting.

"She'll recover." The doctor threw a bag on the table. "I had someone grab your duffle bag. You should get back to the aspirant area so we can free up this bed."

"How can the Halls let this happen?"

The words came out before he could stop them. Dr. Janelle raised an eyebrow.

"Let? You knew what you signed up for." She sighed. "Look, I can tell you from experience that what happens in the trials is nothing compared to what happens in and after the Halls. The world is a dangerous place. Wishing it wasn't won't make it go away."

After the doctor left, he stripped naked and finished cleaning himself. He'd take a shower back at the dormitory, but didn't want to get his clothes covered in blood. As he was leaving, the medical team was rushing in a guy, or girl—he couldn't tell—covered in a luminous greenish slime. He was screaming and the medics looked afraid to touch him. The stretcher disappeared behind a row of screens, followed by the bright auras of complex magics being performed.

Back in the dormitory, he expected people to look at him strangely. When they didn't, he remembered they wouldn't know about what had happened during his second trial.

Yet, anyway.

He checked the scoreboard to find his name much lower than expected. His score was barely above the cutoff line. Not only had going slow to stay with Bobby nearly gotten him knocked out, but he'd nearly gotten his new friend killed. Damon found Bobby's name in the lower section with a score and a note that said "Medical Elimination."

It wasn't the first time he'd ruined someone's life, and he feared it wouldn't be the last.

"Blood and bone."

He pounded a fist into his open palm, remembering that he'd only put a single Hall in the Tome of Record. Without the documents that cursed girl had stolen, it meant even if he managed to survive the third and final trial, he might not make it into Aura Healers because all the slots would be full.

EIGHT

The morning of the final trial Remi stayed in her bunk until Damon had left for the auditorium. It'd gotten harder to avoid him after the second trial when the number of competitors had been whittled down to hundreds, rather than the thousands that had started on the first day.

Remi slipped away towards the tables of food in the central area, stuffing a croissant in her mouth as she shoved fruits and packaged snacks into her pockets. With a score as low as hers, she needed to find allies. The group round was notorious for knocking out even the most well-prepared competitors.

With the flaky bread half devoured, Remi spotted her partner from the second trial. He was standing with a group of other potentials, talking about what they could expect from the final competition.

"Hey, Michael. I'm so glad we made it to the last round."

The flat look he gave her twisted her stomach into knots.

"We? You fucking abandoned me at the first chance. I thought we were supposed to be a team. I barely made it out."

"I didn't know how to help. He was over two hundred pounds, and I can't go outside when it gets too gusty."

The rest of the group turned towards her. A tall girl with auburn hair pulled into a ponytail said, "This is her?"

Michael nodded. "Yeah."

Remi swallowed. "So I guess being a part of your group is out of the question?"

He crossed his arms. "I'd rather ally with an infernal demon."

"Cool, cool."

She gave him an awkward wave and walked away from the group. She could hear them talking about her. It reminded her of the experiment with high school. The only thing it'd accomplished was proving that she didn't belong anywhere. Remi tried finding other groups to join, but either word had gotten out about the second trial or they were already full.

There were more people in the auditorium, but she decided it wasn't worth the risk of running into Damon for the opportunity to be rejected. She stayed near the food tables, eating her fill.

"Most expensive buffet ever," she said with a sigh, thinking about how much she'd spent to join the trials, as a chime announced they needed to enter the auditorium or be disqualified.

Remi stayed in back. The number of potential students was dramatically smaller than the first day, inciting comments from nearly everyone as they looked around at those who had survived. Head Patron Pythia entered to applause and ascended the platform in the center of the room.

"Greetings and congratulations on making it to the third and final day. You have one more task ahead of you, and some consider it the hardest one, because it requires finding a team," she said as she slowly circled.

When the Head Patron's gaze fell upon Remi, she flinched away as if the eye contact burned.

"The third trial will be equally as dangerous as the first two, so be prepared to use everything you know. When you leave this auditorium, you'll be sent to another location where you will compete with your fellow aspirants. The goal of the third trial is to find and acquire colored prize balls. Each one is worth a different amount of points depending on its color. Yellow are ten points, green are fifty, blue are one hundred, and so on. The higher the number, the harder to obtain. And once you've gotten it, you'll have the additional challenge of escaping through the exit portals without getting attacked by your future classmates. There are other surprises, but I don't want to ruin it for you. Keep your eyes out and remember there's more than one way to exit the third trial. Additionally, a word of warning, this third trial is as much, or more, about teamwork as it is about showcasing your creativity and the arcane skill that you'll be demonstrating.

"To keep this less murdery, we're forbidding you from physically or magically attacking your fellow competitors. Directly injuring another competitor will lose you significant points. However, to keep things exciting, we'll be giving you each a stun wand. This will temporarily incapacitate your opponents for ten seconds, giving you ample time to take their prize balls. The wand only fires every twenty seconds, so keep that in mind. If you hang around, they'll just be able to knock you out and take their prizes back."

The entire auditorium chuckled with the excitement of the competition. On the surface, it seemed more enjoyable than the previous two, but Remi didn't put it past the designers to have hidden unusual surprises.

"When you've collected enough prize balls, you can exit the competition area, but know that once you've left, you cannot return. So make sure you're happy with your score when you decide to leave. All decisions are final."

The laughter turned nervous as everyone saw this was the last obstacle to gaining entry into the Hundred Halls. Remi wiped her sweaty palms on her pants as she exhaled deeply, experiencing a surge of adrenaline.

An attendant ushered them through a wide red door where they collected their stun wands. Remi stayed at the back, slowing when she accepted her weapon and the attendant gave her the trigger word.

Remi extended her arm towards the girl and said the command word, which brought a hushed inbreath from the other nearby competitors, but nothing happened.

"Not activated yet?"

"No," said the girl, tapping on her chest, the same location Remi's applicant pin was. "And even if it was, the wand is tied to the pin, so you can't hurt me. I also wouldn't take it off, otherwise your points won't count."

"Thanks," mumbled Remi as she followed the last of the competitors to a large room with a dozen portal archways on the far wall.

She checked for Damon before she made a choice, following the group she thought least likely to be a problem. Remi was the last to step through the portal, and when she arrived the heat and stifling humidity immediately made her gasp. The other competitors at her entry point gave her nasty glances.

She ignored them and examined her surroundings. It felt like the swamps of Louisiana, and as she checked around, she saw willows and swampy ponds between narrow land bridges. Decrepit buildings dotted the nearby landscape, but further in, a taller solid structure rose above the mossy trees.

Behind her, an archway that matched the one back at the auditorium had the word "Exit" etched into the stone and the interior swirled with magical energy. Insects buzzed around her, but she ignored them and tried to figure out which direction was the best way to take, when she was interrupted.

A giant red number ten appeared in the sky at what she assumed was the center of the competition area. A booming voice called out "ten" and then it started counting down.

Seeing that being around others wasn't going to be helpful for surviving the final trial, Remi jogged away, heading perpendicular to the others, which triggered their leaving as well. She headed towards a building as she heard splashing behind her. A burst of cursing suggested they'd tried to fire their wand, but it wasn't activated yet.

Five.

Four.

Three.

Remi ducked into a broken-down building, peering out the opening as she saw other competitors spreading out, looking for colored balls, or watching each other.

Two.

One.

NINE

"Anyone want to partner with me?" Damon asked the group as they craned their necks at the swampy landscape. The side eye and turning away felt like an answer, but he didn't want to give up, not with so much on the line. "I make a good teammate."

"You put your second-round partner and your opponent in the hospital last round," said a girl with short dyed-red hair and a bodybuilder's physique. "I think I'll pass."

The severe glances told him a version of what happened had been passed around the competitors. He'd been getting the cold shoulder all morning, but she was the first one to voice what had been unsaid.

"I didn't mean to," he said under his breath.

His parents always told him his therianthropy was a gift, but it'd always felt like a curse. If he was able to make it into Aura Healers, he would find a way to suppress his urges. He wished he was like his sisters, who managed to channel their rages constructively.

Ten.

Nine.

Damon checked the sky. Then his opponents.

Eight.

Time to get moving.

He jogged off at an angle, keeping his wand down. The long re-charge time meant it was only good in limited situations, especially without a group. The teams of students would have an advantage.

Three.

Two.

One.

The sound of voices quickly followed him.

"Let's take him out right away. We can throw him through the portal and be done with him."

Damon hated giving in to his urges, but for once he needed the anger to fuel his survival. He let rage pump into his legs as he bounded across the soggy soil, looking for a place to hide. He spotted a huge grandfather oak on an island surrounded by murky water, leaped across the gap to land near the roots, then scrambled up the wide trunk and disappeared into the canopy.

Peeking through the leaves, he saw a group of six circle around the water, ignoring the island because they probably thought he couldn't have reached it in the short time. He grinned despite himself. If his whole life wasn't on the line, the event could be fun. As he waited for them to leave, he spotted a green ball resting in the crook of a branch further out.

"Bingo. Fifty points."

Damon edged out onto the branch, which sagged under his weight. The wood creaked as he reached the halfway point, well out of reach of the green ball.

Sensing that he'd break the branch before reaching the prize, he pulled himself into a sitting position and carefully aimed a force bolt at the green ball. The five elements weren't useful in a hospital setting, but he knew they'd be important for getting through the trials, so he'd forced himself to practice each night. He knocked it from its cradle on the second try, and it bounced through the canopy until it settled in the roots.

He worked his way back down and collected his prize, keeping an eye out for others. The ball was fist sized, which made carrying multiples a challenge. He thought about digging a hole and burying it for later, but everyone would be looking out for anything unusual.

The nearby reeds and cattails gave him an idea. He yanked up a few dozen of the thick green fronds and weaved them into a makeshift closed-neck basket, applying a binding charm to keep them together. It wouldn't last for more than a few hours, but it would be enough for the contest. He used another reed to tie the basket to his hip and set off into the swamp in search of more points.

The watery landscape grew more solid the further he went inward. Based on the location of the countdown letters, which he assumed had been placed at the center of the area, he thought the competition zone was across a few square miles. A large area, but not so large when he thought about hundreds of people searching it for the prize balls.

Shortly after, he found a yellow ball, which was worth ten points, floating in lily-covered water. He knelt by the edge, getting his knees wet, and pulled the ball back with a stick. As he fit it into his basket, he heard shouts and growling from his left. Damon padded towards the ruckus, finding a group of three facing off with a lizard-like creature the size of a terrier with gray, mottled scales and a wide toothy mouth. Behind the creature on a mound of dirt sat a red ball.

Five hundred points.

The two balls in his pouch felt meager in comparison. The three approached the creature with their wands in their back pockets. Damon thought about attacking them, but as a solo competitor, his single wand was mostly useless. They fired a mix of force and flame at their lizard-like foe. The magics washed over the creature's back, leaving it mostly unharmed, until it roared and faced the guy on the far left. He cried out and held up his arms, freezing in place.

A basilisk.

Damon knew them from his studies. The paralysis would last hours, sometimes days, depending on the age of the creature. This one looked rather young. The guy would probably be left with lingering dead spots, or stone-like scabs, where he'd never feel anything again, unless he could get treated right away. The other two saw what happened and averted their eyes as they backed away from the basilisk, which didn't stray from the mound.

Seeing an opportunity while the creature was distracted, Damon burst from his spot, running at an inhuman speed. The two guys spotted his movement, but he was on the opposite side of the basilisk before they could react.

The bulky lizard rotated like a semi on ice.

Damon leapt onto the mound and snatched the red ball before disappearing in the opposite direction. The earlier concerns about not having a group faded away as he outran them. Feeling good about his progress in the contest, Damon shoved the red ball into his makeshift pouch. If he could get a few more high-value balls, he'd have a good chance of surviving the third round.

TEN

Remi quickly determined there was no point in gathering the yellow balls. Their point value was too low and they would only hinder her progress. Based on the score she'd received for the second trial, she figured she needed to find a few reds and higher to have a shot of making it past the third round. A group of four had come out of a tower with a gold ball, the value of which was probably enough to put one of them comfortably over the passing line. As they headed the opposite direction, she wondered how long it would take before one of them would betray the group and steal the gold ball for themselves.

It was relatively easy to avoid others, assuming she didn't try to compete for the higher-value balls. As time went on, she worried that she might need to harvest lots of the low-value balls to survive, but that strategy seemed much too tedious and fragile to work. As her parents had always taught, one big life-changing job was better than lots of smaller ones.

She just needed to find the right opportunity.

Creeping across a muddy land bridge, she spotted movement ahead through a line of mossy willows. Remi ignored the insects buzzing around her face and crept towards the trees, using the overlapping leaves to hide her approach.

In a clearing on the opposite side, a guy with a purple Mohawk, built like a football player, was standing near a strange tree with too many thick vines hanging from its branches. The wide trunk had a crack down the center, and at the bottom the glow of a purple ball lay in the crook of the roots. A thousand points would get her close to the number she had in mind before she could exit the competition. She watched as the guy approached, sending out gouts of flame towards the vines, which collectively rustled like snakes shifting in anticipation of a predator.

As Remi observed his attempt to acquire the purple ball, she caught movement out of the corner of her eye. She wasn't the only one watching. The moss hanging from the willows hid her fellow observer, but Remi had the impression that it was a girl around her age with rainbow-colored hair.

Competition.

The action at the tree distracted Remi as the guy, after sending a wave of flame, tried to make a grab for the purple ball. He almost had his hands on it when the vines grabbed his limbs and lifted him into the air. Remi barely had time to wonder what would happen when the crack in the trunk stretched wide, revealing the swirling of a portal. The tree launched the guy through the portal and he disappeared in the blink of an eye.

"Hells children," she exclaimed.

The opportunity of the purple ball seemed less appealing after seeing the guy get sent out of the competition. She checked back to see that the rainbow-haired observer must have thought it too much as well, because she was no longer peering out of the willow.

But Remi wasn't one to give up easily.

She formulated a plan, headed back to the lily pond she'd passed earlier, and collected a half-dozen yellow balls that had been floating in the water, which she carried back towards the portal tree in her arms. Starting at a point right out of the reach of the vines, Remi placed the balls on a path leading back to one of the major trails that led around the competition area.

Once her trap was set, Remi cupped her hands around her mouth and screamed at the top of her lungs for as long as she could hold it before slipping back into the mossy willows. A trio of two girls and a guy appeared, collecting the yellows until they found the purple ball at the base of the vine-covered tree.

"A good one finally," said the short girl. "I don't have any more room for yellows."

"What's the catch? It's got to be guarded like the others," said the guy.

The final member of their team sent an air dart at the tree, which sent its vines into a tizzy. Now that they knew the danger, they continued their debate for a minute before deciding to assault the tree together, figuring three of them could overwhelm the vines.

They started with a series of five elements, and the vines curled back into the canopy, leaving a window of opportunity. As they ran forward, continuing their magical assault, Remi stepped from the willow, moving closer in case an opportunity might present itself.

When the trio reached the roots, the vines shot out like tentacles, grabbing limbs and knocking away five element gestures. The battle had tied up the vines.

Remi darted in and snatched the purple ball as the trio was hoisted up and tossed—one, two, three—through the portal. The crack in the trunk closed with creaks and squeals before returning to its dormant state.

Away from the dangerous vines, Remi examined her prize. A thousand points would put her comfortably ahead of the cutoff line.

She'd done it.

She could leave the competition and pass the third trial, and then the skills she'd learn in a Hall would help her claim the real reward.

The crunch of a stick breaking was her first warning. Remi tried to run but the stun hit her right in the back. Her entire body went stiff as a board and she landed in the mud, face-first, the purple ball rolling out of her frozen hand.

"Nice candy trail, sweet-tooth," said a voice in lilting Irish-accented English.

A pair of pristine black combat boots stepped into view. A hand wrapped around the purple ball with a giggle. The girl with the rainbow-colored hair fled, leaving Remi in the mud with zero points.

ELEVEN

Damon buried the yellow balls in a hole once he acquired the second blue ball. He had eight hundred points, but it didn't feel like it was enough as he'd spied others with the higher-value colors like purple, silver, and gold. The highest balls unfortunately required teams to acquire as the enemies or traps were not easy enough to tackle solo.

He'd made his way to a drier part of the region, so no longer needed to traverse the lily-covered ponds or boot-sucking mud pits.

But it was no less difficult.

The trees grew at strange angles with twisted branches that created bridges between the trunks. He wasn't a botanist, so he didn't know if they were real trees, or had been modified with magic for the contest.

Shouting, followed by the bright lights of magic, rippled in the gaps between the leaves. A pitched battle between two groups was happening in the center of the twisted forest. Damon crept forward. He didn't want to get caught in their crossfire.

He found a spot to spy the action. The two groups were equally matched with six members each, and the recharge time of the wands made it hard to gain an advantage. Damon wondered if it'd been an ambush or if the fight was an accident born from a misunderstanding. They were hiding behind trunks or atop the higher branch bridges. A girl in the back had exploded a bright light over the other team, temporarily blinding them. Not a direct attack, but a clever way to gain an advantage without breaking the rules of the contest.

One of the combatants tried to flank the other side by using a twisted branch when he was caught by a stunning strike. The pouch of colored balls on his hip squeezed out a single silver as he fell onto the bridge. The ball rolled down the incline, staying to the narrow channel until it bounced out and landed beneath a log not far from Damon's location.

He checked his surroundings before he made his way from his hiding location. The participants of the battle hadn't noticed the single lost ball.

A silver.

If he could grab it, he'd be set to pass the final trial and hopefully be invited to Aura Healers.

Using his supernatural speed, Damon sprinted to the log, keeping his head low and hoping no one had noticed. He was so busy watching the canopy that when he came around the log to grab the silver ball, he was surprised to find a mud-caked girl with her hands around the prize.

"You."

A squeak slipped out her lips.

Even if the mud was hiding the details of her face, he could see it in the mutual recognition that she was the one who'd stolen his documents. He'd thought she'd already gotten knocked out, but now that he saw her, he remembered the other competitors talking about a girl who'd abandoned her partner in the second trial.

Everything made sense. No wonder she was alone.

Forgetting where he was, he made a lunge for her, but she drew her wand and blasted him point-blank in the chest, sending him tipping over like a wooden plank to land in the leaves.

As he lay prone, the sound of her retreating had him raging. He fought against the paralysis until the moment it freed him and then he burst to his feet and sprinted after her.

Rage consumed him.

First she'd tarnished his chances at getting into Aura Healers, and now she was taking the final piece he needed for passing the trials.

Damon tracked her by scent, but it wasn't easy because she'd been covered in mud and leaves. He got lost for a moment, but then spotted her fleeing on the other side of a clearing.

A booming voice echoed over the competition area, startling him to nearly lose his feet.

"The third trial will end in exactly five minutes. If you have not exited the area with your prize balls, you cannot pass the third trial."

He caught the appearance of a huge set of red countdown numbers in the sky. Five minutes. If he couldn't catch her and grab the silver ball, then he was toast. He couldn't imagine that eight hundred points would be enough to survive the cutoff.

Damon turned his fear into speed. He threw himself over obstacles, leaping enormous logs and bushes, sometimes running on all fours despite keeping himself from changing. Losing sight of her again brought panic, especially when he realized they were nearing the outer circle where the exits were located. He slowed to a stop, checking all directions in case he'd lost her in his haste.

The countdown was already below three minutes.

He tried to keep himself from hyperventilating, but the walls of panic closed around him. This was his one and only shot to get into the Hundred Halls. His parents would be devastated when they learned they'd put a second mortgage on the house for nothing. Becoming a famous healer had been his life's dream and now it was crumbling down around him.

"Two minutes!"

Damon craned his neck. He jogged forward, hoping to get a new view when he saw her burst away from behind a tree. The swirling archway of a portal could be seen ahead. Damon burned speed to catch up. He tackled her about a hundred feet from the exit, forgetting the wand in his haste to catch her.

She fumbled for her wand, but he knocked it away before she could stun him. Damon knelt on her arms and pried the silver ball from her fist.

"You nearly ruined my life."

Damon couldn't tell what she looked like under all that mud, but he wasn't so angry that he couldn't tell her face had broken with contrition. He wanted to do or say more, but the countdown in the sky was heading towards the final minute. Damon grabbed her by the arms and dragged her to a small tree. He pulled out his belt and used it to bind her wrists to a branch above her head.

"I'm sorry. Someone like you shouldn't be in the Hundred Halls. You're only out for yourself."

With the silver ball safely in his fist, Damon jogged through the portal, relishing the vertigo as he completed the third trial.

TWELVE

Y*ou're only out for yourself.*

The words rang in her head as the voice in the sky counted down the final minute. Without any prize balls, she was unlikely to make it past the third round, which made her almost want to sit and wait for the contest to end.

But she hated being bested, especially by a big bully who'd probably been given every advantage in his life. Remi never gave up. Even if only to prove to herself that she was a survivor. Otherwise she would have said the hell with it a long time ago.

"Relax, Remi. Let's be smart about this."

She tried to pull her arms from the belt, but Damon had constricted her wrists too well.

"Thirty seconds!"

Remi calmed her beating heart and pushed her arms upward rather than pulling them down to give her fingers room to work. She didn't know much magic, but there were a few spells she'd learned in Utica that came in handy when things got tough.

She practiced the gestures once, knowing she wouldn't get a second try. The spell would coat her skin with a slick slime. It was what had saved her when the Scythe sisters had attacked her in the yard. The older one had tried to grab Remi, but she'd knocked her back. The Scythe sister had tripped over a clump of grass and cracked her head on the concrete curb around the basketball court. The younger Scythe sister had managed to bloody Remi's face with a trio of haymakers before the guards reached them. They'd both been sent to solitary while the older sister had left for the hospital, and as far as Remi knew, never left it.

Casting the spell sent a pleasurable shiver down her spine, followed by the feeling of cloying wetness over her entire body. Remi yanked her wrists free as the countdown hit ten seconds.

Nine.

Eight.

She stumbled to her feet as liquid dripped off her skin. The portal was still a ways from her location.

Seven.

Six.

Remi ran as fast as she could, throwing herself through the portal as the countdown hit one.

THIRTEEN

The luxurious hotel suite bed was big enough to hold six people comfortably. But it was just Remi, lying in the center with her feet propped on the pillows, throwing a rubber ball against the wall.

She'd burned an old stolen credit card number to book the hotel room. They'd probably figure it out in a day or two and kick her out, but she wanted to enjoy her last days in the city of sorcery before she found new shores to haunt. The Grand Mage was in the center of the first ward. Her room had a twenty-story view of the Spire, which the top of couldn't be seen unless she pressed her face to the window.

The events of the final trial were burned into her memory. She'd been so close. That damn Damon had tackled her before she'd reached the exit portal. Never mind that physical violence wasn't allowed, but she guessed they made an exception for such a fine, upstanding citizen.

"The Halls are a fucking joke."

She threw the ball, catching it on the rebound as the phone rattled awake.

"I'm not interested," she told the phone without moving from her location.

The hotel menu lay open next to her. She'd picked the three most expensive meals to order, but hadn't gotten around to making the call. She hadn't been that hungry after narrowly missing the cutoff line for the third trial. The silver ball would have put her comfortably into the Halls.

"I guess I can look for ol' Greta and Archer," she said with a sigh, thinking about her parents. She could never seem to get away from them.

The phone started ringing again. It went on for a minute before the message light turned red.

"Still not interested."

Maybe she'd head west. She hadn't been anywhere past the Rockies yet. There had to be lots of scams she could run in those big, rich towns. Ambition made people stupid. Lots of people wanted to be famous actors. She had half a dozen ideas how to exploit their desires without even thinking too hard about it.

A knock on the door made her miss the catch. She rolled over and collected the ball before it rolled off the bed. A second, then third knock made her realize they weren't going to give up, which probably meant they'd figured out that she wasn't supposed to be there. Remi knocked the menu off the bed. She'd really wanted to try lobster thermidor.

Throwing on a Garbage Kings T-shirt with the sleeves cut off, she approached the door and peeked through the privacy hole. A hotel attendant stood outside, rather than a manager and the police, which she was expecting.

"Where's the fire?" she asked as she opened the door.

The hotel attendant wrinkled his nose. "Fire?"

"The urgency. Three calls and now you're banging on my door while

I'm trying to sleep."

"My deepest apologies, Miss Wilde. You have a very important visitor who would like to meet you in the Grand Mage's private dining area."

He handed over a fancy card. At first she thought it was a joke until she saw how serious and awestruck he was.

"Who?"

The attendant swallowed. "I'm not at liberty to say, but I can assure you, she's important."

"She?"

"I've said too much already, Miss Wilde."

He inclined his head and left her at the open door with the card in her hand.

"Miss Wilde. I could get used to that."

She opened the card, which had the hotel monogram on the front.

Remi,

Would you please accept my invitation to lunch to discuss your recent adventures.

Sincerely,

Head Patron Pythia Silverthorne

Remi wasn't sure what she was more surprised about. That the Head Patron of the Hundred Halls was calling on her, or that she was referencing her recent adventures. Or was it a trick to get her out of her room? She checked her attire and decided she didn't care enough to change, not that she had clothes that would match the level of the Head Patron.

The hostess in charge of the private dining area wore a simple black dress and greeted Remi with a warm smile, which sent alarm bells ringing.

"Good afternoon, Miss Wilde. Would you be so kind as to follow me?"

Remi hesitated. She'd expected a comment about her clothes, or the bed head. Would there be police officers on the other side of the door, waiting to throw her in handcuffs?

The hostess tilted her head curiously. "Is there something I can help with? I could send down to the hotel clothing store for something more appropriate if that's your desire."

"My desire?" Remi asked, not even knowing how to take the formality or generosity. "No, I'm fine. Let's get on with it."

When they stepped through the door, she was shocked again by the lack of a police presence. On the far side of the sparsely populated dining area sat the Head Patron, wearing stylish black pants and a matching sleeveless silk blouse exposing a sleeve of tattoos.

"Thank you for meeting me on such short notice. I'd hoped to catch you before you left the city," said the Head Patron.

Remi stayed standing, checking over her shoulder. "Am I in trouble?"

The Head Patron raised an eyebrow. "Not with me. Please sit."

The table was filled with extra plates and silverware. Remi was afraid to touch anything. A waiter in a black suit coat left them waters. The Head Patron made an offhand gesture, and a shimmering sphere appeared around them.

"A little privacy."

The ease and power of the Head Patron's spell had Remi gasping. She'd never seen magic like that up close. It sent pangs of regret that she hadn't made it into the Halls.

"Why am I here?" she asked.

"Straight to the point. I shouldn't be surprised, based on your background."

Remi frowned. "Is this about the bracelet in the first round? I didn't keep it. It should be in the first exit room."

Head Patron Pythia chuckled. "We recovered the bracelet that afternoon. But that's not why I'm here."

For the first time since Remi had entered the dining area, she dared to look at the Head Patron. While she wasn't that much older, ten years or so, and her face had the smoothness of youth, there was a profound weight in the eyes that left Remi feeling like she was in the presence of minor deity.

"Why did you come to the Hundred Halls?"

Remi blinked and looked away. "I didn't have anywhere else to go."

"I read your background. You left Utica Juvenile Penitentiary and came straight to the trials. I didn't see anything about your parents' death. I assume they're still alive."

Remi lifted a single shoulder as an answer.

"I see."

The pressure that had been building up in Remi's mind burst out of her mouth.

"Why am I here, Head Patron? If this is an elaborate sting, just get it over with and send me back to jail."

The Head Patron recoiled with amusement, a smirk on her lips.

"Oh, how I miss not being treated like an antique crystalline glass. But no, we're not sending you back to jail, unless that's what you'd prefer. I'm sure we could find a number of reasons if we dug just a little bit," said the Head Patron, nodding towards the exquisite hotel dining area.

"Then why?"

Remi felt like she was going to break in two. Rich and powerful people disturbed her. She couldn't understand how they existed.

"I want to offer an invitation to the Hundred Halls. That is, if you're still interested."

"What? Why?"

The Head Patron sighed heavily. "We had an unfortunate accident after the trials. A couple of our new students celebrated a little too hard, thinking that their acceptance protected them from their hubris. They were sadly wrong. Now, we have two spots to fill."

"But I wasn't close to the cutoff line. There were dozens ahead of me."

"I know," said the Head Patron, taking a sip from her glass. "But in these situations, we review from a larger pool to pick the best candidate."

"Why me?"

The Head Patron glanced away. "Your history for one. The job that got you thrown in Utica. You stole from some powerful people. The Dreadmarshes are one of the oldest and most secretive families. While that wasn't a main residence, a cottage for visits to the New York countryside, it had significant protections that you easily circumvented. They're still unhappy about the loss. My understanding was it was an old Fae trinket."

"It wasn't hard," said Remi, keeping her face neutral. "I joined their maid service, which got me past the worst of the enchantments. The rest required patience and a few minor spell tricks that any idiot with faez can cast."

She didn't mind talking about the job since most of it had come up in the criminal case.

"Why did you get caught?" asked the Head Patron, clearly curious.

A snort slipped out. "My parents got impatient. They kept pushing me to make my move early. I wasn't ready, but I figured they knew better. I missed one little thing and got nabbed on my way out of the county."

"From what I read, you would have been charged as an adult had they actually caught you with the stolen goods on you. Instead, you were given trespassing and identity theft charges."

Remi shrugged.

The story she'd told the police was that she'd thrown the goods into the river, but the reality was she'd already stashed them in the oak in the park. The way the Head Patron was looking at her made her feel like she knew the pendant was on her person. Remi resisted the urge to touch it.

"Then there are the trials."

"Which I stole from."

"We docked you for those points after the first round."

Remi nodded, remembering the strangeness with her score when she finished.

"But the fact remains that you, despite having a limited magical education, managed to get through the trials using cleverness and wit. The panel judges were particularly impressed with how you used the yellow balls to lure the other students to the tree so you could grab the purple ball yourself."

"Yeah, well, it didn't work out so great."

The Head Patron's forehead hunched. "That seems to be your weakness. The inability to make friends."

"People let you down eventually."

"Do you know your Merlin score?" asked the Head Patron.

Remi shook her head. "Tested once when I thought high school might be the place for me, but didn't stay around long enough to find out what it was."

"I've seen it. Let me say, it's an impressive score. Were your parents mages?"

"My father entered the trials but got knocked out on the third round. Never had enough money to try again. My mom didn't really know she could use magic until she was too old."

The Head Patron sighed. "We lose far too many potential mages for reasons like that. So now you know why I'm here. Are you still interested?"

Remi's hand twitched towards the pendant. It was the key to wealth and never having to worry about anyone else again, but she wouldn't be able to do a damn thing about it without magical training and a patron to protect her from faez madness.

"I am. Would I get to pick my Hall?"

"I'm afraid not. I need to fill the two spots that were opened." The Head Patron narrowed her gaze. "At first I considered assigning you to Arcane Phytology. They're a new Hall this year and need clever students to succeed."

"Phytology?"

The Head Patron nodded. "The study of magical plants. They deal with supernatural foliage like the nekyia tree, discovering new alchemy reagents, and studying the plants of other realms—like the Fae realms or Harmony—amongst other topics. It's an exciting and underdeveloped field. With their new facility in the eighth ward, including a botanical garden, they're posed to make a big impression on the city."

"But that's not where I'm going."

"No," said the Head Patron. "I worried that it wouldn't be a good fit for you, for the same reasons you got knocked out of the trials. You don't know how to trust people."

"I do when they earn it."

The Head Patron smirked. "Sometimes you have to make a leap of faith. The path of a mage is a hard one. Especially in these challenging times. The Event, as everyone likes to call it, put a lot of doubt in regular folk. The Halls are at a crossroads. There's political pressure to change our systems, threats from other realms, not to mention the bad press of being responsible for the deaths of thousands."

"What do I have to do with that?"

"Nothing," she said with a curt laugh. "These are the problems that weigh on me day and night. Which is why I need to make sure we're finding the best possible mages for the Halls. And that means casting our nets wide." The Head Patron's shoulders slumped. "There was a lot of discussion about you for the final spot. Some thought I was being too lenient in overlooking your history because I came from an unusual background myself. That's why we settled on a Hall which is not only a great place of learning, but also one in which you might learn to trust others. To care for them even. Because I can tell you without a shadow of a doubt that I would not be here, or maybe any of us, had we not learned to trust each other. The Halls are filled with a lot of powerful people with big egos and complicated pasts. And I haven't even mentioned the patrons yet." She leaned forward earnestly. "I might be totally wrong about you. Your history, your parents, these might have left you too jaded to ever open yourself up to others. But I have to try. I see that potential in you. In who you might become if you allow yourself the possibility of change."

Remi said nothing because she didn't know what to say. It was overwhelming. She didn't even dare to take a drink of water.

Head Patron Pythia sat back in her chair. She flicked her fingers at the shimmering privacy field, which disappeared, then rose to her feet.

"I have another meeting across town in a few minutes, so I'll have to excuse myself. You can order what you'd like, it's on me."

Remi turned in her chair.

"But you never said the Hall. Which one will I be joining?"

The Head Patron's grin was filled with sharp teeth.

"Aura Healers."

FOURTEEN

Damon rode the elevated train across the city to the sixth ward. He kept catching himself grinning like a maniac. The other passengers kept glancing over to him until an older lady scooted away as if she thought he was contagious.

When he'd gotten out of the final trial and saw that he'd made it over the cutoff line, he'd made a call to his parents. He wasn't sure he'd stopped talking for twenty minutes in a rambling explanation of everything that had happened, but he couldn't help it. They'd barely gotten back home after a leisurely drive across the country, so they were probably too tired to respond. He knew they were happy for him, but they were also concerned. Being a mage in the city of sorcery was a path to greater things, but it came with extra heapings of danger.

The Holistic Institute building known more commonly as Aura Healers was attached to Golden Willow, which was the premiere hospital in the world for treating supernatural and magical diseases. No other facility rivalled it. The place also had the highest incidence of staff fatalities. Working in the hospital was like working in a war zone.

These expectations didn't prepare him for how ordinary the brick building attached to Golden Willow was. It was nothing like the Obelisk, an enormous obsidian spire that was the home of Coterie of Mages, or the ancient castle for Arcanium. Even some of the smaller Halls had buildings fitting their style of teaching. Animalians Hall had its very own zoo in addition to a huge campus.

Maybe it was appropriate that it was a simple brick building. He hadn't wanted to be an aura healer for fame and fortune. He wanted to help people. With his black duffle bag over his shoulder, Damon went inside.

A girl a few years older wearing scrubs and reading from a thick tome sat at a folding table. A hastily scrawled "Welcome New Mages" was written on a piece of paper taped to the front. She looked up from her reading. The circles around her eyes made them cavernous.

"Oh, I didn't see you there."

"I just walked in," he said, jamming his thumb towards the door. He saw her name tag and added, "Veronica."

Veronica looked down with surprise. "Yeah. Forgot about that. You must be..."

She checked a piece of paper with a series of pictures. "Damon Wolfhard."

"That's me," he said, looking around. "This is the new student welcome area?"

Veronica burst into deranged laughter. "You're lucky I'm here. I just pulled an all-nighter, twice. Everyone kinda forgot that the new school year had started. I hope you weren't expecting hand-holding, especially with your teaching professor." She held out a pen and a packet of papers. "Go over there and sign this stuff. Read it if you want, but I can summarize the basics. Joining this Hall is going to be everything, every waking moment of your life, and when you're not studying, you'll be in the hospital treating unresponsive, annoying, and thoroughly disrespectful patients."

Damon recoiled. "That's an awful bedside manner."

Veronica snorted. "Wait until a woman infected with sewer necrorot decides to throw her decaying finger at you and it crawls up your shirt and tries to poke your eye out. Attitudes change real quick."

He gestured towards her arm. "You have something on your elbow. Jelly maybe."

The widened eyes were followed by a slow rise to her feet. "Oh no. Definitely not jelly. Nothic viscera. Someone had a pet that got out of its cage. Made a mess of his shoulder before he managed to beat its brains out with a blender. I should clean this up, it's toxic. In fact, I probably should go take an antidote."

She started heading down a hallway, her pace increasing with each step, so he yelled after her.

"Where do I go?"

Veronica backed up as she said, "Through the blue door, long hallway, third door on your left. There's a fruit loop with rainbow-colored hair ahead of you, and Dr. Decker will be along hopefully. Maybe."

As she ran down the hallway, throwing herself through swinging doors, Damon followed her directions. Until the viscera bit, he'd half-wondered if it'd been an act, hazing for the new recruits. But he'd been around enough hospitals to know when exhaustion wasn't being faked.

Damon had thought the paperwork when he'd signed up for the trials of magic were bad, but entry into Aura Healers came with new categories of legalese that he could only vaguely make sense of. After a time of worried analysis, Damon said out loud, "It's not like you're *not* going to sign."

He examined his messy scrawl after he was finished and threw the papers on the table, wondering if Veronica was going to come back, or if he should check on her. Damon moved the stack of forms to the corner and wrote a note with an arrow pointing to them explaining they needed to be signed. He made a second one so his fellow first years knew which way to go, then took one of the name tags, and after writing Damon in block letters, slapped it to his chest.

The bitter antiseptics of the hallway, combined with undertones of floral, was a comforting smell as his formal shoes rang against the tiles. He'd almost worn the scrubs he had from back home, but decided a more professional presentation was required. The dark slacks and blue button-down was the casual attire that the doctors wore at KC General.

When he came to the location he thought he was supposed to be, Damon hesitated. It looked like a rainbow cotton candy machine had exploded, then achieved sentience and grown legs. He couldn't see the girl's face, only the top of her hair as she leaned over. Wooden charms, colored string, and other detritus were tied into the rat's nest.

"Hello?" he asked as he knocked on the door frame, before cautiously entering, not wanting to startle her.

The deranged smile, as her head came up, was only matched in its intensity by the fierce intelligence in her eyes. She had mellow brown skin with a constellation of freckles across her nose and cheeks.

"I assume this is the right spot?" he asked, edging towards the wide couch opposite the girl. She wasn't wearing a name tag that he could see. "I'm Damon."

"Don't sit there," she said with a heavy Irish accent, pumping her eyebrows with glee as she sat with her legs curled beneath her on the chair. "There's a ghost of a little dead girl at the end of the couch. Bet she saw her unfortunate end when one of the healers made a wrong cut. I can see the scar across her throat."

She made a gesture with the tip of her finger. Damon hesitated near the spot she was referring to, choosing a wooden chair on the opposite side instead.

"She's fucking with you," said a voice from the hallway.

Damon turned to find the girl who'd stolen his documents standing in the doorway, leaning on the frame. She was wearing a cutoff black T-shirt, looking like a skater kid or a wannabe punk rather than a future member of Aura Healers.

"You."

She raised an eyebrow. "For someone who spent their high school jerking off to medical records for extra credit, you sure do have a limited vocabulary."

"You stole my information. I worked hard for it."

She strolled into the room and plopped into the spot where the supposed apparition was located.

"Didn't stop you from getting into the Halls. Besides, I think you got your revenge when you tied me to a tree at the end of the third round."

A burst of laughter came from the girl with the rainbow-colored hair. She covered her mouth with her hand, bright green eyes peering over.

"Didn't stop you from getting in either," said Damon.

"My fairy godmother granted a wish." She turned to the other girl. "I'm Remi."

"Lily."

"He's Damon Arthur Wolfhard," said Remi. "Arthur is your father's name I bet."

Damon hated that she was right.

Lily leaned forward, pointing a long, bright orange fingernail at him. It was the color of a lit cigarette. "You knocked me over at the gondola."

Recognition hit him between the eyes. "I'm sorry. I was trying to get my stuff back from her."

"Ain't right to knock other folks down," said Lily, squinting. "You scared Neko."

The tension was interrupted when a guy wearing a Hundred Halls hoodie leaned into the door. He had a neat afro and wore silver earrings.

"You're in the wrong room. The rest of the class is one floor up."

"That's not where the girl at the table told us to go," said Damon, rising to his feet.

"She was suffering from toxic shock. Sent us all over the hospital. One of the nurses figured out we were in the wrong place. I'm Boon," he said, offering his hand, which Damon shook.

"Damon. I remember you from the auditorium."

Damon found it easy to chat with Boon as they wound through the hallways to the correct room. Remi and Lily followed, talking conspiratorially, which made him want to check his pockets for his valuables.

The room on the second floor was larger, with multiple couches, a wipe board with the words "Delicate Dimpled Demon Balls" written in the corner, a small kitchenette, and three large wooden tables covered in piles of books and tomes.

Boon introduced them upon entry. The first years were a class of fifteen students from all over the country and the world. Damon was relieved he no longer had to interact with the thief, whom he assumed wouldn't last long in the challenging hospital environment. He just had to put up with her until she got kicked out, or left on her own.

"Anyone know who's supposed to talk to us?" asked Ethan, checking his watch. He wore designer glasses and had an artificial foot on his left leg. "We're nearly an hour late. Are we in the right room?"

"Those piles of medical tomes suggest we are," said Sasha in a posh English accent. Damon was no fashion expert, but he imagined her outfit was worth more than the entire room's combined.

A stern voice in the doorway startled the class. An older man, wearing a worn backpack and clothes that looked like he'd been sleeping in them for weeks, stepped in front of the wipe board.

"I'm not late, you're early. Remember that now. Whatever you think you know, forget it. The only thing that matters is that I'm right and you're wrong. Since I have the unfortunate responsibility of being your teaching professor, it means I'm going to spend more time keeping you from killing the patients than actually helping them."

He surveyed the room as if he were picking out victims for a robbery. "My name is Dr. Oren Decker."

FIFTEEN

The scruffy looking doctor who had introduced himself as Dr. Oren Decker looked one step above homeless. The only reason Remi didn't think it was a scam was because this was the last place on Earth she'd imagine trying to run one. While there might be opportunities to line her pockets at a later date, tricking first year Hall students wasn't a profitable venture.

"I'm Damon Wolfhard."

The tall, handsome student offered his hand, which Dr. Decker stared at like it was a live cobra.

"I'll learn your names when I think you'll last more than a week."

Damon hung his head and dipped back to his chair while the new doctor slipped out of his backpack and stretched his arms as if he were readying to take a nap.

"Now, who can fetch me a shot?"

"Of what?" asked Sasha.

"Whiskey, of course. Do you do shots of milk or tea?"

The entire class glanced to each other while Remi was amused. She revised her opinion about it being a trick. The doctor wasn't trying to scam them out of money, but he was doing something. What, she hadn't quite determined, but it sure was entertaining.

"You," said Dr. Decker, snapping his fingers at Boon. "What's in that fridge?"

Boon checked inside, speaking over his shoulder. "Nothing but pop, and a bottle of mustard."

Dr. Decker put a hand to his forehead. "Pop? Okay, fine. Throw me one and the bottle of mustard. Might erase the banger of a headache I've got."

He caught the plastic soda bottle, twisted the cap, and squirted the mustard inside while chanting an incantation under his breath. The mixture boiled and bubbled, a brownish-yellow foam forming in the neck, but before it could escape, Dr. Decker chugged the entire thing in one go. A wall-rattling belch followed, which only brought more collective concern.

"I like him," she whispered to Lily, who was another delightful surprise at the Hall. She'd expected nothing but stiff underwear like Damon, not the loosely wrapped ball of crazy next to her on the couch that may or may not have an animal in her hair.

The doctor looked ready to address them when a middle-aged woman in a white doctor coat, with dirty blonde hair in a ponytail and bags beneath her eyes big enough to count as luggage, appeared in the doorway.

Were any of these doctors not about to fall over from exhaustion?

"No," said the doctor, shaking her head. "No way. No how. I don't know where Patron Jennings is, but we need to have a talk. There's no way I'm letting you back in my hospital, Oren."

"Lovely to see you too, Linda."

"That'll be Dr. Fairlight to you."

He spread his arms. "Sorry, love. I'm all you got. Bill said that Dr. Simmons got hit with a laughing curse that he can't shake and Joanne had a mental breakdown and is somewhere on the Mediterranean coast having sex with hairy men who drink olive oil for breakfast while having doubts about her life choices."

"I don't care, Oren." She hesitated, realizing she was speaking in front of the entire first-year class. "There has to be someone else. Anyone."

"I heard you have a hot shot doctor in charge of the ER. If you don't want me, give her the first years."

"Dr. Morrison is the only thing keeping the ER from descending into chaos. It's been bad these last few years since the Event. Merlin knows we could have used you then, back when you gave a damn."

Dr. Decker raised an eyebrow as he flipped his empty soda bottle into the trash, raising his hands in a mock victory when it went straight into the middle.

"Patient admissions are up?"

"Way up. The city's gone mad. Started last year and has only gotten worse."

He spread his arms. "Then I guess I'm all yours."

Dr. Fairlight reached for the phone on her hip, checking the screen, and then sighed exasperatingly.

"I have to go, Oren. Try not to, you know, try not to be you."

He gave her a magnanimous smile and waved as she left. "Good to see you, Linda. And congrats on making Chief." When she was gone, he jabbed his thumb in her direction. "Dr. Fairlight. Chief of Staff. One of the best doctors I know that has never had a breakdown. Now, where were we?"

No one said anything. He clapped his hands in front of him.

"Right. First year students of the Hundred Halls. Holistic Institute.

What will you be doing under my watch?"

Damon raised his hand. "Helping patients?"

"Wrong. Do not pass go. Do not collect fifty bucks, or whatever that stupid game says. Your job is to not kill them." He walked over to the whiteboard and quickly wrote out a phrase, which he repeated after he capped the marker.

"Rule number one. You don't know shit." He underlined the phrase twice. "You are *not* doctors. Even when you graduate from Aura Healers, you will not *be* doctors. If you're a sadist, you can stay on and get your degree, but until then, you are glorified spell slingers. The only thing you're qualified to do at this point is to keep your mouth shut and your eyes open and maybe, just maybe, after five years of torture, you'll have the distinct pleasure of improving someone's life just a little bit."

He stared at them aggressively.

"Let's see if you were listening. What's the first rule?"

Their collective mumbled answers trampled over each other.

"Let's do it again!"

"We don't know shit!"

At that moment, a man in a white coat paused outside the doorway with his eyes wide as dinner plates. His jaw threatened to bump into his chest.

"Hi, Bob," said Dr. Decker, waving cheerfully.

The man looked like he'd seen a ghost. He continued walking, shaking his head while mumbling to himself.

"That was Bob Morehead. Yeah, I know, bummer of a last name. Head of the Testing Department. You'll get to know him in time."

Dr. Decker rubbed the stubble on his chin as he surveyed the first years as if he was trying to figure out what was next.

"Aren't we supposed to link to Patron Jennings?" asked Ethan with his hand half raised.

"That is true. In a roundabout way. The way things work in Aura Healers is that I'll be your instructor for the entirety of your five years. Patron Jennings prefers to have you link directly to the teaching instructor, which gives us better insight into your work. Everyone raise your fists and, well, you know the drill. Don't fuck it up. I will judge you."

When Remi pulled the faez back into her mind, it wasn't the cool, euphoric feeling she'd felt in the auditorium before the first trial. The sensation was like putting on a wooly sweater that was both scratchy and too warm.

Next to her on the couch, Lily whimpered, her face pinched with pain. She leaned over holding her stomach, which made Remi wonder if the link was making her sick somehow. The inspection was interrupted when Dr. Decker snapped his fingers in Lily's direction. He squinted at Lily, who was playing with the tattered ends of her multihued hair.

"What is that? Is that a rat?" he asked, snapping his fingers and indicating the Irish girl with his outstretched finger.

The entire room turned towards Lily. Remi leaned forward to peer at her new friend to see a pointed furry face sticking out from the mess of hair.

"That's Neko. Don't worry. He's cleaner than a country whistle."

Dr. Decker ran a hand over the top of his head, mussing up his already unruly hair.

"We can't have rats in the hospital."

"I'll keep him in my room. Don't worry, Neko is very well behaved."

"Fine, whatever. Just don't let him become a problem or rat stew will hit the menu."

A tiny squeak was followed by the pointed face disappearing into the mess of hair.

"Right. Where were we?" Dr. Decker sighed. "Who enjoys sleep?"

Half the class raised their hands.

"Wrong answer. The sleep you got last night will be the last you'll have for a very long time. Becoming a healer can't be learned in a book, despite those piles back there. The best way to learn is repetition, and that requires spending countless hours in the hospital, until you're dancing on the edge, having hallucinations so real that you think you've gone mad. It's not a matter of if you'll have a breakdown, but when.

"For the next month, and at various times during the year, you'll be shadowing doctors, keeping your eyes and ears open and your mouths shut. In the course of your five years, I'll rotate you through the different departments so you get a feel for how the hospital operates. In addition, I assume those piles of books back there are for you. Make sure you grab one of each and start working on the first. I expect you to have it read front to back by the end of the first two weeks, and the entire pile by the end of the calendar year."

Dr. Decker stared at them from the head of the room until he raised his arms.

"What are you waiting for? A starting gun?"

The class rose to their feet, scrambling after the books. Each one was as heavy as a boulder. Remi collected her stack, which went from her hands to the bottom of her chin. She hadn't read a book in years. As Remi followed Lily out of the room, she paused by Dr. Decker, who was leaning on a table, thumbing through his phone and eating a cracker he'd pulled out of a random pocket.

"How are we supposed to read all this?" she asked, straining under the weight of the books.

Dr. Decker stared at her with dead eyes for a long moment, before jerking his head towards the door.

"You don't have to be here. Feel free to walk out that door at any time. It'll make my job a helluva lot easier."

SIXTEEN

The dim light in the dorm room was like needles to the backs of her eyes. Lily sat on the corner of her bed with a silver platter in her lap, tracing runic lines across the smooth surface, using blood she'd pricked from her finger. Neko squeaked softly next to her, but she ignored her little companion as she spoke in her native tongue.

"Go rachaidh na spioraid tríom."

The fresh blood glowed intensely for a second before turning to char. A wave of refreshment washed through her, banishing the worst of the migraine. Lily tossed the platter on the floor and leaned against the wall as Neko crawled into her lap. She stroked the rat's silky back as she let relief sink in.

The door opened, sending searing, bright hallway light into the room briefly before disappearing. Remi threw her shower bin onto the floor as she used a secondary towel to dry her hair.

"You okay?"

Lily nodded.

"Better now," she said, hearing the sadness in her voice. There were some things she'd never get to experience again, like circle chanting with her sisters, or the feeling of joy around the Eó Ruis tree. She pushed away the ache. She'd made her choice when she flew over the ocean. No reason to have doubts now when there was still so much to be done.

Remi dropped the towel wrapped around her midsection and began digging through a pile of clothes that looked recently purchased.

"You're no more shy than a proud puca," said Lily.

"Huh? Oh yeah," said Remi as she pulled on a pair of black lace panties. "Kinda forget about privacy, well, in the places I've been."

"Orphanage?"

"No," said Remi. "My parents are still alive...I think."

Lily studied her roommate while she continued getting dressed. Remi had a frenetic energy to her, like a flitting mayfly trying to wring every last moment out of their short life. Little scars marked her back and arms, along with random tattoos that looked like afterthoughts rather than planned choices.

"Brothers and sisters?"

Remi paused, one foot half in her scrubs. "I wasn't in the plan as it was. No reason to add a second mouth to feed. Especially because we were always moving. Sometimes in the middle of the night when things got hot. You?"

"Loads of siblings, cousins, aunts, and uncles. Bit of a stew, mind ya. Lived near Killarney, most beautiful place in Ireland. Already feel my heart wishing I was back there instead of here."

Remi spied the silver, blood-caked platter. "What's that about?"

"A little country remedy for my headache."

"You know magic?"

"Aye. The kind passed down from mother to daughter. I know a fair number of poultices and tinctures. Dreadful concoctions that taste like death, but'll give you a pep in your step or get rid of an unexpected addition in the belly."

Remi hunched her forehead. "Right." She looked to the door. "What do you think of Decker?"

"Dr. Decker? He has a lot of bodies buried in his barn."

"Yeah," said Remi, chuckling. "I heard one of the other doctors call him Dr. O.D. and I don't think they were just talking about his initials." She threw on a shirt and plopped on the bed. "What brought you here? No offense, but you don't look like the type to join the Halls."

A host of images bubbled up in her mind. Her sisters in the Great Hall. Red ribbons around the Eó Ruis. Capturing minnows in the lily-covered ponds. But not all were good memories. She saw the sickness in her sisters, the black lines on their arms and necks, the teeth falling out. The signs on her own flesh had already begun to fade since she'd switched her patronage to the strange doctor, but the pain would remain.

"Not every injury can be healed with the old magics."

Remi stared back, all movements falling to stillness. "I'm headed down to the cafeteria. Heard we get free food and it's not bad. They use spices and stuff. Wanna come?"

The thought of eating made her stomach ache and she wasn't ready to move yet. She'd barely recovered from the trials and the linkage.

"I might join you later."

Remi left their room. The bright lights of the hallway made Lily squint, but she leaned her head into the corner and coaxed Neko into her lap.

"It'll be alright. It'll be alright."

SEVENTEEN

Damon had been standing near the water station for a half hour watching the flow through the emergency room. A man in tattered robes that looked like a Halloween costume was standing on a chair explaining how the end of times was upon them, while at least two babies were bawling at full volume. At the sign-in desk, a woman speaking in rapid-fire Spanish was trying to tell the attendant about her father's injuries. Damon's Spanish was terrible, even though he'd taken four years of it, but he heard something about a man with the face of a grub worm putting a hex on her father. In the short window of time, he'd seen three separate ambulances arrive with bloody victims that were quickly wheeled away to other parts of the hospital.

It reminded him of a video he'd seen once of a busy intersection in Rome, where small cars and mopeds competed for every possible space, moving at random and competing directions. The nurses and doctors moved with an eerie calmness, but he could see the intensity in their eyes. They were barely holding it together.

"Sorry about the wait," said Dr. Morrison, coming from the back hallway. She wore a white coat over her green scrubs. Her hair was braided into a crown. "We had an emergency staff meeting. Apparently the clinic in ward nine had a major power outage. An akurra chewed through a major electrical line." She shook her head. "Damn things were all the rage a few years ago because their scales reflect like a rainbow, but then they get huge and have an affinity for eating anything electronic. They say it'll take until morning to fix, which means this Saturday night is going to get even worse."

"Worse than now?" he asked, glancing to the barely contained chaos.

Dr. Morrison checked out the automatic front doors where the light was fading.

"The evening rush hasn't even started yet. Once it gets dark, the real fun begins. I've already sent word to the school. Anyone who hasn't already had a double shift is being called down. We need all hands, even if they can only push a gurney."

"I'm ready to help. I've worked a lot of shifts at KC General."

She shoved a clipboard in his chest. "Damon. I appreciate the enthusiasm, but you'll cause more harm than good. You've barely been here three weeks. Just stay out of the way unless I give you specific instructions."

For the next hour, Damon followed Dr. Morrison from bed to bed, following up with the doctors and nurses as they dealt with the incoming patients. He was surprised about how many bite wounds there were. Back in his hometown, major injuries were usually caused by guns or knives. Dr. Morrison rarely dealt with patients herself, but helped organize the priorities with a pair of nurses that were in charge of triage. He kept checking out the windows at the fading light, and he wasn't the only one.

When the parking lot lamps switched on, a white-haired older man in faded scrubs came through the emergency room pushing a cart of vials. The tinkling of glass brought the nurses and doctors like moths to a flame.

"Thanks, Jeb," said Dr. Morrison, pulling a vial of swirling orange-brown liquid from the tray, gesturing for Damon to take one.

"I mixed in a touch of dried ghost-eye to help against the toxic slimes we've been seeing lately," said the older man as he ran his fingers through his wispy hair.

"Good idea. I don't know what we'd do without you," she said.

"You're just saying that so I don't retire."

He followed Dr. Morrison's example, downing the mixture, which tasted like oranges dipped in fresh dirt. A warmth spread out through his midsection, climbing to his chest until he felt euphoric like he was floating above the ground.

"Whoa."

"I miss my first taste of Jeb's potions."

Damon rubbed his jaw, which felt tingly. "Is it always like this?"

"No, eventually your body gets used to it, but Jeb keeps adjusting the formula so we're not flagging at three in the morning when the crazy crunch hits."

Damon wasn't sure he wanted to know what the crazy crunch was, and he had no time to ask as the triage nurse called out.

"We've got three howlers on the way. One of them is a troll. Gonna need a ropes team on two!"

"Troll?" asked Damon, barely keeping up with the lingo. He knew howlers were the ambulances.

Dr. Morrison was scribbling notes at the end of a patient's bed.

"Supernatural strength. Either they've got the blood, or are on some enhancers, arcane or alchemical."

"Want me to help?"

She looked like she was about to turn him down, but then she nodded. "Come with me."

Two beefy men and one enormous woman were standing at the automatic doors looking like out-of-place bodybuilders except for their plain white orderly clothes.

"Dr. Morrison," said one of the muscle-bound guys.

Dr. Morrison nodded at the bearded man. "Tavy, this is Damon. He's a fumble fingers." She glanced over. "Sorry. Nothing personal, it's what everyone calls first years at Healers. Anyway. He wants to help with the troll."

Tavy burst out laughing. "First night in the ER?"

"Yeah, but I've—"

Tavy put a meaty hand on his shoulder and gave it a painful squeeze.

"The only thing worse than the ER in Golden Willow is triage near a battlefront, and I should know, I did seven years with Blackstone PMC." He pulled his hand away and looked to Dr. Morrison. "You sure about this?"

"He's not your usual first year," said Dr. Morrison.

"Alright, come with me. The howler should be here any second. Our job is to get the troll into the magical restraints. They said he's been subdued with a heavy dose of spells and sedatives, but don't let that fool you. They like to wait until the worst possible time to make a break for it."

As the first ambulance entered the overhang, they stepped out of the way of the medics that scrambled out and removed a man screaming at the top of his lungs from the back. His eyes were glowing from some spell and he seemed in great pain.

"Gonna be a four beller night," said Tavy, shaking his head.

"Four beller?"

Tavy chuckled. "Back in the early years of Golden Willow, they had a bell outside the ER. Everyone was assigned a bell code. They would ring the bell to bring new doctors and nurses from their sleep or whatever they were doing."

"Out of ten?"

Tavy shook his head. "Five is the max."

"Had many of those?"

Tavy stared into the distance. "During the Event we had ten straight days of five bells."

The tall woman, who had a jaw made of iron, leaned over and spoke in a language he couldn't understand. She was a few inches taller than him, and he was about six foot four. Tavy glanced over at Damon with a grin firmly attached to his lips.

"What she say?"

"Wants to hook up, in a manner of speaking. Not tonight, but you know, when you're free."

"Oh," said Damon, the word falling out of his mouth.

"The Kraks are pretty straightforward when it comes to sex. And insatiable. I don't have the stamina for it anymore," said Tavy.

"Kraks?"

"Krakatow. A mountainous realm that's been in the middle of civil war for the last thirty years. Ash is a refugee." The sound of sirens approaching had Tavy clapping his hands together. "Alright, troll's here. Get ready. Damon, you stand in that corner. We'll wheel the troll into the rope room. Our job is to get him into the magical restraints so the docs can work on him safely."

The adrenaline of the approaching ambulance had Damon bouncing his foot. When the vehicle skidded to a stop, Tavy led them to the back, where the medics threw the doors wide.

"He's out, but not sure how much longer," said the paramedic as they unloaded the gurney, pulling down the wheels for mobility. The patient had his eyes closed, almost peacefully. He didn't look like he had unusual strength, but Damon knew that was deceiving. Something about the patient triggered a lingering concern, so he leaned down and gave him a hearty sniff. He smelled like rich, rotting soil. The acidity had him wrinkling his nose, but he couldn't investigate further because of the pace.

The four of them hurried down the hall towards a room with glowing runes on the frame. Despite volunteering at KC General, the pace and unusual protections left Damon bewildered, but he kept his focus, paying attention to Tavy so he didn't miss a signal.

"Now, this is the fun part. I'm going to unlatch him from the gurney and we're going to haul his ass to the bed. As soon as his arm or leg is in the manacle, snap it closed. On the count of three."

At the moment Damon lifted the patient from the gurney, he realized the guy's eyes were open and staring directly at him. The patient grinned.

"Tavy—"

The word barely left his mouth when the guy ripped an arm free and slammed Damon in the chest, throwing him across the room. He landed on a food cart, which flipped over on him.

The other three went from smooth transition to fighting for their lives. Damon knocked the cart from atop him, scrambling to get back to the patient, who was struggling to get free like a caged wildcat, limbs flying everywhere. The freed arm was doing the most damage, slamming into their jaws and upper bodies, nearly throwing them off.

With fingernails extended to claws, Damon threw himself on the patient's flailing legs, giving the others a chance to finish hauling him to the bed. A punch caught Damon in the right eye, nearly blinding him, but he held on, using his rage to maintain his hold. Ash, the big Krak woman, decked the patient with a right hook that sent him limp, and they managed to finish transferring him to the bed, locking the manacles, which brought a hum of enchantment when they were closed.

"Good job, team," said Tavy, putting his hand on Damon's shoulder.

"Looks like you caught a good one."

Damon couldn't open his right eye and his back hurt from hitting the cart.

"I'll grab you an auto-healer. They work great for little injuries like that," said Tavy.

"Thanks."

"Not a matter of thanks, we need everyone if we're going to survive the night."

Ash leaned over and spoke to Tavy again, which brought another round of laughter. She pointed at his longer nails.

"Oh, now she really wants to bang you, mate."

Damon let himself be led away by Tavy as Ash stared at him like a lion sizing up an antelope. As they passed through the entrance of the ER with two more howlers pulling up, Damon thought back to the strange scents he'd picked up on the patient. It wasn't the first time his sensitive nose had detected the acidic soil, like a garden having gone to rot in the summer heat. He didn't know what it meant, but he didn't have time to think about it as more sirens approached, signaling it was going to be a long night.

EIGHTEEN

A crash had Dr. Paddock checking the hallway while Lily stayed at the foot of the patient's bed. He had pale skin and black lines climbing up the throat. The doctor adjusted his wire-rimmed glasses as he returned.

"Just a Jell-O cart, seems the orderly was careless with his duties."

Dr. Paddock approached the patient.

"Now, for the important part. Our patient is unresponsive, so our investigation will have to be purely physical, which is a blessing in my professional opinion. The sick are rarely truthful with the reasons for their illness."

"Dr. Decker says that even their dishonesty can be a clue to the problem," said Lily.

Dr. Paddock sighed heavily, leaning on the bed. "Your first-year instructor has been away from the hospital system for nearly a decade. I think his practices may be outdated and his methods suspect."

He looked pained by the admission.

"I'm sorry, but it's a tragedy that he was assigned as your teacher given his history."

"His history?"

A groan from the patient had the doctor sighing again, which seemed to be a regular occurrence.

"Let us focus on the task at hand, rather than gossiping about our fellow physicians."

He glanced up.

"And please fix your hair, it's rather distracting. You should consider trimming it. A professional healer shouldn't look like a homeless person."

"My hair is perfectly fine," said Lily tersely.

"Very well then," said Dr. Paddock. "The patient. Can you cast a Nygal's Revealing Aura on him? If you've managed to learn that spell. I realize it's quite difficult for a first year."

Lily ignored the condescending tone and stretched her hands over the immobile patient. The spell in her estimation wasn't particularly challenging, or useful, but she didn't want the doctor to think she wasn't up to the task. The motions for the spell were like conducting a symphony, as she molded and stretched the uncharged faez until it was a pale, golden light above the patient. When it was fully formed, she pushed it into his chest cavity, which lit up the organs and internal features briefly.

The doctor stared at the lingering glow with pursed lips. "That didn't seem to do what I hoped. And your spell work was passable. You should practice it more."

Lily kept a faint smile on her lips. "With pleasure."

"Follow me," he said, heading into the hallway.

"Aren't we going to figure out what's wrong with him?"

Dr. Paddock squeezed his shoulders forward. "It was only so you could practice on him. He seems to be stable and we have more important patients to worry about on such a busy night."

Lily was going to suggest that the patient might have drank water that a kelpie had defecated in. She'd seen similar afflictions in Ireland when tourists swam in lakes that weren't open to the public. The proper course was a poultice of enchanted ginger and crushed pollywart until the sickness passed. He wasn't in danger, but he'd be unresponsive for days until he woke with a major headache.

On the way down the hall, an apparition covered in blood was coming towards them, walking with legs spread and a low moan issuing from his lips. Dr. Paddock froze, holding his hand out to keep her from continuing.

"Do something," said the doctor frantically.

Lily leaned forward, examining the bloody apparition. "That's Boon. He's a first year."

Boon had his arms out. Crimson liquid dripped from everywhere. He looked like he'd taken a bath in a pool of blood.

"What happened?" she asked.

"Dr. Viski had me try to reduce a sanguine tumor with a spell. I bungled the phrasing and it exploded."

"Are you going to be okay?" she asked.

He looked frightened. "I'm on my way to get a round of shots and elixirs. Dr. Viski said I'll be in a lot of pain for a few days, but I won't die."

"You should have been more careful," said Dr. Paddock. "This is why I disagree with the decision to let first years work in the hospital. Your inexperience is a menace. Now hurry along, before the seizures set in."

In the next room, the patient wasn't so still as their last one. The older woman fought against her restraints. Her steel gray hair was wispy and the bags around her eyes had darkened. She spoke in an unintelligible voice that sounded like growls and barks.

"Keep your distance, young lady," said the doctor as he pulled the clipboard. "Here we have a clear case of faez madness, I believe. Using raw magic without a patron has warped her mind and she has no grasp on reality. There's little we can do for her, but hope the worst of it passes or send her to a special facility where she'll ride out the end of her days in this terrible agony. Another black mark against the use of magic, it seems."

"She looks possessed," said Lily right away. "I've seen it before—"

Dr. Paddock cleared his throat, cutting her off. "I'm sorry, young lady, you are not qualified to diagnose this patient. Just because you read a few tomes and passed the trials does not make you a healer. I barely count Dr. Morrison and she's been here for nearly a decade."

"Isn't she the head of the ER?"

"Precisely," said Dr. Paddock. "In an emergency, you can be forgiven for being sloppy and making mistakes. But the real work takes decades to master. Now I'd like—"

He reached for his phone, reading it with the twentieth sigh in the last hour.

"Excuse me, I'm needed on the second floor. There's a patient going through a therianthropic shock, which is a bit of a specialty of mine, so they've asked me for a consult," he said, adjusting his tie and puffing out his chest.

When she started to follow, the doctor said, "Please stay here and don't touch anything. There's already too many people in the room."

Lily frowned after he left and muttered, "Bloody tea sipper."

Without the doctor around, she approached the patient, who stared back with feral intensity.

"I don't think you're down with the faez madness, are you? You look like a woman possessed, but what kind? I don't think it's a spirit possession. That language isn't related to the Veil, or the infernal realm."

Lily reached into her fanny pack, producing a silver coin. She brushed it against the liver-spotted flesh of the old woman, but nothing happened. Then she grabbed for a small vial with an eyedropper, producing a single drop, which she let fall on her fingernail. The nail turned jet black immediately.

"Gladestool poisoning," she said with surprise. "What was an old woman like you doing in the Fae realm? Or did someone bring something over and you couldn't help yourself? Interesting."

Lily closed the door so no one would see what she was about to do. She pulled out a small vial of arsenic and iron flakes. She poured out the ochre dust on the tray next to the bed, then let a single drop of arsenic fall, mixing the two with a tongue depressor from the supply cabinet. Using the wooden applicator, she extended it towards the woman's mouth.

"Just a taste will do."

The woman clamped her mouth shut and shook her head ferociously. Lily checked to see that the door was closed and then punched the old woman in the stomach. When she gasped for air, Lily shoved the flat wood into her mouth and wiped the mixture on her tongue, pulling back quickly to keep from getting bitten.

"There. That should help with the infection." She grinned. "Sorry about the fisticuffs. No one walks far without dirty shoes. It shouldn't bruise too much."

Lily dumped the mixture and applicator in the hazardous waste bin and watched the old woman slowly calm over the course of a few minutes.

By the time Dr. Paddock returned, the old woman was sleeping peacefully.

"What happened here?" asked the doctor.

Lily shrugged. "She calmed on her own. Maybe it wasn't faez madness, but a bit of poisoning of some kind and it worked its way out of her system."

Dr. Paddock stared at the woman with slitted eyes for a long time before sighing.

"Very well. Sometimes we get lucky. Let that be a lesson to you. Come with me, young lady. I have much to teach you."

NINETEEN

The ropes team hurried past Remi and Dr. Decker, who held out his hand, receiving a high five from the beefy guy in front.

"Go get 'em!"

Dr. Decker chuckled as he sipped from a juice box. "Are you sure you don't want one? Got to keep the energy up. We're only at halftime and we still haven't hit the crazy crunch."

"Everyone already looks at me like I'm in grade school and shouldn't be here. If I start drinking juice boxes, they're never going to see me any other way," said Remi.

"Suit yourself. Life gets a lot easier when you stop giving a shit about the little things," he said, checking the nonexistent watch on his wrist. "Now, where were we?"

"On our way to the first floor."

Dr. Morrison came hurrying around the corner. Her normally deep brown skin was flushed and pale.

"There you are, I've been trying to call you for the last half hour."

Dr. Decker feigned checking his pockets for his phone. "I must have left it in the cafeteria. Sorry, Janelle. Whatdya need?"

"Two brothers in Observation Rooms C and D. They were found brawling on the sidewalk in the seventh ward—before Invictus PD showed up, they'd torn down two lampposts and flipped a parked car into a Wizard's Coffee. They're calm now but nobody can figure out what's wrong, and they don't want them at the station unless we can verify what their condition is."

"Aye, aye, Captain Morrison. Myself and Bosun Wilde will report directly to their rooms and discover the truth of this mystery."

Dr. Morrison blinked twice. "Fine. Whatever. Thank you."

She hurried back the other way while Dr. Decker turned and winked at Remi while sucking on the juice box.

"Your loss," he said, holding up the empty drink before launching it into a trash bin thirty feet down the hall.

"Why did you lie about your phone?"

"Huh?"

"It's in your left coat pocket."

He reached in and produced the black case. "Sure enough. Guess I forgot it was there."

Remi didn't know what sort of game he was playing, but he seemed in a strangely good mood despite the chaos that had descended on the emergency room. She'd been studying her tomes when the call had come for all students to support the massive influx of patients. For the first three hours, she was helping the front desk, then Dr. Decker grabbed her to help with his patients. Now it was well after midnight and the rush was still going strong.

Dr. Decker knocked on the doorframe of Observation C before entering the room. The guy in the bed, restraints holding his wrists and legs, looked barely older than her. He was kinda cute with messy brown hair and perfectly placed dimples.

"Hey, amigo," said Dr. Decker, leaning against the bed as if they were old friends. He grabbed the chart. "Dustin, eh? Had a bit of a scuffle with your brother earlier."

Dustin shrugged. "It was an argument that got out of hand. I'm really sorry. If we can be let go, I swear we'll go right home and you won't see us again."

Dr. Decker winked. "See, amigo, you kinda pissed off the PD. When they don't know where to send someone, they'll ship you off to a little jail they like to call Paranormal Hell. So tell me, what had you raging like a demon?"

The patient glanced from Dr. Decker to her.

"Oh, don't worry. She's a doctor in training. Anything you say, she's authorized to hear."

"I swear we were just partying too hard, you know, some powders an acquaintance gave us."

"What if I drew blood? Would that tell me anything?" asked Dr. Decker.

"Please," said Dustin. "If that would help prove to you that it's just a series of really bad decisions."

"Should I get the bloodsucker?" asked Remi, stepping towards the door.

"Bloodsucker?" asked Dustin in horror as he sat straight up.

Dr. Decker put a hand on Dustin's arm. "What our juice box allergic first year means is the phlebotomist, which we affectionately call a bloodsucker or vampire. While those do exist, ours is probably extremely busy, so we'll be taking the samples ourselves."

"Oh," said Dustin, leaning back into the elevated bed.

The doctor rummaged around in the desk until he found a sample vial and a fresh needle. After cinching the patient's arm with a rubber hose, Dr. Decker handed the syringe to Remi.

"You ever taken blood before?"

"What? No. Only watched."

"There's a first time for everything." He checked over his shoulder. "You don't mind, do you, Dustin?"

"I guess not," he replied hesitantly.

"I've never done it before."

"I've read your history, Miss Wilde. I think finger dexterity is the least of your concerns. In fact, I'd call it a strength."

"I, uhm—"

"I insist. Either that or I'm going to make you wear a onesie and drink juice boxes in the cafeteria every night."

She took the syringe. "Are you really a doctor?"

"Are you really trying to be an Aura Healer?"

"Fine."

He held his hand out. "Before you do, there's a little trick I learned in Danir that might make it a little easier since our friend has very small veins."

Dr. Decker cast a spell over the patient's arm that made the flesh glow crimson. She felt warmth emanating from his arm like a hot rock after sitting in sunlight.

"This excites his veins, making it easier, not that I suspect you need it."

The idea of puncturing someone's arm with a needle was not on her wish list. She'd expected to learn spells, which she had, but not to actually touch the patients.

"I'm not planning on being a doctor."

"Not relevant. Trust me. You want to learn this, and besides, you need me to pass you or you'll be back on the streets picking pockets."

Remi growled under her breath. She set the needle against the patient's flesh, sliding it into the throbbing vein until Dr. Decker told her to stop. Then she pulled back the plunger until the vial was full. Removing the needle left a dab of blood, which he covered with a band-aid.

"See? You're a natural bloodsucker."

"Thanks?"

Dr. Decker took the vial, wrote a note on a piece of paper he ripped from a notepad, and handed both to her.

"Take this down to testing. Don't take no for an answer. I'm going to question Dustin's brother until you return with the information."

She looked at the notepaper, which only said: "Test for parasites."

"I don't understand."

"Rule number two with Dr. Decker. Always test for parasites. They're sneaky bastards and their symptoms are a cross-section of every other issue, which makes resolving them a critical piece in understanding how Dustin has been lying to us."

"What? I haven't been lying."

Dr. Decker crossed his arms. "Rule number three. The patient is always lying. But that's okay. There is truth within those falsehoods." He pointed to a fleck of purple paint on Dustin's upper arm. "For example, see this? Paint markers are commonly used in summonings, runic wards, and other enchantments. Our Brothers Grimm were likely involved in some sort of arcane chicanery that left them without their wits."

"Then why am I testing for parasites?"

He shooed her away. "Just do it! And don't come back without an answer!"

The testing laboratory was in the basement of the main building. The head of the lab, Bob Morehead, was loading a centrifuge and drinking a steaming cup of coffee when she arrived. The thunderous drums and guitars of heavy metal were playing softly over the speakers, and Bob was nodding along while mouthing the lyrics.

"You're one of his, aren't you?"

Remi hesitated, holding the note and vial of blood out like a sharp knife. Bob stared at the offerings with flat lips.

"I'm not testing for parasites. It's a huge waste of hospital resources and never amounts to anything. He does it just to prove to himself that he's in charge. So if that's what your little note says, then march back up and tell that fraud to stuff it up his ass."

It was almost two in the morning and Remi's energy levels were flagging. Getting caught between two power structures in the hospital wasn't what she wanted to deal with, but she knew if she tried returning to Dr. Decker, he'd send her right back down.

"I'm just a first year—"

He cut her off mid-sentence. "And in short order, you'll be calling shots on your own. If I don't teach you that he doesn't know what he's talking about now, you'll never learn."

The coffee cup rattled as he set it down, turning to a strange device with runes along the outer frame that were alternating between a pale green and a dull orange. Bob punched in new codes before turning towards another piece of lab equipment.

"Why are you still standing there?"

"Is there anything I can do in return? I'm resourceful. A little trade might benefit us both."

The older man ran his hand through his thinning hair. "I don't do trades. We're not in the eighteen-century barter economy. Now shoo. You're not making a good first impression. Remember I can make your career in Aura Healers a nightmare if I so choose."

With the note and vial in her hand, she trudged back towards the hallway. She made it halfway before she realized that the hospital was like any other organization—driven by egos and power struggles. These were the fault lines her parents had taught her to exploit for personal gain. It was why she'd been able to easily get access to the pendant at the Dreadmarsh cottage, because the owners didn't see cleaning staff as people, thinking that their ancestral history protected them from the foibles of normal life.

"What are you doing back here?" he asked angrily.

Remi put the vial and paper on the counter. "You're testing the blood for parasites and other drugs."

"Did you slip and concuss yourself?" asked Bob.

"No, I just realized who the bigger asshole is, and it's not you. Yes, you can make my life a living hell at Aura Healers, but he can make it infinitely worse. I only have to see how you reacted to his request to know that I'm right. And I probably won't make it to the end of the year, making your threat rather lackluster, while Dr. Decker has an army of first years who rely on his whimsey to pass them. If you don't test the blood now, he'll just send other first years with other stupid requests, or worse, until you break down and give him what he wants. You know he's going to win. Why not give in now and save yourself a lot of pain?"

The longer she talked, the more she knew she was right, but he was so red in the face she wasn't sure he could do the logical thing.

"How about this, you do the other tests, but not the parasite one. Just write up a fake report. It'll save us both a lot of time and heartache. You know the alternative is so much worse."

His jaw slowly lowered and his face slacked until he looked like a zombie. She jabbed her thumb towards a chair in the corner.

"I'll wait. Hopefully the test isn't too long."

A slow blink was the only sign that Remi got that Bob hadn't gone comatose. He swiped the vial off the counter and disappeared into the other half of the laboratory. Remi leaned her head against the wall and in a matter of seconds was soundly asleep.

She woke with Bob shoving a document into her chest. "There's unusual trace chemicals in the blood associated with alchemy. I can run a spectrometer on the chemicals, but it'll take another hour."

"What about the parasites?"

He sighed heavily. "I filled one of those papers out too."

She paged to the back, finding a coffee-stained fake analysis proving the lack of parasites. The report would please Dr. Decker and keep her from getting yelled at again.

"Thanks, Bob."

He said nothing as he trudged back to the centrifuge while Remi hurried upstairs, excited to show Dr. Decker the results. She didn't know how to read most of the information, but the fact that alchemical markers were in his blood was more proof that they were up to something shady as Dr. Decker had suggested.

Remi found him in the brother's room. He looked similar to Dustin but without the deep dimples. Dr. Decker was sitting in a chair next to the bed with his legs crossed, chatting quietly as if they were old friends. She handed him the paper.

"It's not parasites, Dr. Decker. But we found some trace—"

Without looking at the paper, he crumpled it up and tossed it unerringly into the waste bin. She looked from him to the basket twice before shaking her hands at him.

"What the hell? Why'd you send me down to the lab if you weren't going to look at the results?"

The playful mood from before had been erased and replaced with stoicism. He stared back with contempt as he rose and marched into the hallway, beckoning her to follow. When they were safely down the hall, he turned on her angrily.

"Because you didn't listen to what I said. I wanted a parasite test *only*. Not some other pointless analysis which will only tell me what I already know. While Bob and I don't see eye to eye about parasite testing, I do appreciate his reluctance to test for irrelevant data, which wastes valuable resources."

"Pointless? You said in the other room that might be arcane chicanery, which I assume means spells and potions and stuff. Why wouldn't that test help?"

Dr. Decker exhaled through flared nostrils. "While I am pleased that you convinced Bob to test for parasites, which was partially why I sent you down to him, as I wanted to see how you navigate the hospital system. But as for the alchemy test, the last thing I want is for actual results being logged into the system. I thought you more than anyone would understand how the police might use that information to stuff these brothers into a place they don't belong, and might not recover from, even if they're probably guilty of some crime or another."

A cold wind blew through her. She'd been so focused on pleasing the irascible Dr. Decker, she hadn't considered the brothers.

"I'm sorry, I didn't—"

"No, there's no sorry in the hospital and of course you didn't know. That's why I'm in charge. What was rule number one?"

"I don't know shit."

"Do you understand it better?"

Remi hung her head. "I do."

"Now, the next time you go against my wishes, I'll be sending you back to whatever halfway house you crawled out of. You have potential, Remi, but I worry you've spent too much time rebelling against the system to be useful here."

"I was just trying to help..."

"Words that have been used to justify torture and murder countless times in history. You have to do better than that."

Remi wanted to crawl into her own skin and forget the night. Why had she thought she could handle learning to be a mage when she hadn't been in school almost ever? When she looked up, she found Dr. Decker staring.

"Come with me," he said.

She hesitated but followed him into Dustin's room.

"You like a good party?" asked Dr. Decker.

Dustin shrugged his shoulders. "Who doesn't?"

"Come on, Dustin. You're a good liar, but you're not that good."

Dr. Decker grabbed Dustin's hand and pointed at the fingernails while he struggled to free himself.

"There's some skin here from the fight, but look at his cuticles."

"Nail polish?"

"Good, Remi." Dr. Decker released his hand and pulled up his sleeve. "What's that?"

"Looks like glitter?"

"Bingo. You ever been to a rave?"

Remi shook her head.

"There are probably no better raves than in the city of sorcery. The lights, music, illusions, and elixirs make for a potent combination. A euphoric sensory overload that provides a salve against the horrors of the modern world," said Dr. Decker.

For the first time, Remi saw through the cracks of his past. He wasn't talking to her, but about himself.

"Dustin and his brother Caleb mix elixirs for the rave scene," said Dr. Decker eventually. "Pulped thistlewort with rougarou scat provides a base for the most potent euphorics, but if you're careless handling them, you can turn yourself into a raging hulk, which is what drove them to try to kill each other in the middle of the street."

The surprise on Dustin's face told her what he was saying was dead-on.

"I used gloves," said Dustin.

"Gloves are good, but you probably didn't wear high-grade masks. Inhale too much of the off-gases and you'll find yourself angrier than a demon with a bad haircut."

"Shit," said Dustin, shaking his head. "We didn't realize."

Dr. Decker slapped Dustin on the leg. "Remi, can you fetch the keys from the front desk? I'm going to put it in their notes that they had a foreign parasite, picked up from eating bad takeout. Parasites can get you to do all sorts of things."

"Seriously? You're letting us go?"

Remi grabbed a paperclip from the desk, unfolded it, and in a matter of seconds, popped the locks.

"Who needs keys?" she said with a shrug.

She repeated the trick on Caleb's cuffs, and the two brothers stopped by Dr. Decker, thanking him profusely.

"Just don't be idiots next time and wear a mask," he said.

After the brothers left, Remi turned to Dr. Decker. "I don't understand. Can't we get in trouble for letting them go? They're making illegal drugs."

"You wanted to arrest them?"

"No, but, you know, I thought we had to follow the rules. You're not making this very easy for me," said Remi.

Dr. Decker chuckled. "I'm not here to make it easy. Despite what people want to believe, there are no hard-and-fast rules in the hospital. When shit gets hairy like tonight, you have to make things up as you go along, or you'll get buried by the collective mass of human misery."

"What about your rules?"

"Those are different, because you need me to pass," said Dr. Decker. "So the next time you think about disobeying, remember that." He checked the time. "We should be in the calm before the crazy crunch. You should go take a break, walk around outside, or eat, whatever you feel is necessary before it hits."

He didn't wait for her to answer, and headed down the hallway in the same direction as the brothers, which wasn't the emergency entrance.

Remi wandered the opposite way. The emergency room was a normal level of chaos. The same guy that had been there at the beginning of the night was still on his chair. He was mumbling rather than shouting. She spotted Lily heading into a room behind Dr. Paddock. The rainbow-haired Irish girl rolled her eyes behind the white-coated doctor, which made Remi chuckle.

Wanting fresh air, she headed outside, skipping past an ambulance that had arrived. The parking lot was mostly empty, except for the front rows and handicapped spots. The complex of Golden Willow and Aura Healers was set in the middle of a concrete island with tall apartment buildings encircling it like a fortress. Remi wished there was a nearby park or garden where she could lie on the grass or sit on a bench, but the nearest one was at least three blocks away. Too far for a quick excursion. The lack of trees was disappointing, but she was rarely outside the building, so it didn't matter that much.

She stopped when she was surrounded by darkness, away from the bright lights. The night was clear and she could see the Spire at the center of the city. A lamppost buzzed from somewhere behind.

She thought about what Dr. Decker had told her. None of it made any sense. Follow the rules. Don't follow the rules. I'll kick you out if you disobey.

Leaning over to stretch her back, the pendant slipped from underneath her scrubs, dangling from her neck. She stood tall, and wrapped her fingers around the cool metal. The strange designs suggestive of trees and circles were rough against her fingertips. She gripped it and stared into the darkness.

As the events of the night played in her mind, she reviewed her mistakes and wondered how she could ever achieve the levels that Aura Healers would expect of her. Even the worst nurse or doctor had a million times more knowledge. There was no way she was going to be able to learn everything required. Better to learn what she could before going after the reward at the end of the pendant.

A faint glow between her fingers had her looking down, finding it putting off a strange, ghostly light. The metal had warmed. This was a first. She felt a tickle follow her spine, making her shiver. A wind whipped up from the north, even though she saw no storm. The urge to run back into the hospital was strong, but she was too curious to hide.

Remi thought the figure was her imagination at first. He—and she was strangely certain it was a he—stood at the far end of the parking lot near the rows of apartments that formed the barrier between the hospital and the rest of the city. Her feet were rooted to the asphalt. The figure took patient steps in her direction. She was transfixed by his approach.

Her impression was of a grub worm. His face was pale and bloated—a corpse dug up from the soil and set loose upon the earth. He was coming for her. She knew it in her bones, but she couldn't move, or speak. Not even yell out. A White Worm sent to drag her back to some unspeakable horror.

The pendant burned against her palm, startling her out of the trance. The imprint of the design flaired briefly against her flesh, but when she checked a second time, she found the eldritch lights had gone out.

Then she checked the parking lot to find the White Worm was gone. No sign of his existence remained, which she didn't understand, because he'd only been a hundred feet from her location. He couldn't have run out of sight in the brief moment she checked the pendant.

The wailing sirens of an ambulance, followed by a second and third, as if they were a pack of wolves howling to dispel their loneliness, grew louder by the moment. Remi checked for the White Worm one last time, before returning to the hospital. By the time her shoes passed the threshold, she was convinced that it'd been her imagination, brought on by sleep deprivation and the stress of the hospital.

TWENTY

The alchemical laboratory smelled like burnt sage and unspent faez while the sounds of glass clinking made for a soothing song. Damon used a measuring cup to collect the crushed carapace of a pottery ant, checking the scale to ensure he had the proper weight. The lab only had enough room for half the first years, so the others were on rounds with Dr. Decker.

"If anyone needs anything, I'll be in the library, three doors down," said Jeb Anders, the hospital alchemist. He had wispy white hair and bright red cheeks brought on from years of alchemical exposure. Dr. Decker explained that in the early years, Jeb had titrated by mouth, which meant he'd ingested trace amounts of many strange and dangerous reagents.

Damon checked back to the recipe. They were making a simple wound pack. There'd been a rash of bite wounds in the tenth ward attributed to a young camazotz by the papers, but Dr. Decker wasn't convinced because the fang patterns were all wrong.

To his left, the girl Lily was humming under her breath as she mixed the elixir with the grace and alacrity of a master chef. A mass of colored hair perched atop her head, loose curls framing her broad face. After watching her mix a few potions, Jeb had asked where she'd learned, but Lily had deflected the question. Damon didn't dislike her, but he felt like she was hiding something.

Then a crash from two tables up had Damon shaking his head.

Remi.

She'd spilled another tray of reagents.

He'd never seen someone so clumsy. It was the third time today she'd had to go back to the supply room for materials. He still didn't know what she was doing in Aura Healers. The idea that the selection committee thought she'd be a good candidate made him question his own choices.

Fixated on Remi, rather than his own task, he bumped the auto-mixer, tripling the revolutions. The pale purple liquid frothed as he struggled to turn the machine off.

When the mixer no longer hummed, he checked his potion to find it was ruined.

"Blood and bone," he muttered, disgusted with himself for the loss of concentration.

Sure, he was tired, but not that bad. It'd been a good last few days despite the meager amount of sleep.

Damon dumped the mixture into a special container for incineration and grabbed a tray to collect more reagents from the supply room. He wasn't really paying attention when he pushed through the swinging doors to find Remi in the restricted section, removing baggies of tiny mystdrakon embryos from an open long drawer.

Wide eyes betrayed her guilt.

"Is nothing sacred? You know each one of those can save someone who was lucky enough to survive an encounter with a banshee. You're killing someone with your theft."

She shoved the baggies back in the drawer. "I was just looking. I didn't grow up in a hospital like you. I have a lot to learn."

"Bullshit. I bet your pockets are already full. You've been in here three times already. I thought you were incompetent, but now I see what you are. A thief."

Remi closed the cage door on the restricted section and slipped the lock back on the hook. Then she faced him and pulled her pockets out until he could see there was nothing in them.

"Satisfied?"

"I still don't understand how you got in Aura Healers," he said as he found the drawers with the reagents he needed.

"They put me here to keep blowhards like yourself in check," said Remi, leaning against a table. It never looked like she fixed her hair, but the messy mullet had a style of its own.

"Can't you take anything seriously?"

"Can't you get that stick out of your ass?" she replied.

With the drawer halfway pulled out, he glared in her direction.

"Why are *you* here?" she asked.

"I want to help people."

Remi screwed up her generous lips. "Looks like you just want to look cool in a healer's white coat to me. You're always trying to prove to Dr. Decker how much you know and haven't figured out that he doesn't give a shit. I don't know what he cares about, but it sure ain't us. Trying to be the teacher's pet isn't getting you anywhere."

He slammed the drawer shut and placed his forehead on the cool wood.

"Shit," said Remi, blowing out a breath and running her hand through her hair. "I'm sorry. My mouth gets away from me sometimes. I think

I'm just jealous of how much everyone else already knows about magic, or reagents, or all the doctor stuff. I'm way behind on reading and I just don't know how I'm going to pass."

The turnabout had Damon confused. "You are so...weird. First, you're tearing me down about trying too hard, and then you're admitting how much you don't know? What the hell?"

She shrugged her shoulders. "I'm not good with people. Haven't had much practice." She stared at her shoes. "So I heard you're a shapeshifter?"

"A therianthrope."

Remi glanced up. She had luminous brown eyes flecked with gold and thick eyelashes.

"What kind?"

"Wolf."

She shifted her mouth to the side.

"Cool." Then her forehead furrowed. "Why haven't I seen you change? Wasn't there a full moon last week?"

"Therianthropes don't change because of the moon. It happens when we get angry. Rage triggers our transformation, but I can usually keep it to the small stuff like claws instead of fingernails. Changing is hell on our wardrobe."

Remi chewed on her lower lip, before pushing away from the drawers.

"I should get back to my station. Good luck."

After she left, Damon stared at the wall, forgetting why he'd come into the supply room. Eventually, he collected his thoughts, and his reagents, returning to the lab to find the rest of the class in discussion about a string of murders across the city.

"When I was in the ER last night," said Boon, tugging on his diamond earring, which he seemed to do whenever he was speaking, "we had three separate cases of people going flat out crazy, trying to strangle tourists near the Newtown Fishmarket. Was weird. They all had slaver on their mouths."

"The *Herald* is calling it the Season of the Witch," said Sasha, looking excited about the prospect. "They say it's a cult in the city trying to bring back the Event."

"What a stupid, fucking gobshite to write such a thing," said Lily, frowning. "Witches ain't crazy, power mad mages."

"How do you know so much about witches?" asked Sasha, crossing her arms.

"There's a fair number in Ireland. Good for an elixir to make a boy fall in love with you," said Lily with a wink.

Sasha shook her head. "I can never tell if you're fucking with me or not."

"What even is a witch?" asked Remi. "I thought it was just another name for a mage."

"Witches and warlocks don't have a patron like the Halls," said Lily. "They pledge themselves to supernatural beings, usually ones that have been around a long time. That's what I've heard anyway."

"I don't think it's a cult," declared Damon. "But there is something, or someone behind it. Been too many coincidences like that."

He wanted to explain the signature smell he was picking up on the worst patients, but even at KC General, they'd been unappreciative of his sensitive therianthrope nose.

"Or maybe," said Remi, holding her arms wide. "Hear me out. The world is a fucked-up place filled with bad people. Those three probably had a bad batch of street drugs, or maybe some weird gas floated up from the Undercity. I know I haven't been in the city long, but this place is in constant turmoil."

"What about the White Worm you saw?" asked Lily, furrowing her brow.

Remi shot her a withering look. Before Damon could follow up, Jeb returned to check their work.

"You need to be more careful," said Jeb after Damon explained what had happened. "You don't get do-overs in alchemy, especially in the hospital. An incorrect mixture could kill someone."

Damon had to stay around to finish the project. He was the only one in the lab since everyone else, Remi included, had completed the mixture on the first try. After Jeb gave him the thumbs-up, Damon headed back to the dormitory wing of the hospital. When he was passing Dr. Decker's office, he saw the light on and chanced a knock.

"Speak, friend, and enter."

Damon stuck his head through the opening. "Friend?"

The doctor had his feet on the desk. He was levitating a stress ball using a continuous flow of air magic, which was knocking papers off his desk, but he didn't seem to mind.

"How are you doing that?"

Dr. Decker adjusted the flow, and the ball shot towards Damon. He caught it and set it on the desk, not knowing how to take the instructor.

"The more important question is why, but nobody ever seems to care about that."

"Why?"

Dr. Decker put his feet on the floor. "There is no extra credit in Aura Healers, if that's what you're here for."

"I'm not here for extra credit," said Damon, taken aback. "But I wanted to talk to you about all the deaths and injuries that the hospital has been treating lately."

"Too much for you?"

"No, not at all. I've just been keeping notes, not only about the ER, but the murders reported in the *Herald*, and I thought there seemed to be some pattern with it. We get streaks of similar injuries. The police see the same types of deaths. They pop up mostly on the eastern half of the city. I feel like there's something going on."

"And what are you planning to do about it? If such a thing was true?" asked Dr. Decker, studying him intently.

"I don't know. Is there someone who we can tell? A detective at Invictus PD?"

Dr. Decker leaned forward. "What's the first rule?"

"I don't know shit, but I swear, if I can bring back my data, I think you'll see what I see," said Damon.

"Here's a fundamental truth about the world. Bad shit happens. Yes, occasionally, there are people or creatures that cause multiple deaths, or injuries. There was the Canal Killer a decade ago. Or when the Soul Thief terrorized the school, but those are far and few between and they had very specific victims. A single cause for all the death and misery in the city? That's a bit farfetched."

"I'm not saying it's all the causes. But I think it's the reason for the increase these last few years."

"Damon, I appreciate your enthusiasm for the work, but you're an idealistic first year who desperately wants to save the world. You're seeing patterns because you want them to exist, not because they do. I read your file. I'm sure you want to redeem yourself for past mistakes, but that's not how things work. We do our best to survive each day. Those mistakes. They're just something we have to deal with."

He grabbed his white coat from the back of the chair and slung it over his shoulder.

"Dr. Decker, if I could explain, there's a smell—"

The doctor shuffled past, leaving Damon standing in the open door. "Now if you would excuse me, I have a date with a bowl of blue Jell-O in the cafeteria."

Damon knew he shouldn't have brought his theory yet, because he lacked concrete proof that the others would understand, but he also knew his nose was smelling something important. It'd saved his life before, he had no reason to distrust it now.

"I know I'm right," he told himself.

TWENTY-ONE

Remi threw the carryall over her shoulder. She'd gotten it at the Golden Willow lost and found. The interior smelled like an old perfume bottle had leaked, but it wasn't strong enough to make her not want to use it.

"Takin' a holiday in the city? Want company?" asked Lily from the corner.

She was sitting cross-legged in a chair wearing soft green pajamas with Neko in her lap, stroking his velvety white back. Remi hadn't been too keen on living with a rat, but the critter spent most of his time nesting in Lily's bed.

"I, uhm, had some errands I wanted to run," said Remi.

A smile formed on Lily's broad lips. "If you're going to sell those reagents you've been stealing, it's not my trouble, but two makes the road shorter and I've been meaning to get out and see the city."

The eager look on her face made it hard for Remi to say no. Dr.

Decker had given them a day off for relaxation and threatened them with expulsion if he caught them studying or working in the hospital. Probably because Ethan had flubbed a simple spell so spectacularly that it nearly caught an oxygen tank on fire and blew up the south wing.

"I'm not doing anything fun."

"It's settled then," said Lily, hopping up and grabbing a heavy shoulder bag.

She let Neko crawl in. After a moment of settling, the rat stuck his pointed face out of the top.

"Where to?"

Seeing she wasn't going to shake Lily, Remi led them out of their room and then the hospital. Besides, she'd never had a close friend—not that they'd achieved those levels—but running errands with another person was a novel experience.

The red line train station was busy despite it being a Monday since it was Thanksgiving week. The regular folk were bundled in sweaters and hoodies on the chilly autumn day, but Remi was wearing a simple black T-shirt, relying on a weather enchantment to protect herself from the cold.

Her Irish companion leaned against the window, staring at the view as they circled the city. They passed the Canal District in the seventh ward filled with college students drinking cheap elixirs on a long break, while the Menagerie and Cryptozoo in the eighth was filled with families to see the unusual animals. The Glitterdome could be seen for the entirety of their trip, and closer in the second a botanical dome had been constructed. Remi had planned on lifting a few wallets on the journey, but Lily's presence and the soul-worn exhaustion from months of working nonstop had left her feeling thin.

The ninth ward was a mix of residential and community business. A smattering of smaller Halls made their home there, but mostly along the outer edge. It was the kind of place Remi thought she could live if she had to pick one in the city. Buskers worked the corners outside the bodegas, playing upbeat jazz, or performing illusionary theater, their collection plates stuffed with bills and coins. She made sure to give each and every one of them at least a five-dollar bill.

"I expected you to take, not give," said Lily after she'd given a burning mime a ten-spot.

"I appreciate the hustle."

Lily bumped shoulders, grinning maniacally. "Game knows game?"

Remi groaned. "Nobody says that, unless they're some online poser."

The rebuke didn't seem to faze Lily, who always seemed to look like she carried the answer of the universe with her. There was something both annoying and refreshing about her outlook, especially as Remi had seen her roommate in great pain at times.

"Why did you join Aura Healers?" asked Lily. "No offense, but you don't look like you're the kind with magical ambitions."

"It was the only Hall that would take me."

"Fair point."

Catching Lily's good mood, Remi shouldered her back. "What about you?"

"Like our tall, handsome friend, I only put Aura Healers in the Tome of Record."

"He's not my friend."

"Aye, not yet, but maybe eventually."

Remi screwed up her face. "Not likely. He's an arrogant do-gooder. I'll concede that he's an unnatural amount of attractive, bordering on supernatural, but even if I was interested in him, he'd never be into me given *my* history."

"Oh, I doubt that. He's like a kid on the playground, throwing rocks at the girl he likes."

Lily rolled her eyes.

Remi had never stayed in one place long enough for romantic entanglements. They would only get in the way of her goals.

"I wouldn't have time even if I was interested. What about you?"

"My favorite romances are the ones that my friends have," said Lily, blowing a strand of colored hair out of her face.

Catching sight of a window full of magical devices resting in velvet catches, Remi shuddered to a stop. A whirling gyroscope provided a mesmerizing distraction at the center of the window.

"Here we are. The Tinker's Delight."

Remi had researched all the tinker shops in the city. There were hundreds, but she'd settled on this one because it also bought and sold alchemical reagents and it'd been around for decades—emphasizing its discretion.

A bell announced their entrance, but the front desk wasn't in view. Given the high price tags of the items near the front, Remi assumed there were other protections to dissuade thieves from making off with the valuables. It seemed like the kind of place she would avoid stealing from. There were too many easier targets in the city.

A row of shelves containing old tomes caught Lily's notice. She looked like she wanted to hug the entire structure.

"I'll be over here when you're finished."

Remi slowed near a shelf when she spotted an exquisitely made dagger with an onyx-inlaid hilt. The blade looked as sharp as a razor and the back half had marbled dark spots. A handwritten card beneath the weapon explained that it'd been enchanted against infernal beings. The price tag had five digits before the decimal.

There were dozens of interesting items like the blade, but she pushed through her curiosity, eventually finding a desk near the back. As soon as she saw the owner, she understood the reason for the location.

He was a non-human, probably not even four feet tall, sitting behind a desk made for a person of his stature with rich, orange-brown skin like polished wood and a full head of white hair and a stylish goatee. He wore a three-piece suit, which looked like it belonged in the early twentieth century. People called them goblins, or trogs, the latter being the more offensive term, but she knew that they came from a variety of realms and were completely unrelated.

"Greetings, young lady," said the owner in an English accent. "How may the Tinker's Delight serve you?"

Remi dug into her bag, producing a collection of baggies with a variety of reagents including the mystdrakon embryos, and other valuables. She dumped the pile onto the low desk, spotting the name tag on his jacket that read: Albi Seventoes.

"I'd like a quote on selling these, and I also have a separate inquiry about a magical item in my possession."

Albi picked through the baggies. He lifted one that had the Golden Willow logo printed on the side and raised an eyebrow.

"Your website said you were discrete."

"I am," said Albi with a nod. "But that *does* change the price."

She nodded, mostly mad at herself. She'd been so tired lately that she wasn't even sure she'd checked them once. After a few minutes of sorting and looking up prices, he wrote a number on a piece of paper. It was smaller than she'd hoped, but still a tidy sum for virtually no work.

"That's fine," she said, catching a disappointed frown as he was clearly hoping to barter. "Assuming you can answer my questions about this pendant."

His face brightened as she pulled the chain from beneath her shirt, then over her head, handing it to Albi. He reached out his hand, but yanked it away before it could touch his flesh.

"What is the meaning of this?" he asked, nostrils flaring.

"What do you mean?"

The corners of his eyes creased before he relaxed slightly. "You don't know?"

"It was an heirloom that I got after my parents died. I don't know anything about it, and the few people I've asked couldn't help me. I want to know what I've been carrying around all these years. I'm sorry if there's something wrong with it."

"That pendant stinks of the Fae."

Remi collected the pendant in her palm to study it. The designs suggested trees and circles, though it was hard to tell because whenever she examined it too long she found herself looking elsewhere.

"This is Fae?"

"Reeks of it," said Albi. "Hold up the pendant so I can spell it."

She let it dangle at the end of the chain. Albi reached into a drawer and pulled out a jar of black powdery material. He scooped a tiny chunk into his mouth with a silver spoon, then spoke in a low voice, using a language she'd never heard. When he was finished, he breathed out a black mist, which collected around the silver pendant. Bright lines and other details that she hadn't seen before came into focus.

Remi found herself transfixed. Her mind leapt to faraway places. She was still in the shop, but she was also in a deep, dark, twisted forest. The scents of rotting vegetation were thick, choking her.

She was trapped.

Remi clawed at her own throat, not able to breathe in the unbearable heat. Through the gaps in the vines and overwhelming growth, she saw a figure in the distance.

She was being hunted.

That much she knew.

The fear tasted like ashes.

The first impression she had was of antlers, but then when she looked back, she saw the White Worm staring back at her through the trees.

"Begone Daemhan!"

A bright light, followed by a painful shock reverberating through her body, had Remi flying through the air. She landed on her back, air struck from her lungs, groaning until she looked up to see Lily standing over her. Lily helped Remi to her feet, and she held onto her friend, not trusting her legs. The pendant lay on the floor, the chain curled around it like a serpent.

"Are you well?" asked Albi, face wracked with concern, leaning forward on his desk to see over the front.

The vision had left Remi with an oily feeling that she wanted to scrub from her skin with steel wool and a long, hot shower. She felt like part of her mind was still in the forest being hunted.

It was both rich and rotten. A bountiful harvest rotting on the vine.

"I'm not sure." Remi checked her hand which for a moment had the imprint of the pendant as if she'd been burned by its magics. The swirling patterns flaired for a second before fading into her flesh. "Thank you for whatever you did."

"I did nothing," said Albi, nodding towards Lily. "That was your friend."

"A simple ward, nothing more," said Lily, staring at her as if she had bugs crawling across her face.

Albi spoke in a language Remi didn't understand, which Lily answered fluently. The two conversed for a minute before turning back to English.

"What did you experience?" asked Albi.

"I was somewhere else. A forest choked with greenery. Rotting. I couldn't breathe. Someone was hunting me."

"Someone?" asked Lily.

Remi gave her a look, lifting a single shoulder. She didn't want to talk about the White Worm in front of the shopkeeper.

"Do you know where your family got the pendant?" asked Albi.

The pendant had been in a simple wooden case at the Dreadmarsh estate. There were wards, but she'd managed to trip one of the other cleaning ladies into the glass, shattering it. The pendant had been left in an unguarded area until the owners could secure it, which was when she'd made off with the item.

Remi shook her head.

"I wish I knew. Is it dangerous?"

"I think your experience should be instructive enough," said Albi with a bushy eyebrow raised. "Though I may have triggered the unfiltered magics when I sought to bypass the glamour."

Remi nodded as she recalled images she'd seen on the pendant that hadn't been there before.

"What is it for?"

"If I were a betting man, I'd say it was a key. Of sorts. Someone from or associated with the Fae placed specific magics on the pendant to be revealed when certain conditions are met."

This wasn't news to Remi, but she didn't want Lily or the shopkeeper to know, so she kept her expression bewildered, which wasn't difficult because she was still suffering from the aftereffects.

"A key for what?" asked Lily.

"That's a good question," said Albi. "But I wouldn't know the first thing about how to find out."

Remi crouched down and collected the chain in her fist. "Is it safe to touch?"

"Mostly," said Albi with forehead hunched. "The glamour has returned, but I wouldn't hold it close to your skin. That gives the magic a chance to affect you, if it hasn't already."

"I'll keep that in mind," said Remi, collecting the pendant in her palm and shoving it entirely into her front pocket. "Would you be able to find out more about the pendant?"

"For a price."

Remi handed the paper with the value of the reagents back to Albi.

"Will this do?"

"It's a start," he said with a grin.

She left after leaving how to get ahold of her. Outside the shop, Lily frowned.

"That's not a family heirloom, and your parents aren't dead."

"People want to help you more when you've seen hardship," said Remi, scratching the back of her head.

Lily pursed her lips and crossed her arms. "The Fae aren't to be messed with."

"Is it really the Fae? Rotting vegetation and the White Worm don't sound like them to me."

"That's true," said Lily, nodding. "But I smelled it too. And I know that smell like the beating of my own heart. It was the Fae. The other stuff, it's a complication. Maybe they were owners of the pendant at one time. What is it for, Remi Wilde? You already knew it was a key. I haven't known you that long, but I know that much."

"I know it's valuable. That's it."

"Nothing with the Fae is worth the wealth you think you might enjoy. They love nothing more than impaling humans on their own desires," said Lily.

"I know. I know."

"You certainly don't sound like it, offering your hard-earned money for more information."

"Curiosity is all."

Lily raised an eyebrow, to which Remi responded with a playful grin and a pat on the shoulder.

"We've run my errands and we still have most of the day. What would you like to do now?"

Lily's eyes lit up. "I heard the Menagerie and Cryptozoo has a young ollipheist."

"Ollipheist?"

"Aye, like a river dragon, but not a real dragon. Can get as big as a bus. Never seen a young one before."

Remi hooked her arm around Lily's.

"Then let's see this river dragon."

They marched off towards the train station, and Remi thought about the pendant in her pocket.

TWENTY-TWO

A week after the trip into the city, Lily woke in the middle of the night when Remi was snoring from across the room. She lay silently, watching the slow rise and fall of her roommate's chest until she was certain she was deep asleep. Sliding out of her covers in a pair of soft cotton pajamas, Lily grabbed a small bathroom kit at the end of the bed and slipped into the hallway.

She passed a few workers on the way to the hospital chapel. No one gave her a second glance. The hospital was its own ecosystem—no one questioned how the other parts worked.

Lily slipped into the nondenominational chapel. There was no lock, so she just had to trust that no one would enter in the middle of the night. The space wasn't big. Benches enough for twenty people and a marble altar at the front. A big box on the side was filled with implements of various religions in case someone wanted to hold a specific ceremony, but

Lily had brought her wares with her.

A small potted tree sat to either side of the altar. Lily hauled one pot on top of the marble surface. The weight made her muscles burn, but she managed the feat on the first try.

Using a green paint marker from her kit, she drew two concentric circles around the pot, then added runes between them. Lily worked carefully and slowly, despite the risk of discovery, humming under her breath the entire time. With the wards complete, she pulled a penknife from the kit, and after digging away the soil from the base of the slender trunk, etched more runes in the bark.

With preparations complete, Lily placed her hands flat on the cool marble and began the incantation. The chant lasted until the runes glowed warm with light, reflecting into her down-turned face.

"Seo dom mháthair. Is mise d'iníon na bhfiántas."

Lily repeated the phrase, keeping her faez at the ready. She kept it up for a long time until the leaves of the potted plant shook. A voice returned both gravelly and thin:

"Cén fáth a bhfuil tú ag glaoch orm, Lilith? Tá na fréamhacha lag agus lofa."

The connection felt distant, leaving Lily to ache for familiarity. The words she wanted to use fell to ash on her tongue, but she knew she couldn't keep Medb waiting.

"An bhfuil leigheas aimsithe agat?" asked the voice from the tree.

"No, Mother, I have failed thus far. But I continue the search. There is a lead, but I fear it may be false."

She'd slipped back into English, but repeated the phrase because Medb preferred it that way.

"Cén fáth a ghlaonn tú?"

"Tá an lobhadh anseo."

The runes flashed crimson for a moment.

Lily bowed her head deeper as a sickly green light emanated from the soil, tendrils reaching for her neck. The mist burned against her flesh, making her choke and stammer, until she dismissed the connection, throwing herself away from the altar before she could become entrapped.

"Bough and branch."

Lily pulled a bottle of isopropyl alcohol from her kit and used it to clean the paint marker runes from the marble, then returned the potted plant to its original location, covering up the carvings with loose soil.

When she slipped back into her room, Remi half woke, hazy expression staring from her pile of covers.

"Everything okay?"

"I just went to the bathroom," said Lily, holding up her kit.

Remi stared back blankly. "I had a bad dream. Rotten vines were crawling from under the door, trying to choke me."

"Just a dream," said Lily, offering a reassuring smile. "Just a dream."

TWENTY-THREE

Remi trailed behind Dr. Paddock on rounds feeling like a lost duckling. The glasses wearing doctor barely talked to her, except when he gave her instructions for the spells she needed to cast, half of which she hadn't learned yet.

"After you, Miss Wilde. Let's see how we can *not* perform our duties with the next patient," he said derisively.

"Yes, doctor," mumbled Remi as she trudged into the room.

A twentysomething, attractive young man with a mane of blond hair was sitting up in bed, grimacing and breathing shallowly. Sleeves of tattoos stuck out from his hospital gown.

"How are we today...Mr. Lyons," said Dr. Paddock as he read from the patient's chart.

"It's fine. Am I going to get out of here soon? I have a show tomorrow, I really need to get back."

"A show?" asked Dr. Paddock.

Remi didn't need the explanation to know that Gerald Lyons was a singer in a rock band that was playing at clubs around the city. Nearly every woman in the hospital, plus a few men like Boon, had been discussing his arrival and every move.

He'd been singing at the Bang Factory in the Canal District when a jealous girlfriend cursed him while he was on stage. He'd been in undetermined pain for two days since. Nothing they'd done had helped, though there was a lot of explicit discussion about how they could help him get over his problem.

"I'm the lead for the Krakens," said Gerald.

He had luscious eyelashes and pouty lips. After he'd arrived at Golden Willow, the entire class of first years had watched a video of him strutting around the stage with his shirt off.

"And what are the Krakens? Do you work at the zoo?" asked Dr. Paddock.

"The zoo?"

Gerald looked confused, so Remi spoke rapid fire.

"He's a singer for a band. It's called the Krakens. He got cursed by a jealous girlfriend."

As soon as she finished speaking, her cheeks grew warm, then grew hotter as Gerald rested his gaze upon her. She'd never been one to swoon around a guy, but he was supernaturally attractive and it was making it hard to think. Some of the first years thought he might be related to a siren.

"Thanks, Remi."

The wink was almost too much. It helped her get her feet back beneath her. Gerald looked past them both as a pair of nurses came stumbling into the room looking giddy with glee. They were both in their forties but were acting like they were teenagers.

"We're here for his sponge bath," said the first nurse, waving a sponge.

Dr. Paddock checked the chart. "I'm afraid he's been marked down for no physical contact due to his pain sensitivity."

"Sorry, ladies," said Gerald. "Even the covers and clothes hurt. I've been really considering stripping down and just lying naked atop the bed, but I'd hate to cause any trouble."

The two nurses went blank and left the room with hurried steps. Remi had a pretty good idea where they were going.

"No counter to the curse has been identified?" asked Dr. Paddock.

"They sent a recording of the event, but the music was so loud that we couldn't hear the spell," said Remi.

"Am I going to be like this forever? Because I really have to piss. I've tried to go on my own, but since everything hurts, I don't know how to go," said Gerald, his mouth twisted.

Dr. Paddock hung the chart on the end of the bed. "That, son, is something we can help with. Remi, are you familiar with Antony's Forced Pollakiuria?"

She wracked her brain, paging through the book in her mind. "Yes, I think I do."

"Are you, or are you not?"

"I'm pretty sure."

Dr. Paddock sighed heavily and pulled his phone out. "I keep a copy of all the Hall tomes in here for times like these. I'm very sorry, Mr. Lyons, we are a teaching hospital, and not all of our students are as prepared as they should be."

"It's okay, Doc. I don't always remember my lyrics either. I bet it's tough memorizing everything, especially in this city, when anything can happen. I get it, Remi."

She swallowed met his gaze despite feeling a little dizzy.

"Thanks," she muttered and accepted Dr. Paddock's phone.

She reviewed the instructions twice to make sure she remembered how to cast it.

"I think I've got it."

Remi held her hands over Gerald's crotch, which brought a sly grin from the patient. She had to work to get her mind moving again as being around him made it hard to think. She started the spell after a deep in-breath.

"Speak up, Remi," said Dr. Paddock, looking on clinically.

She started again, feeling Gerald's gaze upon her. The finger gestures weren't difficult, but a few motions were suggestive enough to bring embarrassment. The words were mostly nonsense, but most spells were like that. She dipped into her well of faez, sending the raw magic into the covers as she finished the spell. A small flash of light emanated from his crotch and then she stepped back.

"That should be it," she said, looking around the room rather than at his luminous eyes. "I can grab the bedpan for you."

As she turned, she saw the furrowed brow from Dr. Paddock as he reviewed the spell that she'd finished. The look made her worry that she'd done something wrong, so she checked back with Gerald.

"Oh," he said with a grunt, leaning over. His face was going through contortions.

"Oh," he said a second time, more forcefully.

He glanced up, eyes wide with what she first thought was terror. He tried to speak, but seemed distracted by whatever he was going through.

"Is something wrong? Can I get you something?" asked Remi.

"Miss Wilde," said Dr. Paddock, pointing to the phone. "The second gesture on the third stanza. I believe you might have twisted your wrist incorrectly."

"What?" she asked, as Gerald moaned again, this time louder. "I'm sorry. Did I make the pain worse?"

"Oh," he said with an upward lilt.

Then again. And again.

Gerald leaned back in the bed. His hips were arching towards the ceiling as he continued his refrain.

There was a bit of self-awareness as his mouth opened wider and his exclamations grew louder. Before long, he was practically shouting.

"Ohhh! Ohhh! Ohhh!"

The moans were loud and rising at the end. His eyes were wide and his hands were gripping the bedcovers into tight balls.

It was at this time that realization of what was really happening set in. Remi didn't know what to do. Should she leave, should she stay, what was the protocol for a patient going through the opposite of pain? Dr. Paddock hadn't figured it out yet as he was staring at the phone and back to Gerald, mumbling about the incompetence of Dr. Decker's charges.

"Is everything okay?" asked a nurse, sticking her head through the open door.

Gerald was at full shout. His "Ohhhs" were musical, forceful, erotic.

The nurse's jaw dropped as she responded with a soft, "Oh." Then, "What did you do?"

"It was to help him pee," said Remi, grimacing at the use of the word. The proper description would have been urinate, but she hadn't gotten used to using the right terminology at the hospital, which always made her feel like a fraud.

"Oh, I see," said Dr. Paddock, seemingly oblivious to the display happening in the bed. "The spell was successful, but in a different way."

Gerald's hips were raised high as he gripped the covers, his face etched in either pain or ecstasy.

"Oh, heavenly fucking hellfire!"

Much to Remi's horror, his shouts had brought a crowd including half the first years who were all on rounds, and Dr. Decker, who was watching the whole affair with his head tilted and an air of amusement on his lips.

If there was any doubt what was happening, it was removed the moment Gerald started screaming, "Ohhh, yes! Ohhh, yes!"

A wetness began to spread at his crotch, growing wider and darker as he shouted and slammed his fists into the bed. It went on for two minutes. When he was finished, Gerald fell back into the bed, looking like he'd just finished a marathon, with sweat beaded on his forehead.

"Shadows below, that was amazing," he said, smiling at the audience.

Dr. Decker started clapping, which spread to the rest of the crowd, which Gerald seemed to enjoy as he smiled in response.

"I think I just blew a half pint's worth," said Gerald.

Dr. Paddock turned around and faced the assembly. "Really? Is this proper decorum in the hospital? Begone, all of you! And you, Dr. Decker. What kind of example are you for your young healers? You should be ashamed!"

The rebuke sent the nurses and students scattering, while Dr. Decker ached an eyebrow at Remi and said, "We'll talk later."

Dr. Paddock spun around to Gerald. "Please, sir. On behalf of the hospital, please accept my apologies for this travesty. If you would like to file a formal complaint, I will send for the hospital lawyers. This was unacceptable."

Gerald smacked his lips and took a long drink from a juice box on the tray.

"Complaint? I'd like to file for Miss Remi to receive an award. Not only was that the most amazing experience of my life, but I think that she made my problem go away. I'm not in pain anymore. Remi fixed it."

"But that had to be embarrassing," said Dr. Paddock, huffing with indignation.

Gerald looked down at the massive wet spot. "Ain't no shame in having a good time, right, Remi?" he asked with a wink.

Dr. Paddock turned on her, clearly wanting to punish her, but since the patient hadn't agreed, he was flustered.

"You should go see Dr. Decker as requested. I think you're well and done here."

Gerald saluted her. "Thanks for the good time, Remi. Maybe I'll see ya around."

Remi stumbled out of the patient's room. She couldn't remember which way to go until a pair of nurses walked by.

"Nice job, Half-Pint," said the taller one.

Remi shook off her stupor and headed up to Dr. Decker's office. He was carving a piece of soap with a knife when she arrived.

"Am I in trouble?"

"This time? No. Lucky for you, the spell, which was intended to reduce the swelling in his prostate so he could urinate, stimulated it instead. Quite spectacularly. I'm going to guess the curse the jealous girlfriend put on him had some component about never letting him cum again, which was why he was in so much pain."

"I thought blue balls were an urban legend."

"Mostly," he said. "But in this case, the curse was designed to make him hurt. But you unknowingly fixed it. The fact remains that you flubbed your spell. And this isn't the first time."

"I'll do better."

He sighed and set the soap and knife onto his desk. "While I agree that you have a lot of promise, we haven't seen that come to fruition just yet. It might be your lack of proper schooling all these years has left you without the tools to succeed in a place like this."

"Are you kicking me out?"

"No. Not yet. But I want you to take today as a lesson. You got lucky, but you might not next time. I can tell you there's nothing worse in this world than knowing you're the one that caused someone's pain and suffering due to a mistake. If I kick you out, it won't be because I don't like you, or believe in you, it's to protect you from the misery of failure and, more importantly, to protect your patients."

"I understand," she said, nodding. If she got kicked out, everything would be ruined. No pendant. No career in the Halls. Nothing. She'd be forced to petty thievery to survive. "I'll do better."

Dr. Decker picked up his soap and knife and started carving again.

"You should get back to Dr. Paddock. Rounds aren't finished, but you know, try not to fuck any more spells up, Half-Pint."

TWENTY-FOUR

The entire group of first years was crowded around the patient's bed. There were only fourteen of them now. A week after Thanksgiving, Donald had left in the middle of the night with only a note under Dr. Decker's door as explanation. It had simply read: "I can't do this anymore."

"Who here can tell me what the proper spell to check Chuck's wound is?" asked Dr. Decker, leaning against the bed. A middle-aged balding man with his left arm wrapped in a tube covered in runes sat cheerily as the class scratched their heads.

Damon reviewed the tome in his mind, trying to remember the right spell.

Before he could answer, Ethan spit out, "The Field Finder."

"Could you demonstrate for me? Minus faez," said Dr. Decker.

Ethan stepped forward, his artificial foot clunking on the tiles. He performed the gestures and words with the practice of a concert musician.

"I'll give you nine out of ten for spell work, but unfortunately, Ethan, you killed poor Chuck. Zero out of fifty. The problem with most spells when the patient is wearing a regeneration tube is you have to worry about the runes *and* the solution inside the tube." Dr. Decker picked up the patient chart. "In this case, due to receiving a bite from an unknown critter in the sewer system, our Chuck has been given an exotic mixture to protect against infection and what, class?"

Damon added his voice to the droning response: "Parasites."

"But there was no parasite found in his bloodstream," said Ethan.

"That's because Chuck is an experienced sewer maintenance professional. As soon as he was bitten, he drank the correct elixir and hurried straight away to the ER. As you can see, his arm grew scales during that short window before the right spells were applied."

"Ain't no way I'm going down like Levi in section eight," said Chuck in a thick New England accent. "They found him covered in white slime and gnawing on a rat while his eyes were completely black."

"Anyone else?"

Damon shouted out, "The Perceiver."

Dr. Decker bobbed his head side to side. "Good marks for safety, you didn't kill Chuck, but it won't tell you anything."

"The Double Kilter," said Lily in her lilting accent.

Dr. Decker pointed right at her. "Bullseye again. Lily's a stone-cold marksman. The Double Kilter keeps from interacting with the elixir while providing the necessary analysis for the doctor." He held out his hand to Chuck, who shook it as if they were old friends. "Thanks for playing another round of Let's Not Kill the Patient."

"No problem, Doc. Happy to be of service."

"Everyone out!" said Dr. Decker. "On to the next room. And Chuck, thank you for keeping our sewers clean. A healthy shitter is the key to running a good city."

On the way to the next room, Sasha asked, "Why do we keep checking for parasites? We never find any."

"Rule number one, Sasha. Rule number one."

The class shared bewildered glances between themselves as they squeezed into the next hospital room. There was a collective bet amongst the first years whether or not Dr. Decker was messing with them. At the end of the year, if they hadn't found a single parasite in all their tests, then the three-fourths of the class that had bet that way would win. Damon had decided against his better judgement that Dr. Decker had an actual medical reason for rule two, but every week it was harder to believe that he would be proved correct.

The murmuring grew as Damon worked himself into the back of the room. As one of the tallest members, he tried not to stand in front.

"Our patient died a half hour ago," said Bryan, reading the chart.

The covers had been pulled over the body. "We'll stop here anyway. Even the dead have something to teach us. Hand me that chart."

He spent five seconds reading it, before tossing it on the covers. Damon thought he saw the body move but that was probably his imagination.

"Unknown causes. They found him in an underpass near the ring road wandering around like a lunatic. He attacked a police officer, who hit him with a limb-lock spell, and he fell unconscious. They thought it was a concussion at first, but they found no signs of trauma to the back of the head. Thoughts?"

A sniff brought the aroma of rotting vegetation. Damon coughed. He wanted to get out of the room. It was choking. He looked around to see no one else was reacting the same way, not even Dr. Decker.

"Did he work on a farm?" asked Damon.

Dr. Decker tilted his head. "Why did you ask that?"

"Is it just me?" said Damon, pointing at his nose. "No one else smells that? It's like the produce section went bad and no one cleaned it up."

The entire class lifted their chins, sniffing at the air. Everyone but Remi, who was staring at him as if something was wrong, but when they made eye contact, she looked away.

"I think I can smell that," said Ethan.

A few others nodded.

Dr. Decker, however, ripped the covers from the patient. He stared at the lifeless body, which lay with its eyes open and mouth slightly agape, then leaned over and started smelling the corpse from inches away. When the doctor had moved up the chest and was hovering over the open mouth, Damon saw the hand twitch into a curled claw.

"Watch out!" screamed Damon, before he even knew why he was yelling.

Dr. Decker stood upright and half turned, still in range as the body snapped upward like a marionette being controlled by a novice puppet master. Damon thought that he was going to be bitten or grabbed, but at the last second, Dr. Decker spun around.

"Shayut!"

A wall of white mist slammed into the patient, throwing him back into the bed with half his body threatening to tip over. Dr. Decker had his hands up, ready to deliver another arcane strike, but the patient had returned to its previous motionless state, limbs limply hanging over the edge of the bed. Dr. Decker grabbed a measuring stick from a drawer and poked the body while the class looked on, then reached out and checked the pulse.

"Nothing."

He followed up with pair of spells: Hafer's Heartbeat and The Waves of Consciousness. Neither came back positive.

"Is he a zombie?" asked Sasha.

"Contrary to popular fiction and the occasional conspiracy theory, there is no such thing as zombies. There's no spell to bring someone back from the dead, a fact confirmed by the greatest arcane minds of the Halls."

"Then how did he move?" asked Sasha.

"The body may not have a spirit, but that doesn't mean other things can't decide to use it like a puppet."

"Like the zombie-ant fungus," said Lily.

"Ahh, yes, *Ophiocordyceps unilateralis*. A nasty little trick of nature that does a number on those poor ants," said Dr. Decker. "It's one of those areas where nature has done better than magic."

He yanked the body back to the center of the bed and, using a wooden tongue depressor, poked and prodded the corpse while the class watched. When he got to the mouth, he made noises of understanding.

"Forceps?" he asked, holding his hand out. When no one moved, he dug through the drawers to find a pair. Dr. Decker shoved the thin pincer-like instrument into the open mouth, then with a yank, produced a long piece of thin vine that was spotted black.

"That's what I was smelling," said Damon.

"Interesting," said Dr. Decker.

Boon raised his hand. "Should we be worried? Like is this an airborne fungus or something that's going to turn us into zombies like him?"

Dr. Decker raised an eyebrow. "If it is, it's too late, but no. I don't think so." He gestured to a gray panel on the wall. "It would have turned orange or red if there were airborne particles."

Grabbing a sample jar from the cabinet, Dr. Decker stuffed the rotting vine inside before closing it up and writing a note on the side. He snapped his fingers at Remi.

"Take a blood sample for me, since it's something you're actually good at."

Damon started to feel jealous, since he'd spent a month with the phlebotomist at KC General and felt like he was a pretty decent bloodsucker, until he heard the rest of what Dr. Decker had to say. He knew she was doing poorly on their tests, which required demonstration of the various spells and concepts they'd been learning these last four months.

"Will I be able to? He's been dead a bit. The blood has congealed."

Dr. Decker furrowed his forehead. "Right. Uhm, inject a bit of saline with warmed faez into the vein, then give it thirty seconds. That should thin the blood enough to pull a sample."

While Remi worked the corpse's arm in an attempt to pull blood, Ethan asked, "What was that spell? The one when the corpse attacked you. I don't recall that in any of the tomes."

"Oh, it's an Animalians mark. A hunter friend in Harmony taught me. When you're dealing with dangerous supernaturals, being able to react quickly is important. Marks are faster than the five elements."

"How many realms were you in when you were away from Golden Willow?" asked Ethan.

"A dozen or so. Lost track. You go where the work takes you, and there's a need for a medic everywhere. But I learned a lot of techniques and spells I wouldn't have otherwise. When you don't have the resources of a hospital at your beck and call, you have to improvise. That's how I learned the blood one too."

"Here's the sample," said Remi, holding up a vial filled with dark blood.

"Excellent. I won't have to fail you just yet." Dr. Decker checked his watch. "That should be it for the day. Who'd like to take these—"

Damon surged forward. "I would."

"Don't forget."

"Rule number two. Got it," said Damon as he headed for the basement.

"Let Bob decide what else needs to happen. He'll know best," yelled Dr. Decker as he left the room.

Bob Morehead was drinking coffee and directing one of his assistants on a new machine when Damon arrived. The excitement in the head of testing's eyes dimmed when he saw who had darkened his door.

"One of Dr. O.D.'s minions, wonderful," he said with the excitement of a headsman. "Parasites I assume?"

"That too," said Damon, handing over the sample jar and blood vial. "A corpse tried to attack the doctor. He pulled these from the mouth, and here's a blood sample."

Bob whistled softly as he stared at the spotted vine. "Isn't this a beauty. What are you?" He checked up to find Damon standing nearby. "This is going to take a while."

"That's okay. I'd like to learn."

"Nobody likes a kiss-ass," said Bob.

"I'm serious. I smelled something on the patient and I wanted to understand if that had anything to do with these samples."

"Smelled something?"

Damon gave a description.

"Sensitive nose? Oh, that's right. You're the therianthrope."

Bob's assistant, a young woman with blonde hair pulled into a ponytail, glanced up, visibly disturbed by the news.

"I am."

"Lucy, take this vial. Start the standard profiles, including parasites—"

Lucy gave him a strange look before nodding with understanding. Damon didn't understand the exchange but he was too tired to worry about the politics of the testing lab.

After his assistant left, Bob put the rotting vine in a closed box and cut samples using rubber gloves. He took five different pieces and put them into separate containers, adding drops of colored liquid to each one. It took an hour for all the tests to be run. When they were finished, Bob handed Damon the ten-page report.

"Can I get the Cliffs Notes version?"

Bob tapped on the front page, a fresh copy with a small coffee stain in the corner. "No parasites, imagine that. But I did find something interesting in the blood. Ficus altissma arcana. It's an extract of the Strangler Fig, a vine-like plant that kills the trees it attaches itself to. That's what the vine was as well."

"Strangler Fig?"

"A variation on the plant is commonly used in a wide-variety of elixirs. Sometimes called a Strangler Vine. It's a base reagent, modified decades ago due to its affinity for attaching itself to other molecules, particularly in the brain. Big Alchemy, like D'Agastine Industries, uses swimming pools of the stuff."

"So it'd be hard to track down where he was exposed?"

"Exposed? This gentleman must have drank an entire glass of it. There was that much in his blood system, which is why the vine grew I believe. I'd bet his entire interior cavity was filled with the plant and it hit some nerves causing the body to move, making Dr. Decker think it was alive." Bob tapped on the paper again. "Interestingly enough, I've been seeing trace amounts of ficus altissma arcana in more samples than I would expect. That in itself isn't unusual, given its properties and usage, but it has started feeling like a trend."

Damon slumped. He was hoping for something more concrete that would help him explain his theory. "But if it's easy to get then it wouldn't mean much."

"Oh, no, not at all. Ficus altissma arcana is a restricted reagent. D'Agastine Industries makes their own, but anyone else would have to get it from Cyclone Reagents, because it grows in jungle climates, so you can't just throw a seed into a pot and expect a vine to pop out. Getting more than a few ounces is a big pain in the ass. Jeb uses it in the alchemy labs from time to time and even that much requires additional levels of security. Whoever gave this gent an entire glass full should be easy to track down.

There aren't that many people authorized to use it."

"Why is that?"

"Because the most common use is in potions or salves that affect the mind. It can be used to heighten senses or magical use, or to help control dangerous animals during transportation. It's quite an interesting reagent." Bob shrugged. "If you could get into Cyclone Reagent's customer logs, it'd probably be easy to narrow down who might have been capable of this."

Damon saluted the head of testing. "Thanks, Bob. That's great information."

"It is?" he asked as Damon was jogging out of the room.

On the way back up, Damon contemplated passing along the additional information, but decided that Dr. Decker would remind him of rule number one. Their last discussion on the subject had made it abundantly clear that he wouldn't entertain the theory unless he had overwhelming evidence. Damon decided if he could find out who might have had a large enough quantity of the strangler fig extract, then he might be able to narrow down who was behind all the chaos in the city. The only problem was he had no way of acquiring the information. Cyclone Reagents would never open up their books to him, which meant he was at a dead end.

There was another way, he realized as he stepped into the elevator, but the thought nearly made him sick when he considered it. He'd never be able to get the information legally, but he knew someone who had a dimmer view of rules and how they might apply to her.

"This is a bad idea, Damon Wolfhard. A very bad idea."

TWENTY-FIVE

Remi was sitting in the first year lounge with Lily practicing spells on the dummy when they were interrupted. Dr. Decker had privately given her the ultimatum to improve or he wasn't going to allow her to come back after the new year. Lily had volunteered to help, but it felt like trying to learn music from Mozart.

"Sorry, Remi, I'm worse than a kicker in heels at this. I don't have the words to explain what comes naturally to me," said Lily.

The plastic facsimile of a human body was lying on the big table at the center of the room. A cartoon of the zombie corpse attacking Dr. Decker had been sketched on the whiteboard by Ethan the previous day.

Remi cracked her knuckles.

"It's not you. I suck at this. I can get the finger gestures right, but it's hard to juggle the other parts. Manipulating images in my mind, pronouncing those completely bullshit words, and adding faez to it the entire time? I don't know how anybody becomes a mage."

"I don't know how you managed to take the chain from my neck, despite me knowing you're going to do it, but you get it every time."

Remi lifted a single shoulder. "That's easy. The more you think about something, the easier it is to steal."

"As if that makes a bloody bit of sense," said Lily, perched on a fluffy armchair. She turned her head, rainbow strands falling into her face. "Mr. Wolfhard, how are ya?"

The handsome fellow first year stood in the doorway, frowning as he always was, but she detected it was a different frown from his normal judgy one.

"Could I talk to Remi alone?" he asked Lily.

"Not suss at all," said Remi. "I think I'd prefer her to stay on that note."

"I have something I have to ask you that's really private," he said, scratching the back of his neck.

A bark of a laugh slipped from Lily's mouth. "Are you finally going to ask her out? I see the way you two look at each other."

"No," she said at the same time as Damon, bringing flushness to her face.

"I don't know where you're getting that," said Damon. "She tried to ruin my life."

Lily shrugged her shoulders as she twirled a strand of hair around her finger.

"Maybe I think the two of you need to get laid. Wouldn't be so bloody tense all the time. Everyone else in the class has been sleeping with each other."

"I'm tense because I'm trying not to get kicked out," said Remi.

She'd thought she'd be able to spend a few months at Aura Healers and learn enough to go after the pendant, but magic was much harder than anticipated. If she got kicked out now, she'd be screwed on both ends.

"What did you want to talk to her about, Wolf Boy?" asked Lily.

Damon massaged his temples with his fingertips, muttering, "Maybe this wasn't a good idea."

"Either speak or get out," said Remi. "I'm trying to fail here."

He exhaled deeply. "Fine. You two remember the zombie guy that attacked Dr. Decker?"

Remi gestured to the whiteboard with the cartoon like a game show hostess.

"Right." He sighed and picked at his fingernails without making eye contact. "I have a theory about him and the other weird shit going on in the city."

"Yeah, we heard you think it's a cult or something like that," said Remi.

"How did you?"

"You haven't been shy about it."

"I guess I haven't been. But I found out something interesting about the zombie guy. He was jacked up on some plant extract, which is why he had vines growing in his interior cavities. The same stuff has been showing up in other cases, albeit in trace amounts, but there's a pattern."

"Okay, great. Tell Dr. Decker. Not sure why you're bothering us with this," said Remi.

Damon massaged the bridge of his nose with his forefinger and thumb.

"I did. He reminded me of rule number one."

"I can see why he did."

"I'll admit, the evidence isn't lock tight. Yet. But I have a lead. There's only one company that supplies the extract. If I can get into their records, maybe I could find out who has been using large quantities of the stuff. It'd give me a lead."

Remi crossed her arms. "Isn't all the crap we have to do for the hospital enough? Now you have to go invent new problems to occupy your time? Merlin's tits on a stick. I'm barely surviving and you're trying to be Nancy Drew."

"Think about it. If there was a small group creating all these problems and someone could stop them, then Golden Willow wouldn't be overloaded with patients all the time. You'd have more time to study, Remi."

"Sounds great, but I'm not betting the farm on an inside straight."

"What?"

It was Remi's turn to sigh. "Never mind. You really didn't have a life outside of the hospital."

The comment clearly stung Damon. He tried to hide the recoil, but Remi could almost see his interior monolog on his face.

"Damon, look. It sounds really interesting, if you're into that sort of thing, but I'm barely passing. If I don't get my shit together, Dr. Decker is booting me, and I don't blame him. Except for drawing blood, I'm as useless as an empty saline bag."

In all her time in the hospital, she'd seen Damon as a blowhard teacher's pet who despite what he said, was only trying to make himself look good. But she couldn't help but see how much he wanted this to happen. If things were different, she'd consider it, but she didn't see how she could under the circumstances.

"I'm sorry. But even if it was possible to help, this sounds like a pipe dream."

He chewed on his lower lip and took a step towards the open door.

"I have an idea," said Lily. "Why don't you help him in exchange for tutoring? I'm useless as a teacher, but Damon here is probably a great one."

"Lily..."

"Would you?" he asked right away, hope blooming in his eyes. "I would help you. Please. I have to know why I smell this rotting vegetation in so many patients."

"What?" asked Remi, standing tall.

Lily was equally shocked.

"My nose. I can pick up the smell of a garden gone to seed in the summer heat. It's why I started researching this idea. When Bob told me that he was finding the extract in lots of samples, I knew I was right." He screwed up his face. "Have you smelled it?"

Remi shared a glance with Lily, who was probably thinking about the day at Tinker's Delight when she'd had the vision. "No, it was just interesting, is all."

She looked away.

"But I don't think I can consider it. Cyclone Reagents sounds like a tough place to break into if they keep valuable reagents on site..."

"Remi?" asked Lily, opening her hands.

"I know I have a past," she continued, "but breaking into a business like that… It's not like you can just pick a lock and waltz in."

"Oh," said Damon, deflated again. "If it's not possible...maybe I was asking too much."

"Yeah," said Remi, gesturing with her hand. "Breaking in is almost always the wrong move. It's like attacking someone exactly where they're strongest. Better to find a weak spot, a vendor that makes frequent visits and impersonate them, or even better get invited in as a third party. Government maybe. I mean, it'd be a huge pain in the ass, forging documents and stuff, and I don't have the tools to make them."

"So it's not possible?" he asked.

A name popped into her head. An old friend of her parents. She was aware that he was in the city, but hadn't wanted to bother him. Not that she'd had time.

"There is one possibility, but it'll cost you."

"How much?"

"More than you probably have, unless you can see to helping me the next time we're in the alchemy lab?" she asked.

"You're kidding me, right?"

"Damon. Come on. You just asked me for help breaking into a place of business with tight export controls, but now you're balking at a sleight of hand with some of the more expensive reagents? If you're right about the cult, or whatever, isn't it worth doing something just a little wrong? It's not like the hospital even notices."

Damon buried his face in his hands, moaning softly as if he were in pain.

Lily perked up, a delirious grin on her lips. "You can't curse your rival without sacrificing a few chickens, Damon. Just say yes, you know you want our help."

"*Our* help?" he asked, letting his hands drop.

Lily shrugged. "I'd hate to miss out on all the fun, and if I join, it'll make it harder to kick all three of us out if we get caught."

"What do we need to do?" asked Damon. "Do I need to buy a ski mask?"

"Fuck," said Remi, realizing it was going to happen. "No ski masks. That bullshit is for amateurs. I have to talk to someone before this has a chance of working. If we don't have the right documents, we'll never get past the front door."

Damon clasped his hands together, sporting a face-wide grin. "Thank you. This means a lot to me, and I think it'll mean a lot to the hospital and city too." He checked the time. "I have to meet with Dr. Morrison for rounds in a bit, but I can come back later and help you with your spells."

Remi gave him a nod, and he disappeared down the hallway.

"This is probably a mistake," she said to Lily, who was cradling Neko in her arms and making baby noises at him.

"You need the help and he needs a thief."

"Why did you agree to get involved? I don't buy that 'they can't kick us all out' stuff."

Lily looked up from her pet rat, who seemed perfectly content in her arms.

"What? You mean you're not curious about his idea? Especially after what happened to you in Tinker's Delight?"

"A coincidence, nothing more."

"Sure, people have visions of a decayed forest and a worm-faced man all the time when they touch a Fae-kissed pendant," said Lily.

"You really think they're connected?"

Lily shook her head, which made the mass of rainbow-colored hair dance around her face.

"Probably not, but you'll find answers one way or another. And if he's right, it'd be a boon for the hospital. Merlin knows the staff is getting close to breaking. I heard Boon trying to talk Sasha into staying. She was thinking about quitting before the holiday rush smothers us."

Remi ran a hand through her black hair. "I'll need to find time to leave the hospital. We don't have another day off for two weeks."

"I'll cover a shift for you," said Lily. "We can tell Dr. Decker you have a family emergency in the city. He won't be happy, but he'll let you go."

"Fine. Let's do it. I'd like to tackle a task I'm actually good at for once." Remi leaned against the table. "I don't know what I did to deserve a good friend like you."

Lily offered an odd smile that bordered on maniacal. "Don't worry. We all get what we deserve in the end."

TWENTY-SIX

An early winter storm whipped down from the north, bringing cold winds and pink noses. Despite using weather enchantments, Remi was miserable as she hurried down the sidewalk in the eleventh ward. The area seemed like it had an identity problem, with every other block falling to ruins, while the good sections were filled with expensive sports cars in front of high-end restaurants.

The Charm & Hammer was away from the gentrified region. Remi stepped over the legs of a bum wrapped in a tarp and blankets while a scruffy black-and-white dog curled next to him. She pulled out a food bar she had in her pocket and gave it to the dog, who munched it down in a few bites.

The bar was a few doors down. It looked like a concrete box, with murals of guys in military gear fighting demons with spells and rifles spray-painted on the outer walls.

The gray December afternoon disappeared as she stepped into the dimly lit Charm & Hammer. Growling, guitar-heavy music played at an annoyingly high volume, forcing Remi to squint. She wasn't twenty-one, but no one gave her a second glance. It was early enough in the day, the place was sparsely attended. The only others not at the bar were a trio of guys clad in black gear drinking whiskey and a larger group of twenty-somethings huddled around a table speaking quietly.

The bartender was ringing up a customer at the bar, an old man with a half-empty beer glass in his fist. Remi watched from a distance before approaching. The bartender was leaning against the rail, thumbing through his phone when she stepped up, raising an eyebrow briefly before returning to what he was viewing.

"I need to talk to Warnock."

The bartender didn't react. She could see a video reflected in the cracked mirror behind the bar. Multiple naked bodies were writhing around on the screen. She rapped her knuckles on the hard wood, but he continued ignoring her.

"I'll show you my tits if you get Warnock."

"What?" he asked, eyes wide, looking up from his phone.

"I said I won't tell everyone you're looking at trog porn if you get Warnock."

The bartender screwed up his face. "Listen here, you little bitch."

"Either that or I can tell him you're skimming from the till. I saw you slide that twenty into your back pocket. I know for a fact Warnock has video cameras, so don't think you can move the money somewhere else before he catches you."

He balled his hand into a fist, snarling at her.

"Your call. Be a lot simpler if you just got him for me. Or better yet, take me to his office."

The bartender closed his eyes momentarily before nodding. "Come with me."

She followed him into the back. The walls had scars that looked like knife wounds and there was a faint aroma of piss, which surprised Remi, because she'd always been under the impression he was doing much better. A bang on the door brought a muffled voice.

"All yours," said the bartender, before heading back to the front.

Remi swung the door wide.

Even from behind the messy desk, Warnock was an imposing figure. His ice-blue eyes contrasted with the dark umber skin tones that glowed in the soft light beneath his head full of gray dreadlocks. The pulsing jaw suggested that she'd arrived at the wrong time.

"Who the fuck are you?" He leaned to the side. "How did you get back here?"

A moment of panic in her breastbone had her wondering if she'd made a mistake.

"Uncle Warnock. It's me, Remi. Archer and Greta's kid."

He stood up from behind his desk. The cramped room seemed like it was going to explode outward from his size and presence as he circled the desk, intensity burning in his ice-blue eyes.

"Remi?"

The question was followed by his expression breaking into a grin and his arms opening wide.

"When the fuck did you grow up?"

Warnock lifted her off her feet in a hug so long and smothering, she didn't want to let go. When he let her down, she was glad she'd already wiped away the tear. It'd been a long time since she'd enjoyed a familial physical connection.

"I got into the Halls."

"Whoa," said Warnock, grinning. "You really have grown up. Which one?"

She chuckled, anticipating his reaction. "Aura Healers."

"That makes not a lick of sense. What do your parents think?"

The cheery mood faltered. She gave him a brief rundown of Utica Juvenile and her decision to join the Hundred Halls, without revealing the pendant.

"They didn't show up? That doesn't sound like them," he said, rubbing his jaw. He had an apologetic cast to his gaze as if he knew he was giving them too much credit. "I assume this isn't a social visit?"

"I need a favor."

Warnock raised an eyebrow. "A con?"

"Not the usual kind," she said, and proceeded to explain Damon's theory and request.

"Remi. That's not the kind of work you want to get involved with. Very little reward for the risk. I know your parents taught you better than that."

"But where are they now? And as far as I'm concerned, getting help so I can stay in Aura Healers is worth it. I'm going to fail otherwise."

"You? A doctor? I just don't see it."

The accurate analysis stung, but she didn't disagree. "There are a lot of ways to make a living."

Understanding smoothed away his concern. "I get it now. You've got some other job lined up."

"I'm keeping my options open, but none of it's possible if I can't use magic."

Warnock leaned against the desk. "I never liked how your parents kept pushing you to use it without patronage. I know you were young, but madness can come for anyone. Anything I can be of help with?"

"It's too early, but I'll keep you in mind. For now, I have to pass my classes, and for that I need that tutor."

"The werewolf."

"Yeah, him."

"What clan?" asked Warnock.

"I heard someone mention he was clanless. Was Zev, or something like that."

Warnock leaned back and whistled long and slow. "Zev. Wow."

"What?"

"His entire clan got wiped out about ten years ago. Somewhere not too far south of here. Was a big thing on the news. They killed everyone but your friend and his family."

"Merlin's tits...who?"

"Nothing ever came out. Lots of speculation. Most people assumed it had something to do with criminal elements, but the ruthlessness and power required to kill that many werewolves without a trace? That seems like something bigger and badder than a few gangbangers getting spicy over a bad deal. The bodies looked like they'd been thrown into a blender."

"They printed that in the papers?"

"Oh, no, but it always comes out on the Internet," said Warnock, visibly disgusted. "Wish I'd never been that curious."

Remi reviewed her opinion of Damon, wondering if she had him all wrong. She'd assumed that because he'd come from a healthy family that everything had been easy for him.

"So this Cyclone job? You need papers, uniforms, and a chip reader? Those don't come cheap."

She reached into her carryall, pulling out a handful of individually wrapped baggies and dropping them on the edge of the desk.

"These should cover it."

"A little short," he said after picking through them. "But I'll give you the old friend discount. Should take a week or two, I'll contact you when they're ready."

"Thanks, Warnock. It's nice to see a familiar face." She glanced around. "Though I thought this place would be a little nicer? Or were my parents lying to me?"

The self-satisfied grin told her she'd misjudged something. He left the room and gestured for her to follow. The hallway led to a dead end, but he tapped on a hidden compartment, and it slid wide revealing a set of darkened stairs. A steady thump-thump of music emanated from below.

"The customers have a different entrance." He paused at the door, shaking his head. "I can't believe I'm taking Archer and Greta's kid down here. Promise me you'll never tell them."

"I'd have to see them for that."

Warnock led her into a different world beneath the seedy bar. They entered an expensive and large office filled with leather couches with a one-way mirror on the wall looking into an enormous space. Remi didn't know what to think as she saw at least a hundred customers spread out across the multiple bars. Neon lights shifted colors with the groove as patrons gyrated on the dance floor. In the corner, a group of businessmen were sitting around a hookah pipe looking delirious as they blew out colored smoke.

"Where are all the cars? The block looked empty," she said.

He chuckled. "I have a shuttle bring them around to the private entrance in back."

"So that shitty bar above is just a front?"

"The Charm & Hammer specializes in some illicit magics that the authorities would frown upon. Not here, but in the private rooms. Nothing dangerous, but it's not for the faint of heart."

Remi stared in disbelief, thinking about how profitable the venture was. Based on the quality of his customers' clothes, she assumed Warnock was charging a hefty premium.

"Need any new blood in your operation?"

Warnock gave her a long, hard look. "I loved your parents like family, but one thing I never liked was how they used you for their personal gain. It reminded me of those parents that push their kids to be professional athletes, or child actors. They weren't doing it for your education. I'm happy to do that other favor for you, because it sounds like your werewolf friend has good intentions, but maybe this Aura Healers thing is the right change for you. Get out of the shady bullshit and find a real career, one that you can be proud of. Not this. Not here."

"You're not proud of this? This is impressive. Genius really," said Remi, gesturing towards the endless party before her.

He grew real serious.

"Nothing like this happens without some hard choices. I've done things that would make your skin crawl. This looks good on the surface, but I assure you that your parents would be furious with me if I got you involved. I'm sorry, Remi. I'm not taking any apprentices. Stay in Aura Healers, get a good Hall education, and do something better with your life than the one your parents wanted."

The rebuke felt like getting sent back to the kids table when she was old enough to sit with the adults. She'd grown up idolizing Warnock and the other characters her parents had connections with. To have him tell her she shouldn't want this life almost made her want it more, because it was all she'd ever known.

She couldn't imagine herself working in a medical setting, caring for people who lied about their conditions or grew violent because they were stuck in a hospital. She'd rather work in food service. At least people were nicer when you brought them something tasty to eat.

When she looked up, Warnock was typing furiously on his phone with his thumbs. He gave her a nod, so she responded with her own, before heading out of his secret office. The lights and sounds quickly faded as she climbed the stairs to the seedy bar. By the time she returned to the chilly, gray skies of the city, the secret bar felt like a dream.

Remi pressed her hand against the pendant under her shirt. Since Tinker's Delight, she'd wrapped it in cloth so it wouldn't rest against her flesh and trigger any more visions.

Maybe what Warnock had said didn't matter. Working for him would be a lateral move, not the ramp to riches she desired. When she finally solved the mystery of the pendant and claimed the Horn of Brân Galed for her own, she'd have enough money to buy a dozen bars. Maybe even the Charm & Hammer. She pulled her jacket tight as the chill winds whipped down the street and marched back to the train station with visions of becoming stupidly rich on her mind.

TWENTY-SEVEN

Damon stared at the two sets of navy blue jumpsuits hanging from a hook in the back of the panel van. He checked the name tags for the third time, trying to comprehend how this was going to get the information he needed. Outside the van, a car backfired, making him jump.

"I don't get it. Decanter Printer Technicians? We need their customer lists, not a box of toner. This is what we've been waiting weeks for? I thought you'd be breaking in and stealing the customer records. And where's my jumpsuit?"

The smug smile on Remi's lips brought heat to his cheeks. He buried his hands beneath his armpits so she wouldn't see the extended claws.

"Never hit them where they're strongest. Cyclone Reagents keeps millions of dollars of alchemical materials on-site, and their customer lists are worth almost as much as that. They use top-notch security with so many enchantments and cameras it'd make your head spin," said Remi while Lily looked on from the passenger seat.

"But a printer repairwoman is going to get the information?"

Remi smirked. "Trust me. As for the missing jumpsuit, that's because we're going to need an additional distraction. I don't want the front desk or security to know what we're doing, which is where you come in."

"I do?"

"You're going to wear your best suit, which is in that hanging bag on the other side, and at the appointed hour, be the most annoying potential customer to ever step foot in their place of business," she explained.

"Why am I doing that? Why not Lily?"

"Because you exude a self-righteousness that borders on fanatic, which is exactly the right personality to keep our mark busy."

The description cut deep, but he kept his face neutral so she wouldn't know that it'd hurt. Remi was back to fussing with the uniforms, muttering about creating ink stains to make them look used.

"You broke into my room?"

"Hardly a great heist, you can breathe on the locks and get them to open." She gestured towards the hanging bag. "Get dressed. I want you to practice a few times before we ship you out."

Remi carried the two jumpsuits to the front of the van. The girls slipped into their uniforms while he undressed and put on his best suit, which didn't quite fit him anymore. The cramped van made it hard to maneuver and he hit his head on the roof twice. When he was in his skivvies, he caught Remi checking him out from the front seat, but she quickly looked away.

She handed him a briefcase and a folder of documents. "Memorize that."

"Shouldn't I get more time for this?"

She sighed.

"This is the first day we've all had off for a month. I got the package from my contact late last night. If you want to wait until spring, we can do that."

Damon put a hand to his forehead. "No, it's fine. This is all just new to me."

"It's bloody exciting, is what it is," said Lily, patting her jumpsuit. "I've never stolen anything before. Not like this anyway."

"What about her hair? She hardly looks like a maintenance tech."

Remi reached into a black bag and pulled out a jar. "The rainbow hair is exactly what a tech would have, but so you're not so obvious, run this powder through your locks. It'll turn it black for a day or two."

She made him run through his backstory a few times while Lily changed the color of her hair.

"You're a natural, Damon. The key is you've got to keep him as busy as possible. We're doing a full court press, because we want him to be distracted, and the last thing we want is for him to make any decisions we don't like. If you overload someone's decision-making, they default to the simplest and easiest solutions, which means letting us do our job."

"An annoying customer is hardly overwhelming," said Damon.

Remi winked. "You're not the only player in the game. Now, get out of here. Come around from the other direction, circle the block if you have to. Wait until you've seen us go into the front office and then after two minutes, come inside and do exactly what we just went over."

"That's it? What if something goes wrong?"

"Let me handle that."

A surge of adrenaline made him dizzy. He grabbed a safety handle for support.

"You okay there, big guy?"

"Nervous I guess. Feels like I'm about to jump off a cliff."

"Perfectly normal. The first time I did a big job, I puked on the sidewalk and got some on my jeans. The mark kept sniffing as if he thought something was wrong," said Remi with a shrug.

Damon climbed out of the van and he started walking down the street when Remi whistled at him. He checked back to find her holding the briefcase.

"Blood and bone," he muttered. "Thanks. I'll need that, won't I?"

Before he could turn away, she grabbed his sleeve. "Remember, you came to me. So if you get nervous, have second thoughts, and try to bail on me, I will make your life a living hell in this one and the next."

"Aye, Half-Pint," he said, saluting her, which brought heat to her face. She slammed the van door closed, and he continued around the block, shaking his head.

"Aye, Half-Pint? What the hell am I doing?"

Damon put one foot in front of the other, reviewing the information she'd made him repeat in his mind, but it was getting harder to remember.

"Breathe dammit. You memorize medical tomes every day. This is barely half a sheet of information."

He opened the briefcase to check the paper, but the wind whipped through the alley, grabbed the document, and sent it soaring up and over the building before he could even blink, leaving his entire body chilled with sweat.

TWENTY-EIGHT

Remi gave Lily a last second rundown before they left the van. The Irish girl was the opposite of Damon, which could be its own problem.

"Stop smiling so much."

Lily put a hand to her lips. "Am I?"

"I might be an idiot for dragging you two amateurs into this, but you have to work with the tools you have."

"This is fun," said Lily, who kept touching her newly colored, jet-black hair. Remi reached up and collected Lily's hands, squeezing them tight as she looked her in the eyes.

"Stay focused. And act bored, you know? The life of a printer technician is not what you or I wanted. So act like it. Frown, grumble. Anything but that grin, please."

Lily made an exaggerated frown, which only made her look like a petulant child.

"I'll be fine, luv, don't worry about me. Just having a bit of fun before the real business starts."

Remi rolled her eyes as she climbed out of the van. "Keep quiet and follow my lead. If anything goes sideways, let me improvise."

"Aye, aye, Half-Pint."

Remi wanted to tell her not to call her that, but doing so would only make it worse. She threw the bag over her shoulder and marched towards the entrance of Cyclone Reagents with the resigned ambivalence that came with being an hourly worker. The building didn't stand out and the only thing marking it was a simple sign above the door.

The interior was a smallish space with a simple desk and a lone door leaning into the main area. The receptionist was typing on his phone when they arrived. His eyes shot to their name tags.

"Decanter? I didn't call you."

Remi threw the clipboard on the counter with feigned exhaustion.

"The printer sent a request for maintenance and a checkup."

"The printer did?"

Remi shrugged.

"You should see the new models. They've added some tiny enchanted creatures that keep up with the little things like paper jams and other crap like that. I have to interrogate the little critters for information because they're afraid they'll be out of a job."

"Wild," he said, eyes wide. "IDs?"

He checked them both, squinting as he read the details. He reached for the company phone as if he was going to make a call to confirm when Damon entered behind them. The receptionist looked up and sighed as he set the phone back in the cradle.

"It's in the room behind me," he said, gesturing through the glass where boxes of office supplies were waiting to be put away.

Remi led Lily into the printer room as Damon introduced himself.

She left the door open a crack so she could hear if he screwed up enough to put them in danger, but so far, he was passable even if he was talking too fast.

"...opening a new alchemy shop, but I need a high-volume supplier..."

When she turned back to the printer, Lily was staring at the papers on the exit tray, so Remi knocked them out of her hand and nodded towards the camera in the upper corner.

"Sorry."

"Help me pull the printer away from the wall," said Remi.

The access panel was in back. They made enough room for her to squeeze behind and reach the electronic innards. As she pulled the chip reader out of the bag, she caught the receptionist glancing in their direction. Regular maintenance wasn't normally done through the back, and he seemed to be catching on, so she pulled out her phone and sent a quick text to a friend of Warnock who was waiting on standby.

Almost immediately, the phone rang, which forced the receptionist to answer. Damon, to his credit, continued talking, which annoyed the receptionist. More phone calls came in, requiring switching and answering each one in turn. With the receptionist thoroughly distracted, Remi hooked the cord to the back of the printer and set it to download the entire history. The bar denoted that it would take about ten minutes, which meant there was more information than she'd planned, but hopefully they could keep up with the distractions until it was complete. The marvel of modern printers was that they kept the entire history of what they'd copied or printed, making them the weakest link to acquire stolen information.

Despite all the distractions, the receptionist kept glancing back at her through the glass wall. Remi grew worried as his expression grew pinched and severe. Not even Damon or the calls could keep him pacified.

"Just hold your fucking spiel for a second, my dude," said the receptionist as he slammed down the phone and turned to march into the back.

Damon grabbed his wrist to keep him from entering the room, which only angered him further. It was the last thing she would have wanted him to do, but he'd clearly panicked. She maneuvered herself out from behind the printer, preparing to intervene until the download finished, which was going to take more than a minute.

"If you don't let go of me, I'm going to call security. Something is not right and I want everyone to stop talking to me," said the receptionist as he broke from Damon's grip and marched into the printer room.

Remi met him with her hands up before he could reach the printer.

"What's going on? Is there a problem?" she asked.

The receptionist pointed at the printer. "That's not how you do maintenance, and I checked the records. Someone was here just last week. This isn't right."

He reached for the walkie-talkie on his hip.

"Hey, whoa, no need to cause a scene, we're new to the job," said Remi. "Maybe they sent us here as a test to see how we perform. Please, you'll only get us all in trouble if you do that."

He shouldered away from her and toggled the walkie-talkie, preparing to call security when Lily stepped forward.

"Bi socair."

"Hey," he said, visibly confused.

Remi wanted to intervene but something about Lily's supernatural calmness told her to let the Irish girl continue. She kept speaking in a melodic tongue. The longer she went the more the receptionist stilled until he was completely motionless. Lily put a hand on his shoulder and led him back to the desk, glancing back to Remi, who took it as a signal to continue.

She squeezed behind the printer, checking that they had a few minutes left. Remi watched as Lily interacted with the receptionist at the front, chatting like old friends. His responses were delayed, and unnatural, but he made no motion towards the walkie-talkie again.

When Remi caught Damon's attention, she nodded to send him away. He grabbed his briefcase and left. Not long after, the device finished downloading and she unhooked it from the printer and pushed it back against the wall.

"All done here," she said to Lily.

Lily patted him on the shoulder. "Thank you and have a great day."

He repeated the phrase twice as they walked out the door. As soon as they were outside, Remi said, "What did you do?"

"A little Gaelic charm, nothing too deep."

Remi glanced over her shoulder, expecting guards to come rushing out.

"Will he remember?"

Lily shrugged. "It'll be fuzzy."

They made it back to the van. Damon appeared not long after. He looked pale as he clutched the briefcase.

"Are we screwed?"

"I don't think so," said Remi. "Lily saved our bacon."

The Irish girl curtseyed. "I didn't know the bacon was in danger, but pleased as a woodland fairy I could be of help."

"What were you doing with the printer?" asked Damon.

"Copying everything it'd printed or copied in the last year," she said, receiving a low whistle from Damon.

Remi pulled out the device and hooked it to her phone, using it to download the records, which she immediately sent to Damon. When his phone chimed, he checked it.

"This is it?"

"Everything you wanted."

He shook his head. "Wow. I halfway thought this would end in failure."

Remi didn't want to tell him that except for Lily's intervention it almost did.

"Let me drop you two off at Golden Willow. I need to return the equipment and the van."

Damon stared at his phone as if it were a pot of gold. "This is amazing. I can't wait to dive into the data."

Remi started the van and put it into gear. As she pulled out of the alleyway and into traffic, she glanced over to Lily, who was sitting in the passenger seat, humming and playing with her newly blackened hair. Remi wasn't sure if she should be impressed or frightened about the ease with which Lily charmed the receptionist, but by the time they reached Golden Willow, she'd pushed those thoughts out of her head. She had bigger problems than her unusual roommate, namely, if she couldn't figure out how to memorize the enormous stack of spells that Aura Healers required, she wasn't going to be in the Hundred Halls much longer.

TWENTY-NINE

Night was a familiar friend to Lily as she stalked through the streets of the tenth ward with Neko hiding in her rainbow-colored hair. The lack of stars was a bit depressing, but the city lights made their own constellations. The city of sorcery was truly a wonder. Through a gap in the apartment buildings, Lily saw an illusionary dragon doing battle with a giant above the second ward.

But she wasn't getting fresh air, or enjoying the city sights. Since she'd arrived in Invictus, Lily had kept her ear out for those who might be able to help with her problems. She'd sensed the unusual presence on a visit to the tenth previously, but it'd taken weeks of research to find her hiding spot.

The air grew warmer, despite the chill, bringing a rising mist that coated the street in dreamy ambiance. The old-timey gas lamps turned to hazy eyes in the distance, halos of light making her feel like she was wandering on the edge of Fae. Lily made three trips around the block before she realized she was being warded away, glamours hiding the true path to her desired destination.

"A little bit further, Neko."

Lily spoke the words that protected her in the forests of her home. They had less potency in the streets of Invictus, but they held enough power to help her carve her way through the enchantments to find herself standing at the end of a long street looking towards a soft crimson glow. The building looked like it'd been built in the early 1900s, with glass bulbs buzzing with the name above the double doors.

The Mists.

As Lily neared her destination, the shapes of men and women—mostly women—peered out of the darkness from balconies, leaning on the cast iron fencing. A woman with skin the color of autumn and a feathered boa wrapped around her nearly naked body whistled down at Lily.

"Come on up, darling. Ask for Princess. Best night of your life at the Mist."

If it were another location, or another time, Lily would have made wards against glamours and charms, fearful of being ensnared, but the Mists was exactly what it advertised. A brothel. But why Lady Nimueh had chosen this as her home was a mystery.

Lily ignored the other offers as she entered the red double doors. Outside the music and chatter had been muted, but stepping inside turned the volume up until it was rattling around in her head.

"Take that beastie elsewhere before I send you into the abyss," said a woman's voice from the top of the stairs. She was elegant and refined, wearing a crimson-and-gold dress sculpted of silk and lace, both revealing and powerful, with a high neck befitting a queen. The woman oozed magic, which meant she was who Lily was looking for.

"Neko isn't a danger, Lady Nimueh."

"I know what that beast is and where he hails from. He stinks of *kalkatai.* I know corruption of Fae anywhere," Lady Nimueh growled as she sauntered down the curved stairs, keeping her hand on the smooth dark wood of the railing.

Lily sniffed her jacket. "It's not Neko. I work at the hospital."

Lady Nimueh twirled her wrist, and a trio of glowing sprites spun towards Lily, who held her ground, hoping they were benign. The apparitions circled Lily for a few rounds before dissipating into the ether.

"It seems you are correct, but the question of your beast remains."

"He's my guardian."

"The only reason you need fear me is because of his presence," said Lady Nimueh.

Lily sensed danger radiating from the mistress of the house. Neko squeaked and disappeared, burrowing deep into her rainbow hair.

"Please, I've come a long way and have little time before I need to return to Golden Willow."

"You're a creature of the Halls?" asked Lady Nimueh, squinting. "This confuses me. Why is one of your sisterhood chained as so?"

"It's why I need to talk to you. I'd heard many of you left the Old Country and hoped I might find answers at your door."

A pair of giggling half-naked women came rushing into the entryway as if playing a game. They squealed when they saw Lady Nimueh.

"Apologies, Mistress, we were just having fun."

Lady Nimueh smiled generously. "You're fine as wine, children. Go about your evening. This is a safe place."

After the women left, Lady Nimueh turned her attention back to Lily, scowling as she approached. "Come with me. I'll at least give you a chance to ask your questions, but know that if I sense even a single claw or tooth, I will destroy the both of you."

"Thank you," said Lily, inclining her head.

She followed the Lady to a back room. On the way, Lily saw half-naked men and women lounging on Egyptian divans, drinking wine and laughing.

In a private room, her host approached a bar and poured two drinks of golden liquid out a crystalline decanter. Lily gave hers a sniff before daring to drink.

"Kvasir?"

"I thought you might enjoy a taste of the Old Country."

"I am humbled by your generosity," said Lily, being careful to take only a sip as the potent liquor could make fools of powerful men.

Lady Nimueh drained her glass. "You want to know why I left?"

"It's not why I came, but I'm curious."

The older woman, in age not looks, stared into the distance. "Because it seemed pointless to be guarding old relics when the world was filled with powers that made them nearly obsolete. The city of sorcery itself is a marvel that even the old gods couldn't conceive in the ages of darkness. Some of the maids stayed, beholden to the old rituals, but many left, finding purpose in new ventures."

"A brothel?"

The frown on Lady Nimueh's lips suggested disappointment in the question.

"I wandered these lands for decades in search of purpose, new relics to guard, something, anything. I came upon this place on accident, but found there was something more precious than an ancient artifact.

"The men and women that work here are free to come and go as they please. This is the life they choose. In exchange for things they would otherwise not miss, I keep them safe and healthy from the ravages of this world."

"A brothel is a great place for a healer."

Lady Nimueh looked down her nose at Lily. "I'm not merely a healer."

"I meant no offense."

"Yet, your lips gave it." Lady Nimueh approached and sniffed. "Your scent confuses me. Many masters hold your leash."

"Like you, I made my choice freely."

"Illith'd fa no mein kalkatai," said Lady Nimueh.

The language of the Fae was hard to understand with her human ears, but she'd studied it enough to know what she was trying to convey. Lily had to summon the words to her lips before she could speak them.

"Fa no Medb il'canto kalkatai."

The words scraped across her tongue, leaving Lily exhausted.

"Medb?"

Lily inclined her head. "Il'canto deamaze..."

"You may speak in a more comfortable tongue if you choose."

"Thank you for your generosity, Lady Nimueh. The kalkatai reaches even here to the city of sorcery. Chonaic mé White Worm."

Lady Nimueh narrowed her gaze. "This concerns me not."

"But for Medb."

"I can do little to affect the kalkatai. That is a greater problem than my powers."

"I see," said Lily, trying to hide her disappointment as not to insult her host. "Do you know who I might speak to that might? Or is there an old artifact I should seek out?"

"The ones that might are lost to time, or are being hoarded by powers greater than you or me. Sadly, the reason the maids have been able to guard what they have is because those tools aren't important enough for anyone to bother. Even the blade seems silly in this day and age."

Lily sipped at the golden mead, no longer worried about losing her senses as Lady Nimueh could not help her.

"I see this is sad news," said the madam. "I could offer a night with one of our hosts or hostesses, whichever you prefer, to ease your troubles?"

Lily finished the drink, girding herself against its effects.

"Thank you for the offer, but I must decline. My shift starts in a few hours. I need to return to the hospital."

When she looked up, Lily expected to give her last goodbyes to Lady Nimueh, but instead found herself in the middle of the street, surrounded by cool fog. Lily found her bearings and headed in the direction of the nearest train station, mist swirling behind her like an ethereal cloak.

THIRTY

Remi was sitting at the Diamond Café on an early January morning waiting for her tutor to arrive. She fidgeted with her cup of coffee, spilling the hot liquid on her hand. By the time she got back from the front with a stack of napkins, Damon had entered, which meant it was too late to escape the fate she'd made for herself.

"You okay?" he asked, forehead hunched as he unslung his backpack.

Damon was wearing hospital scrubs. He'd clearly just gotten off the midnight shift by the smudges on the shirt and the haggard look to his gaze. When he arrived at the beginning of the year, he'd been a tan tower of muscle, but the five months at Golden Willow had depleted his vitality, turning his skin ashy.

"You know, the usual existential crisis of what am I doing with my life," she said, slumping into the chair. "I regret coming here and seeing all the smug businesspeople eating their breakfasts and talking about their jobs as if they know that's exactly what they want to do with the rest of their days."

She wasn't sure why she was being so verbose with Damon. Maybe it was exhaustion. Maybe she felt like she knew him a little better after the printer heist. Or maybe it was that he'd actually asked a question, rather than accusing her of doing something shady.

"I'm having doubts myself," he said, taking the spot across from her.

"You?"

"Not that I *want* to do it, but that I *can*." He sighed heavily. "Last night we had a little old lady come in. Cutest little thing, at least until a patient came in covered in blood and she turned into a full-fledged langsuyar. I threw her through a window after she nearly took Dr. Paddock's head off."

Damon stared into the distance, his face etched with the memories of the night.

"Merlin's tits, that's awful." She checked back to the pile of school tomes on the table. "We can reschedule if you want?"

"No. Please, no. I need something normal. Tangible. I don't think I could sleep if I wanted to. Nor do I want to."

"Right, yeah."

The hospital had a lot of great moments when you were able to help a patient with a problem, but there were far too many horror shows between. Which only made her chuckle aloud.

"Care to share?" he asked.

"This place is tearing me into tiny little balls of mush, but I'm here with you trying to stay."

"Finally understanding the purpose?"

Remi didn't want to tell him that it had nothing to do with the hospital and everything to do with learning enough to go after the pendant, but she didn't want to hurt his feelings after a hard night.

"Something like that."

He grabbed a tome from the pile. "Shall we start?"

For the next three hours, he went over the latest medical spell tome with the patience of a saint. They practiced without faez, and while she knew that his experiences were vastly superior, sitting one-on-one with Damon was only more proof of her lack. He accessed the endless lists of spells as if he were a tenured professor and demonstrated them like a concert performer while she fumbled through the gestures and stumbled over the words.

It wasn't that she couldn't use a single, well-practiced spell, but the mass of information she had to hold in her head was too much and interfered with her execution. After flubbing a heart rate dampener, Remi let her forehead crash into the table, rattling the empty coffee cups.

"I suck."

The delayed response didn't help her confidence.

"It's not that you suck, but it's like you're rushing through every spell as if speed matters."

With her forehead still on the table, she turned slightly, peering at him with one eye.

"It's too much. I've missed too much school and never learned how to memorize. Isn't there a potion or spell to help?"

"If there was I'd be taking or using it, but it's hard to improve magic with magic. They cancel each other out. There's no shortcut, Remi. But I don't think you should beat yourself up. You've come a long way since the beginning of the year."

"You're placating me. I just bungled the last three spells we practiced."

"Okay, maybe a little," he said with a wry grin.

She leaned back in the chair and stretched her arms upward. "Am I fooling myself?"

"I can't answer that for you. I can only tell you that when I first started volunteering at KC General, I mistakenly put my drink into an empty urine sample cup. Unused, but still. Some of the orderlies called me Mr. P."

"Ouch, I think I like Half-Pint better than that one."

"You're not wrong," he said.

Remi put a hand on her forehead. "Am I delusional?"

"You might be a morally suspect thief, but you're also a talented morally suspect thief. If you learned all that stuff that helped me get the Cyclone data, I think you can learn these spells. But you're going to have to put more than a few hours a day into it."

"More than a few hours a day? When am I supposed to sleep? Every time I think I'm going to get a few hours to myself, there's a new emergency requiring all hands on deck. There's been more four bellers in the first semester than most first years have their entire five years!"

He clinked his coffee cup against hers. "There are spells to keep us from getting ulcers."

"I thought being a mage would be more glamorous. And easy. That getting into the Halls would be the hardest part," she said with her face in her hands. Remi peeked through a gap in her fingers. "Speaking of Cyclone...learn anything?"

"Why do you care?"

"I don't, but I'm being nice because you're being nice to me."

"I keep my end of a bargain," he said, lifting his coffee cup. "But the data has been more interesting and less enlightening than I originally thought. There are very few places who have ordered enough strangler extract to prove my theory. Very few isn't even correct. There's only one."

"One? That's good, right? It should make proving it even easier."

His shoulders deflated. "That would be true if it were a normal business. I'm not even sure where I could begin, nor do I think it would be wise to even try. I'm at a dead end."

"Why give up now? What's so different about this place that it makes you want to give up?"

Damon reached into his backpack and pulled out a leaf of stapled papers and handed it over. It looked like the printout of a webpage. A circular badge contained a pure white antlered beast. She turned her head to read the words going around the badge.

"Society of the White Stag?"

He tapped on the paper. "There is no official listing of members, but when I did some digging, I came up with the elite of the elite. Names like DuPont, Severe, Lockwood, Dreadmarsh."

The last name sent a spike through Remi's heart. *Dreadmarsh.* That was the family that she'd stolen the pendant from, but she couldn't let Damon know that.

"Those names mean nothing to me," she said with a neutral tone.

"Nothing but the oldest and richest families in the world. The last one in particular might as well be its own cult. Rumors are that the heads of that family have been around for centuries, much longer than the Halls, which puts into question who their patron is."

Remi paged through the documents, freezing when she came to a crest that seemed both familiar and alien. It took a moment, but she realized it was a memory from when she'd been in Tinker's Delight and she'd had the vision from the pendant.

"Something wrong?"

"Flagging," she said, shaking her head as if she were tired, but she was nothing of the sort. The idea that the pendant might not just be a key, but part of a private society, sent her thoughts into a whirl.

"What does the society do?"

"They're very guarded and secretive. No one really knows, though there's a lot of speculation online. Some call them the real illuminati.

Rumors are that some of the top Patrons are members along with the city's mayor, governors, and other political figures and they make decisions about everything that goes on in the world."

"That seems like a little much," said Remi.

He screwed up his mouth. "Probably, but the fact remains, it's a dead end."

"One thing's for sure, they have the power to do what's been happening in the city," said Remi, musing aloud.

"You don't actually think that I might be right?"

Remi lifted a single shoulder. "Chaos is a useful tool. People are upset about the crime and murders. Most blame the Head Patron for not putting a stop to it, and I know they don't like her because she's young and she wasn't one of their own." She took a sip of her cold coffee as she thought about their first meeting at the beginning of the year. "Can't you find a way to get in? An invitation, or volunteer to be a worker?"

Damon tapped a long nail against the ceramic cup. "There's no place to apply and even their charity events are highly restricted."

"There's always a weak spot."

"Are you volunteering to help?" he asked, clearly surprised. "Weren't you just complaining about having too much work?"

Remi stared at the image that had reminded her of the visions. She was at a dead end with the pendant until Albi found more information. Maybe the Society could illuminate the path.

"I need a distraction or I'll go mad," she said.

Damon accepted her explanation without question, nodding as if he was struggling with the same issue.

She spotted the time on the wall clock and sighed heavily. "It's been fun but I've got a double shift, the second half with Dr. Decker."

"Ouch."

Remi shoved her books into her backpack. "If you want to check it out on a night we're both off, let me know." She left him staring out the window with the weight of the world on his shoulders.

THIRTY-ONE

His scrubs were covered in blood and other fluids Damon didn't want to think about. Even at KC General he hadn't had to deal with so much *splattering*. Everything he did, everyone he interacted with, had to explode liquids everywhere. Damon didn't have time to shower, so he yanked off his clothes and threw them in the corner, vowing to burn them later. Not having a roommate was both freeing and disappointing as his room was lonely and a bit of a mess because there was no one to judge him.

He checked his watch to see he was late. Remi was going to kill him, or think he'd chickened out, but Dr. Morrison had been teaching him how to deal with supernatural spider bites. A group of preteens, who'd been playing in an abandoned house near the twelfth ward, had stumbled into a nest of ghost spiders. The poison gave the kids hallucinations making them think they were being beset by beings from beyond the Veil. It took a mix of antidotes and spells to calm the kids. For now. Damon didn't think they were going to be alright for a while. They'd seemed pretty shaken by the event.

Using a cleansing spell, Damon washed himself as best he could, finishing with a wet wipe to scrub the stains on his arms. He almost threw on a new pair of scrubs out of habit, but managed to find a pair of jeans and a hoodie sporting his sisters' lacrosse team.

As he headed out of a side door, he heard the announcement bells ringing in the dormitory, making him hesitate. This request for help in the ER was voluntary, but he hated turning them down when they were clearly going to need it. Damon reminded himself that what he was working on *was* help. His phone buzzed the moment he reached the station. It was Remi. He quickly typed a response. OMW! And added an emoji of a person wearing surgical scrubs.

It was a clear mid-February night with a bright moon that gave the city a silver glow. He was surprisingly awake despite the late evening time, but the year in Aura Healers had made him a night owl, less dependent on sleep than he thought possible.

The train car was filled with people around his age, some fellow Hall mages, headed out to the bars and clubs in their stylish outfits, wearing colored beads and adorned with enchantments to give them a supernatural appearance. Crimson eyes that flashed other colors occasionally were all the rage. Damon saw five sets in his short ride to the third ward.

Remi was sitting on a bench outside a tavern when he arrived. She looked like she would fit in with the crowd on the busy Friday night, wearing a black silk jacket over a crimson top. A raised eyebrow had him questioning his fashion choices.

"I guess you look the part of the high school jock who never got over his former glories," said Remi, tugging on his lacrosse hoodie. "Especially since this barely fits you."

"It was a fundraiser for my sisters' team. They're the jocks of the family."

"The Demons, huh?"

"In mascot and in playstyle. Every other team in the league hates them." He glanced around. "Where's the Society?"

"About that," she said, frowning. "Come with me."

She led him down the street, which was mostly closed shopping establishments and a few scattered bars and late-night dining. A group of twentysomethings in fancy clothes and colored beads climbed out of an SUV laughing and stumbled into a flashy bar at the other end of the street.

"This isn't the area I thought the Society would be located, not with a clientele list like that," said Damon, craning his neck.

"Exactly. I was confused at first too." She checked the sign on the traffic light and oriented herself in an eastern direction.

"See over there. That should be the Society at 180 Crowley Avenue, right between the One Spell and the Hi-Lonesome Boutique."

"That says The Ane's Chic House," said Damon, squinting.

"Right. Looks like a high-end women's clothing store on the surface, but I've been sitting down the street, doing my best not to think about or look directly at the place, and what I saw were strange looking vehicles pulling up and letting people out at the front door. Yet when I turned my head, everything disappeared."

"It's an illusion?"

"A Look Away enchantment. Or a version of it. Keeps you from seeing what's really there. The clue's in the name too," said Remi, frowning.

"Ane's Chic House?"

"Reverse the words. Chicane. To deceive."

Damon widened his eyes. "Wow. I would have never figured that out. This sure makes a stakeout more challenging and explains why this isn't in the first ward."

"I kinda wondered that myself. But it makes sense. Don't put your secret clubhouse in the place everyone would be looking for it," said Remi.

"What do we do now?"

"We're not getting anywhere near the front entrance, so let's take a stroll around the block."

Damon shoved his hands in the front of his hoodie as they walked at a leisurely pace.

"What are their names?" she asked after they crossed the street.

"Huh? Oh, yeah. Nat and Talia."

"Short for...?"

"Natasha and Natalia. The Terror Twins. I miss being able to watch their games. Minus the complaints from the other parents. You'd think their games involved world peace by the way people act." He looked down to Remi, who was staring back blankly. "Not a jock I assume? What were you? AV club? Theater kids?"

Remi ran a hand through her black hair, mussing it. "I have literally no idea what you're talking about."

"High school. What clique did you run with? Everyone was a part of some group."

"Not everyone it seems," said Remi. "I didn't go to high school. Well, except for a brief few months that was an unmitigated disaster."

"Didn't go to high school? Homeschooled?"

"In a way, but not the kind of lessons you would understand," said Remi with a shrug. "I don't know much about history or science, but I can break into a car and get it started in less than thirty seconds, or tell you the fifteen major brands of safes and how to crack every one of them."

"Oh," said Damon. "Sorry. I guess I understand what you mean now about not knowing how to study. The kind of things you've been learning are more kinetic, practical. Well, practical in a criminal sort of way."

"Thanks," said Remi, rolling her eyes. Then she slammed to a stop, craning her neck in all directions. "Damn. We're back near the front. I don't remember walking around the back of the building. Do you remember any alleyways?"

Damon put a hand to his forehead. "No, but I have a pinpoint migraine right between my eyes."

"That's the enchantment. Your brain is trying to make sense of the illusion and it's giving you a headache."

"That sucks."

"No, it's good. The more things are different, the more our brains work. I don't have the headache. It might have to do with your physiology. Your werewolf senses are more attuned, which makes the difference more painful. We can use that."

"How?"

"We're doing another lap, but hold my hand and squeeze when you feel the migraine the worst."

The difference in their hand sizes was almost comical. He was comfortably over six feet tall while she was barely over five feet. It felt like he was smothering her hand. He also worried it might feel awkward, given their previous animosities, but she seemed to accept it like a professional, focused on the job rather than their physical connection, which bothered him despite his best effort to make it otherwise.

When they reached a spot about thirty feet past the entrance, Remi stopped as a taxi pulled up. The vehicle looked like every other yellow cab in the city.

"Look across the street at the windows," muttered Remi under her breath.

The tension at the center of his forehead increased, but he did as she asked. In the reflection on the opposite side of the street there wasn't a yellow taxi, but a carriage being pulled by a pair of jet-black horses with crimson eyes. Damon was so startled he checked back to see the cab still in its previous spot and two regular looking people climbing out of the back door. The backs of his eyes wanted to implode from the pressure, but he checked back to the window to see two figures in masks with antlers sticking from the tops and wearing black shapeless clothes. The squeeze of her hand suggested that she was seeing the same thing.

After the taxi left, Remi said, "That was wild. What did we just see?"

"I have no idea."

Before they could move on, two more vehicles pulled up. Using the window trick they saw two gorgeous women with angel wings climb out of a cloud, and a single masked figure wearing crisscrossed chains on his nearly naked body exit a black vehicle that looked like it'd been designed in a hellish furnace.

"We should move before someone notices," she said as she dragged him forward.

Damon massaged the bridge of his nose. "Did we really just see that? I'm not the sort to believe in lizard people conspiracies, but..."

"Shit. I know what it is," said Remi.

"What?"

"Did you see a lot of people wearing purple, yellow, and green beads on the train?"

"Yeah."

"Mardi Gras. It's the middle of February."

"I barely remember January," said Damon.

Around the side of the block, the tension in Damon's forehead increased until he wanted to lie down.

"Here."

"Here?" she asked, looking around at the brick wall.

Remi released his hand and started feeling around, so he joined her. When his arm disappeared through the brick, he motioned for her to follow. The illusionary wall was one-way, so they could see the city street as a car sped past.

"Wide alley," she said.

"Tire tracks. I bet this is the service entrance."

At the end of the short alleyway, they found a courtyard that wasn't open to the sky. Loud music came from the direction where they'd seen the vehicles drop people off. Remi hid them behind a dumpster while they watched the back door.

"Should we try to go in?"

"No way. Not with the kind of protections this place has. Did you notice the building is only two stories from the outside, but it's clearly bigger than that based on this covered courtyard? I bet it's at least five stories."

"How do you notice all that?"

"My brain is trained to look for the lie."

Remi pulled him down when the back door opened. Two guys and one girl in waiter outfits stepped outside and lit up a couple of cigarettes. Damon's hearing was good, but it was hard to pick out what they were saying other than complaining about the way they were being treated by the assholes inside.

"Sounds like a heck of a party," said Remi after they went back inside, wagging her eyebrows.

No one came out for another three hours, leaving them to stand quietly behind the dumpster amusing themselves with small talk about the trials and tribulations of the hospital. Remi smelled clean, while he abhorred the lingering scent of the hospital on his flesh.

Well after midnight, two of the three waitstaff they'd seen before headed out of the back door wearing backpacks and looking haggard, forcing Damon and Remi to hide behind the dumpster when the workers went down the hidden alleyway. When they reached the illusionary wall, Remi yanked his arm forward to follow. For the next twenty minutes they trailed the two workers as they meandered deeper into the third ward, eventually entering a bar called the Silent Hare.

"Come on, this is our chance," said Remi as she surged towards the entrance, leaving Damon to wonder what kind of trouble she'd get them in next.

THIRTY-TWO

The Silent Hare was exactly as advertised, with music playing at a low volume over the speakers. The late hour meant the place was nearly empty, with a few knots of people enjoying alchemical smokes at the bar, including the two workers. Remi had been hoping it would be busy, making her job easier.

"Come on," she said, grabbing his hand. "Follow my lead."

Remi stumbled towards the bar, hesitating before the empty chairs.

"This one taken?" she asked one of the workers.

The Asian girl set her billowing glass of smoke down, the effects smoothing away the crease lines from the long night, and gave an apathetic shrug.

"Can I help you?" asked the bartender, gesturing towards the board on the wall when she stared back blankly. Remi squinted at the list of alchemical smokes with names like Breathe In Breathe Out, A Trip Down

Memory Lane, and The Plummet.

"Recommendations? We're here on vacation, first time in the city," she said, squeezing Damon's arm as if they were dating.

"Two Wonderous Weekends coming up," said the bartender, turning back to the wall of levers and spigots.

"Isn't this place cute?" she cooed at Damon, who stared back in horror before she kicked him under the stools until his expression cracked.

"I guess?"

"The twins would love it. Too bad they couldn't come with us," she said.

"I hope they win their lacrosse tournament instead," he said.

Two brass jars filled with a bluish smoke were set before them.

"How do I?" she asked honestly, having never sampled an alchemical smoke before.

"Lean forward and inhale. Not too much at first, take your time. It's about six to eight shots of smoke per jar, depending on your metabolism."

Remi placed her nose over the fluffy smoke. It smelled sweet like cotton candy. She inhaled more than she planned. The smoke went right to her brain, filling her with a peaceful euphoria. She stared at the levers with a grin on her lips until the feeling drained away, leaving her with a strange contentedness she hadn't felt in a long time.

"Merlin's bloody balls..."

The girl to her left snorted. "Is this really your first time?"

Remi nodded in a daze, being truthful. Never in her life had she had the time or inclination to visit a smoke bar. "I had no idea."

The look of derision wasn't lost on Remi, but she was playing the part of the dumb tourist and ignored it.

"We both work in the hospital back in Kansas City. Not many smoke bars there, and we never have time anyway."

"Oh, wow. I bet it is good to get away. Honeymoon?"

Before she could answer, Damon kicked the back of her calf. "No. We're just dating. I'm a resident, he's a nurse in training."

Another kick.

"Welcome to the city of sorcery," said the girl, raising her glass of smoke.

"You work here?" asked Remi.

"Just got off."

"What do you do?"

The girl opened her mouth, but it was as if an invisible hand closed her lips, which pinched as she narrowed her gaze.

"I'm sorry. Did I ask something improper?"

"No, it's just, we work for some very private people with strict work requirements."

Remi shrugged. "That's okay. Do you have any recommendations for us while we're in the city? I'd buy you a smoke in return."

The girl, whose name they eventually learned was Abigail, nodded, and Remi moved next to the two workers. For the next forty-five minutes, Abigail and Dexter waxed about the sights and hidden gems of the city. The information was quite informative, as they'd been stuck in Golden Willow for the past six months. The pair had moved to Invictus, drawn to a place awash in magic, but had found it more difficult to live due the city's struggles and the high cost of living. By the time Abigail and Dexter decided it was time to leave, they were sharing hugs and laughing like old friends.

"If you're ever back in the city, Remi, look us up," said Abigail. "And good luck at the hospital."

After the workers left, Remi dragged Damon out of the bar.

"Let's get back to Golden Willow. I'm tired, and if I stay here, I'll just order another Wondrous Weekend."

Damon furrowed his brow. "Did we learn anything? I don't understand."

Remi pulled a handful of papers, including a few large bills, from her pocket. "I haven't got a chance to look at it, but let's see what we've got. I guess some of the Society members are good tippers. That's a surprise." She lifted a folded sheet that looked like a calendar. "What do we have here?"

"Work schedule, but that's not useful," said Damon.

Remi tapped on the paper, a spot in early March. "This one's different. There's an address written in her handwriting. Where is this?"

Damon had his phone open. The map didn't accept the information as if it didn't exist.

"Maybe she wrote it wrong?"

"Doubtful. It doesn't matter. There's a town. Arcadia. We can use that. It's a few hours outside of the city," said Remi.

"What if it's like the club with all the protections?"

Remi thought about the cottage she'd gotten the pendant from. "It might be, but probably not. Whatever this place is, they put it out there for a reason. A remote location might be enough to keep the curious away. Either way, we've got a few weeks to learn what we can before we check it out."

Damon stared with flat lips. "This isn't about helping me, or finding out what's going on in the city. You've got another angle brewing." He crossed his arms. "I'm not letting you come with me if you're just going to try to rip them off. I didn't sign up to be the accomplice to a petty thief."

"Petty thief? If I was going to rip them off, it certainly wouldn't be petty."

"I was talking about Dexter and Abigail, they needed that money you just stole, but I guess I should have looked further than that. So you *are* going to rip off the Society?"

Remi let out a curt laugh. "Are you crazy? Did you see those protections at the club? I'm good, but I'm not *that* good. Maybe if I had five years of training at Assassins or Coterie I might be able, but then again, I probably wouldn't need to do it if I could have gotten into one of those."

"Then why are you helping me? And don't tell me it's to solve the city's problems so you can have an easier time at the hospital. I'm naïve but not that naïve. Watching the way you navigated those workers, making them feel at ease so you could empty their pockets made me realize you were doing the same to me. You're using me, but I just don't know what for."

He'd seen right through her. Remi didn't know how, but he had. She was busted and the only way out was to reveal something important. Personal.

"Do you know where I was before I entered the trials? A juvenile penitentiary for kids with magical abilities. I ended up there because my parents had me steal something I shouldn't have and then when it was time for me to leave, they didn't show up to pick me up. So I thought I'd try to join the Hundred Halls, find a new path for myself. Fucked that up too.

"When you took the ball from me at the third trial, I thought I was out. I should have been. But when I was lounging in an expensive hotel I was staying at using stolen credit cards, I had a visit from the Head Patron."

"What?"

"Yeah, tell me about it. Thought I was in trouble, or hallucinating, any reason but the one she was there for."

"If this is bullshit—"

"It's not bullshit. I can drag you to the hotel and have the staff vouch for me. They were as unbelieving as I was."

The anger in his expression had softened. "What did she say? What was she like?"

"Not what I expected, that much is for sure. Not what the media says about her. Anyway. They lost two applicants to stupidity after the trials and needed to pick two to replace them. I was her choice. Said I showed promise, but also, she was concerned about my history and general selfishness. Told me that I could be better and escape the future my parents wanted for me, but I had to learn to trust people. Had to learn to do things for others and that's why she sent me to Aura Healers."

"I still don't follow the connection."

Remi thrust out her hands. "I'm trying to be helpful. That's it. You're the most honest boy scout, try-hard person I've ever met in my life. So I thought, if he cares about something, maybe I should too. Is that so hard? If you're lost in the forest without a clue on how to get out, and you see someone who seems to know where they're going, you follow them. I'm following you. That's all. And it just so happens that I have some specific skill sets that are helpful. But if you don't want my help, then I'll understand. I don't know if I'd trust me either in your shoes."

Damon stared back blankly for a long minute. She almost thought he'd been paralyzed, or had gone comatose until he shoved his hands into the pocket of his too-small hoodie.

"You've given me a lot to think about."

Then he turned and marched off in the direction of the train station. Sensing he didn't want her company for the walk, Remi stayed on the corner until he was out of sight. The night was late, but she wasn't tired. Remi almost headed back to the Silent Hare, but it was probably closed by now. She wandered in the general direction of the station, taking her time. The streets were virtually empty.

Remi neared the train station. A few blocks more and she could sit down for the forty-five-minute ride across the city. She hadn't been worried about walking alone, but then the realization that she didn't have a six-foot-four werewolf at her side hit her around the time a strange, eerie sensation crawled up her spine. She smelled the rotting vegetation before she turned.

A figure stood on the opposite side of the street. Robes and a hood hid the entirety of his form, except for the pale, bloated face sticking out from the darkness.

The White Worm.

He was only a hundred feet from her location. She thought to run, but her feet were strangely rooted to the concrete. The White Worm took a step off the curb. She was trapped. Could barely breathe, just like the vision she'd had in the trinket store. In her mind, she was surrounded by trees and vines, all competing to grab her and hold her in place. There was nothing she could do.

Then the whirling lights of a siren appeared from around the corner two blocks down. An ambulance. To Remi it was her savior, a sign from Golden Willow that she would be safe. The vehicle sped past her location. She almost waved it down, but knew that they wouldn't stop on their way to the hospital. When she looked back to the spot, the White Worm was gone and she was alone once again. The feeling of confinement and strangling was absent.

Remi ran the rest of the way to the station.

THIRTY-THREE

In the weeks after the Society stakeout, Remi found it harder to maintain the illusion of being a student in Aura Healers. It wasn't that she wasn't improving. The tutoring with Damon had given her the confidence and insight to tackle the enormous tomes of spells required for first years and she was still meeting with him, but the sessions were brief and impersonal after their blowup.

The way he'd exposed her motives made her feel like an imposter. Damon had been right. She wasn't there for school, not like the rest of the students, but to learn enough magic to go after the prize at the end of the pendant. The urge to steal as much as she could and disappear kept her awake each night, but she hated the idea of giving up, especially when it'd been so hard to get into the Hundred Halls.

"Miss Wilde, are you with us today?" asked Dr. Decker on rounds.

She'd been with him all morning.

"Yeah, a little tired I guess," she said.

Dr. Decker gestured to the patient, a middle-aged man with a missing arm. A creature had torn it off a few days prior. He'd been walking his dog after midnight and had survived only because of a neighbor who'd heard his screams.

"Mr. Jacobs isn't feeling tired."

The admonishment stung. Remi put up a brave face. "I'm sorry, Mr. Jacobs."

"Don't be sorry, Remi, take the blood sample as I asked," said Dr. Decker in a surprisingly brusque mood.

Remi grabbed the phlebotomist gear and circled the bed to take Mr. Jacobs' blood. The patient stared back apathetically. He hadn't come to terms with losing his arm yet. She'd heard him sobbing the night before when she passed his room, which was understandable, given the man was an electrician. It'd be hard to make a living once he recovered.

Remi took his blood as efficiently as possible. When she handed the sample to Dr. Decker, he stared at her as if she had two heads. He placed the vial on the tray.

"Come on, we have full rounds this morning." Then to Mr. Jacobs, "I'll come by later this afternoon when the game is on. I might even have some non-hospital approved beverages."

Mr. Jacob's eyes lit up, the first sign of life since she'd entered the room. "See you then."

"I thought giving alcohol to the patients was forbidden. A firing offense," said Remi as they returned to the hallways.

"Ethics, morality, and rules are three entirely different things. If you weren't busy moping the days away you might learn the difference, especially for an enterprising girl of your background."

Remi opened, then closed her mouth, sensing that Dr. Decker might know she'd been stealing reagents from the alchemy supply room.

The next three patients, Dr. Decker inexplicably had her take blood samples even when it seemed like there was no obvious need. After the last one, she confronted him in the hallway.

"What's going on? Am I just a lab tech to you?"

"I think you need to ask yourself that. You barely interact with the patients except at my direction, and frankly, it doesn't appear that you care about being in Aura Healers or Golden Willow."

"Rule number one? I thought I didn't know shit, and that the patients always lied, and some bullshit about parasites, which seems hilarious now because we haven't found a single one in all the tests we've brought to Bob."

Two nurses and an orderly had turned the corner, but immediately went back the other way upon her outburst. Dr. Decker stared her down, almost daring her to continue. She felt like she was on the last thread before getting cut from the school. It would be appropriate. She'd never fit in anywhere. Why would Aura Healers be any different?

"Come on, we have more patients to see," said Dr. Decker, leaving her in his wake. She had to hurry to catch up to his long strides as he left the wing of the hospital where his patients were located, going up two floors to one of the special wings of Golden Willow where the more challenging cases were cared for.

An old woman there was clearly dying based on the awful smell that was thick like smoke in her room. She was hooked to dozens of wires and tubes, her eyes cavernous and her flesh emaciated.

Remi didn't mind the injured, or sick, but those on the precipice of death made her skin crawl. The beeping on the monitor came slow and irregular. Remi stayed near the doorway where the air was better.

"Odette," said Dr. Decker, leaning down and giving the old woman a kiss on the cheek. "How is my leading lady doing today?"

Odette pressed the button on her bed, bringing her upper body into an upright position. Despite the ravages of her flesh, her eyes were bright and intense. Powerful. Remi shifted over to examine the chart.

"This is the worst hotel I've ever stayed in, Oren, but at least the staff is handsome and kind," she said with a wink.

Dr. Decker was holding the old woman's hand. "This is Remi Wilde. First-year student. If you can't tell due to the unblemished scrubs, she wears the arrogance of youth."

Odette broke into a coughing laugh. Remi could hear the fluid in her lungs.

"Age makes fools of us all," said Odette, grinning up at Dr. Decker like old friends.

"Oh, damn," said Dr. Decker, checking his phone. "I'm sorry, milady, I have to make a run for a quick meeting with the top brass. I'll be back in a flash."

Remi had let the clipboard drop to follow Dr. Decker, but he shooed her back.

"Peasants aren't allowed in the castle. Stay here with Odette. I'm sure you two will have a lovely conversation without a stuffy old guy like myself present."

Before she could protest, Dr. Decker hurried down the hall. Remi stayed near the wall with her hands behind her back as Odette examined her from her bed.

"I don't bite."

Remi looked to the open door, willing Dr. Decker to return and save her from having to interact with a woman who looked like she didn't have many days left. The tube under her nose shifted with life-giving liquids.

"You're very lucky to be working under Dr. Decker. There's no finer healer in the hospital," said Odette after a few minutes of silence.

"Him? He's a bully and a tyrant," said Remi, the words escaping her lips before she could rein them back in.

Odette raised an eyebrow. "You judge him on all the wrong things." She tilted her head. "Are you trying to run out of the room? I swear, I'm not dangerous anymore."

"What's wrong with you?"

Remi groaned internally at herself. Those were the most unprofessional words she'd spoken in the hospital, and that was saying a lot.

"The excesses of my youth have finally caught up with me," said Odette with a laugh.

Remi didn't know if the old woman was messing with her. Taking tentative steps, she collected the chart and read through the information. Since she didn't have a doctor's training, most of the wording was foreign, but she did see the word *therianthrope* under the supernatural section.

"Are you a werewolf?" asked Remi.

"It's not polite to inquire about a therianthrope's true form. It's something I only tell my closest friends."

"True form? I thought this was your real form and the change, well, that's just another version."

Odette's bright eyes twinkled. "When I was young, I thought as much. Most therianthropes spend our lives trying to hide who we really are. It's only with age that we understand it's that form that brings out our best if we learn to embrace it. You should give it a try."

"I'm not a therianthrope."

Another round of silence was followed by a question from the old lady.

"Do you like it in the hospital?"

Remi looked at her shoes. "It wasn't my first choice."

"I can tell. You look like you have one foot out the door."

"Did Dr. Decker tell you to say that? Is this a trick?" asked Remi, checking the hallway for the doctor.

"No, young lady. Oren and I have wonderful conversations. Not as often as I would like, but I understand how busy he is. As difficult as your young mind might find it hard to conceive, we've never discussed you."

"Conversations? Aren't you his patient?"

"No, dear. I'm an old woman walking the final, lonely path. Oren is just an old soul here to see me on my way with dignity and honor."

Remi didn't see how lying in a bed covered in tubes and wires was dignified or honorific, but she wasn't about to disagree with a dying woman.

"Would you like to touch my wrinkly old flesh?" asked Odette, holding up her arm with surprising vigor.

"Why?"

The old woman chuckled. "You're standing near the door as if you expect me to lunge and rip your throat out. But you also keep staring at me. I thought it might dispel your worries if you could touch my skin and confirm that I'm just a brittle old woman."

"It's not really necessary, I'm just waiting for Dr. Decker."

"I don't think that's true at all. You're not waiting for the doctor."

"What's that supposed to mean?" asked Remi.

"I know your type. You're looking for a shortcut, or trying to hurry through the hard stuff to get it over with. But the truth is, even the hidden path is filled with thorns. And flowers. Best to enjoy whatever road you're on because it all leads to the same place."

Stung by the analysis, Remi crossed her arms and leaned against the door frame. If Dr. Decker was trying to teach her a lesson, she didn't know what it was, nor did she want to learn. Odette watched her with what felt like pity, which only hardened her heart against anything the old woman was trying to say.

After another twenty minutes of silence, Dr. Decker returned. He didn't say a word about Remi's location near the door and approached Odette with his arms wide.

"I need to return to the chaos pits. I'm sorry I didn't get to stay longer. I'll find time in the next few days. I hope my first year wasn't too annoying while I was gone."

Odette nodded. "We had a lovely conversation. Isn't that right, Remi?"

"Yeah," said Remi tersely, feeling like she was being made fun of.

Dr. Decker kissed the back of Odette's wrinkly, liver-spotted hand. "Another day, milady. Come on, Remi. The hospital never rests."

Before she could leave the room, Odette called after, "Come back anytime, dear."

Remi hurried after Dr. Decker, relieved to escape the smell of the dying woman.

THIRTY-FOUR

Damon was returning from the bathroom when Tavy ran past, his sneakers squeaking on the white tile. The big orderly slowed, turning sideways.

"Lend a hand?"

"Lead on."

Tavy ran into the west side of the wing. The sounds of painful moaning echoed into the hallway, where passersby looked visibly disturbed. The Krak, Ash, was outside the room, bent over, expression cracked with horror. Given the things she'd seen when fleeing her homeland, Damon was worried as he followed Tavy into the room.

Damon didn't know what to expect, nor did he know what was going on as Dr. Decker was directing the mass of nurses and orderlies around the patient's bed. A woman wearing a bathrobe hastily thrown over crimson lingerie was apologizing profusely, tears streaming down her face.

"It wasn't supposed to do this. The spell was only meant to make things a little more wiggling and fun. Simon, baby, I'm so sorry!"

His fellow first year, Boon, was staring at the patient while Tavy and the other orderlies were holding the man in the bed down. Dr. Decker followed Boon's gaze and snapped his fingers.

"You two, I'm going to need an assist."

Damon hurried to the doctor's side, still not comprehending what was wrong. The only thing he saw was a patient sitting in bed with something large stuffed into his pants. He was sobbing as the orderlies held his arms back.

"What's wrong?" asked Damon.

"A spousal enhancement gone wrong," said Dr. Decker. "We don't have time for researching the proper counter, so we're going to have to improvise. Boon, I need you to calm the patient with a Hypnotic Pulse, while Damon you're going to need to hold it tight while I put blocker runes on it. You're the only one strong enough."

"Hold it tight?"

"Jackie," said Dr. Decker to the nurse on the opposite side once Boon had started chanting and the patient stopped thrashing. "Cut 'em."

The explosion of fabric was met with a sight that Damon certainly was not expecting. Doctors and healers in Golden Willow had to get used to seeing and examining all parts of the natural human body.

This was not one of those times.

As the patient's pants tore apart, rather than his manhood appearing, it was a hooded reticulated snake. As the creature reared back, Damon did the first thing that came to mind and punched it.

When the man screamed through the hypnotic spell, Damon realized his error.

"What are you doing?" asked Dr. Decker, eyes wide.

Damon grabbed the delirious snake beneath the head. "Sorry. I thought it was a real snake!"

Using paint markers from his white jacket, Dr. Decker made neat runes along the length of the snake's body. He had to circle the bed to complete the spell.

When he was finished, he said, "Let's tame this bastard!"

The spell was both simple and complex. Damon would have never thought to use the modified inflammatory reducer to tackle the transformed member, but the runes and the swirling magics reversed the damage the botched spell had done. In the span of a minute, the patient's snake-cock had shrunk down to a normal size, the fanged mouth turning back to the pink mushroom head. When it was finished, the patient's eyes rolled back and he seemed to pass out.

"You can let go now," said Dr. Decker.

The entire staff stuffed into the small room stared in wonder at the tiny flaccid penis as if it were a priceless work of art.

One of the nurses said, "That's one way to tame a python."

As the staff tried to congratulate Dr. Decker, he thanked them for their excellent work, shaking hands and commending each and every one of them by name. Damon was in awe of his rapport with the staff.

"Good job, Boon. Damon."

Dr. Decker turned to the woman, who appeared shaken by the experience.

"What was the spell?" asked Dr. Decker.

She jawed at the air. "It was a lexology modification. I should have planned it out better, but I was high and horny." She glanced to the unconscious patient. "Simon's great and all, but our nights are only one way."

Dr. Decker put his arm around the woman's shoulders and spoke with her quietly. She nodded while wiping her face, before throwing her arms around the doctor.

Out in the hallway, Boon asked, "What did you tell her?"

"I told her I'd leave her a few spells I learned in Hythia which are much safer than a lexology modified one to improve their bedroom experiences."

"That was the weirdest experience of my life," said Damon, shaking his head.

"Nice right hook," said Boon, grinning from the other side of the doctor. "I almost lost concentration on the spell when you punched it."

Dr. Decker checked his phone. "Come on, Boon. We have a checkup on the second floor, green ward."

Damon had a few hours before his shift so he headed to the first-year common area. On the way, he ran into Ash, who went straight for him like an arrow.

"Damon," she said in her heavy accent, putting a hand on his arm and giving it a squeeze. Her English had improved since he'd first met her earlier in the school year. "You beat snake."

"Yeah..."

Ash had gray-tinged blonde hair that looked like a wheat field covered in a dusting of old snow. She had a few inches on him and if it weren't for his supernatural strength, probably would be stronger than him.

"It was very warm," she said, leaning close.

"Very warm?"

"How you say, make me want you."

"Oh, hot," said Damon, blushing. He'd had a girlfriend a few times in high school, but once he started volunteering at the hospital, he had little time for romance. Ash put her face in the crook of his neck and licked him, which both turned him on and confused him.

"That was…nice."

She grinned in his face. "I like to lick."

"That's…a…really good."

Damon couldn't think, and that was before she put her hand on his crotch.

"You like?"

He nodded profusely.

Before he could do anything else, she dragged him towards a supply closet. The small space smelled like bleach and old mop water, but Damon didn't care as Ash tore his clothes off while biting his neck. He lifted her onto the industrial sink, using the meager light under the door as illumination. Twice during their coupling the sink turned on, spraying her muscular ass with hot water, and once someone knocked on the door before eventually leaving them alone.

When they were finished, Ash cleaned herself off in the sink and dressed alongside Damon. She smacked him on the rear before opening the door.

"It was good."

She left him in the supply closet, bewildered and a little sleepy. Damon finished dressing and headed to the common area. Ethan was studying at the big table, tapping his artificial foot to the music in his headphones. Damon grabbed a caffeinated drink from the refrigerator, wishing he had one of Jeb's elixirs instead.

While Damon was trying to piece together the last hour, a little delirious from the session in the supply closet, half the class, including Remi, who didn't make eye contact, entered from their meeting with Dr. Morrison in the ER.

He knew casual sex in hospitals was common. Dealing with life and death on a regular basis and the constant interaction with the same people left few options other than banging your co-workers. Damon thought as a first year, he was either immune or above that, but he had zero regrets as he enjoyed the bubbly drink.

He looked up to see Remi staring at him, but she turned her head. They hadn't spoken since the stakeout at the Society for the White Stag.

He regretted his words, not only because they'd been harsh, but he still needed her help if he wanted to continue the investigation. Damon had been wanting to apologize, but busy schedules had made it nearly impossible.

"Nice job, Professor Python," said Sasha from across the room. "We heard about the dick-snake and how you punched it."

"Not my finest moment. I just sort of reacted. I didn't realize that the snake was him."

Not everyone had heard the story, which required a retelling. It wasn't the strangest thing that had happened in their first year, but it was up there with Bryan flubbing a spell when a patient kicked him in the stomach and the rebound sending him to the ceiling where it took Dr. Decker two hours to come up with a counter and get him down, but then the aftereffects had Bryan belching bubbles for three weeks.

"It clearly paid off," said Sasha, grinning. "A group of nurses heard you and Ash in the supply closet. I guess she gets turned on by snake handling."

Everyone demanded he tell that story as well, but his face burned with embarrassment, especially when he caught Remi frowning in his direction.

"We're lucky those two didn't knock down the wing," said Lily, perched on a seat with her legs curled underneath. Strands of rainbow hair had fallen into her face. The comment brought laughter from the group and more ribbing about the experience.

"She's been gunning for you since the first week," said Ethan with his headphones around his neck. "I'm surprised it took this long. She already got Sasha a couple of weeks ago and Donald before he left."

Sasha put her arms up in a victory V. "It was on an empty food cart in a room with an unconscious patient. Ask me six months ago if I'd ever do that and I thought you'd be crazy."

Another round of laughing was interrupted by Dr. Paddock's entrance, which put a damper on the humor.

"One of the fourth years will be casting out a benign ghost from a nine-year-old girl if you'd like to observe. It's on the third floor in the Veil wing."

The majority of the class got up to follow Dr. Paddock. Damon would have joined them but he had his shift in fifteen minutes. When he saw Remi leaving the room last, he saw an opportunity and surged forward, putting a hand on her arm.

"Hey. I'm sorry."

Remi screwed up her face in confusion. "It's not a big deal. Fuck who you want."

"No, not that. The other night, what I said." He stared at his shoes to see if his thoughts were located there. "It was a long night and, I don't know, I saw how easily you manipulated Abigail and whatever his name was, and I had this thought that you were using me and it made me mad."

Remi searched his face, but said nothing.

"I can't fathom the life you led before you came here," said Damon. "It was unfair of me to assume so much."

"And you still need my help."

He closed his eyes and nodded. "And I still need your help. If that's okay."

Remi lifted a single shoulder. "I understand transactional relationships." At that moment, Ash strode by the room, which prompted Remi to nod that way. "I think you understand them too."

"I—"

"Don't worry about it. I'm a little jealous. Maybe half my problem these days is I'm not getting laid." She glanced at the clock. "I have to go. I don't want to miss this ghost girl business."

Remi hurried down the hall after Ash and when she caught up, she met her pace, talking quietly. Damon couldn't hear what they had to say, but the Krak woman glanced backwards at him, which made him blush again. He slipped back into the room, which had returned to its nearly empty state with only Ethan at the big table, his headphones returned to his ears.

THIRTY-FIVE

Remi was standing outside the parking garage with Lily when Damon pulled up in an old rusted Toyota Charmer truck. He leaned out the window.

"Lily's coming too?"

"Is that a problem?" asked Lily, crossing her arms.

"No." He looked into the truck. "I might have found a bigger vehicle had I known."

"Given the unknowns, I thought she could help. Where'd you get the truck?" asked Remi as she climbed in first, sitting next to Damon in the driver seat. Her hip was pressed against his as Lily slid in next, making the cab cramped.

"Dr. Morrison lent it. She thinks we're heading out for a night of camping." He gestured to the truck bed, where camping equipment was tied down. "The truck belonged to a friend of hers who left it at the hospital when he embarked for another realm."

"Wicked," said Lily.

The drive to Arcadia took more than three hours, most of it in complete silence either from exhaustion or the awkwardness of being in close quarters. They got lost on the back roads that didn't show up on any map. There was no "town," only a collection of gravel roads that circled a heavily fenced area. They reached the only paved road away from the highway, but it was blocked by a huge metal gate with a security building. Damon drove on before the guards got suspicious.

"I bet that's where Abigail is supposed to go for work," said Remi, checking over her shoulder as the guards watched them leave.

"There was a gravel road that ran along the trees towards the back side of the property," said Damon, eyeing the fading light.

"You're the boss."

Damon gave her side eye, but pointed the truck in the direction of the trees. Twenty minutes later they came over a rise. The gravel road continued perpendicular towards a big ranch, but Damon drove the truck into the trees, burrowing it deep where casual inspection wouldn't find it. He handed them daypacks, explaining they were part of the cover in case they got caught.

The sun was setting by the time they reached the fence line, sending dappled light through the trees, which had sprouted their leaves earlier than the rest of the region. The old leaves from winter crunched beneath their boots. Remi admired the way Damon looked like he belonged on the cover of a hiking magazine.

"What are you staring at?" he asked as they stopped at the fence.

"The outdoors suits you."

Damon screwed up his face. Clearly he was trying to find the insult hidden in the compliment. He marched away, catching up to Lily, who was staring at the fence. It was twenty feet tall with a thick board at the top facing inward and heavy cut-resistant chain that was coated in a light green plastic to make it invisible from a distance.

"Expensive barrier," said Lily. "What again do you think they do here?"

"I have no idea," said Damon. "But this is the only place that's received enough strangler extract to cause the problems in the city. I was hoping we could sneak onto the property and discover enough to bring to the authorities."

"Something odd about this fence," said Lily, leaning close.

"Doesn't look that odd to me," said Damon, craning his neck back.

Lily grabbed a moth flitting by her head and tossed it at the links. The winged insect hit the wax-covered wire and stiffened, before falling to the ground. She knelt down and poked the critter.

"Not dead. In stasis. I bet if we try to climb it, we'll be just like that moth, except someone will be notified to come pick us up."

Damon sighed heavily as he stared at the wire cutters in his fist. "It wasn't going to be easy, was it?"

"What do you expect?" asked Remi. "We're trying to break onto the property of some of the richest people in the world. They're probably trying to keep away paparazzi more than thieves, who would never be stupid enough to break into this place."

"Really? Even if they had a lot of juicy artifacts or something here?"

"Risk and reward," said Remi.

"I thought thieves want to pull off the heist of the century and be known for all that," said Damon with his arms crossed.

"That's only in the movies. Anonymity is better than infamy. Real thieves want to hit the easiest mark possible. Why make it hard when you just want to pay your bills?"

"Are you two done flirting yet?" asked Lily, who was digging in the cloth fanny pack around her waist. Her youthful, freckle-filled face and rainbow hair contrasted with the outfit she wore, which made Remi think of an old woman who spent her days knitting before a warm fire.

Curious, Remi ignored Damon and stood by Lily's side to see what she was doing. After seven months as her roommate, Remi knew when Lily was going to do something both odd and interesting. The Irish girl pulled out a skein of colored twine and approached the fence. She loosened the string and, letting it rest on her palm, started singing softly in a language that Remi assumed was Gaelic. The string's head lifted like a tiny snake then slithered forward, wrapping itself around the wire and then maneuvering through the links at a steady pace.

Damon opened his mouth to speak but Remi shook him off. She didn't know what kind of spell Lily was working, but she seemed to know what she was doing.

Lily kept singing and the string kept gliding through the fence. She formed a giant oblong circle and when the head of the string reached the beginning, she trilled a little whistle and it tied itself into a knot. She gathered golden faez in her mouth and blew it on the links, which sparkled like fireflies at dusk.

"Should be as green as gold to cut now."

"What did I just witness?" asked Damon, jaw hanging low.

Remi was equally curious. She thought she knew everything about her roommate, but the display proved there was more to the eye than the strange Irish girl let on.

"The Crown tends to be greedy when it comes to land. There are many sacred areas to my people that are bound by fences like this. I learned as a young girl how to bypass them from my older sisters."

"Someday I want to hear more about your family," said Damon. "Okay to cut?"

"Give me the cutters," said Remi. "If you get hit with a stasis field, we're not strong enough to drag you back to the truck."

He handed them over. Remi put the shears around the wire and, using both hands, squeezed until she heard a pop.

"I guess it worked."

She continued cutting for a few more links until Damon took the shears and sped up the bypass. When the inner fence peeled away leaving a man-size hole, Remi whistled.

"Nice one, Lily. We'll make a thief of you yet."

"It's not thievery if you owned it in the first place."

Remi didn't know what her friend was referencing but she started to step through, only to be pulled back by Lily, who was sniffing the air with a wrinkled nose.

"Something don't smell right."

"I think meat hands had to disimpact someone earlier today," said Remi.

Damon sniffed his fingers. "I don't smell."

"Not that," said Lily, leaning into the hole. "There's potent magics here." She dug into her rainbow hair, pulling out Neko. The white rat squeaked as she stroked his head. "Gonna need you to stay out here, my little friend. These charms might be rather painful if I try to take you through."

"The enchantments are blocking Neko?"

Lily smiled oddly. "I put enchantments on him to keep him safe. Rather not unravel them just to bring him through. Better if he stays out here. I'll leave my pack and he can nest in there."

Remi was sure there was more to the story, but if Lily got them past the fence, the last thing she wanted to do was question her friend's motives. She followed Lily through, but when Damon followed he cried out in pain, jumping back to the outer side of the fence line.

"What was that?"

"Is that because he's a werewolf?" asked Remi.

Lily was staring at the top of the fence. The thick board was actually an electronic marquee with bright runes displayed.

"What is that?" asked Remi.

Lily shook her head. "Bough and branch. That's the most expensive enchantment I've ever seen. It's all electronic, so they can change the charms around the entire facility without having to reapply them by hand. Must have cost millions."

Remi's stomach tightened. "I'm liking this less and less. You don't have this kind of protection unless you've got something important inside. Look at all the land, space to keep prying eyes out. And this fence? This is a lot more like the Society building in the city than I thought it'd be."

"Are you injured?" asked Lily.

Damon rubbed his arm. "No marks, but it hurt like hell. Like my skin was on fire."

"It's detecting your supernatural blood," said Lily, pointing to the marquee.

"Am I stuck out here?"

"You can come through, but it won't be pleasant."

Damon moved back a few paces. He paused before throwing himself through the gap, a sharp scream leaving his lips as he collapsed on their side, heaving in the leaves. He climbed to his feet slowly.

"Blood and bone, that was awful. I hope we can find another way out. I don't know if I want to do that again."

"Where to?" asked Remi, gazing across the rolling green hills that led up from the fence line. Daylight had faded, leaving a nimbus on the horizon.

Damon straightened his daypack and started up the hill in long strides. The tree line fell behind them, which left Remi feeling exposed. Other patches of trees dotted the hillside, but they were too far away to make her feel safe. She kept checking back to the fence to lock the location of their escape in her mind, catching the runes on the marquee switching to a new set.

"Hold up," she said, stopping them halfway up the hill. "The runes changed."

"Sure enough," said Damon, half turning, but looking ready to continue.

"Something changed for sure. That's not good," said Remi.

"And it might not be bad either. Probably nothing to do with us. You're just paranoid," said Damon.

"Paranoia has saved my ass more than once."

"Do you have a suggestion?"

Remi checked back to the fence. "Not really."

"Then let's keep going. I feel like we're really close to some answers."

Remi agreed, but worried the answers wouldn't be pleasant. When they reached the hilltop, a cup-shaped valley spread out before them with a massive set of buildings at the center. The brick buildings had sweeping roofs with turrets and glass house wings, lit from within. The sprawling campus had a half dozen structures surrounded by lush, manicured gardens with huge fountains. It was too dark to see if there were many people below, but she could see movement near a building at the edge that looked like stables. She hoped Damon didn't want to head down, but he seemed so focused on his goal he was oblivious to the dangers present.

A pulse of horns sounded in the distance.

"What was that?" asked Damon.

Lily extended her arm towards a set of buildings on the ridge, surrounded by towering trees. "I saw a flash of light over there."

Remi was still focused on the property at the center. The shifting of shapes at the edge of the light was hard to pick out, but she was certain that people were moving up the ridge in a group on horseback.

"I don't like this," said Remi. "I think we should leave. Like right now."

"There's something oddly familiar about this," murmured Lily.

The horns sounded again.

"Yeah, maybe we shouldn't be standing out in the open," said Damon, looking around.

He started jogging around the rim, staying on the outer side, heading towards the buildings on the ridge where Lily had seen the flash of light. The dim light had faded to black and her eyes weren't adjusted, leaving her to feel like she was blindly wandering across the hill, using Damon's blue and white daypack as her guide as she hurried to keep up.

Damon halted, putting his arms out to keep them from passing. He turned his head sharply.

"Did you hear that?"

"What?" asked Remi.

Damon appeared disturbed by the sound he'd heard. "It sounded like a tiger."

"I heard a wolf," said Lily, who had reached into her cloth fanny pack and grabbed something small that was hidden by her fist. "And I think I know what this is. The horns, the property. If I were home, I would have recognized it right away, but I thought it might be something else."

"What is it?" asked Remi.

Before Lily could answer, a low growl from above them on the ridge had them freezing in place. Remi looked up to see a faint silhouette of two creatures standing so close to each other that it was hard to make them out separately with multiple tails undulating over their bodies hypnotically.

Cold fear shot down her spine as the creature turned slowly towards them, which made Remi realize it was not two creatures, but one, and the heads sprouted from the same body.

And the tails.

She didn't know what they were, but she knew they'd made a big mistake sneaking onto the property.

Damon sidestepped while keeping himself between them and the creature, which let loose both a gut-rattling roar and a horrific howl.

"Run! To those trees!"

THIRTY-SIX

The two-headed beast bounded down the slope at Damon, keeping its crimson eyes locked onto him. The girls had burst towards the outbuildings surrounded by trees. It was the closest point of safety, but they'd never make it if the beast turned on them, so Damon let rage consume him.

Claws ripped painfully from the end of his fingers as his back stretched outward, muscles expanding and growing rapidly. The pain was mixed with the euphoria of release—the gestalt of becoming.

Darkness cloaked the beast's approach once it had left the ridge, but he could smell its potent blood, smell the old flesh lodged in its dual heads. The meaning of the monstrosity was lost to fury as he prepared for impact. The roar on Damon's lips was cut off when the beast pounced, and the only thing that probably saved him was the leap forward.

Damon was knocked off his feet, tumbling down the hillside, but he found his feet right away. The beast was at least three times his size, which meant his werewolf claws and teeth wouldn't be enough. The creature was on his left, having tumbled upon impact, but had found its feet just as quickly.

At close range, he saw one head more clearly. A tiger. And the tails weren't tails at all, but velvet-covered tentacles sprouting from its shoulders. The monstrosity growled, preparing to leap, and this time Damon was certain it wouldn't miss. He hoped the girls had reached the tree line and could find safety.

As the beast lowered its forepaws, readying to leap, a bright flash, followed by the swirling of brightly lit insects, distracted the creature. It tried to eat one of them, before growling and barking.

"Come on," said Lily, motioning to follow.

He didn't know what kind of magic she'd displayed, but wasn't going to question being saved. Faster than his fellow first year, he scooped her up and sprinted full out, hearing the roar and howl of hunting from behind. When he reached the trees, he didn't see Remi.

"Up here!"

The thick trees had long trunks, but that was nothing for his claws.

"On my back."

Lily climbed on, and as the beast bounded towards them in loping strides, he pulled his way into the tree, following Remi's voice. He'd managed to reach the first level of branches, which were at least twenty feet above the ground, when he heard Remi tell him to watch out.

Damon leapt, barely avoiding the snapping jaws from below, and landed on the branch. The impact nearly knocked Lily loose, but he grabbed her hand before she could fall to the beast below.

Using one hand to hold himself on the branch, Damon regripped to keep Lily aloft as the beast prepared to leap again. At the last moment, he yanked her up, right as the teeth clacked on empty air. She landed on the branch, holding tight as he hauled himself up. As the beast growled below, he helped Lily climb higher to where Remi had found a wide spot to rest upon.

"Whoa," said Remi.

He thought she was talking about the beast, but he found her staring at him. Her lips were parted and her eyes were wide. But not scared.

"All your clothes are ripped to shreds. Wild."

Speaking in his wolf form came out rough and gravelly. "Do you think that thing can climb?"

She peered through the gaps. "We'll find out soon enough."

Before he could answer, a trio of horns sounded from nearby, nearly startling Lily from her perch. Damon reached out to steady her, but the claws cut into her arm and she yelped, pulling herself away. The fresh blood went right to his head. He knew he had to keep calm. He'd never been like the rest of his family. The coppery scent filled his mind with visions of tearing flesh from bone. He could crush Lily's head with the squeeze of his fist. She sensed it and started backing away, heading further onto the thin part of the branch.

"Damon, what the fuck are you doing? You're scaring her," said Remi from above.

She smacked him on the head with a thin branch, not much more than a stick, but it startled him out of his rage. He bared his teeth at her, not in anger, but frustration at his loss of control.

"Hush, they're coming."

She pointed the stick away from the trees. The two-headed beast had quieted as well, sensing the approach of others. Damon heard the thunder of hooves before his friends. He saw ghostly lights through the leaves as a group of mounted men circled around the copse.

The beast barked and burst away, bounding across the grassy hill with the horsebacked riders in pursuit. The light was faint, but the enormous lead rider wore antlers and rode a jet-black warhorse with bits of bone poking through flesh. He led the hunting pack after the two-headed beast, oblivious to their presence in the trees. He watched until they were away and the horn sounded in the distance, marking that the beast was no longer a danger.

"Is everyone alright?" he asked.

"Are you safe now?" asked Lily right away, a heavy scowl in her voice.

"I'm sorry. I meant to grab you, but I missed. It was an accident."

"What the fuck just happened?" asked Remi. "Was it just me, or did I see a bunch of animal-headed people riding skeletons after a two-headed wolf?"

"I saw a tiger head," said Damon.

"Tiger? Wolf? Who cares? What did you get us into, Damon?"

He was still breathing heavily, the smell of fresh blood keeping him from calming.

"I don't know."

"How are we getting out of this tree?" asked Lily, swaying on the branch. "I'm not a good climber."

"I'll help you down," he said as Remi shimmied past without fear of falling.

Lily pouted, but as she looked through the gaps at the distance below she edged back across the branch. He offered his back and after a heavy sigh, she climbed on.

Back on the ground, Remi seemed the least affected by the near-death experience. She eyed him up and down.

"You can stop staring at me."

Remi squinted. "When do you change back?"

He didn't want to explain that the scent of fresh blood was making it hard to calm himself. He didn't feel a danger, but he knew he presented a fearsome presence.

"It doesn't go quickly the other way." He checked his clothes, seeing them tattered from the transformation. "We can head back if you want."

"No," said Lily. "I didn't survive that to give up. We should check out those buildings."

The structures in the trees had soft ambient lights inside. The larger one was the size of a warehouse. He hoisted Remi up so she could see through the window, which elicited a hushed exhale of surprise.

"Merlin's balls," she said.

"What?"

Remi hopped down. "Better see it for yourself."

If there was a lock, it didn't slow Remi, who was through the door in an instant. He saw the cages right away, smelled the potent flesh of supernatural creatures.

In the first enclosure was a gorilla-sized beast with hooks for arms and the head of a vulture. It sat against the thick bars of the cage, deliriously staring forward, barely acknowledging their existence. The other cages held similar chimeric beasts constructed from a variety of origins.

"They're all stoned," said Remi, picking up a rock and throwing it at the vulture-gorilla. She received a weak squawk for her effort.

"I know what this is," said Lily. "It's a hunting preserve. The kind that rich people like to enjoy. No competition, beasts tailored to their interests and released on command."

"What about the antler-head guy and the skeleton horses?" asked Remi, kicking at the loose straw on the ground.

"It was the bloody Wild Hunt is what it was," said Lily.

"Where are they using the extract? This place goes through buckets of the stuff," he said, feeling himself again. It would take another hour to completely look human, but he had control of his thoughts and instincts.

"I bet they mix the elixirs that keep them docile in the other building," said Remi.

The two structures were connected by a breezeway. True to Remi's guess, it was an alchemy laboratory. He sniffed out the industrial-sized barrel of strangler extract on a heavy, reinforced shelf.

"I don't think this is the source of the chaos in the city," said Remi.

Damon crossed his arms, disappointed. "No, I don't think so. We should leave before someone finds us."

Remi stuffed her backpack with reagents from the lab, but he said nothing since they were already trespassing.

The center of the valley was alive with lights and hollering when they returned outside. Climbing to the ridgeline, they saw the two-headed chimeric beast had been killed and dragged to the hunting lodges near a huge bonfire that sent fireflies into the sky. Damon couldn't make out faces, but he saw the people had taken off their helmets, and servants were removing the skeletal armor from the horses.

"Bloody fools," said Lily, making signs and spitting in the grass. "The Wild Hunt is not to be trifled with."

"They seem like they can take care of themselves," said Remi.

"What's the Wild Hunt?" asked Damon.

"The huntsman of the Fae. Some say it's the Oak Father on a hunting party, others say it's an older eldritch Elder from the Fae, who exists on an eternal hunt. It doesn't matter which one is true, because when we heard the baying of their spectral hounds, we stayed in our home and warded the doors. Even masquerading as them could be conceived as an insult, inviting their wrath. These rich people are fools to cosplay as ancient powers."

Damon didn't believe Lily that there was an actual Wild Hunt, but he wasn't about to disagree after she'd saved him from the beast earlier.

"I think it's just a bunch of rich people playing dress-up, so we're probably safe," said Remi with a shrug. "Let's get out of here. I have a shift tomorrow early. I'd at least like two hours of sleep before we get back."

"You can sleep in the truck. I won't be able to rest for hours," said

Damon.

The return to the fence line was uneventful, except for the passage through the gap, which hurt as bad the second time for Damon. He was back to human form by the time they reached the truck, which allowed him to change into the extra pair of scrubs he'd brought.

As soon as they left the gravel roads, Remi was asleep, snoring softly on his shoulder while Lily sat with Neko in her lap, stroking his white fur and occasionally mumbling about the Wild Hunt.

THIRTY-SEVEN

The beeping and wheeze of oxygen machines reached Remi outside the room. She huddled by the door with her hands shoved under her pits, ignoring the strange glances from the nurses and doctors walking past. Remi couldn't figure out why she was here, but she couldn't leave either.

"I can hear you breathing out there. Why don't you come in?" asked Odette.

Remi almost scurried the other way, but felt foolish enough that she'd been lurking outside the door that she decided it was better to enter. She skulked into the room as the old woman, covered in wires and tubes including an oxygen line beneath her nose, lay in her upright bed. There was an odd smell of decay as if the body no longer cared about regular maintenance.

"Did you need to check on me, it was Remi, correct?"

Remi nodded, looking at her shoes rather than the old woman. "Yes."

She screwed up her face. "No. I'm not here to check on you."

"Wanted to see if I'd kicked the bucket yet?" asked Odette with a wry grin.

"No," said Remi. "That'd be weird."

"Not as weird as standing outside an old lady's room not saying a word."

Remi put a hand to her forehead. "I shouldn't be here. This is, I don't know what it is, but I'm sorry."

"Remi, please. I don't get many visitors and Oren has been so busy lately." Remi had made it to the doorway when Odette added, "I don't have much time left."

The words were like quicksand around her feet. Remi turned and went back to the foot of the bed, but couldn't meet the old woman's gaze.

"How is your first year going?"

"Terrible? But better. I'd like one night of sleep, but that won't be for a few years, maybe a decade," said Remi while staring at her shoes.

"Oren's very hard on you, isn't he?"

Remi glanced up, the sympathetic smile breaking her inner struggle.

"He's an asshole, but patients seem to love him."

"He's a good doctor, you could learn a lot from him," said Odette.

"But he's not your doctor and as far as I understand, there's nothing left to do for you," said Remi.

"Both of those things are true, but that doesn't mean what he's doing isn't impactful."

"I never meant to sign up for Aura Healers, but it was my only choice if I wanted to be in the Hundred Halls. I don't know if I have what it takes to be a healer, and especially not a doctor," said Remi, letting the words unburden her.

"Oren wasn't always a good doctor, dear."

"You've been in the hospital that long?"

She chuckled. "No. But he told me himself. Told me some interesting stories about his past. Illuminating even. He's led a difficult, but fascinating life."

"Like what?"

"Those are his stories to tell. I wouldn't dare to presume."

Remi shifted two steps to the middle of the bed. "What about you? Did you lead an interesting life?"

"To some, no, but for me, absolutely," she said, staring into the middle distance. "I was a botanist."

"Plants and stuff."

"Yes," said Odette. "Plants and stuff. I worked in a greenhouse in upper New York, run by a billionaire with interest in the science."

"Like supernatural plants?"

"Some, but mostly no. This was real research-driven science, not profit like D'Agastine Industries or Pyramid Health, or any of the others in the alchemical market."

"Are you...?"

Remi waggled her fingers.

"No, not a mage. Just a therianthrope with a love of plants, particularly water based. But again, not all. It was a wonderful facility with ample resources for our research. I truly miss it, but as they say, all good things must come to an end."

"What's wrong?"

"I developed a unique cancer in my lungs and other organs. It's slowly eating me alive, turning me to mush. Even Golden Willow, with its amazing doctors and history, hasn't been able to do much more than keep me comfortable."

"Unique?"

"We specialized in research with plants from other realms. While we were exceedingly cautious, the doctors assume I picked up something that attacked my system, but they've never been able to figure it out."

"That's terrible."

"That's life," said Odette with a shrug. "There are no guarantees. But let's not dwell on that. Tell me something about yourself."

Remi hesitated, not wanting to reveal too much, but the woman's short future loosened her tongue. She spent the next half hour telling Odette about the early jobs her parents pulled with her. The older woman was delighted by the tales and by the end when Remi had to leave for rounds with Dr. Paddock, Odette had her promise to visit again when she had a free moment.

THIRTY-EIGHT

The blood pustule was at least three inches in diameter when it exploded, throwing sticky liquid all over Damon's fresh scrubs. He'd already had to change twice and he was only two hours into the shift. The purification spell would keep him safe from any bloodborne pathogens, but he was getting tired of having to cast it.

Three more howlers hit the entrance to the ER, and the EMTs got into an argument about which one was a higher priority. The influx of patients had been constant, strange attacks happening all over the city.

"Damon, they need you in Room 2F for a translocation," said a nurse, hurrying past.

He jogged into the room, which had been partitioned for additional beds. Dr. Morrison was holding the patient in stasis, a golden blanket of light covering his quivering body. The veins in her forehead were bulging from the strain and she was too busy keeping the spell in place to speak, but he didn't see the reason for the translocation request.

"What do you need me to do?"

She grunted, drawing threads of golden light and wrapping them around the patient's limbs while he struggled to escape.

"The nurse said a translocation. Not a translocation?" he asked as she shook her head.

Damon studied the patient. He looked like a middle-aged man in the middle of traumatic shock, but without a visible wound.

"Necrosepsis? No, then a possession?"

Dr. Morrison jutted her chin at the patient's legs. Damon examined the man's stiff limbs until he found marks on the back of his calf that looked like a wicked non-human bite. The pattern was unknown to Damon, and the request for a translocation didn't make sense.

He snapped his fingers. "Transfusion? RBF?"

Dr. Morrison gave a sharp nod, making her braids shake. A rapid blood filter was a spell technique that tried to remove toxins from the blood. It was used when the source was unknown, and it was the equivalent of sucking the venom from a snake-bitten leg.

While the doctor was holding the patient, keeping him from convulsing, or attacking, it was hard to tell, Damon worked the spell. It wasn't simple, requiring exact movements and rotating two different shapes in his head while speaking the command words. Then once the spell was active he had to coax the blood through the filter gate in the leg. Damon worried that he'd picked the wrong spell, or that toxins were the problem when nothing came out of the patient's leg after the first minute.

Then the patient arched his back, screaming mutely as Dr. Morrison tried to keep him still. A regular person shouldn't be able to resist the stasis, but something was overcoming her advanced spell, which made him want to hurry. He pulled harder, and the man silent-screamed again, followed by the bulging of his calf. A black tarry substance came snaking out of his wound. Damon kept drawing it out while he kept up the RBF. When the last trailing speck of black tar exited the wound, hovering in the air like a glossy ebony snake, Damon let the spell collapse and the liquid fell onto the bedcovers, hissing as the toxic material ate through the fabric.

Damon grabbed the spill kit from the desk and threw the alchemical neutralizer on the substance, which worked enough that he could get it into the bin with a spell assist. When he was finished, Dr. Morrison let the stasis collapse. The patient let out a low moan with his eyes wide, and before he could feel the worst of his injuries, the doctor injected him with a painkiller that would knock him out.

"Good work," said Dr. Morrison, leaning on the bed. "That was quick analysis and a great RBF, especially for a first year."

"Thank you. Any idea what bit him?"

"No idea, but shit like this keeps happening. I don't know if we can keep up. I asked Dr. Fairlight to bring in more doctors, but she says it's hard to get people to commit to a place in full-fledged chaos. On the other hand, I think the current Aura Healers class, if you can survive it, will turn out to be one of the best due to all this practice."

Damon examined the wound again. The teeth marks suggested incisors, but they were uniform rather than off-kilter like most sets of teeth. He explained his thoughts which brought nods from Dr. Morrison.

"This isn't the first bite wound like this I've seen," she explained.

"Supernatural creature?"

"No. Like you said, the teeth are too uniform. Unnaturally so."

Given Dr. Morrison's dual major in both Aura Healers and Animalians, Damon was primed to believe her.

"You seem to have a theory brewing behind those eyes," said the doctor. "What do you think?"

Damon explained what he'd learned about the strangler extract but not how he'd acquired the information. She nodded along.

"Sounds plausible. I like how you're thinking."

Dr. Morrison moved to the computer and pulled up her account.

"Let me show you some of my notes."

She pulled up a group of pictures showing bite marks similar to the one on the patient's leg. More than similar. Almost exact.

"I know, I know," she said. "Besides being too straight, they match too. Down to the spacing between the teeth. Whatever it is, either it's not natural, or is something I don't have the experience to understand."

"Not natural? Like a golem or something constructed?"

Dr. Morrison shrugged. "Possibly. But that wouldn't explain what's been happening to the bite victims. Each one has reacted differently to the bite."

"What do they say about how they got it?"

"They don't remember. Not just these either. Lots of others practically wake up in the ER having no recollection of how they got here or why they went temporarily crazy," said Dr. Morrison.

"Maybe it's parasites," said Damon.

"You've been around Dr. Decker too long," said Dr. Morrison wryly. "But none of the blood tests have come back with any signs, otherwise it'd be a plausible answer. Parasites can do some crazy and awful things if they're left unchecked."

"I wish we could figure it out. I feel like things are getting worse."

"You and me both. When I get a few moments to myself I like to sit on the roof and study my notes on a datapad. The sounds of the city, the lights of the Spire, the bright flowers wrapped in the trees—they make for a peaceful place to imagine myself anywhere but here," said Dr. Morrison.

By the end, she seemed to realize she was talking to a first year rather than a fellow healer or doctor, and looked away.

"If you want, I can send you my notes and you can see if you find anything interesting that I've missed."

"I would love that. Thank you, Dr. Morrison."

"You're very welcome," she said with a smile that reached her eyes. "You remind me of some friends of mine."

"Good friends?"

"The very best." She checked her watch. "I need to give the follow-up orders for our bite victim. You can head back to the ER and see how those howlers are progressing."

Damon saluted and ran out of the room, feeling like he was actually accomplishing something at Golden Willow. It made the long double shift that didn't let him sleep until the sun was rising worth the struggle.

THIRTY-NINE

Remi had two cups of blue Jell-O in her fists on her way to see Odette for the afternoon chat session when Lily waved her down. Remi shoved the plastic cups in her scrub pockets and jogged to the attendants desk in the ER. The entire class of first years was standing in a semicircle around Dr. Decker. Daylight streamed through the front windows, so it was too early for a major emergency, but the nurses clearing out space and hauling in folding cots and privacy shields they kept in the basement told her something bad had happened.

"There was an incident at the Newtown Fishmarket," said Dr. Decker. "About two dozen people went crazy, started attacking each other, clawing, biting, the works. Took Invictus PD's riot squad to put things to order, but now we have a couple buses of injured folks on the way here. Maybe five minutes away. Probably less. Unfortunately, Dr. Morrison is off today, so I'm in charge of the ER. We're going to full triage mode. I'm going to assign you each to a nurse or doctor—help in any way you can. The ropes team will be on hand if necessary, but there's going to be a lot of chaos because half of them are in cuffs and still wild."

She shared a look with Damon, who was clearly thinking the same thing about this incident, but she didn't have time to talk to him as a nurse shouted about the buses arriving. Remi caught a phalanx of police vehicles escorting the buses and nearly missed her name being called.

"Remi, you're with Mandy on vamping..."

Under normal circumstances, Remi might have complained about being relegated to taking blood samples, but she understood the need to compartmentalize duties. It would make surviving the chaos easier.

Mandy was pulling her gray-tinged hair into a bun when Remi found her. A cart filled with phlebotomist gear was already organized, which didn't surprise Remi, since Mandy was one of the nurses the first years loved best. Not just because she was extremely competent, but she had a soft touch with them as students while other nurses could be rough.

"You ready?"

Remi nodded. "Just tell me what you need me to do."

Mandy winked. "That's my girl. Whoa, look at that. This is going to be fun."

She wasn't kidding either, grinning at the line of middle-aged men and women being dragged towards the front doors by officers in riot gear. Almost as soon as the first few entered the ER, a slight woman with steel gray hair broke free from her handler and leapt onto a table, eyes bright with rage. She leaned back her head and howled, then leapt right into the ropes team coming to grab her. The ensuing wrestling knocked over two tables before the smallish woman was subdued.

The next five hours passed in a daze.

Remi moved from table to table, taking blood samples and occasionally casting a simple tetanus spell if the patient had been hit with anything metal, or soothers for the anxious but non-wild patients.

The entire time, she heard nothing but screaming from the incoming injured and yelling from doctors and nurses trying to be heard over the chaos. Towards the end, Remi's fingers were stiff from tying the tourniquet, but she kept up with the grueling pace.

"I think we're caught up," said Mandy, wisps of gray hair free around her temples. She stretched her fingers. "I'm going outside for a vape. It's got a unicorn tear base, which makes it excellent for the comedown after a wild afternoon if you want to join me. We can enjoy the lovely views of laundry hanging on the back railings of the apartments."

She snorted softly as she reached into her scrubs for the vape pen.

Remi hadn't even realized that it was night already. The parking lot lamps were on and the normal ER evening pace was picking up, but thankfully the night shift had arrived. She wanted to join Mandy, not only because she could use the break, but nurses really ran the hospital and getting on their good side was a recipe for future success.

"I would, but I have someone to check on," said Remi, holding up two cups of Jell-O.

Mandy's eyes creased with a smile. "I understand. Let me know if you want to hit this when you come back."

The elevators were packed, so Remi used the stairs, feeling dizzy from the lack of nutrition. The elixirs that Jeb had brought after the first crazy hour had helped, but they were wearing off and her knees were shaking.

Remi reached Odette's room only to find the older woman asleep. She checked to make sure there was mist in her oxygen line when she didn't hear a pulse beat. The finger catch was lying over the edge, which made Remi smile. Odette hated wearing it and turned off the monitor whenever she could. *I'm here to die, why does it matter if the nurses can see my pulse?* she'd asked on more than one occasion.

Remi thought about waking Odette up because she wanted to talk to her about the afternoon's craziness. The old woman loved to hear about Remi's day, which made her feel like she wasn't as useless as some of the doctors made her feel. But Odette rarely slept these days, the pain in her gut was getting to be too much. Even as the old woman slumbered, her lips tightened with occasional grimaces.

"I'll come back later," she told the sleeping woman, setting a cup of Jell-O on the table.

Remi jogged back the other way, hoping to catch up with Mandy outside, but she was already gone by the time she got there. The curb made for a nice, quiet spot to enjoy her snack. Remi realized she'd forgotten a spoon, but it was easy to squeeze the plastic and push the Jell-O into her mouth, using her tongue to capture the colored gelatin.

Clouds had blanketed the city and she'd heard a storm might come later, but the layer only reflected the lights, especially the illusionary battles over the second ward, which she couldn't see directly, but the flashes against the glass on the Spire or the clouds above gave her ideas of what might be happening. As she stared into the night sky above the city, the events of the evening filtered through her mind.

Since she hadn't had a chance to talk with Odette, Remi imagined their conversation. Remi had been contemplating telling her about the pendant. The old woman loved to hear about her thieving adventures, so the idea that Remi was planning some magical heist would make her day. Sharing secrets wasn't advised in a profession like hers, but Odette didn't have much time left, and Remi wasn't feeling like a thief much these days. She hadn't stolen anything from the alchemical storage room in over a month.

And even if she didn't tell her about the pendant, Remi enjoyed hearing about life in the greenhouse. It sounded like she got to live in her own little protected bubble away from the aches and pains of the world. Sometimes, Remi wished she could have a life like that.

"Oh, to live in a greenhouse..."

As soon as the words left her lips, she felt the significance as if a lightning bolt had hit her. She sat up straight and let the nearly empty Jell-O cup drop to her side. Then she burst to her feet, heading into the hospital to find Damon.

It took a few tries, but eventually she tracked him down to the children's virology ward where he was on rotation with a doctor Remi didn't recognize. He came out to the hallway after excusing himself.

"What's wrong?"

"Greenhouses," she said, spreading her hands wide as if she were an announcer at the circus and she had just introduced the main act.

"Greenhouses?"

"The strangler root. That's why you don't know who's doing it. They're growing it in greenhouses. You can simulate jungle environments, or any environment really in one."

Damon's eyes widened and then he threw his arms around Remi, before realizing what he'd done and pulling away.

"When did you become a greenhouse expert?" He shook his head. "It doesn't matter. I'll start researching greenhouses in the city right away. There can't be that many. Thank you, Remi. Maybe this will be our big break."

"I hope so too. I don't know if we can handle many more Newtown Fishmarket incidents."

"Yeah," he said. "Feels like each new thing is getting bigger. Like they're a warmup for something worse."

Remi had more to say, but the doctor waved him back into the room. She headed back down to the ER until she found Dr. Paddock.

"There you are. Always late, these first years," he said to the nurse at his side. "To think they'll be healers or doctors someday gives me heartburn. The world we created is wasted on the youth."

Normally, Dr. Paddock's pronouncements would have spoiled her mood, but she was feeling buoyant after telling Damon about greenhouses.

Since coming to Golden Willow, she'd felt like the hospital was stealing away her life force one incident at a time, but after surviving the Fishmarket triage and having the greenhouse idea, she wondered if there might actually be a place for her in Aura Healers.

FORTY

In the few hours Damon had between studying and his shifts, he took trips into the city to investigate any greenhouses he could find online. A few were open to the public including one associated with the newest Hall at the university, Arcane Phytology, which studied the magical plant world. But after researching them online, he quickly knocked them off his list. The smaller greenhouses were owned by private citizens, and it was easy to see that they didn't have strangler root vines, because the environment they grew in was much hotter and more humid than most other plants could sustain, and they required a host tree to attach to—which would eventually result in the tree's demise, making the vine an unlikely addition to any normal greenhouse. As well, the strangler vines matured regularly with bright crimson and purple flowers that were said to look like open wounds.

After two weeks of searching, he was left with the lingering feeling that whoever was behind it was hiding their greenhouse in a place no one thought to look. The city was huge, and filled with areas that weren't regularly lived in, like the twelfth and thirteenth wards on the western side. Some of the buildings had been torn down, replaced by overgrown fields. When he read about those areas, he was met with a lot of descriptions of strange happenings and leftover magical wards, which could indicate where the strangler root was being grown, or some unrelated other enterprise. The other and most depressing possibility was that it was being grown outside the city. If so, discovering the source would be impossible.

On a Tuesday afternoon in early May, after checking a greenhouse in the seventh ward, one of the last on his list, he returned to the first years' common area, finding a bunch of his classmates, including Remi and Lily, lounging on the couches.

"Did the hospital blow up and get replaced with illusions while I was gone?" he asked.

Boon was lying on his back, throwing a wadded-up surgical hat into the air and catching it. He lifted his head slightly.

"We've been given a reprieve from the chaos. The ER was empty and Dr. Morrison said we should go relax and enjoy ourselves."

"It's not a trick, is it? Dr. Decker's not going to show up in a moment and give us a test or something?" he asked.

"Dr. O.D.? He's not in the building," said Ethan. "Heard he was on a date last night, but that can't be true, because doctors aren't supposed to have personal lives, so we decided he fabricated the rumor to sound cool."

"I heard he has an ex-wife who used to work at the hospital," said Remi, who was eating a cup of Jell-O without the spoon. Damon tried not to be distracted by the way she was working with her tongue, so he grabbed an energy drink from the fridge and made Ethan scoot over.

"No way he has an ex," said Ethan, dropping the makeshift ball. "For one, time, and second, he's a barely put together mess that moonlights as our instructor."

"Is that what our destiny is if we stay here?" asked Remi. "Loveless, sexless slaves to the grind?"

"Sexless?" asked Boon. "Girl, I've been on my best streak since I figured out I *liked* sex."

"What?" asked Remi, sitting up. "Who? When? Where?"

Boon tilted his head. "The more fun one is how, but I'll save you all from the delightful details. Remember, we're not the only ones stuck here. There are a lot of the other doctors, residents, orderlies, whatever, who just want a quick hookup. Right, Damon?"

When the entire room turned to him, his face turned bright red.

"I, yeah, but I wasn't looking for it."

"Exactly," said Boon. "He wasn't even looking for it."

Damon accidentally made eye contact with Remi, who was staring at him with a look he couldn't quite comprehend, so he took a long drink as a distraction.

Sasha cleared her throat softly. "Is anyone else having regrets? Not like, I'm going to quit or anything, but is this way worse than you'd thought it'd be?"

No one spoke for a time. Even Damon found himself contemplating his choices. He would do it again in a heartbeat, but he had to wonder how he could keep up with the pace for five years, or longer if he chose to stay in Golden Willow.

"Half the staff have addictions of one kind or another," said Ethan. "Did you know Dr. Paddock drinks these weird lime green elixirs two or three times a day?"

"I think those are for his stomach," said Boon.

"Fuck his bloody stomach," said Lily. "He's a right bastard and a shite doctor. I swear half his patients would be better off without him."

"Hasn't Dr. Paddock won the doctor of the year two out of the last four years?" asked Sasha.

"Political bullshit is what that is," said Lily, uncharacteristically scowling.

After seeing the rainbow-haired first year in action at the Society hunting grounds, Damon respected her opinion on matters of healing more than the others. He just wished he understood why she was so talented, or had bothered to attend Aura Healers.

Remi sat up and looked around. "Do you all feel like you know what you're doing? For real. After nine months, I feel like I'm barely above a blood tech."

Boon burst out laughing, bending over and slapping his knees. "Did you know I ordered the wrong elixir for a patient last month? Thankfully it was only a laxative and the patient spent the next twenty-four hours in the toilet, but Dr. Morrison reminded me it could have been fatal. I don't even know how I did it."

"Not as bad as when I mixed up two words in a calming spell and the lady I cast it on grew a beard in about a minute," said Sasha.

A round of laughter had everyone smiling. The stories continued with each first year explaining their worst screwups during the year. When Damon started to speak, Ethan slapped him on the leg.

"We know, Damon, you punched a dick-snake right in the face," said Ethan. "But if we're having a contest for the best one, Half-Pint has to be the winner."

Remi slumped into her chair. "Did you know he invited me to see the Krakens? I guess he made up with his girlfriend, because she was the one to make the offer. Sounded like they had more than the show in mind."

Boon hopped to his feet. "Don't tell me you didn't go."

"Sorry," said Remi. "It's not like I had time. I don't know how you guys find hookups in the hospital. Taking a night off to go to a club sounds impossible."

Boon fake swooned, falling back into the couch. "My heart."

"It's not your heart that was missing out," said Lily, grinning. "You horny bastard."

Boon stood up and stretched. "On that note, I think I need to go back to my room and work a few things out." He winked at Ethan. "You might want to give it fifteen before you return."

Ethan followed him out. "I need food, so you're good. Going to swing by the cafeteria for a burger if anyone wants to join me."

In a matter of a minute, the room cleared out except for Lily and Remi, who were staring at him expectantly.

"Any progress?" asked Remi.

He shook his head. "None of the greenhouses in the city are set up for growing strangler vines. Either the greenhouse is incredibly well hidden, or isn't in the city at all. For now, it's a dead end."

"What about the information Dr. Morrison shared with you?" asked Remi.

"Nothing that we don't already know. It's helpful, it just doesn't point in any new directions. The only thing it really does is tell us that we're not the only ones thinking that something larger is going on."

"Dr. Decker doesn't think so," said Remi.

"Rule number one," said Lily with an eyeroll.

"It would make a lot more sense if rule number two had ever shown up," said Damon. "Not a single parasite found the entire year, which I heard from one of the nurses is a record."

Remi screwed up her face as if she'd smelled something awful. "Any ideas about the weird identical bite patterns? Seems like that should be a solid clue."

"Nothing," said Damon.

"At least we've been given a reprieve," said Remi, stretching her arms. "I'd forgotten how good it felt to lie around. Maybe I'll take a nap."

"Need any tutoring?" asked Damon, shrugging. "You know, since we have time."

Remi chewed on her lower lip.

"I think my bed is calling. As much as I appreciate the offer."

She left the common room. Lily was the only other person remaining, but she was busy fussing with Neko, who had crawled out of her hair and was perched in her lap, eating pieces of dried fruit from her fingers. Seeing that she was busy, Damon grabbed his energy drink and headed back to his room for more greenhouse research.

FORTY-ONE

The tray crashed onto the ground, shattering the half dozen vials, spilling bright pink liquid across the tiles. Remi froze with her arms up, a mask of horror on her face.

"I'm so sorry, Jeb. I should have been more careful when I came around the corner."

The alchemist scowled at the mess.

"Those were for the surgery in a half hour. I don't have time to remix them."

A pit formed in her stomach. She felt like the worst person in the world. The alarm hadn't gone off and she'd woken up late, which meant she was going to hear an earful from Dr. Decker once she found where he was on rounds.

"Can I?"

"No," said Jeb sharply. "You've done enough already." He jutted his chin down the hall. "Just go. You're clearly behind."

Remi found Dr. Decker on the fourth floor, following up with a patient suffering from a severe reaction to Ur-Bear poison. The guy was an Animalians Hall mage who'd gotten too close to the creature at the Invictus Menagerie and Cryptozoo. Dr. Decker didn't acknowledge her arrival while he gave follow-up instructions to the patient.

"This kind of response to the poison is unusual, so you'll want to be careful in the future. Talk to Professor Park about a regimen of shambler toxins to help you develop a resistance. In your line of work, you're going to need a healthy immune system."

"Thanks, doc," said the guy sheepishly.

Outside the room, Dr. Decker turned on her.

"No excuses. You're nine months into this program. You should have learned to be on time by now."

"I'm sorry, Dr. Decker. I'll do better next time."

He leaned over, peering at her scrubs. "What's that liquid all over you? Never mind. We have a heavy schedule. Time to move."

The next few hours were a whirlwind.

Dr. Decker was in a foul mood, which only made her day worse. She kept wondering about the surgery, hoping that it had been successful despite her destroying the elixirs the doctors performing it were going to take. The distracting thoughts only made her less than attentive, receiving multiple reprimands from Dr. Decker when she wasn't responding right away. After she failed to take a blood sample on three consecutive tries, Dr. Decker pulled her outside.

"Do you still want to be in Aura Healers?"

"What? Yes."

He flattened his lips.

"Sure doesn't seem like it. You're not all here today." She opened her mouth but he waved her off. "Whatever is going on, you need to fix it. The next few stops aren't that important, so I want you to go outside, get some fresh air, whatever you need. Then come back in a half hour and stop by Jeb's to grab the secondary antidote ordered for our clumsy Animalians mage. It should be ready by then. I didn't like his pallor. He's probably fine, but that elixir should make sure he's good to go in case he has a weakness to the toxins. You can do that, right? No more issues?"

"Yes, Dr. Decker."

Remi left with her head down. She swung by Odette's room, but the doorway was filled with the lung regeneration machine that she used on an every-other-day basis to try to extend their use. Odette hadn't been doing well lately, coughing and wheezing constantly when they chatted, which made missing out on seeing her even worse. Remi just wanted a friendly face.

The elevators were full with a line waiting outside, so she veered into the stairs, catching Dr. Morrison coming down from the roof.

"You doing okay?" she asked.

Remi lifted a single shoulder. "One of those days."

"We all have them," said Dr. Morrison. "Try not to let it get you down."

On the way out, Remi looked for the nurse Mandy in hopes of bumming a vape from her, but she was somewhere else in the hospital. The ER was moderately full, though it was still daytime. The night rush would start in a few hours. Remi stood on a concrete island near the parking lot, staring at the apartment buildings surrounding the hospital, wishing there was a better view.

"Fucking concrete jungle."

As soon as the words left her lips, she remembered something that Damon had said about Dr. Morrison's trips to the roof. Remi craned her neck at the six-story building. She'd never been up there, because it didn't seem that interesting. But Dr. Morrison had told Damon that she liked it for the view of colorful flowers. It didn't appear any of the apartments had a garden on their balconies. Mostly she saw laundry and a few chairs for enjoying the outside.

Remi checked her watch. There was still plenty of time before she had to get back to the patient. She jogged back into the hospital, found the first stairwell, and climbed to the roof. The effort left her bent over and heaving by the time she reached it.

The roof was a wide area with a helicopter pad on one wing and dozens of HVAC units dotting the rest of the surface. Remi didn't immediately see where Dr. Morrison took her breaks, so she circled the edge until she found a picnic bench and a trio of wooden Adirondack chairs facing the city.

Remi didn't see it right away until the scattered clouds shifted, sending a sunbeam reflecting off the towering glass.

A greenhouse.

It was west of the hospital, past the ring of apartment buildings, and the reason it hadn't appeared on any of Damon's investigations was that it was on the roof. She couldn't see inside due to the glare, so she ran back down and headed out the ER automatic doors, past an incoming howler, and across the parking lot.

The run tired her quickly. She'd never really been in shape, and outside the fear-induced run when the wolf-tiger beast was chasing her, she'd never gone that far. By the time she passed the apartments, she was covered in a patina of sweat. Finding the greenhouse was harder than she thought as she kept craning her neck upward. It wasn't until she cut down a side street that she caught the glint of greenery.

"No wonder no one saw it."

The gothic-style brick building wasn't completely out of place amid the shotgun-style housing, but the greenhouse on the roof certainly made it unique. A black wrought iron fence surrounded the estate, which had high bushes that blocked sight of the lower windows. Not that it mattered since the shades were pulled down.

An eerie sensation trickled down her spine as she crept closer. The fence kept her from seeing through the windows but she caught the sign of movement behind the curtains. But she needed to see in the greenhouse. Not the interior of the house.

Remi circled the block until she found a fire escape on the back of a nearby apartment building that she hoped had a good view. The metal rattled as she climbed, but no one came out to see what a short girl in dirty scrubs was doing outside their window. The flat roof provided a path to the opposite side, where she had a straight view into the greenhouse, but the sun's glare made seeing inside impossible.

"Come on," she said to the clouds.

The sky was filled with big, fluffy ones meandering across the city like bored bovines. When a cloud finally covered the sun, the reflection disappeared, leaving Remi with a straight view into the greenhouse. At the center of the interior were colorful purple-crimson flowers attached to vines on a dying tree. There were other planting beds and strange leafy plants, but she couldn't keep her eyes off the wound-like flowers.

Strangler root.

Remi reached for her phone when she saw movement in the greenhouse. She threw herself to the gravel-covered roof, slamming her shoulder on impact. The pain receded quickly, giving her a chance to peek over the edge to see the White Worm. He had his hood pulled back, revealing a bald head with a pallid complexion and tendril lines clawing up his neck, while he drank a cup of coffee, staring in the direction of the hospital.

The world slowed down in that moment.

For most of the year, she'd wondered if the White Worm was real or a hallucination brought on by the pendant. To see him standing in a greenhouse a few blocks from the hospital was both a revelation and a horror.

The root cause of their problem had been right under their nose.

When he glanced her direction, she dropped below the roof edge, heartbeat thudding in her ears. The urge to grab her pendant was strong. Almost geas-like. As she lay staring up at the cloudy sky, she realized that it hadn't been a vision when she'd seen him in the parking lot. He'd probably been passing through on the way home.

Remi stuck her phone above the edge and snapped a few pictures, sending them to Damon and Lily as she lay on her back. The White Worm was still in the greenhouse, gaze firmly planted on the hospital as if he were plotting its demise. And in a way he was, as the constant influx of crazed wounded was putting a strain on the entire staff.

Her phone exploded with replies asking a host of questions, which she tried to answer. But both of them were in the middle of patient care and couldn't leave, which reminded her she had to get back to Golden Willow. She was ten minutes late and still on the roof.

"Stop drinking coffee and go do plant stuff," she whispered when she saw he was still staring out the glass.

Using her phone, she made plans with Lily and Damon to come back after their shifts were over, which would be well after dark. Luckily, none of them had double shifts as the break in chaos had given them a chance to breathe.

Realizing that Dr. Decker was going to kill her for being late again, she crawled to the metal fire escape stairs and oozed over the edge, keeping her profile low and hoping that the White Worm didn't see her.

Once she was off the roof and out of sight of the greenhouse, Remi ran full out. The way back seemed twice as long. She'd sweat through her scrubs by the time she returned to Golden Willow, heading straight to Jeb's lab.

"Oren already sent a nurse down to retrieve the elixir," said Jeb when she skidded into his area.

The world dialed down to a pinpoint as she made her way back to the floor where the Animalians mage was located. When she arrived the room was empty. She found the attending nurse to learn that he'd gone into shock and had been wheeled into surgery.

"You're Dr. Decker's first year, aren't you?" asked the nurse.

The look was eviscerating.

Remi nodded.

She ran into Dr. Decker before she could leave the area. An emptiness filled her chest, worse than the day she was caught after the Dreadmarsh job, or when she was sentenced to a year in Utica. It was worse because someone else was paying for her mistakes.

"Is he—"

"No," said Dr. Decker, his voice rising, which attracted the notice of the nurses at their station. "No, you don't get to ask that now. If you don't want to be here, don't take it out on the patients, grow some courage and leave."

"I do want to be here. It was a mistake, it's been a bad day," she sputtered out.

Dr. Decker's jaw pulsed with anger.

"Bad day. Bad day? Do you know that every last person that comes to Golden Willow is having one of the worst days of their life? You know, when you come in on a stretcher, or in the back of an ambulance, your day has gone to absolute shit, so don't tell me about a bad day. *We* don't get bad days."

He tapped on his chest.

"That's not why we signed up for this. The people here, like that poor kid you were supposed to treat with a simple, fucking elixir which might have kept him from getting sent to surgery, are at their lowest. No one wants to come to a hospital. They're sick, or dying. They've been shot, or bitten by some toothy sewer creature, or have some disease that's tearing their life down inch by inch and they're hoping we might have an answer for them. Their world has been shattered, broken into a million pieces, and they look to us to put it back together. That's why we don't get bad days. We're their last hope in a world gone mad.

"And it's not like a hospital is a friendly looking place. It smells like antiseptic and death. The walls are white, the scrubs impersonal. Everyone who steps into our halls has to contemplate their mortality, even if they're not the one sick. Which means it's *our* job to make them feel like it's going to be okay, to give them hope, or at least a comforting hand as they make their final slide into eternity."

He marched away, then spun on his heel and pointed his finger at her as if it were a wand that would disintegrate her on the spot.

"If you don't want to be here, fine. It's not for everyone. It takes a person who can have empathy for others, who can see beyond their own needs, and who isn't *stealing* from the very place that is trying to change their life."

"But I haven't—"

He was in her face, towering over her.

"Haven't what? Stolen anything recently? Is that what you were going to say?"

Her world turned to ash.

Remi couldn't feel the lower half of her body. She wasn't sure how she was still standing, mouth jawing like a fish out of water.

"I..."

"Go, just go. You're dismissed from your duties for the rest of the day. I'm sick of having to protect the patients from your incompetence, or is it indifference? Which only makes it worse because it was your choice to let them fail."

Numbness overtook her body as she left the nurses station, feeling all eyes on her. She couldn't think, or breathe. When she hit the elevator, she went up rather than down, which would take her back to the dormitory. The phone in her pocket buzzed with messages, probably from Damon and Lily, but she didn't care anymore. She'd tried. She'd really tried, and this was the response? How could one give every waking moment of their lives to their care and then after screwing up once while trying to fix the *actual* root cause of the problem get vilified for it?

Her feet brought her back to Odette's floor without even thinking about it. She wanted a friendly face. A comforting hand. But what she found was an empty room that looked like it'd been prepared for a new patient. None of the accoutrements Odette had collected like the ceramic swan figurine or the picture of her in the greenhouse were sitting on the dresser in the corner.

Remi checked the number on the door to confirm she was in the right place.

"Excuse me," she asked a passing nurse. "Is Odette in surgery or tests somewhere else in the hospital?"

The rounded eyes and furtive glance towards the empty room sent shock waves through Remi's body.

"I'm sorry—"

"No," said Remi, screwing up her mouth, trying to keep the truth away. "No. Not now. Not now."

The nurse put a hand on her arm. "She was on her last days..."

"But I didn't get to say goodbye," said Remi, her voice cracking. "What happened?"

"The treatments weren't working anymore—during the lung rejuvenation, her body started shutting down. We would have revived her but she had clear instructions not to. I'm sorry, I know you visited her often, which I'm sure she appreciated. She was a special lady."

The numbness went down to her soul. She'd never cried for anyone. Why start now? They just disappointed you, left you on the side of the road when you got out of juvie, or treated you like scum when you made a simple mistake.

"Are you going to be okay?" asked the nurse, resting her hand on her arm. "We have grief counselors available."

"No," said Remi, shaking off the touch. "No more feelings. No more hand-holding. Or caring. Especially not that."

She marched away, feeling untethered. Drunk on grief. She could barely breathe, and when the phone buzzed in her pocket with an incoming phone call, she put it to her ear.

"I don't care about the greenhouse anymore, so you can just forget about me."

"Miss Wilde?" came an Englishman's voice. "Do I have the right number? Is this Remi Wilde?"

"What? Oh. Is this Albi?"

"Yes, Miss Wilde. From the trinket shop. You asked me to investigate a lead for the information about the item in your possession. Are you still interested?"

Remi leaned against the wall. It was hard to use her legs. "I think so. I mean yes, yes, I'd almost forgot about it."

"That's good, because I happened to be speaking to a fellow practitioner who is quite knowledgeable about trinkets related to the Fae."

"That's good."

"Yes, it is good. Very good. The only problem is he's on his way out of the city. Out of the realm actually. I set up a meeting for you, but you'll have to get on a train right away. He said he would wait. He's south of the city about an hour. You're quite lucky he agreed to meet. If there's anyone that can help you, it's him. I'll send along a profile once you're on your way to help you with your meeting, but you have to leave now. There's no time."

The miasma parted, giving Remi a clear view of her future. While she hadn't learned exactly what she wanted to know about magic, the year in Aura Healers had given her the basics, enough she could manage the rest on her own. It wasn't like she was without resources.

"Miss Wilde? Are you there?"

"Yes," she said, startling to awareness and hurrying down the hall past a stretcher with a moaning woman with blood covering her chest. "I'm grabbing my stuff and I'll be on my way."

"That's wonderful. I'll let him know you're coming and send along the information. Good luck, Miss Wilde. I'm excited for you."

The whiplash left her dizzy, but she pulled together enough brain cells to swing by the alchemical supply room. No one was present and the locks were laughably simple. She loaded a bag full of materials that would give her a head start on the cash she'd need to go after the pendant.

Remi was relieved when Lily wasn't in their room. Of course, she was on rotation. Remi thought about leaving a note, but decided she didn't have time, nor the mental space to formulate a proper goodbye. Maybe she'd send along a note at a later date. Or maybe it was easier to never say anything.

"Bye, Neko," she said to the white rat, sitting on Lily's blankets. "Take good care of her for me."

Changed into street gear and with her clothes and stolen reagents stuffed into a bag, Remi headed out of a side door to avoid being spotted, and hurried in the direction of the train station.

She had the urge to look back, to see Golden Willow one last time before she returned to her former life, but looking backwards had never been something she was good at. Better to keep heading forward to new ideas, new opportunities, and the prize at the end of the pendant rainbow.

FORTY-TWO

Damon paced in the alley while Lily looked on, stroking the white rat in her lap. He kept checking the time, then his phone, then back to his watch before looking down the street, expecting Remi to come strolling up at any moment.

"She'll be here," said Lily in her lilting voice, though her expression wasn't so confident. "She wouldn't leave us with shite up to our trousers like this. Not after being the one to find the greenhouse."

"It's an hour after her shift. She should have been here by now, which means she bailed on us."

"Unless there was an emergency. It's not like you'd leave if you were elbows deep in it," said Lily, brushing her brightly colored hair out of her face.

"But she would have answered. Sent a thumbs-up or something."

"Aye, that's true too," said Lily, clearly dejected.

"She chickened out. That has to be it. She's not answering because she doesn't want to put herself in danger." Damon put his hands on his hips. "I should have known she was a coward."

"A selfish petty thief with parent issues and a pear-shaped moral compass, sure," said Lily. "But I wouldn't call her a coward."

Damon ran his hand through his hair. So close to the answer, so close to solving the problems in the city, he was ready to burst through the door.

"I can't wait. If you don't want to come, I understand, but this is too important."

Lily climbed to her feet, letting Neko crawl back into the giant nest of her hair. The tail disappeared neatly as if there was an extra-dimensional space inside.

"I'm not lettin' ya get yourself skewered all alone. You can count me in," said Lily.

His chest heaved with relief. "Glad to have you." They crept to the corner, staring at the gothic house, lit up from within while the rest of the block was muted, given the late hour. A howler in the distance could be heard heading to the hospital.

"Wish she was here to get us inside."

As he crept up to the front gate, he kept expecting the shades to burst open with the White Worm staring them down, bracketed by an army of crazed followers.

"What now?" he whispered.

Lily shrugged and pulled the gate open, the creaking sound dissipating immediately. Concrete steps led to wooden double doors with a brass knocker in the shape of twisted antlers. He put his ear to the surface, but couldn't hear anything out of the ordinary. Testing the handle revealed that it was unlocked.

The interior looked like it'd been furnished in the 1920s. An antique gramophone sat on a darkwood desk. He wasn't ready to head up the stairs, so he stepped into the study. A bookshelf of ancient tomes drew him near. He read a few of the foiled spines. *The Lies of Fath Fiada. A Kornik in Murias Hill. Alchemical Mysteries of the Ancients.*

Lily clucked her tongue, pointing up the stairs. He followed, stepping carefully to keep them from creaking. The Irish girl moved like an apparition. The second level seemed a living quarters, but they kept going up towards the greenhouse. Humidity blanketed the final staircase until they were presented with a steel door.

He shrugged when she put her hand on the handle and checked back to him. Damon had no idea what they'd do if they got caught. The surety that he'd enjoyed outside seemed thin in retrospect as he crept through this unknown person's house. He had visions in his head of being cuffed by Invictus PD while they explained that the owner was an eccentric millionaire with a passion for odd plants.

The greenhouse brought beads of sweat to his forehead, the stifling air like breathing through a straw. He saw no one else amid the plants and trees, but spotted several doors leading to other parts of the building. They stopped at the strangler vine that had wrapped itself around a tree like the upper part of a noose. The bruise-colored flowers smelled like rotting meat and fresh fruits, making Damon screw up his nose in disgust. The greenhouse was filled with plants unknown to Damon, like a wedge-shaped tree with dozens of thick vines resting on the dirt like braids.

A cluck of the tongue had him turning to find Lily holding up a metal jaw. He didn't realize what it was until she made it clamp down. A cursory inspection revealed the same bite pattern that Dr. Morrison had recorded in her notes, but he couldn't understand the purpose of the device. Lily had the same thought, offering a shrug as her answer.

Then he spotted the containers along the far wall. Six cylindrical opaque vats, two containing a greenish liquid while the other four were pale yellow liquid with metal stairs giving access to the opening on the top.

He examined each one, finding them bursting with tiny worm-like creatures swimming in circles. The green vats contained worms twice the size of the yellow. There had to be thousands in each vat. Probably more. He used a scooper to capture a worm, which was only the length of the end of his pinky and as wide as a couple of hairs wrapped together.

"Parasites."

Lily joined him on the metal stair, scowling at the wriggling worm in the liquid.

"Insanius vermis." She glanced up. "Crazy worm. A parasitic creature from the realm of Illithusus. This is why people have been going mad as a hatter. There's enough in these vats to take out an entire ward."

"It can't be," said Damon, staring at the critter in horror. "Rule number two. We tested for parasites. A lot."

"Maybe these don't show up on the tests."

A deep voice from the other side of the greenhouse startled them both.

"Oh, these show up in the tests. But insanius vermis don't hide in the bloodstream. They lurk in the brain tissue, reproducing and creating instability in the mind, especially in those that can use magic. But they're killed easily with antibiotics, or simple antiseptic spells, and leave the body quickly, making them perfect for my purposes."

Damon nearly toppled off the stairs trying to see who was talking. He grabbed the top of the vat to see a pale, bald man wearing thick robes approaching through the lush foliage. Damon jumped off the metal stairs, landing between two planter beds with his claws extended. He wasn't ready to unleash his rage, but could feel his muscles rippling with anticipation.

"What purpose is that?" he asked as Lily joined him by his side.

The White Worm was exactly as Remi had described him. His skin was bloated like an old corpse, and his flesh had a clammy look, a pallor usually found on rotting melons.

"Il'math no gammali," said the White Worm, gesturing artfully towards them.

Before Damon could guess the purpose of the words, thick vines wrapped around his limbs, dragging him back to the wedge-shaped tree. His back slammed against the trunk, knocking the wind out of him, and the vines encircled him further. Lily joined him against her will, fighting the vines, but losing the battle.

"Neko, ionsa air!"

The white rat leapt from her mess of multicolored hair, landing on the soil as it transformed before his eyes. The creature doubled in size, growing thick claws and expanding its head, but before it could finish, the White Worm hit it with a spell covering it in crackling electricity. Neko fell over in the dirt, and the White Worm grabbed the malformed beast and tossed him in a cage, putting on a padlock, then adding a spell that reduced the poor rat to its original size.

"That was a foul trick," said the White Worm, pointing a thick, yellowed fingernail at Lily. "And explains why I could never get back into the hospital once you arrived. Your ag athrú was protecting it."

Lily spat on the ground and cursed at the pale man. Damon wished he understood what she was saying, but the venom of her speech gave him a good idea.

"How do you know the Old Tongue?" asked Lily, still struggling against the vines.

The White Worm smirked. "That doesn't matter." His speech was more erudite than his dress suggested.

Damon reached into himself for his rage. His eyes snapped open as his muscles expanded and his head leaned back with a war cry. The vines tightened around his body, cinching simultaneously as his clothes split.

The White Worm approached, examining him as if he were a flowering plant. Damon couldn't wait to rip his head off with a swipe of his claws. He could feel the transformation approaching critical mass.

Then his captor reached into a pocket, pulled out a packet of violet dust, and blew it in his face. The powder burned Damon's eyes and the rage burning in his chest evaporated. Damon spat and struggled, trying to regain the momentum of escape. He needed his muscles, his anger.

"What did you do to me?"

"Wolfsbane," said the White Worm. "I was aware you were searching for me. I would have taken care of you and your other friend a long time ago, but this witch and her pet have kept me from penetrating the hospital more deeply."

Damon stared at Lily. He knew she was unusual and powerful in ways he didn't understand, but she was clearly more than he understood. Lily stared back through her colored hair.

"Where is your little friend? Is she sneaking around the house alone?"

The White Worm stepped onto the soil and put a thick, yellowed nail beneath Damon's chin.

"Tell me, or I'll cut your throat. I saw her spying on my home earlier today. I would have taught her a lesson then, but she got away before I could grab her."

"She didn't come. I don't know where she is."

"Liar," said the White Worm, splitting flesh with his nail.

"Check my phone. You can see my messages."

The White Worm narrowed his gaze, before reaching into Damon's pocket. The pale man read the messages before throwing the phone into the dirt.

"Not much of a friend to send you here and run away."

"She's not my friend," said Damon.

There'd been a time, especially after the Society visit, that he thought they could be friends. But those days were over. Not that it would matter much longer.

"What are you going to do with us?" asked Lily.

The White Worm wandered to a vat of greenish liquid. He lifted the lid and using a sample jar, scooped out two wriggling worms.

"I'm going to let you experience what some of your patients have been going through. It's taken some time to get the breeding right. These worms are variations on the insanius vermis, modified with magic and combined with other species to achieve the right amount of control."

"Why? What are you going to do?" asked Damon, the words tumbling over his tongue.

The White Worm stared into his vial of greenish liquid. The worms were the length of his pinky and twice as thick as the others.

"I know, quite beautiful, aren't they? With this in your head, you'll be much more amenable to my suggestions. Once the city has been properly infected, and chaos reigns, I'll send you back to your precious Golden Willow where you can finish the job."

Using a pair of tweezers, the White Worm pulled out a wriggling critter and tried to lay it upon Damon's cheek. He swung his head back and forth to keep the worm away, but more eldritch words were spoken and the vines grabbed his head and held it tight.

"This city of sorcery is an abomination. A travesty to the natural order of things. The events of the last decade should be proof enough that it shouldn't exist as it threatens the entire webbing of realms through its arrogance. I've come to cut the rot out, destroy the roots so the tree will die."

"The roots? Tree?"

"He means the Halls," said Lily, frowning.

"Why?" asked Damon. "Why destroy the Halls?"

The White Worm lifted the tweezers and set the wriggling creature on Damon's cheek. For the first time, he noticed the White Worm's hands had a patina of dusty green as if a coating had washed off when he'd scooped out the worms. But Damon quickly forgot about the unusual skin tone as the wet critter scooted up his cheek, headed towards his eye. He tried to shake it off, but his head was held fast by the thick vines.

"So that others may flourish. When a tree dies in a forest, it nourishes the seeds growing in the soil. A new biome cannot grow until the old one is destroyed." The White Worm grinned, his pale flesh cracking with stiffness as if he wore a mask. Cracks of green shone through. "And if your little friend comes back, then you'll be quite the surprise once I'm finished with you both."

Damon barely heard the White Worm's words as he watched the tiny worm inch up his cheek. Every sloughing wetness was a horror. He was forced to watch as the worm lifted its tiny head—magnified by its closeness—and as the creature touched his eye, Damon screamed.

FORTY-THREE

The elevated train rumbled along the tracks, circling the city encased by night. Remi leaned against the window, feeling the rattle against her skull, trying to soothe away the miasma of emotion caught in her chest.

It was harder than she thought to leave Aura Healers. Despite the bone-deep exhaustion and constant abuse from doctors and patients, Remi already missed the place. It was so different from anything she'd ever experienced before. It'd almost felt like—

She shook her head, dismissing the warm thought before it could take root. *My time there will help me find the Horn. That's the only reason I even bothered with that place.* If this associate of Albi's had the information she desired, she could be on her way to fame and riches. One big job was all a good thief ever needed. She'd pull off what her parents couldn't do and teach them not to leave her outside of Utica as if she'd never existed.

Remi stretched her legs, kicking the black duffle bag filled with clothes and a hefty load of reagents taken from the alchemy supply room. Glassware clinked with the shifting train car. She'd cleaned out the most expensive reagents, leaving just enough of each one to hold over the hospital until a new shipment arrived.

She fiddled with the lockpicks she kept in her coat as she thought about Odette, wishing she'd been given a chance to say goodbye. The old woman wouldn't approve of her choice, but she'd had a great life of privilege and wealth, working for a rich businessman who lavishly funded her studies. Odette would never understand the kind of life that Remi had been forced to lead.

Lily would be mad, for certain. The Irish girl had been a bit of an enigma, but Remi thought they'd been friends, despite not knowing a lot about her. But Remi understood that. It's not like she'd divulged much about her past either.

Damon was a different situation entirely. They'd been at cross-purposes almost the entire time, except for the Society visit and a few other fleeting moments. He was nice to look at, but she wasn't sure she'd ever allow herself to be mixed up with him, given their opposite views on the world.

"Don't get too close," she reminded herself.

It was a tenet her parents had instilled in her. When you're pulling off a job, don't make friends with the marks. Don't feel sympathy, or concern about their situation.

But that's what she'd done. She'd gotten too close to her fellow first years and some of the patients. Well, maybe even a few of the doctors and nurses. For a while, she'd forgotten why she'd come to the Halls in the first place. Her parents would have laughed had they seen her in scrubs, surrounded by bed pans and beeping machines, taking blood samples as if she belonged. They would have called her a fool.

As the train rumbled into the eighth ward, Remi spied an oblong glass dome filled with trees and rope lights with thousands of people in black ties and dresses wandering the paths. It appeared an event was in progress. Charity probably. More rich people jerking each other off while the world fell apart.

Remi sighed and diverted her attention elsewhere. Further out, near the center of the second ward, she witnessed the illusionary battles near the Glitterdome. An enormous version of a Hall mage was battling a shadowy dragon. The bright displays of magic were nothing like the real thing in her estimation, but that was the point. They were meant to entertain, not instruct. As Remi watched, she realized that it wasn't just any Hall mage. She recognized the short black hair, artfully spiked, and the tattoos on the forearms. Head Patron Pythia Silverthorne. It could be no other.

The day at the Grand Mage's dining area came back as if it'd only happened yesterday. Not that it was hard to remember meeting one of the most famous people in the world. Remi hadn't put much stock in what the Head Patron said, but those words came back as if she were hearing them again for the first time.

These are the problems that weigh on me day and night. Which is why I need to make sure we're finding the best possible mages for the Halls. And that means casting our nets wide. There was a lot of discussion about you for the final spot. Some thought I was being too lenient in overlooking your history because I came from an unusual background myself. That's why we settled on a Hall which is not only a great place of learning, but also one in which you might learn to trust others. To care for them even. Because I can tell you without a shadow of a doubt that I would not be here, or maybe any of us, had we not learned to trust each other. The Halls are filled with a lot of powerful people with big egos and complicated pasts. And I haven't even mentioned the Patrons yet. I might be totally wrong about you. Your history, your parents, these might have left you too jaded to ever open yourself up to others. But I have to try. I see that potential in you. In who you might become if you allow yourself the possibility of change.

"You were wrong about me," said Remi.

An older woman with a pair of knitting needles in her hands looked up, startled by the half-conversation. Remi faced the window and tried to ignore the reflection of herself. It was hard not to see the doubt in her own face.

"I could have changed," she whispered. "If they would have let me."

Remi closed her eyes and set her forehead against the cool glass. Damon's words at the end of the final trial "you're only out for yourself" came back to haunt her. The further she got away from the sixth ward, the more her heart ached. She pulled the pendant from underneath her shirt, unwrapped it, and stared at the swirling designs. Then she pulled out her phone, staring at the dozens of messages from Damon asking where she was at.

"Idiot probably went into the house."

Not that she thought it would matter. He was a werewolf and Lily was a powerful mage. The two of them should be fine against the White Worm. She could imagine their disappointment, but not surprise. They should have known she'd eventually abandon them. It was what she'd learned from her parents. That's what Dr. Decker had seen in her and why he'd been pushing her hard. He'd wanted her out of Aura Healers before she really screwed up.

"That's not true, Remi, and you know it."

Why else would he have introduced her to Odette? Remi had never gotten to learn what kind of therianthrope she was, not that it mattered now with her dead. Remi hoped there would be more than just Dr. Decker at the funeral. She felt bad that she wouldn't be there. Odette deserved better.

The phone and pendant were still in her hands. The last message from Damon just said: Where are you?

"I can't go back, can I?"

The pendant weighed on Remi. A chance to escape the misery of her life, the constant wonder of where the next meal was coming from, checking over her shoulder expecting the cops to show up, or an associate in crime deciding to give them the hard way out.

The hospital had been a burden.

It had required every waking moment of her life. More than that. Her sleep too. Sanity even. But she'd seen the way the patients had looked up to Dr. Decker, even when he told them bad news. They respected him because he'd dedicated his life to their improvement. *Why am I even thinking about this?* She could see Lily and Damon's faces. The others of her first year too. Lying around the common area, laughing about death and sex had been one of the happiest moments of her life, even if it'd been meaningless. But it wasn't. Hadn't been.

The lure of the pendant was strong, but the idea of being in a place she belonged, that she had friends and maybe even family—that was stronger. Remi closed her eyes, laughing quietly that she'd changed her mind.

"I'll come back for you later," she said to the pendant, rewrapping it and tucking it in her shirt.

The train was slowing as it approached another station. She grabbed her duffle bag and headed towards the doors. After running across the empty tracks, Remi loaded into the train headed back towards the sixth ward. She typed a message to Damon and Lily to let them know she was coming, but no answer returned.

The ride away from the hospital had passed in the blink of an eye. Heading back took forever. Her feet were bouncing before she reached the seventh ward. By the time the train pulled into the station nearest Golden Willow, Remi was at the doors, ready like a racer at the starting gate. A locker took the contents of her duffle bag. She waved down a taxi outside, throwing herself in the back and giving the driver directions to the White Worm's house.

The downstairs lights were off when she arrived, which wasn't a good sign. Remi crept to the door, expecting the White Worm to fling open the windows. When she made it inside, she decided that he wasn't present and it wasn't a trap. A cursory inspection of the downstairs gave her the impression that the White Worm had a fascination with older times. She spotted a Roman gladius in a glass case and other antiques that would be worth a fortune. Remi ran her fingers over the glass, contemplating a diversion until she remembered why she'd come in the first place. A check of her phone proved that they hadn't yet responded.

Remi eventually found the stairs, avoiding the creaky wood by staying close to the wall where the supports were best and few nails existed. Pale light filtered down from another stairway, which led to the greenhouse.

A side door distracted her. She peeked in to find a cluttered room filled with toolboxes and shelves full of maintenance supplies like brass pipes, spray nozzles, and pump engines. Remi closed the door, since the equipment was unimportant to her investigation.

She listened at the greenhouse door before daring to enter. The air was stifling. It was like being in the Midwest during the summer. Beads of sweat formed on her forehead, which she wiped away while peering around the thick foliage. Remi spotted Damon and Lily standing near a wedge-shaped tree. They were facing the opposite direction, staring at something she couldn't see from her vantage.

"Hey," she whisper-shouted. "It's me, Remi."

Their stillness triggered concern, and she checked around before daring to step closer to her friends.

"Damon. Lily. What are you doing?"

The pair turned slowly, their faces blank of emotion, which sent alarm bells through her head. When she spotted Neko in a cage, she knew something was wrong. Very wrong.

Remi dove behind a planter bed right before Lily launched a spell at her. The sonic dislocation ripped apart the trees, sending shredded leaves into the air. She peeked above the wooden wall to see Damon, already wearing tattered clothes, lean his head back and howl with the intensity of an angry wolf.

"Oh no."

She didn't know how, but the White Worm had taken control of her friends, much as it had turned the people of the city into mindless rage-machines. Remi made a lunge for the greenhouse exit, but Damon cut her off, so she dove onto the planter beds and scrambled through the thick plants while Lily blasted her with potent magics.

"Hey! It's me, Remi!"

Their automaton stares told her that simple begging wasn't going to get the job done, but she was the weakest of the three. How was she going to survive her friends when they actually knew how to use magic? Damon roared again, his throaty call echoing in the greenhouse. He hadn't changed to full-fledged werewolf, but he was on the verge with his muscles bulging and his eyes burning bright. The only thing keeping her alive was that they weren't pursuing her with vigor but rather followed with eerie patience, knowing she was outgunned on all fronts.

"Come on, whatever the White Worm did to you, you have to fight it. Merlin knows I'm a shit healer, I'm not going to be able to counter it."

As Remi danced through the trees and bushes, her smaller size giving her the advantage as long as she stayed off the paths, she tried to remember which spell might bring her friends back. When Lily tried to cut her off, Remi scrambled behind a row of empty vats with three at the end filled with yellow liquid, teeming with tiny wriggling worms. She made the connection with her friends' behavior.

"Fucking parasites. But why didn't they show up on any tests?"

But Remi knew the answer.

She'd told Bob the head of the laboratory to lie about the results to keep Dr. Decker off his back.

"Oh no, this is all my fault."

Remi looked up in time to see Lily launch another spell. The air turned glossy black at the end of her finger, rippling forward with hypnotizing speed. Remi dove to her left as the plastic vat exploded, sending yellow liquid and parasites everywhere. As she came to her feet, Damon appeared, and Remi scrambled past the thick vines covered in awful smelling flowers to hide behind the dying tree. She expected Damon to follow, but he paused at the edge, his nose wrinkling with disgust. She thought it was his enhanced nose until Lily stopped at the same location, hesitant to follow her through the strangler vines. Something about them was keeping her friends from attacking, which wouldn't help her escape, but at least provided a moment's reprieve.

"Can either of you tell me what the spell is to get rid of those parasites? No? You're my tutor, Damon. You have to tell me," she said, hoping something about the worms or extract would convince him that she was to be listened to. Both of them stared back with lingering menace.

Remi reached into her pocket, pulling out her phone. She dialed Boon.

"I'm in the middle of a patient—"

Remi shouted over his answer. "It's an emergency. Please. I need your help. It's fucking critical. Like five-bell critical."

The last part shut him up. She could hear one of the nurses yelling at him as he left the patient's room.

"This better be important, Remi, because otherwise I'm in big trouble."

"I don't have time to explain why, but I need to know a counter for parasites. One that I can cast on the, well, patients at a distance."

A pause. "What the fuck is going on, Remi?"

"Please. I need that spell. STAT."

"Okay, okay. At a distance? Are you sure?"

She squeezed her eyes shut. "Deadly sure."

"That's a tall ask. I'm running back to the dorm to grab my books."

She peeked around the tree trunk. Lily looked like she was contemplating a new spell. Her head was tilted and her fingers were dancing before her as she mumbled.

"Hurry."

After the sound of heavy footfalls, she heard Boon enter the first year common area and ask about the spell. Remi heard murmuring voices.

"I put you on speaker. Can you explain what's going on?"

"If you don't get me that spell, I'm going to be dead and then so are a whole bunch of others," she said, thinking about the emptied vats. "Just get me the spell. I'll explain once I'm in a better position."

She heard Ethan, Sasha, and Bryan's voices discussing the counter she requested, followed by the turning of pages. After a few false starts, Boon said, "I think we have one. It's not easy and I'm sorry, it doesn't work at distance. You have to be at least five feet away when the spell completes or it won't work. The closer the better."

"Five feet? Are you sure?"

"I'm afraid so."

"Fine. Explain it to me."

They went over the details three times, making her repeat the words and explain the gestures. It wasn't the hardest spell she'd ever cast, but it was more challenging since she wasn't going to get much time to practice. She repeated it without faez a few times before she thought she might have it down.

"If you hear me screaming, or nothing at all, call the cops and send them to the old Gothic house west of the hospital behind the apartment buildings and then prepare for a five-bell night."

"Are you sure?"

"Just do it."

She set the phone down in the dirt and grabbed the bruise-crimson flowers, stuffing them in her shirt and pockets in hopes that it would keep them off her until the spell was completed. Lily was still mumbling in earnest, which didn't make sense until Remi saw that the flowers and vines were turning brown and dying. Including the ones she was using as a ward. The way Damon was staring told her she had little remaining time before he leapt onto the soil and tore her limb from limb.

There were a lot of things Remi wasn't good at. Memorizing spells. Caring for patients. Not stealing things from everyone around her. But she was good under pressure. It was why her parents kept throwing her into difficult situations, because they knew she could handle it. If it hadn't been for their impatience, she would have never been caught and sent to Utica.

As Lily's spell continued to kill the flowers on the vines, Remi stepped forward and began her counter for the parasites. She stayed within the safety of the vines, but would have to move closer when the spell completed. Remi focused on Damon since he was the bigger danger. The words danced across her tongue as she manipulated faez in her mind, shaping the spell until it was nearly ready.

But it was a race against Lily, who had a head start in destroying her defenses.

Remi hurried through the last few parts, knowing that delay was as bad as fumbling it. At the latest possible moment, she rushed forward and completed the spell, throwing the cleansing energy at Damon, who appeared ready to pounce.

A crackling white light appeared around him, freezing him in place as he cried out. While he was in silent internal battle, Lily ended her plant killing spell and switched to something more immediate and potent. With nowhere to run, Remi prepared to dive out of the way. At the spell's completion, she flinched, but Damon reached over and put his arms around Lily, interrupting the spell. The Irish girl squirmed and cursed while Damon held her fast.

"Cleanse her quick. She's stronger than she looks."

Remi repeated the spell without issue, which allowed Damon to release Lily.

"I was like an observer in my own body," said Damon, shaking his head. "I'm sorry."

Remi scrambled back to the phone in the dirt. "We're good. They're good. I'm safe. No cops. Not yet anyway."

"What's going on?" came a chorus of voices from the phone speaker. "Is there still going to be a five beller?"

Remi glanced to her friends. Both of them nodded.

"She's right," said Damon. "Something terrible is going to happen tonight."

"Damon? When did you get there?" asked Boon.

"Don't worry about it. Just go get Dr. Decker and tell him to prepare the hospital."

"What about you two?"

"Three," said Lily. "We're going to try to stop it."

Remi gave the final word and hung up the phone. They gave her a brief rundown of what happened and what the White Worm had said. As soon as they finished repeating his soliloquy, Remi put a hand to the back of her head and squeezed her hair.

"I know where he's going."

"You do?" asked her friends simultaneously.

"The Invictus Botanical Gardens in the eighth ward. It's part of the new Hall, Arcane Phytology. It looks like they're holding a big fundraiser tonight. I saw it from the train. Everyone was in black ties and dresses."

Lily hurried to the cage where Neko was being kept and knocked off the lock with a quick spell, then let the white rat climb into her hair. Damon stared at the pair with a strange look, but there was no time for frivolous questions.

“Come on, we have to go,” said Remi, heading towards the stairs. “If the White Worm infects all the richest people of the city, he can destroy the city with a few words.”

FORTY-FOUR

The taxi driver swerved through traffic with the three of them in the back seat. Damon was on the right side, sticking his head out the window like a dog to catch fresh air. He still felt like he was trapped inside himself. It'd been like watching a puppeteer work his body. If he'd been forced to rip Remi's limbs off like the White Worm had said, he would've never been the same.

"I need you to send your best cops to the Botanical, yes, this is real."

Remi growled under her breath while she spoke on the phone.

"I'm a first year at Golden Willow, or Aura Healers, whatever. But I'm telling you that this guy, no I don't know a name, is going to use a bunch of parasites to infect everyone at the Botanical Gardens and destroy the city."

Remi paused, stared at the phone.

"Stop laughing! I'm serious."

She jammed her thumb into the red button.

"Fucking cops. The first time in my life I actually want to see them and they think I'm nuts."

"Can you go any faster?" he asked the taxi driver. "I'll double your fee and pay for any tickets."

The guy leaned his head back momentarily, shrugged, then the vehicle accelerated, pushing them into their seats. Damon pulled his head back into the car.

"How are we getting in?" asked Lily. "It's a black-tie event and we're in scrubs and Damon's are practically falling off him. Remi, you can get us in, right?"

"Fuck if I know," she said. "We'll see when we get there."

The lighted botanical dome was visible the last few blocks. The driver had to let them off up the street because the line of black limousines letting out their guests at the red carpet was backed up. They couldn't get any closer than a hundred feet due to the crowd and paparazzi, snapping pictures of the celebrities, Hall patrons, and politicians of the city entering.

"I think I saw Celesse D'Agastine just go in with the mayor at her side," said Lily. "If the White Worm gets her, this whole place is going under faster than a dropped pox bottle."

"How the hell is he going to get in?" asked Remi, pacing the sidewalk. "He looks like a bloated grub worm."

Damon shared a glance with Lily. "I think he's been wearing a mask. When he got in my face with the worms, I swear it looked like he had something over his face. His arms were greenish and when he touched me it was, I don't know, wooden."

Lily spat on the concrete, but Remi grabbed her arm and dragged her back the other way.

"Come on, we need to find the workers entrance. You said he had multiple vats of worms. He can't just walk through the front door with that."

The botanical dome stretched over two city blocks, glowing like an enormous jewel at the edge of the eighth ward. Asphalt paths meandered around the outside through manicured bushes until they came to a side entrance with huge garage doors leading into an administration building. Catering vans from Licensed to Feed were lined up near the sidewalk. Further back was an ambulance with the lights off suggesting no one was inside. The rest of the parking lot was filled with the run-down vehicles of the event workers.

"The entrance has a security detail," said Damon, nodding towards the double doors near the vehicle drop-off. "Can we convince them we're here for an emergency? Someone had a heart attack? There's an ambulance over there."

Remi raised an eyebrow as she looked him over. "You look like you're a stripper who survived a middle-aged women's bachelor party, and I doubt they have extra scrubs." She hurried across the concrete. "Come on, our way in is over here."

They jogged to the catering vans. Remi popped the lock from the back and they climbed inside.

"What is it with you and vans?" he asked.

Remi shrugged as she dug into the shelves built into the side panel, producing white catering outfits. She tossed one to each.

"Time to get naked."

The speed at which she stripped off her clothes without a hint of modesty made Damon feel jealous. He climbed out of his tattered scrubs, feeling Remi's eyes upon him in the close quarters. He opened his mouth for a quip when a searing headache had him bent over and seeing bright flashes against the back of his eyes.

"What's wrong?" asked Remi.

"I feel like my head's going to implode," he said, gripping his skull.

"Merlin's balls. That's the parasites," said Remi. "The spell killed them but now you have the little critters in your head. There's an elixir for removing them, but we'd have to be in the hospital. I hoped it wouldn't happen until we got back."

The tension in his head passed, allowing him to open his eyes again. He exhaled heavily while screwing up his face.

"What if you didn't get them all?"

The pained look in her expression was answer enough.

"Better now," he said, even though he had a lingering ache, but he concentrated on putting the catering clothes on. The pants weren't long enough, leaving his ankles exposed.

"How do I look?" asked Lily, expanding her arms and grinning beneath her enormous mess of colored hair.

Remi put her hands on her hips. "Like you own a food truck that may or may not be selling hallucinogenics on the side."

When they approached the guards, Remi said, "Let me do the talking."

The security detail had automatic weapons and their black armor glowed faintly with arcane runes, but they looked completely bored and barely fit into their gear.

"IDs?"

Remi opened her hands. "I'm sorry, we were at another job when they said to come here STAT because they were getting behind with serving. We forgot to swing by the office and get our credentials back."

The security guard frowned. "No ID, no entrance."

"Please, dude. I like this job and I don't want to get fired again. You understand, right?"

The guy looked unsympathetic to her case, which meant they weren't getting in.

"Hey man," said Damon, leaning forward. "If you want, I can bring some filets out later. They've been enchanted and spiced with unicorn horn powder. Supposed to be divine. Packaged in a bin of ice so you can cook them later at your leisure. They won't miss 'em."

The two guards stared at each other until one of them said, "Sure, man. Just have your supervisor swing by and let us know who you are so we can enter it into the logs. And don't forget those filets."

Damon fist-bumped with them both before they were let inside. Remi scowled at him.

"How did you do that?"

"Maybe you should pay attention to the patients more. Everyone has a comfort food and those guys looked like they've BBQ'd their fair share of meat."

The administration building had multiple hallways. Remi led them through, avoiding the pockets of people until they reached a door leading to the interior. The dome was breathtaking. A wonderland of rare plants and botanical marvels, which was slightly unsettling after the horrors of the greenhouse. Softly glowing magelights hung in the air above the paths meandering around the flowers and plants, each one meticulously cared for while men and women in their formal outfits strolled peacefully with flutes of pale liquid.

"There's a pavilion at the center," said Lily, extending her arm towards the sloped roof filled with tables and chairs, where a jazz band was playing on a stage.

"That's probably the most likely place for the Worm to infect them," said Remi.

"Can't be in the food, cooking it would destroy the parasites," said Damon.

The three of them stared at the botanical gardens.

"You've been studying him," said Remi. "How is he going to infect this many people?"

Damon bit his lower lip. "I don't know. Except for the steel jaw, which he was using to hide the injection of the worms, I never figured it out."

"What about the Newtown Fishmarket? That was a mass event. Probably practice for this," said Remi.

"I never determined how it was happening. There were no common factors from the patients. Different people ate at different stalls. There were no commonalities."

Lily crossed her arms. "We should split up and see what we can learn. Keep in touch with our phones. I'll check the paths."

The way the Irish girl was staring into the distance with pinched lips, as if she'd seen someone she recognized, but didn't want to admit it, confused Damon. He followed her gaze but saw no one interesting in that direction.

"I'll swing by the pavilion, since that's where it's probably going to happen," said Damon.

"I'll check the red carpet entrance and then join you at catering," said Remi. "But we better figure it out fast. The Worm isn't going to wait long to make his move."

FORTY-FIVE

The lingering scent of Fae tickled Lily's nostrils as she strode across the meandering concrete pathways, cutting around guests in their formal attire. The taint faded past the koi pond, leaving her shoes scuffing to a stop. She checked around only to see she was far away from the central area where the event was happening.

Lily didn't understand the presence of the Fae, nor why she could detect it. Normally, they hid their existence with charms and glamours, but the White Worm didn't seem to care. His aura in the greenhouse hadn't been so strong, but now that he was close to completing his plan, he'd not bothered with the protections.

She spun around searching, hoping to pick up the scent but it was gone. The reason she'd chosen the paths was because she thought he was out here. The only others she'd seen were the guests, enjoying the sights and oblivious to the danger.

The idea that the White Worm was a Green Man had been in the back of her mind, even before the greenhouse, but those events had nearly confirmed it. What she didn't understand was why. They were caretakers of the Fae wilds. The city was the last place in all the realms one should find a Green Man. Unless he was so infected by the kalkatai that he'd lost his good sense. It was the same corruption that was affecting her former patron, Medb. Answers weren't forthcoming as she'd hoped they'd be when she gave up her former life and came to the city of sorcery. The maid of the mist had been unable to point her in a fruitful direction, but now she had a chance to question a Green Man, one infected by the kalkatai, the great corruption. The only problem was if the others found him first, they'd either kill him or he'd escape and then she wouldn't get the answers she needed to save her family.

A pointy nose stuck out from her hair, sniffing and wriggling its whiskers.

"Not yet, Neko. But stay ready."

Her companion was restless. A cool paw was placed against her cheek.

"I know, you're still mad about getting shocked and thrown in a cage. But we have to be careful. We came all this way for answers, we don't want to lose our chance."

But where would the Green Man be planning on unleashing his parasites? And what about all the strangler root extract? Unlike the vats of worms, there'd been no sign of the elixirs that could have been used to drive people crazy, unless she was missing something. Lily didn't think that he could sneak the potion into their drinks, as the potent liquid was far too bitter not to notice, and alchemy required precise mixtures. Combining the extract with other materials to hide it would only ruin the effect. The only thing Lily was sure about was that the last year of chaos had been testing for the Green Man and now he was ready to unleash it on the city at large by infecting the most powerful people in all the realms.

"How will he do it, Lily? You've come all this way, given up so much, don't be a right gobshite at the final bell."

As she scanned the dome, she worried that the pavilion was a distraction. It was far too open and obvious to be the main way the Green Man was going to infect everyone, especially since the attendees were sure to have arcane protections against poisons or harmful elixirs. There were three other main buildings at the edges of the dome. The entrance where the red carpet had welcomed its treasured guests, the classrooms where Arcane Phytology taught its craft, and on the opposite side, closest to the pavilion, was a third structure hidden by a wall of greenery. The other two buildings were filled with lights and people, attending or running the event, while the third was dark and with no visible people outside.

Lily pulled out her phone and thought about messaging her friends where she was headed, but decided that if the Green Man was there it would give her a chance to question him. And this time, she wouldn't let him surprise her with his Fae tricks. It would be her turn for an ambush.

FORTY-SIX

Damon was worried about being found out as an imposter, especially since he lacked an ID, but no one gave him a second glance. Unlike his time spent in Golden Willow in scrubs, which gave him an air of authority, the catering uniform acted as a Look Away enchantment. As he passed men in their tuxedos or woman wearing glittering gowns, it was as if he didn't exist.

The pavilion was more grandiose up close. Most guests were standing in clusters with flutes of pale golden liquid in their hands. Beneath the sloping white roof an illusionary galaxy swirled as if the event was being held in the deepest parts of space. The illusion was so good that he could barely see the structural beams or fire suppression lines that hung in the ceiling, which was probably the point.

As he glanced to his right, his heart started racing when he realized he was staring at Celesse D'Agastine, the Patron of Alchemists Hall. Damon knew that older mages could smooth away the years with potent sorcery, making them appear youthful, but the effect scrambled his thoughts.

"What are you doing?" came an agitated voice from his left. "You're not supposed to stare. Weren't you listening in the orientation?"

"Huh?"

Damon turned to find a woman in an all-black outfit with a data pad in her arms and a Hall pin shaped like a glowing flower attached to her shirt.

"You should be over there with the rest of catering. Seeds and stones, are you deaf? If you have to use the bathroom, head the other direction to the little outbuilding behind the *lapis arboreous* exhibit."

He nodded and headed in the direction she indicated. The catering area was off to the side of the pavilion. Damon had no intention of joining them, but another all-black-outfitted woman with a Hall pin ushered him to the group.

"I don't remember you from the orientation," said the woman, tapping on the data pad as she spoke.

"I was a last-minute replacement."

She screwed up her face, but before she could launch into a diatribe, another member of the Hall came running up.

"Phoebe, there's a problem at the drink station. They've already run out of ambrosia and some old lady in a tiara is throwing an absolute fit."

"Already?"

Damon started to slink away, but Phoebe grabbed his sleeve. "You. Join the others. This is the last warning about wandering around, or I'll dock your pay."

Damon nodded and hurried away as Phoebe was dragged to the next problem. He tried to skirt the catering area, but the two guys on the end spotted him and waved him down.

"Come on, we're behind. We need to get these plates ready, you know these rich people aren't going to serve themselves."

The next ten minutes Damon was plating the food and putting it back into an enchanted warmer that would keep it fresh until it needed to be served. He barely had time to watch the event while he plotted how to escape until they were waiting for another cart of food to arrive, giving him a chance to observe the guests in the pavilion.

Almost as soon as Damon looked up, he saw a familiar face. He didn't recognize him at first, because he'd previously seen him at a distance, but the height was unmistakable. It was the man wearing the antlered helmet at the Society hunt. Damon remembered him from when they were standing near their prey, celebrating the successful hunt. The tall man had a potent vitality much like Celesse.

Damon leaned over to a fellow worker. "Who's that?"

"Seriously? What is this, your first day?"

"Humor me."

"Aleksander Grimm."

"Am I supposed to know that name?"

The guy guffawed and shook his head. "You been living in a box all year? The *Herald of the Halls* has been fawning over him all year. That's the Patron of Arcane Phytology, the guy that's putting this fancy shindig on. He's been the talk of the town, or at least that's what I hear all these rich mucky-mucks talking about. It's why they've been so hard-assed about every little detail. This event is supposed to be a big coming out party for the newest Hall. A celebration of a successful first year."

"Blood and bone, this is bad," muttered Damon.

"Bad? This looks like it's a pretty fade party, if you ask me, not that I've ever been invited to one like this. I bet recruitment for next year is through the roof. Reporters from every paper in the city, and even some of the national ones are here."

Aleksander was laughing with a group of older folks with white hair.

They looked like they were having the time of their lives.

"I have to go."

"The next round of food is almost here," said the guy.

"Bathroom."

As he pushed towards the exit, dodging around the cart of expensive alcohol bottles headed towards the drinks area, a voice called out sharply after him.

"Hey you. Damon. You're the guy."

He slowly turned around, his gut tightening as if it were caught in a taffy machine. Damon recognized her right away. It was the girl from the smoke bar. Abigail. He saw Dexter over her shoulder on the next station.

"You're the asshole that stole our tips. You and that girl, Remi. You're not a hospital nurse from Kansas City at all, are you?"

Damon started backing up with his hands in the air. "I don't know what you're talking about."

At that moment, Phoebe returned from the drink station disaster and Abigail grabbed her arm.

"Hey, this guy is a thief. He's not supposed to be here. He doesn't have an ID."

"I was just—"

Damon burst into a run, knocking over a girl with an armful of drinks as a host of shouting rose up behind him. He zigged around a cart hauling food to the banquet only to run into a group of security guards with automatic weapons. For a split second, he almost unleashed his rage to get away, but they trained their guns on him and he was forced to halt.

"Put your hands behind your back."

Damon backed away. "You can't take me. This whole place is under threat from a madman who wants to turn everyone into mindless zombies. Please."

As soon as the words came out his lips, he knew he was screwed.

They shared incredulous glances. The lead guard gestured to Damon, indicating a support structure for the pavilion.

"Over there, hands behind your back and around the beam."

Damon complied but he kept talking as the dining staff watched from their space.

"Please, I'm not screwing around."

"Lower your voice, sir."

The ruckus was hidden from the main area by a line of coolers. A quick shout might alert Lily or Remi, but he had no idea where they might be. The plan had gone to shit. "Please." The click of cuffs around his wrist was followed by the ripping of duct tape.

"You don't under—"

The guard slapped the tape over his mouth and turned back to the others.

"I don't trust this guy. We're going to need a paddy wagon to make sure he's not a rager. I'll call one in. Steven. You guard him until his ride arrives and then we can ship him off to the precinct. Shock him if he causes an issue; otherwise, he's out of sight, so it shouldn't cause any stress to the event."

Cuffed to the steel pole beneath the pavilion, Damon looked through the gap between the machines at the luxurious party about to turn tragic. He banged his head against the pole and cursed his bad luck.

FORTY-SEVEN

The idea that she was making an awful mistake was not lost on Remi. Rescuing her friends from the White Worm was one thing, but getting involved with a charity event with the richest people in the city felt like an extremely bad idea. Her parents would call her a fool. Hell, *she* thought she was a fool. But once they'd gotten rolling after the rescue, she found it hard to disengage.

"Find the Worm, and then let it be someone else's problem," she told herself as she jogged around the outer paths in the all-black outfit she'd stolen from the lockers at the worker entrance.

The front had more security than the place she'd come in, but that wasn't unusual, and most of it was focused on people sneaking into the building from the outside, rather than from her direction. Remi made it into the building through a side door that hadn't been locked.

The building had been converted to a red carpet entrance, but it was a set of classrooms like the other location, except it looked unused. She imagined it'd been built for the upper classes that didn't yet exist in the new Hall.

"This could have been your Hall," she said aloud.

Had things gone a little differently with Head Patron Pythia, she would have been studying plants instead of taking blood samples and tracking down murderous White Worms. Remi went up the stairs, telling herself she wanted a bird's-eye view of the dome, but really she wanted to see what she was missing.

The sleeping quarters were twice the size of her small room with a single luxurious queen-sized bed and a private bathroom with a shower. Remi imagined herself sprawled on the duvet, studying a normal amount of spell work rather than the mammoth stack of tomes they were expected to know in Aura Healers. *No one feels guilty if they kill a plant.*

Despite not wanting to believe him in the moment, Dr. Decker had been right. She'd never fully committed to Aura Healers. Even now, standing in the Hall she could have been assigned, she had regrets. Remi pressed her face against the glass, observing the rich people wandering the paths, enjoying their drinks in peace.

There was no peace in the hospital. It was a constant churn of chaotic struggle to keep people alive against all odds. It was a task doomed from the start. Magic was powerful and could perform miracles under the right conditions, but it wasn't omnipotent.

"I'm sorry, Odette."

The words came out of nowhere. She hadn't even been thinking of the older woman, but it only reminded her that she'd passed away earlier in the day. *I didn't get to say goodbye.* Remi banged her fist on the glass and headed out of the room. She'd meant to steal one of the data pads the staff were using in hopes that it might provide her information to help her find the White Worm, but she'd gotten distracted by "what if's."

Remi put her first foot on the stairs when she saw a door with alchemical warnings on the side. They had them on the hospital alchemy room too. She crept forward and peeked through the window to see a modern alchemy laboratory that made the one at Golden Willow look like it was made for a hobbyist.

"Merlin's balls..."

The lock fell quickly to her picks and she was inside, examining the automated testing and mixing equipment that would make elixir mixing a dream. Remi ran her fingers across the cool metal until she came to a Phoenix Corporation Reagent Modifier. The big black box didn't look like much, but she knew from her studies that it contained enchanted platinum sensors that were worth a few hundred thousand dollars. Even on the black market, she could get most of that value since it would allow underground drug makers to increase the potency of their products, or make new ones they couldn't with normal equipment.

"No one will even miss it."

The building might not see use until the fall at the earliest and maybe not even for another year or two depending on their recruiting class. It was the easiest heist in the world. A king's ransom placed freely into her lap. How could she not steal it? The disassembly would take at least an hour. She knew this from when they had to clean the ancient modifier at Aura Healers, and she'd have to find the tools first. But if she let her friends deal with the White Worm, she could have the enchanted platinum sensors out by the time they left the party.

But as she considered the theft, she couldn't help but be reminded of her earlier arguments when she was headed off to see Albi's contact. *Once I go down that route, there's no turning back*. It was nice having friends. Especially one as easy on the eyes as Damon, even if she had no intention of ever sleeping with him.

"I guess I *am* a fool."

Remi left the alchemy lab, locking the door behind her, and headed down to the lower level where few guests were coming in. It took two minutes to find an unguarded data pad, and after standing near another student, she lifted the password. A host of information appeared at her fingertips in an organized manner that made her cry when she thought about the antiquated systems on Golden Willow's network.

"Okay, Remi Wilde. If you were the White Worm, how would you infect everyone in the dome?"

FORTY-EIGHT

Lush vines had been artfully grown to hide the building from the paths. Lily recognized the sorcery used to sculpt them as it was a technique she'd learned from her older sisters when she was only six. *Good, little Sprout, you'll make a proper de Meath woman yet.* They'd called her a prodigy. The most powerful young witch in the family in ages, which was why she'd volunteered to be the one to come to the Hundred Halls.

She crept to a set of double doors painted dark green to blend into the foliage, finding them unlocked, which was a relief since Remi wasn't with her. The girl moved through locked doors as if she was using magic. The fact that the longtime thief actually came back to save them had been more of a surprise to Damon than to her, but Lily suspected that Remi was looking for a better life than the one her parents had designed for her.

The interior was a huge open space filled with giant plastic vats, criss-crossing pipes, and the hum of motors. Lily could tell by the height of the roof that there was a second floor, though she didn't see stairs leading up. The purpose of the equipment wasn't readily apparent to her, but she suspected it was made for water treatment. She found a chemical station and sampling jars with printed materials showing the proper levels of the various additives.

Seeing that there was no sign of the Green Man, Lily looked for the stairs, finding metal ones at the far corner of the building. As she climbed to the second level, the earlier scent of Fae came back stronger, except this time she could smell the corruption. The underlining rot reminded her of a garbage dump she'd passed on the bus ride to the city. It brought bile to the back of her throat.

The second level was more compartmentalized. The spaces were large, but there were big walls between them. She entered a room with three large diesel generators rumbling. With no one visible, Lily made her way to the next area but the door was locked.

A set of platforms went above the big generators and through the wall at a higher level. Lily climbed up a ladder and crept across the metal grating until she reached the second room.

To her surprise, three people were working in the area. She thought she might be mistaken about the presence of the Green Man when she saw someone in a maintenance jumpsuit working on a big red machine, but then she realized the other two were security personnel. Both were standing at a table, staring blankly ahead as if they were mindless automatons.

It appeared the maintenance worker was hooking up a series of barrels to the red machine. Lily had to move to see the machine better, but once she was over it, she realized it was the fire suppression lines. She caught a whiff of strangler extract—the bitter liquid was unmistakable, especially after she had been prevented from killing Remi by its flowers.

He's going to spray the crowd in the pavilion with his crazy juice.

The plan made perfect sense. All the rich folks would be sitting together when the charity portion of the event started. Once the spray nozzles were triggered, they'd be dosed in the potent liquid, turning everyone temporarily insane.

That's what he must have been testing at the Fishmarket. The Green Man probably sprayed people with it by hand.

But this didn't answer all her questions. For one, the Patrons and other top mages would hardly be affected as their protective enchantments and charms would save them from the worst effects, but also she didn't see the vats of mind control worms that were missing from the greenhouse. He wouldn't have taken them out of the greenhouse unless he was planning to use them.

Lily examined the parallel rows of pipes heading from the building towards the outside, hoping to find a shutoff valve. At worst case, she could destroy the pipes and completely invalidate the Green Man's plan. She thought she saw a viable candidate when she heard a rifle chamber clicking into place. Three sets of faces peered up at her through the metal grating.

"How you escaped the worm shouldn't be a surprise given your family, but I wonder what one of your lineage is doing away from your lands," said the Green Man.

It was hard to see through the metal and the light was dim, but Lily could see the edges of the mask he used. Normal folk wouldn't be able to tell, but she'd never been normal.

"I could say the same about you. Why aren't you tending the wilds of the Fae?" she asked as she held her hands behind her back, working a potent spell that would stun the Green Man. While the bullets in the two charmed guards' weapons could kill her outright, it was his sorcery that worried her most. "Now more than ever with the kalkatai, the land needs you."

The Green Man hissed out his answer. "As if that would save them. I've come to the heart of the corruption. The Halls are destroying the realms, perverting them to its hungry needs. Not even the Fae can withstand its influence."

"The Halls are a problem, but they're not the one destroying the Fae."

The moment he started speaking, she unleashed her magic. The air around him turned crumpled brown, encasing him in a containment field. He froze, words half formed on his lips. The two guards continued to stare upward with their rifles, but they would be ineffectual without his commands. She was preparing a second spell to knock them out when the Green Man lifted his arm and the entire metal bridge she was standing on electrified.

Lily was knocked off her feet, face slamming on the grating because she couldn't control her arms to cushion the fall. Neko leapt from her hair, landing on a red machine below and scurrying away before the Green Man could catch him.

"Get help. Find Remi or Damon," she called to Neko.

Moving brought agony. She struggled to climb to her knees, but trembling muscles wouldn't cooperate. The sound of footfalls on metal rang in her ears and then rough hands carried her back to the lower level.

The Green Man got in her face. She could smell the rot beneath the mask as his emerald eyes searched her.

"Why are you doing this? You are a Green Man. This, whatever you're doing here, is beneath you. Please. The Halls are not your enemy."

Lily had only ever met a Green Man once when she was younger. Her older sister, Evangel, had taken her to a shimmering during a blood moon to see the heart stags run. He'd been lurking at the barrier between the two realms, and had revealed himself to her, which had been another sign to the family of her promise. The Green Man had been covered in leaves, completely invisible to the untrained eye. The potency of his seelie sorcery had been humbling.

"I would spill your blood for interfering but the de Meath family holds a place of honor in the Fae. When I'm finished with my appointed task, I will take you back and give you to the dagmana tree. That way you can serve the Fae for all eternity."

"No," said Lily, trying to struggle but her arms were held fast.

The Green Man before her was nothing like the one she'd spied years ago. His essence had been twisted like a gnarled old bush that looked like a collection of knots.

"Not that."

The dagmana tree would keep her alive, bound to its essence. She would become a spirit in the realm of Fae, never to see her family again. The Green Man might see it as an honor, but it was a death sentence.

She didn't see him ascend to the upper deck, but then he was standing over her. The Green Man leaned into view, extending a lumpy finger towards her forehead. The nail was blackened by corruption, sap leaking around the cuticles. When it touched her flesh, a warm bath rose up and carried her into oblivion.

FORTY-NINE

The squelch of a speaker startled Remi as she moved across the paths, acting like she belonged, while keeping her head on a swivel. She knew she was missing something important. Neither entrance had signs of the White Worm, which meant he was setting up somewhere else. It had to be.

Remi checked her phone. No messages. She hadn't seen Lily or Damon since they split up, and the main event was about to start, which would be the perfect time for the White Worm to strike.

She paused at the corner of the drink station as a tall, handsome man in a tuxedo climbed to the stage. The sorcerous vitality radiating from his skin told her he was a patron, even before he opened his mouth.

"Good evening, ladies and gentlemen. I'm Aleksander Grimm, Patron of the newest Hall, Arcane Phytology, or for those of you who don't like tongue twisters, the plant Hall," he said in a Norwegian accent.

A wave of laughter passed through the seated crowd. Remi scanned the faces, looking for the White Worm, in case he'd hidden himself as one of the members, but she couldn't see him. The whole thing stunk of wealthy, elitist bullshit. She was surprised she was bothering to protect them. If it weren't for her friends, or the impact to the city, she'd never think to concern herself with their plight.

She pushed the patron's speech out of her mind as she continued looking for where the White Worm had set up. She spotted the building hidden by the trees and avoided interaction on her way to investigate.

A row of vine-covered trees cleverly hid what appeared to be a maintenance building. An eerie feeling traveled down her spine. Remi checked around her. Nothing. It was like a ghost had traveled through her.

Looking back to the party, she thought she saw movement as if someone had snuck past. Remi was going to investigate when she heard scuffing in the leaves. And a whine.

"Back off or I'll fry you like bacon," said Remi with her hands up. She was more likely to singe the hair off her hands, but whoever was lurking nearby wouldn't know that.

The crunch of a stick breaking sent up alarm bells. She almost ran. Then she saw a creature between the bushes, a short and powerful four-legged being with a smooth, hairless body that shimmered as she stared at it. Fleshy tendrils undulated from its hindquarters, waving like sea fronds in a current. The beast gave off vibes of the Fae, even though she'd never seen its like before.

"Back off, whatever you are," said Remi, taking backwards steps.

The creature lowered its head and pawed at the ground. Remi halted. Its behavior was odd.

"Are you lost? Or part of an exhibit?"

The hairless creature mimed cleaning its face with cupped paws, and the resemblance was like a spike to the brain.

"Neko?"

The creature nodded quickly. Remi didn't understand but she was sure she was right. Before she could ask another question, Neko burst down the path towards the building. She didn't understand until it stopped and checked back to her.

"Right, follow."

Neko led her through a side door in the building. It was hard to look directly at Lily's companion as the air around it wavered like heat on a desert highway. The shape briefly coalesced into a cat-like creature, and then a fox with a rat's head, before returning to the hairless version. Neko paused at the corner of a big room with diesel engines rumbling.

Remi tried to step around, but Neko blocked her. The reason was apparent when she saw the two guards standing over an unconscious Lily, bound to a support beam near a chemical testing table. The guards had automatic weapons. *What am I going to do?* She was a thief, not a fighter. And there was no sign of the White Worm. He could be lurking around the corner, out of sight. She could walk right into his grasp.

Before she could formulate a plan, Neko stepped into view, walking confidently towards the guards, who bristled as soon as they saw him. Neko's tail swished dangerously, like a panther on the prowl as it approached the guards. The mustached one in front set the butt of his gun against his shoulder and aimed down the sights. Neko made no effort to evade. Remi was sure Lily's companion was going to be shot.

The squeeze of a trigger made Remi flinch. But Neko was unharmed. The guard had sent bullets right through Neko, pinging off the concrete and bouncing through the equipment. The shimmering around Neko popped like a soap bubble. A more solid version appeared behind the guards. Two screams later, they were unconscious on the concrete.

Remi ran forward and kicked their guns away while Neko stared unnervingly at her.

"That was awesome, and very creepy," said Remi, thinking about how she'd shared a room with the beast for an entire year. "You have a lot of explaining to do when you wake up."

She checked on Lily, shaking her, but the Irish girl wouldn't wake. Zip ties bound her to the support beam.

"Come on, come on."

Neko pressed his forehead to Lily's chest, and like a defibrillator, she jumped slightly, before opening her eyes. A slow, sleepy grin formed.

"Remington."

"What happened? Where's the White Worm? And what the hell is Neko?" asked Remi as she checked around for a pair of clippers to cut the ties.

Lily blinked twice before her consciousness seemed to come forward.

"The Green Man is in the party. You have to hurry. Stop the machines. It's going to spray everyone with the strangler extract potion."

"What?"

"The Green Man. White Worm. He's using the fire suppression equipment to spray the entire party. I don't know how he's using the parasites, but the extract will be bad enough. Turn off the machine."

Remi moved to the equipment Lily indicated, but when her hand brushed the equipment, a shock knocked her back. A field of arcane energy formed over it.

"What the hell?"

"Branch and bough, that's a forbidding."

Remi grabbed a rifle. She wasn't experienced, but she knew enough to use it. As she aimed at the machine, Lily yelled, "No!"

"Why not?"

"It won't work. A Green Man's sorcery is too strong and he's more powerful than any other I've seen. It's the corruption."

"How do we stop him?"

"Get everyone out of the pavilion before they're sprayed."

"Sprayed? He's sending the extract through the pipes?"

Lily nodded. "He used a version of the aerosol spell."

"Aerosol spell?"

"Third tome. You and Damon worked on it last month."

"Great, we know how he's doing the extract. What about the parasites?"

"I don't know, but you have to get them out before the machine turns on. It's on a timer."

"But how do I—"

The words fell apart in her mouth as she realized she was holding a quick and easy method to make people flee the party, but firing an automatic weapon near the world's most powerful people was not going to end well.

"Oh, Remi, being a thief was much simpler."

"Hurry," said Lily from her spot.

With a heavy sigh, Remi took a step towards the outer door when the big red machine rumbled into life. Lights appeared over the control panel and she could hear the equipment pressurizing.

Remi aimed the gun at the machine and squeezed the trigger. Bullets ricocheted into the building while the machine continued pumping. She had no way to stop it. Her shoulders slumped and she let the rifle clatter to the concrete.

"We're too late. We lost."

"Not yet. We can't let the Green Man win."

Remi looked back to Lily, attached to the pole.

"Are you crazy? We need to leave."

"No," said Lily earnestly. "Take Neko and stop him. Please. Before it's too late."

Remi hesitated.

Why couldn't this be easy?

FIFTY

Damon was listening to the head of Arcane Phytology's speech from his pole when the fire suppression kicked in. It was a pretty good speech. Not that Damon was experienced with the art of speaking in public, but Aleksander was giving a good breakdown of what he intended as the mission for the newest Hall. Discovering new alchemical reagents. Developing cures for regular and supernatural diseases. Improving knowledge of paranormal plants and the creatures that make their homes on them. The speech brought a sense of hope even to Damon and the crowd loved it, applauding at the carefully choreographed pauses that Aleksander made. This new Hall would make a great partner with Aura Healers. He could imagine Jeb working with Aleksander to improve outcomes in Golden Willow.

And then the sprinklers burst open.

The misty spray filled the air with a potent aerosol.

Damon hoped it was a ploy at first. That it was Remi's plan, a way to get everyone out of the pavilion in a rapid manner.

Then the bitter scent of strangler extract hit. It was pungent. Mixed with other reagents, but the underlining base was unmistakable.

Guests were shocked.

They knocked over chairs as they made to hurry away. The guards and waitstaff were hit too. A few of them started laughing as the mist covered everything and everyone.

Damon got a glimpse of Aleksander Grimm on the stage, looking like a kid who'd just found a turd in his birthday cake. The entire party was a disaster.

And then it got worse.

Damon watched as the majority of the guests, staff, and guards collapsed to the ground. Not unconscious, but they were writhing and crying out as the aerosol elixir entered their bodies through the skin.

Not everyone was affected. The Patrons and the other super-wealthy were protected from the aerosol with enchantments and trinkets. The head of Alchemists Hall, Celesse D'Agastine, strode from the event in a golden dress, not a drop of liquid on her pristine skin, disgusted by the interruption.

Confusion reigned.

But no one realized except Damon what was going to happen next. He'd read the reports from the Newtown Fishmarket event. A wave of unconscious attendees had resulted in emergency services called, but before they could arrive and potentially apply an antidote, they rose up and started attacking people like mindless zombies.

The mist stopped spraying from the fire suppression lines, but the damage was already done. Damon wondered why he wasn't affected, but assumed it was his therianthrope blood. He tried to access his rage, so he could break free, but the urge was suppressed, which told him he was right about his guess. Little solace for when they rose up and started attacking everyone in sight. He'd get ripped to shreds. Or shot once the guards started firing their weapons into the crowd.

It was going to be a bloodbath.

As the ambulance approached from the opposite side with its lights on, Damon sensed something was wrong even before his logical brain could figure it out. When he saw a man in an EMT uniform step out of the vehicle, he knew what was going to happen. It was the White Worm. He'd changed disguises. His face was slightly off, but no one seemed to notice.

"Universal antidotes! Hurry, we can prevent any adverse effects if you take it quickly," said the White Worm, hauling a white sports drink cooler from the back.

The people that hadn't been affected by the extract were heading in his direction as he pulled out drink cups and started filling them to hand out. Damon yanked at his cuffs, but he had no way to free himself, or tell anyone that it was a trap. The drinks would be filled with parasites, probably hidden with glamour. The line of rich and powerful would not just be mindless zombies, but ones bound to the White Worm once the parasites took hold.

Please someone free me! Don't take them!

But it was too late.

The first few guests were sucking down the "antidotes" as the first of the others writhing on the ground were slowly making it to their feet.

The slapping of soles on the concrete had him turning, expecting to be attacked, but instead he found Remi and a strange hairless dog-like creature at her side. She ripped the duct tape off his mouth. After shaking off the initial sting, he said, "The White Worm is going to feed them parasites at the EMT truck. Hurry!"

Remi took one look at everyone lining up at the ambulance and her jaw dropped. Before she could move in that direction, a woman in a white catering jacket rose to her feet, eyes blank of emotion. She surged towards Remi, grabbing her arm and slamming her head against the pole.

FIFTY-ONE

The scene was overwhelming, leaving Remi frozen by Damon's side. Hundreds of people in formal attire were laid out on the ground, or knocking over chairs as they climbed to their feet. The line leading up to the ambulance where the White Worm was handing out parasite-laden "antidotes" was full. Even the Patron of Arcane Phytology was at the back of the line, glancing over his shoulder in shock.

Remi didn't see the caterer until she had her arm and slammed her into the pole. Stars burst into her vision as her head impacted the metal. The woman dug her fingernails into Remi's arm, so she kicked her between the legs. The kick infuriated the mindless woman, and she reared her arm back. Remi, too stunned to avoid the coming blow, was saved when Neko barreled the woman over and nudged her in the head, knocking her back out.

"Hurry, stop them from drinking the parasites," said Damon, still bound to the pole with handcuffs behind the portable refrigerators.

She briefly checked around her for something to pick the locks, before remembering she had her gear in her jacket.

"It's too late. We have to leave before it gets really bad."

"No, Remi. We don't."

She looked at the tall first year. "Are you crazy?"

"You could say that. We did all willingly sign up to be kicked, punched, and spit at, and that's just the doctors."

Remi looked between Damon and the ambulance. "There's nothing left to do."

"There's always something more to do. Even if we only save one person. Please, Remi. You can do this. I know Dr. Decker is always giving you shit, but it's for a reason. That's why we signed up for Aura Healers. To help people. This isn't ideal, but here's your chance. We can still help them. And if we don't, shit's gonna get a whole lot worse in the city. Do you really want to leave everyone at Golden Willow to the mess about to happen?"

A burning frustration rose up in her chest. Every ounce of her body was saying to flee. Her parents would call her a fool. Or a dupe. A mark. She glanced briefly at the building where the enchanted platinum sensors were located. She should have stayed on the train and learned about the pendant. Being a hero was a mistake. She realized that now. Odette's death had her all confused. There hadn't been a chance to say goodbye.

"I hate you, Damon."

Remi sprinted to the ambulance, waving her hands and screaming, "Don't drink that! It's a trap! He's a Green Man from the Fae and it's going to poison your mind!"

The entire line of rich folks stared at her as if she were crazy. *She* thought she was crazy.

The Green Man caught her eye. His lips snarled briefly before returning to a mask of professionalism.

Then Neko surged forward. The hairless beast rippled like a heat wave. The Green Man dropped the cup he was about to hand over when he saw Neko bounding forward.

Remi thought Neko was going to attack. Instead, the strange creature leapt onto the table, knocking over an older woman in a black dress. A man in a tuxedo lifted his hand as if he were going to punch Neko, but then the beast sent out a wave of dislocating air. When it passed over the "EMT," he changed from a relatively normal looking human to a humanoid-shaped pile of rotting leaves in an EMT uniform with menacing green eyes staring out from the depths. Brown goo dripped from the arm of the corrupted Green Man. The gentleman at the front of the line recoiled then vomited onto the concrete path.

The Green Man raised its arm as if it were going to send a bout of sorcery into the crowd, but a hearty voice called out in Fae language.

"Il'thus na danar!"

The head of Arcane Phytology gathered up eldritch energy and sent it rippling towards the Green Man, knocking him into the side of the ambulance. The people in line scattered as the Patron sent more magic against the fallen Fae creature. Remi checked around for Neko, but Lily's strange companion had disappeared again.

The relief that the parasites had been stopped ended when Remi saw the entire crowd that had been dosed by the sprinklers rising to their feet. She ran back to Damon to unlock his manacles.

As she worked the lock, she asked, "Why aren't you like them?"

"It's my blood. Therianthropes aren't easily affected, but it's blocking my rage, or I would have broken the cuffs already."

"Your blood?"

The words came out of her lips as her mind whirled. Damon started explaining the medical properties as her lockpicks dangled in midair, no longer working the cuffs. She glanced up, following the line of pipes from the pavilion back to the maintenance area.

"Remi? Are you okay? Did you get sprayed?"

"No," she said, shaking her head. "But I have an idea. A really stupid one. I have to go."

She was running away before she'd finished speaking, heading straight to the back of the ambulance as those in line were now wrestling with the ones hit with the extract. Someone on the far side fired a gun into the scaffolding. A scream erupted from the drink area. Sorcerous flames burst from another region. The chaos was starting to coalesce into something dark and menacing as the collective madness picked up steam.

But the year in the Golden Willow emergency room had taught her to stay calm. She dove into the back of the ambulance, finding the phlebologist kit in a labelled drawer. She grabbed extra tubing and other gear before running back to Damon, who was staring at her as if she'd gone mad.

And maybe she had.

"Now is no time for a blood sample."

Remi ignored him and set an IV line. She attached the tubing and climbed onto a table to reach the fire suppression lines.

"Are you crazy? The pressure will blow air bubbles into my arm."

She held up a one-way valve. "Don't worry, I have a plan."

The spell was something she'd forgotten about. It'd been years since she'd learned it. Certain house systems relied on pressurized pipes surrounding the wires which would trigger alarms if the pressure dropped, but the spell allowed her to access them without letting out the condensed air that was being forced through the line.

Remi ignored the battle going on inside the pavilion. Out of the corner of her eye she saw a blonde woman in a slinky dress repeatedly punching a guy in a tuxedo straight into his balls while she screamed like a Viking on a raid.

Using the wrench she'd taken from the ambulance, she unhooked the spray nozzle. Air came rushing out. Remi applied the spell to the one-way valve before shoving it into the hole and filling the gaps with binding tape. Then she hooked the tubing up to the hole and hopped down, connecting the other side to the IV line.

"Blood and bone, Remi, what are you doing?"

"You wanted me to help. This is my help. Trust me, please."

His face broke with concern, but he nodded. She applied the aerosol spell to the IV line and then turned the valve so his blood would start pumping out. It started climbing the line, headed towards the one-way valve. The next part was the trickiest. He wouldn't have enough blood for her purposes, but there were spells for just about everything. Remi started chanting over the line, which would make the blood more voluminous once it was turned to aerosol. It traveled up and into the fire suppression pipes. She checked to the part to see nothing happening, but she kept chanting, using her fledgling magic to expand his blood. *Don't focus on the patient, focus on the spell.* With her eyes closed, she didn't realize a second person was standing across from her until she looked up to see Lily. The Irish girl added her magic to the spell, which picked up in potency.

Then blood sprayed from the fire suppression nozzles. It started as a drizzle and then turned to an oscillating pulse before hitting stride and spraying fully across the pavilion. Between the volume increaser and the aerosol spell, the few pints of Damon's blood filled the air with a crimson mist.

The effect was immediate.

And gross.

The white food service jackets were soaked to pink. Exposed skin turned soggy and hair was sticky with pale blood. Men and women in fancy clothes punched and kicked each other in a rain of crimson.

It looked like something out of a bad vampire movie.

But in a matter of seconds, the pitched battle ceased as soon as the therianthropic aerosol blood hit their skin. Combatants went from clawing each other's faces to standing apart, confused at why they were acting that way.

Remi was so pleased by the effect, she almost forgot about Damon until she glanced back to see him pale as a ghost with his eyes rolling into the back of his head. She turned the valve, shutting off his blood flow, and unhooked the line. Lily caught him after the cuffs came off. He didn't completely collapse, but suddenly looked drunken.

Sensing that she didn't want to be anywhere near the place once the authorities arrived, Remi helped Damon stagger from the pavilion. Arriving police and ambulances rushed towards the blood-soaked party, oblivious to the three of them who looked the least affected by the chaos. Good triage meant ignoring the walking wounded. Another gunshot got them moving at a faster pace.

They managed to get Damon out of the dome and down the block to the train station before flopping onto a bench. Nearby riders moved as far away from them as possible. While they hadn't gotten directly sprayed, their clothes were splattered with dark pink stains and Damon looked like a walking corpse. Relief set in as the train rumbled into motion while Damon, drained of multiple pints of blood, leaned his head on her shoulder. The ride back to the sixth ward passed in a daze until they reached Golden Willow.

FIFTY-TWO

Dr. Decker found them in a side room near the ER, putting blood back into Damon. The first-year instructor burst in with his stethoscope hanging over his shoulder ready to admonish them, but he stopped, mouth hanging open as if he couldn't quite understand what was happening.

Remi stared back as he studied them for a long time. She could see the gears turning as he saw the splattered blood and their outfits. When the intercom crackled to life, announcing the incoming wave from the charity event, Dr. Decker sighed heavily.

"When you're finished with the tin man over there, I'll see you three in the ER. And since it isn't Halloween, make sure you change out of your costumes."

After he left, Remi turned to Damon, who had regained a slight pink to his cheeks.

"You okay?"

"Getting better. Keep the oil coming," he said while Lily rubbed his back. "What are we going to tell him?"

"Nothing," said Remi. "We weren't there and he has no right to know."

"Are you sure?" he asked.

"Completely." Remi tilted her head at Lily. "What's with the rat?"

Faint splatters covered Lily's freckled nose making it appear that they'd spread.

"Tomorrow when all this is over, I'll explain, but only if you tell us where you went for half the night."

Remi nodded with her eyes closed. "That's fair."

"I'm good to go," said Damon, pulling out the IV and hopping from the table. He staggered for a moment, holding himself up with the steel table.

"You sure?"

"I'll eat a few cookies and pound some of Jeb's best elixirs. I'll be fine. Besides, you heard Dr. O.D. We've got incoming."

Remi checked the time, seeing that she hadn't slept since Merlin knew when.

"Let's do this."

§

The ER was slammed with a dozen howlers filled mostly with fancy clothed rich people. Gunshot wounds. Clawed faces. Concussions. There was no shortage to the variety of wounds. Everyone covered in pinkish blood and a dazed expression that suggested they didn't think that could happen to them.

It was strange for Remi to have been on the other side of the wounds for once. A few times, the doctors started speculating about what could have caused the chaos, and Remi had to work to keep her lips clamped shut, especially when they suggested the wrong course of treatment. Unless they said something that would harm the patient, she stayed silent, knowing that most of the wounds were superficial.

Despite the chaos, the late night had none of the anxiety that usually came with a flood of ER patients. She guessed it was like cleaning up after a hurricane, when the waves were still choppy and the beach was covered in debris, but you knew it was the end so you could remain calmer about the exhausting work.

At times, she caught Dr. Decker staring at her or her friends. She guessed he was piecing together what had happened. Remi hoped that no one recognized their role in the events, but during a break in the action, when someone turned up the TV in the waiting area, she saw Patron Aleksander Grimm being interviewed.

"The tragic events from tonight were caused by a rogue creature from another realm intent on killing and injuring people at my charity event," said Patron Grimm.

"What happened to this rogue creature and do you know where it came from?" asked the reporter.

Patron Grimm stared straight into the camera as if he were speaking directly to the city.

"That remains to be understood, but I can assure everyone that this creature was destroyed completely by my sorcery once he was identified. While I am horrified at the scale of tragedy that unfolded at this celebration of my Hall, I think that only my quick action prevented more people from being hurt or killed. We have much to be thankful that the casualty numbers were rather small considering."

The reporter put the microphone into his face. "What about the rumors of parasitic infection or mind-control enchantments?"

"Vicious rumor. I assure you that whatever happened was more chaos than reality. But know that anyone injured is currently being treated at Golden Willow hospital. I'm certain the great nurses and doctors of that facility can handle any injuries or illnesses that resulted from tonight's events."

The staff watching the TV cheered in response. Remi missed the final part of the interview because she couldn't hear, but she guessed nothing important was said because they switched back to the anchor desk and she returned to caring for patients.

§

As the sun was coming up, Remi hauled the duffle bag full of reagents to Dr. Decker's office. She wasn't surprised to find him sitting at his desk folding a piece of paper into tighter shapes. He normally had a quip, but his silence spoke volumes.

"I won't take any more from the hospital supplies."

"Take?"

The words caught in her throat. "Steal. I'm sorry."

Remi set the bag by his desk. He leaned over and unzipped it, whistling softly at the contents.

"I didn't take everything. I left enough so there were no interruptions in care and replacements could be ordered."

Dr. Decker leaned back in his chair and crossed his arms. "I should give you an award."

"You should kick me out."

An eyebrow raised. "Is that what you want?"

"No. But I know that's what you should do."

"What happened at the plant Hall?"

Remi placed her hands behind her back and shrugged speculatively.

"Hard to tell from the injuries, but it looks like it was quite a mess."

Dr. Decker furrowed his forehead. "Snitches get stitches?"

"No one ever says that unless you're a TV mobster. Criminals are the first person to sell you out if they think they can profit from it."

He held up a piece of paper. "I had an analysis done on some of the blood. Very interesting results. Do you have any theories on how the entire party was exposed to therianthropic blood?"

"Will it turn them into werewolves?" she asked with feigned concern.

"That's not how it works."

The corner of her lip curled slightly, which brought a shaking of his head.

"No, I'm not kicking you out, Miss Wilde. I'd hate to lose a student who shows such promise. The creativity required for that kind of solution is remarkable."

Her chest uncoiled. "That's good to know. Is there anything else? I'd like to catch a few hours of sleep before my next shift."

"That's fine. Unless you have any theories about tonight which might be helpful."

She stopped halfway out the door. "Theoretically. It might be good to test for parasites despite what Patron Grimm said on TV. Also, you'll want to talk to Bob about those tests. He might have been fudging them to keep you off his back."

"Theoretically."

"Is there anything else?"

His expression crashed. "One more thing. Services for Odette will be later this afternoon in the chapel."

In the chaos of the evening, she'd forgotten about her death. It seemed like weeks ago.

"Thank you."

"Remi?"

"Yeah."

"I'm glad you came back."

"Me too."

FIFTY-THREE

Remi had never been to a memorial service before. Her parents had moved them around constantly and personal attachments were discouraged. If you might have to get up and leave the county at a moment's notice, you didn't want anything interfering. Which meant the only friends she'd ever had were her parents—which really weren't friends at all.

The chapel felt claustrophobic when she stepped inside. Two pots of flowers sat on the simple altar while the benches had a collection of nurses Remi recognized from caring for the old woman. Remi didn't know what to expect, so she stayed against the back wall by a potted tree.

Dr. Decker appeared shortly after in his white jacket over green scrubs. He spotted her against the wall and gave a brief nod, before taking a spot near the front.

The nurses eventually left, leaving a small item on the altar before heading out of the chapel. They smiled at her as they left, which helped her feel like she belonged. Even when she didn't. *Of all the times to get to know someone, I had to pick someone that was going to die.* After the chaotic night, Remi wished she still had the chance to sit in Odette's room and tell her about everything that had happened. The old botanist had loved her stories. It'd made Remi feel like she had some worth. She enjoyed listening to Odette's stories too.

Dr. Decker checked his phone and then rose from his bench near the front. He set something small on the altar before heading down the aisle.

"She left this for you," said Dr. Decker, handing over a sealed card from the gift shop.

"Me?"

His eyes creased with a smile. "She enjoyed your visits very much. You made an old woman's last days bearable."

The card trembled in her hands. What could Odette have said? Dr. Decker left her at the back of the chapel. She shoved it in her back pocket.

Remi was planning to leave when the doors opened, revealing Damon and Lily in their first-year scrubs. Without saying a word, they stood to either side of her. Hands grasped hands. Tears welled up in her eyes as a sob escaped her lips. She'd never been good at crying. What was the use when there was no one to care if you did, but having them at her side made them flow in a river of grief.

When she couldn't take it anymore, Remi broke contact and strode to the altar. An origami swan sat at the center. It was what Dr. Decker had been folding when she'd entered his office last night. She touched the graceful neck as an answer popped into her head.

"Oh."

Her friends were waiting for her outside of the chapel. They swung by the cafeteria for coffee before climbing to the hospital roof. A helicopter was landing on the pad on the far side, but they found the peaceful spot with a picnic table and Adirondack chairs that overlooked the city. Puffy clouds kept the sun from blinding them as they sipped their coffees. A set of sirens, police not ambulance, came roaring up the side street headed in the direction of the White Worm's house.

She raised an eyebrow.

"Someone may or may not have sent a tip to the Invictus PD." Damon sat up. "That's okay, right?"

"More than okay. I'd hate for someone to take up his insane plan." She paused. "Is now the time for spilling secrets?"

"A good a time as any," said Damon.

When Lily didn't speak, they both looked to her. She wrinkled her nose.

"I'll feed the fairies if that's what you're looking at me about."

"Who first?" asked Remi.

Lily sighed. "Since we're talking about the Green Man, I guess that should be me. I don't know about you two, but I didn't come here to become a healer. I did, but not the kind you're thinking of. I come from a long line of witches."

"I knew it," said Damon. "That explains why you're so good at magic."

"Aye, that it does. When we're old enough to access our faez, we pledge ourselves to Medb."

"Medb?" asked Damon, leaning forward.

"An ancient Fae who came to the island many centuries ago. She's been our family's patron for as long, keeping us safe in return for certain sacrifices."

"Sacrifices?"

"Not like that, you big dolt," said Lily with a wry smile. "A little blood from ourselves, sure, but mostly our time and magic. We care for the sacred Yew tree. Eó Ruis. But now the goddess and the tree are dying. And we don't understand why."

"That's why you came here," said Remi.

"It is. The kalkatai is causing it. The corruption of the Fae. It's turned the summer realm into a place unrecognizable by my family."

"That's what I saw in my vision," said Remi, nodding with understanding.

"It is. And the White Worm, or Green Man, is a part of it too. Or was." Lily hung her head. "I came to the Halls in hopes of learning how to fix the corruption, or fight it, if that's what it requires."

Remi put a hand on Lily's knee. "Neko?"

"He's a changeling. A powerful one. We were bonded when I was a young witch, barely old enough for the rites. It's why I volunteered."

Remi sucked in a breath. "You had to give up your connection to Medb."

"Aye," said Lily, her lips wrinkling with uncharacteristic sadness. "But it'll all be worth it if I can heal Medb and my family."

Remi reached into her scrubs and pulled out the pendant. "Is this connected in any way?"

"I don't know," said Lily. "It might be. Or not. The Fae is a wide realm, not counting the other courts. What do you think it is?"

"Riches and wealth. My parents were convinced, which is why we stole it from the Dreadmarshes."

"The Dreadmarshes?" asked Damon, aghast. "Are you insane? They're one of the most powerful families in the world."

"It was in a minor cottage that they rarely used, and except for my parents' impatience, I would have gotten away cleanly. Instead I had to spend a year in Utica."

"What does it lead to?" asked Lily.

Remi pursed her lips, unsure if she wanted to reveal all her secrets.

"I really don't know," she lied. "But I know my parents, they were dead certain that it was a path to riches. The one big job that if we could pull off, we'd never have to steal again."

"Is that where you went?" asked Damon.

"I did. I was supposed to meet with an expert in the field, someone who would tell me the next steps."

"Why did you come back?"

Remi clutched the pendant which felt warm against her palm. "Because I'm an idiot? My parents always warned me about getting involved with other people's lives, and that's what I did. I got involved. I can't say exactly why I came back, but I knew that if I kept going I wouldn't like the person I'd come to be."

"We're bloody glad you did," said Lily with a wink.

"Me too." She screwed up her face. "Does anyone else think it's strange that two people connected to the Fae became friends?"

Lily shook her head. "Not at all. The seelie and unseelie worlds work in mysterious ways. Your pendant and my past probably drew us together."

Remi tilted her head at Damon. "What about you? Do you have any Fae connection you're hiding under all that werewolf muscle?"

"Me?" His forehead furrowed. "Not at all. I think our connection came from you trying to steal from me."

Remi wasn't sure she quite believed him, but she didn't want to upset the mood. Their phones buzzed collectively, summoning them to a meeting with Dr. Decker in the first year lounge.

"I'll be along in a moment," said Remi as her friends headed back.

After they left, Remi approached one of the big metal HVAC units. She reached under the curve of a vent until she found the magnetic lockbox she'd fixed underneath. After punching in a passcode and adding a breath of faez to unlock it, she examined the wads of cash inside along with other valuable items she'd picked up in the last year.

Most of it she'd stolen before she'd decided to make a go of it at Aura Healers, but she wasn't about to give it back now. Returning the reagents to Dr. Decker had been hard enough.

Remi dangled the pendant from her hand, letting it twirl in the wind before dropping it into the box. Not only was she not going after the Horn at the end of it, but as she'd learned this year, its connection to the Fae was dangerous. After closing it up, she reattached it to the bottom of the vent and returned to the picnic table.

She pulled out the envelope from her back pocket and using a fingernail, sliced it open. A smile climbed to her lips as she realized the card had come from the gift shop in the hospital. The front had a picture of a swan gliding across a lily-covered pond. When she opened it, a single fluffy white feather slipped out and landed in her lap.

On the inside, the cursive script read:

For each hex, there's a counter...
For each demon—a sword...
For each ordeal—the will to battle on.
For each curse—a ward...
For each silence—a horn...
For when the deathless king comes,
All the halls will sing forlorn.

A single handwritten phrase graced the empty space on the opposite side. Remi hugged the card close as she read it.

Don't give up hope.

Remi reread the note a dozen times before she carefully returned the feather to the card. She gave the city one last look.

"Time to get to work."

§ § §

This ends the first book of the Aura Healers Hall series. Stayed tuned for the second book:

FULL MOON DEMON

Special Thanks

From the ashes of failure, new growth can form.

As my newsletter readers know, this series started off as something entirely different. I wrote a book that once I got to the end I realized was neither a Hundred Halls story, nor was good enough to publish. Yet, without it, this series wouldn't exist in the wonderful form that it does. For that I have to thank my best friend and wife of twenty-seven years, Rachel, for her excellent advice as we discusssed what I should do with that failed book on the way to see Phish in Denver for four days. That conversation helped me find clarity of where I'd gone wrong as well as how to start over with fresh eyes.

I must also thank my team who help make each novel as best as it can be: Sasha Almazan & Gene Mollica from GS Covers, Tamara Blain from A Closer Look Editing, the beta reader team (Tina Rak, Andie Alessandra Cáomhanach, Lana Turner, Phyllis Simpson, and Melanie Coupland), as well as my writing group that we affectionately call the Murder Cabin (Andrea Stewart, Anthea Lawson/Sharp, Annie Bellet, Megan O'Keefe, Marina J. Lostetter, Jamie Thornton, and Tina Gower). Additionally, the Vanguard plays defense for little errors that sneak through the cracks, and for this book, I have Leslie King, Debbie Davis, Phyllis Simpson, and Brian Busby to thank!

ABOUT THE AUTHOR

Thomas K. Carpenter resides in Colorado with his wife Rachel. When he's not busy writing his next book, he's hiking, skiing, and getting beat by his wife at cards. He keeps a regular blog at www.thomaskcarpenter.com and you can follow him on twitter @thomaskcarpente. If you want to learn when his next novel will be hitting the shelves and get free stories and occasional other goodies, please sign up for his mailing list by going to: http://tinyurl.com/thomaskcarpenter. Your email address will never be shared and you can unsubscribe at any time.

www.ingramcontent.com/pod-product-compliance
Lightning Source LLC
Chambersburg PA
CBHW030421310726
48979CB00009B/1561/J

* 9 7 8 1 9 5 8 4 9 8 2 3 1 *